Dear Reader:

We were delighted that the folks at Waldenbooks asked us to participate in their Romance Club membership drive by preparing four special books, each containing two previously published *LOVESWEPT* romances from favorite authors. Of course, we are pleased to be reissuing these marvelous love stories . ... but we are especially pleased to be doing so because of the wonderful support you and the people behind the scenes at the Romance Club have given to our authors in particular and to our *LOVESWEPT* line in general.

Why not use these special editions with their twin tales to introduce a friend to the *LOVESWEPT* line and to the Waldenbooks Romance Club? Everyone would benefit . . . and I can assure you that we would be most grateful!

We certainly hope you enjoy these old favorites.

Warm regards from everyone at *LOVESWEPT*,

Sincerely,

*Carolyn Nichols*

Carolyn Nichols

## WHAT ARE *LOVESWEPT* ROMANCES?

They are stories of true romance and touching emotion. We believe those two very important ingredients are constants in our highly sensual and very believable stories in the *LOVESWEPT* line. Our goal is to give you, the reader, stories of consistently high quality that may sometimes make you laugh, sometimes make you cry, but are always fresh and creative and contain many delightful surprises within their pages.

Most romance fans read an enormous number of books. Those they truly love, they keep. Others may be traded with friends and soon forgotten. We hope that each *LOVESWEPT* romance will be a treasure—a "keeper." We will always try to publish

*LOVE STORIES YOU'LL NEVER FORGET*
*BY AUTHORS YOU'LL ALWAYS REMEMBER*

The Editors

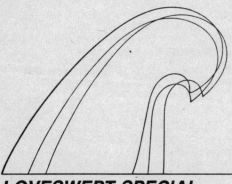

# LOVESWEPT SPECIAL

## TWO GREAT ROMANCES IN ONE VOLUME

# Billie Green

### A Tryst With Mr. Lincoln?
- previously published as Loveswept #7

### A Very Reluctant Knight
- previously published as Loveswept #16

 BANTAM BOOKS
TORONTO · NEW YORK · LONDON · SYDNEY · AUCKLAND

A TRYST WITH MR. LINCOLN?
A VERY RELUCTANT KNIGHT

*A Bantam Book / September 1986*

A Tryst With Mr. Lincoln? *was first published in June 1983.*
A Very Reluctant Knight *was first published
in September 1983.*

*LOVESWEPT® and the wave device are registered
trademarks of Bantam Books, Inc. Registered in U.S. Patent
and Trademark Office and elsewhere.*

ISBN 0-553-21804-2

---

*Bantam Books are published by Bantam Books, Inc. Its
trademark, consisting of the words "Bantam Books" and
the portrayal of a rooster, is Registered in U.S. Patent and
Trademark Office and in other countries. Marca Registrada.
Bantam Books, Inc., 666 Fifth Avenue, New York, New
York 10103.*

---

PRINTED IN THE UNITED STATES OF AMERICA

O    0 9 8 7 6 5 4 3 2 1

# *A Tryst With Mr. Lincoln?*

(Previously published as Loveswept #7)

*To Dixie*
*She loved fiercely and was fiercely loved.*

# *One*

"Oh my God!"

Needles of sunlight pierced Jiggs's tightly closed eyelids as shock held her body rigid beneath the covers. Very carefully she opened one eye, praying that she had been mistaken.

It was no mistake. There was very definitely a man in the bed! With both eyes opened wide in horror, she cautiously took in the broad expanse of bare chest beside her. She stared at the long, lean body as though mesmerized by the dark hair that curled down the middle of the bronzed chest, narrowed on the flat plain of the stomach, and disappeared into the blanket that was casually draped across the lean hips.

Her eyelids closed over confused, panic-stricken green eyes. What am I doing here? she wondered wildly. In her twenty-nine years of life, Jiggs had sometimes found herself in awkward situations. What woman hadn't? And she could usually rely on common sense and a deeply ingrained, natural

1

dignity to carry her through the most embarrassing scene—but waking to find herself in bed with a total stranger was beyond her range of experience! There had been nothing in her life to establish a precedent for handling this type of thing. Promiscuity was foreign to her. It was a horror to her. It didn't fit into her well-ordered life. Jiggs was a neat, tidy person. Casual affairs were neither neat nor tidy.

So, what do I do now? she wondered silently. Her first inclination was to leave before the sleeping man beside her awoke. Never having considered herself a coward, she balked at not tackling a problem head on. But she had no recollection of this man and she didn't know how she was going to explain that diplomatically. The pounding in her head left her in no mood to cope with a wounded male ego.

"Good morning, Jiggs."

The deep male voice jerked her gaze upward to a smiling face set with laughing gray eyes. He had propped himself up on one elbow, dark brown hair falling forward across his forehead, and was watching her closely.

"Good morning . . . um . . ." She desperately searched her memory, but could not, for the life of her, come up with a name. Jiggs eyed his strong, unconventional features warily. Handsome was too tame a word to describe his face. No, not handsome, but breathtakingly striking—a stone sculpture before the rough edges had been polished away. His deep tan was not the smooth brown acquired lying on a beach, but spoke of long hours of hard work under the hot Texas sun. The whole effect was one of barely controlled barbarianism. She didn't trust him—not for a minute—but it was too late for second thoughts. She had obviously trusted him last night.

He stretched his muscular body contentedly, then dropped his eyes to her body above the blanket where a lacy strap had slipped off one white shoulder. After a brief, disconcerting moment, he looked into her confused eyes. "You don't look too pert this morning, darlin'." A secret amusement lurked around the corners of his eyes, but was quickly concealed as he said silkily, "You don't regret last night, do you?"

Regret what? she wondered, mortified, as she shrugged the camisole strap back in place. She had no idea what had taken place last night, but how do you tell a man that you can't remember his lovemaking? Oh, well, when in doubt—fake it. "No, of course not . . . um . . ." What in the world was the wretched man's name? "Of course, I don't regret it." Liar, she silently accused. "But I really must be going now." She kept her voice matter of fact and avoided his eyes. "I've got *so* much to do today."

"Why, Jiggs, I do believe you're shy." His hand came up to rub his jaw, effectively hiding a devilish grin. "You weren't shy last night, sweetheart. I'll never forget the way you seduced me with your willow-green eyes and tantalizing touch." His reminiscent smile had Jiggs gritting her teeth. "And the way you turned into a wildcat in my bed— biting and scratching while in the deep throes of passion." The strangling sound coming from Jiggs's throat stopped him for a moment and he looked at her with innocent eyes. "I beg your pardon? Did you say something? No? Now where was I? Oh, yes—the deep throes of passion. It was wonderful. It was good for you, too, wasn't it, Jiggs?"

"Well . . . actually . . ." She could no longer keep up the pretense. She simply wanted to go home and spend the rest of the day soaking away the pain in a hot tub. "The fact is . . ."

"Don't tell me you don't remember! Jiggs, you wound me." The accusation in his eyes was at odds with his strangely twitching lips. "You mean you don't remember the way you undressed me? You seemed very impatient."

"I undressed you?" she squeaked.

There was no doubt about it, the grin now appearing was very definitely wolfish. "Undressed me is putting it mildly. I should have said you ripped the clothes from my body." He gave her a knowing look. "You're so impetuous."

"Oh, no," she groaned, sliding lower in the bed.

"Oh, yes. Would you like to see what you did to my shirt?" He moved, as if to rise, and the blanket slipped precariously lower on his hips, revealing the drawstring waist of black silk pajamas resting indecently low on his hips.

"No, please." She squeezed her eyes shut in embarrassment. "I'll take your word for it. I'm sorry if I ruined your shirt. I can't understand it. Nothing you've told me makes sense. In fact, this whole situation makes no sense." Her earnest green eyes pleaded with him to understand. "I know this will seem difficult to believe, but I don't normally do this sort of thing. I'm totally, completely, painfully confused and I . . . I think I would like to go home now."

"But you can't leave now. Aren't you curious about last night? You can't leave everything up in the air." His long-fingered hand slid under the cover and rested on her warm thigh, his voice growing husky. "Maybe if we recreate the scene it will refresh your memory—kind of like an instant replay."

"No!" she said in a gasp, pushing his hand away. She began to sit up, then fell back with a groan, as pain pierced her temples. "I'll . . ." Her voice came out high, unnatural and she swallowed to begin again. "I'll probably remember the whole thing when the fog in my brain lifts." Jiggs felt lost and so vulnerable, a feeling that she hated. She gathered her strength and with a new firmness said, "May I have my clothes and privacy to dress, please?"

"I don't understand you," he complained in an exasperated tone. "You obviously came to my room expecting me to make love to you or you wouldn't have been in my bed when I arrived. So why play hard to get? Look, darlin' . . ." His voice softened as he swiftly, surely moved to half-cover her body with his own. "I'm sorry last night didn't turn out as you expected, but we can make up for it now," he whispered huskily, nuzzling the sensitive skin below her ear.

Jiggs stifled the unfamiliar shudder of pleasure that such intimate contact with his hard, masculine body sent rippling down her spine and focused her cloudy brain on his earlier statement. "In your bed? Didn't we arrive together? Weren't you at Max's party?" A nebulous memory floated through her mind. A crowded car. She was in someone's lap, fighting wandering hands. She winced as a stab of pain in her temples chased away the elusive visions.

"Jiggs, you don't have to pretend," he chided gently. "You weren't pretending last night. You wanted me and you came after me." He seemed not to notice her furious glare, his smug look congratulating her for her good taste. "I don't know anything about a party. I only know that when I saw you snuggled up on my bed, waiting for me, I didn't care where you had come from." His admiring gaze slipped from her face to her partially concealed body below. "You don't question a gift from the gods."

Jiggs's anger was lost in her growing confusion. What was he saying? If he hadn't brought her here, how did she come to be in his room? In his bed? She tried to give her voice a semblance of dignity as she asked, "If we didn't arrive together, when did I get here? Was I alone? When did you get here?" A note of hysteria crept into her voice as she realized how little she knew about the night before. "And where in the hell are we anyway?"

"You're serious, aren't you?" he said, studying her flushed features intently. "You really don't know how you got here?" She moaned in frustration, giving her head a short, negative shake. "Look," he said, his voice now firm and efficient. "I'm going to get dressed. While I'm in the bathroom, try to organize your thoughts, then we'll see if we can piece together what happened."

From his manner, Jiggs gathered that he was used to dealing with problems, and dealing with them promptly. The change was so remarkable, she simply stared in fascinated silence. As he finished speaking, he sat up abruptly and she nervously shifted her eyes to the ceiling.

Upon hearing the door close, she scrambled from the bed and surveyed the large room for her things. She found them lying neatly on a chair in the corner and hurriedly slid into the crepe de chine dress. A grimace marred her features as she caught sight of herself in the dresser mirror. The low-cut, midnight blue dress looked out of place in the brilliant light of day—it was clearly a dress for the soft lights of evening. Maybe there was a back way by which she could escape unseen. She looked anxiously about the room for a clue to her whereabouts. That she was in a hotel room was evident, but which hotel? The beautifully reproduced eighteenth-century Georgian furniture and plush carpet gave the room a look of subdued elegance. She mentally complimented the decorator who had echoed the room's chocolate brown and navy blue color scheme in the delicate pattern of the cream colored wallpaper. This was obviously one of Dallas's better hotels. She moved to the large window and pulled the drapes aside. In the distance, she could see the unmistakable shape of Reunion Tower, but before she could get her bearings, she heard the bathroom door open and she knew she was no longer alone. Jiggs turned cautiously to face him, feeling uncharacteristically shy. She had never been in a situation where she felt less sure of herself. She didn't like the feeling of having no control over her life.

His deep voice jolted her from her depressing reverie. "Come over here and sit down, Jiggs," he commanded, his voice brisk. "Just relax. We'll get to the bottom of this. I'm sure there is a very simple explanation."

She hovered nervously beside one of the brown velvet chairs before sinking abruptly into it as he gave her an impatient glance.

Lowering himself into the matching chair, he shifted slightly to face her. "Now, tell me just exactly what you *do* remember about last night."

She blinked in annoyance at his curtness, but swallowed a sharp retort as she realized that someone had to take charge and her fuzzy memory ruled her out completely. The fire dwindled in her spring-green eyes and she said with relative composure, "Last night I went to a celebration party given by a friend."

"And the name of your friend?" he interrupted to ask.

"Max Bueller."

"How close a friend is he?" he queried, gazing at the navy carpet with studied indifference.

"What difference does it make?" Jiggs couldn't understand his line of questioning.

"It could make a lot of difference," he muttered obscurely. Catching her puzzled glance, he added hastily, "Who knows—you may be a thief. That would make Max an accessory."

"What are you talking about?" Somehow she had slipped through the looking glass. Nothing was real anymore. "Accessory to what?"

"That's what we're trying to find out," he said, infuriatingly patient. "Go on—was the party held here at the hotel?"

"No, it wasn't here—wherever 'here' is—it was at Max's townhouse in North Dallas."

" 'Here' is the Beresford House," he informed her.

"We're making progress. At least I know where I am. Now if I could just find out how I got here!" She sighed in despair. "I knew I shouldn't have drunk so much on an empty stomach. I skipped lunch yesterday and Max's gluttonous friends ate everything in sight before I even arrived." He seemed fascinated by her face, his steel-gray eyes glued to her thoughtful features as she continued to explain. "I rarely drink, but Max kept proposing toasts and it would have seemed churlish to refuse."

"You said it was a celebration. What were you celebrating?"

"Max's new assignment. He's a free-lance photographer and he's just been assigned to do a peace series. It means he'll be traveling all over the world. Naturally, he wanted to celebrate." She recalled the mischievous gleam in Max's eyes as he refilled her champagne glass again and again. "I suspect he was trying to get me drunk. It's just the kind of dumb joke Max enjoys." She stopped to massage her throbbing temples as though trying to force the elusive events of the night before to the surface. "I can remember checking my watch at ten-thirty and that's the last truly clear thing that I can recall."

"Clear? You can remember things that are not clear?" At her nod, he asked, "For instance?"

"I have a very hazy memory of being in a crowded car." She leaned her aching head on the high back of her chair for a moment, then jerked upright as she remembered something else. "Abraham Lincoln!"

"I beg your pardon?" He looked at Jiggs as though he expected her to start foaming at the mouth at any second.

Unaware of his astonishment, she leaned forward, triumphant at having recovered a bit of her missing past. "Someone—I can't remember who—told me that Abraham Lincoln wanted to see me. I recall being very impressed that such an important person had asked for me." It took a moment for what she had just said to get past the pain in her head and sink into her brain. "Abraham Lincoln?" she whispered, turning tear-filled eyes to the man beside her. "I'm crazy, aren't I? I thought *you* were, but it's really *me*," she murmured incoherently.

"Jiggs?"

The gentle concern in his voice was her undoing. It released a trail of tears that ran silently down her lovely, confused face. Then strong arms came around her, lifting her, and she was in his lap, being rocked like a baby. Jiggs leaned against his strength, resting her weary head on his shoulder and letting him rock away her fears.

"Thank you . . . um . . . I'm sorry, I don't know

your name." She glanced up at him and sniffed pathetically.

"You're quite welcome and my name is Matt." His encouraging smile, viewed from this close range, brought a strange feeling to the pit of Jiggs's stomach. He smoothed back the hair that had fallen across her forehead, apparently unaware that he still held her clasped to his chest. "Would you like to tell me what that was all about?"

"Don't you see," she asked miserably. "I wake up in bed with a strange man, foul creatures are playing the Anvil Chorus in my head, I find out I'm totally insane, and . . . and my hair's a mess," she finished on a wailing note and buried her face in his shirt.

"Matt?" The word was muffled against his broad shoulder, which was, unreasonably, shaking.

"Yes, Jiggs," he answered in a strangled voice.

"May I go to the ladies' room?"

Low, rich laughter burst forth and filled the room. She stared at his face in startled wonder, mesmerized by his laughing features.

"I'm sorry, Jiggs," he said, controlling his laughter with difficulty. "I've been a pig, haven't I? Badgering you when you don't feel well and I didn't even offer you the use of the bathroom. After all the champagne you had last night, you must be in agony. Honestly, I wasn't being sadistic—I just didn't think."

"Really, there's no need to go into detail." She turned her head and began to memorize the pattern in the wallpaper as crimson flooded her face. "May I go now?"

"Of course," he said, releasing her, then handing her the satin evening purse which had lain on the table between the chairs.

Realizing that he was barely suppressing his laughter, Jiggs hurried from the room in embarrassment. Minutes later as she surveyed her disheveled appearance in the bathroom mirror, she railed at the fates that had led her into this predicament. "When I get my hands on Max," she muttered, "he'll wish he had never heard of Jiggs O'Malley."

She pulled the comb viciously through her tangled auburn locks, viewing the results with displeasure. "Mirror, mirror . . . well, come on," she urged, "who's the fairest? Bo Derek?" She turned from the mirror in disgust and complained, "Don't you ever read fairy tales? That's all I need—an honest mirror." Directing a rude gesture at the unobliging mirror, she squared her shoulders, took a deep breath, and made up her mind to be out of the hotel and back in the real world as quickly as possible.

Matt was still sitting where she had left him. Like the Raven, "never flitting," she thought, then wondered if she was becoming hysterical again.

Sensing her presence, he turned his head and said, "Feeling better now, Jiggs?"

His hastily stifled grin had her mentally wincing, but she answered calmly, "I'm fine, thank you." She sat down in the chair she had vacated earlier and faced him with what she hoped was a dignified expression. "Matt, I've told you all I know about last night. Could you do the same? Leaving out the intimate details," she hurried to add. "Just tell me what you know about how I came to be in your room. Please."

"I honestly don't know how you got here, Jiggs," he answered seriously. "I returned to my room about twelve-thirty this morning and you were asleep on my bed."

"Asleep . . . on your bed. I see." She swallowed her mortification. "Then what?"

"Well, I wasn't bothered at first because I had

been expecting a visitor—her coloring is similar to yours." His swift examination of her body seemed to say it was the only similarity. "Once I had realized my mistake, I tried to wake you. You revived long enough to tell me your first name . . . and that I was cute. . . ." Jiggs shifted in embarrassment at his mocking glance. ". . . then you passed out cold, so I made you comfortable and let you sleep. I just assumed you were looking for a good time and had bribed someone to let you into my room."

She looked at him curiously. "Do women often bribe their way into your room?" His wicked grin brought an answering smile to her well-shaped lips. If you smile at them like that, she thought, I can't really blame them.

She glanced away from the distraction of his smile and began to concentrate on what he had told her about the night before. He said he had made her comfortable and let her sleep. Since she had been wearing only her camisole and panties when she woke up, Jiggs decided not to probe into *how* he had made her "comfortable." Suddenly, the gears in her foggy brain began slowly turning. "Matt, just now you said that you let me sleep, is that right?"

His outspread hands were joined to form a peak and he was whistling softly under his breath, carefully looking the other way. Finally, as if just hearing her words, he glanced at her. "What? Oh, yes. So I did."

"Then, all that business about my scratching and biting and . . ." her voice rose as her fury mounted, " . . . and ripping your clothes off. That was all a lie, wasn't it?"

"Do you know," he said, regarding her closely, "when you're angry, your eyes do the damnedest things."

"Matt!"

"No, honestly," he said, leaning closer. "They turn deep emerald green, but there are these crazy little flecks of gold that sparkle right next to your pupils. It's weird. Beautiful, but weird."

"Matt, why did you tell me those things?" she asked in exasperation. She knew she should be furious at his deception, but relief that she had not made love to a stranger outweighed her anger.

"I don't know. It seemed a good idea at the time. You were so certain that the worst had happened, I just hated to disappoint you."

His assumed innocence brought a reluctant smile to her face. "I'll accept that—for the moment—but why did you let me go on believing it?"

"Scout's honor, Jiggs," he said, raising his hand, "I thought that you had figured that part out yourself." His quizzical look seemed to question her intelligence. "You're not very experienced, are you, Jiggs?"

"I have been engaged," she defended herself heatedly. "And I really don't see that it's any of your business."

He conveniently ignored her irate comment. "You were so shocked at the idea of being carried away by passion and if the ex-fiancé didn't provoke that kind of reaction in you, then it's best that you broke it off." He gazed deeply into her eyes, as though he were trying to penetrate her very soul. "Because it's there, Jiggs, I can see it in your eyes."

His low, husky voice and sensuous gray eyes caused a tingling warmth to spread throughout her body. Her eyes dropped in uneasy tension to her clinched fists. He's right, she conceded silently. Roger's lovemaking had been "nice." And that insipid, unforgivably damning word applied to his personality as well. A nice, quiet, boring man who made love in a nice, quiet, boring way. However, she wasn't willing to discuss her limited sexual experience with Matt. Under normal circumstances, Jiggs would have given a bone-chilling reply to any such personal comment. But these were anything but normal circumstances. A more bizarre situation she had never encountered. The sooner she was out of it the better. She lifted her head, intercepting his thoughtful gaze. "Matt, you don't really think I'm a crook, do you?"

"Well . . ." At her sharp glance, he chuckled and continued, "No, I guess not. Why?"

"I just wanted to make sure before I leave."

"Leave! But we haven't had breakfast yet."

"No, really, Matt. I've got to go." She stood and looked down to brush an imaginary speck of dust from her dress. Now that it was time to leave, she felt awkward and strangely hesitant. She caught his movement in her peripheral vision and a moment later he was standing before her. His hand gently tilted her chin, forcing her to look up at him.

"But you're my guest, Jiggs, and I've given you a rough time. Let me make it up to you by giving you breakfast." The words were spoken softly, his breath a gently seductive caress on her face.

Jiggs shifted to move away from the disturbing closeness, only to find herself caught in the circle of his arms. She threw him an inquisitive look and was stunned by the desire burning deep in his gray eyes. She opened her mouth to deliver an indignant protest, but found his mouth eager to take advantage of her half-parted lips.

His fingers spread across her back and moved down her spine, smoothing the thin material of her dress over her curving buttocks, shaping her body against his. His hands skillfully caressed her hips before sliding over her stomach to her rounded breasts. Delicious shivers ran down her spine as he lowered his mouth to her neck, his firm lips and moist tongue teasing the sensitive skin.

The softly provocative exploration continued, spreading a warm languor through Jiggs's lower limbs. Without her volition, her body arched against his hardening length. He groaned deep in his throat at her response, intensifying his hungry caresses. "Your body is perfect, Jiggs." His voice was raspy, urgent. "Last night when I took off your dress and found you were only wearing those silly little pieces of lace underneath, it took all my willpower to stop myself from touching you. God," he breathed sharply, "I deserve a medal for that."

Jiggs caught her breath, shocked by the thought of him looking at her nearly naked body; then her brain, dulled by unfamiliar emotions, came to life as she felt him undo the hook at the back of her dress and begin to ease down her zipper. She knew that unless she took action soon, the situation was going to be totally out of control. Matt had an uncanny effect on her senses. If she stayed, her fears of sleeping with a stranger would become a reality. She had to find a way to divert his attention and make good her escape.

She brought her hands, which had somehow become entangled in his thick hair, down to push against his strong shoulders.

"Matt, wait." Her plea was lost against his lips as he once again sought the honey of her mouth. She pushed harder, her efforts meaningless against the concrete hardness of his muscular chest.

"Oh God, Jiggs, you're delicious," he moaned, his lips moving over the softness of her throat before sliding lower to encounter the rounded tops of her firm breasts.

"Matt—please!" She had to make him listen before she was lost in the enchantment of his touch. "Matt, you promised me breakfast."

Her words seemed to penetrate for he lifted his head and stared at her blankly. "Breakfast?" He shook his head as if to clear it. "You want breakfast . . . *now*?"

"Yes, please."

"I can't say much for your sense of timing, but I did make the offer. Okay, breakfast it is." He released her to run long fingers through his disheveled hair as though wondering what to do next, then turned toward the bed. "I'll have room service send something up. Would you like to see a menu?"

The moment he turned his back, Jiggs picked up her evening bag and headed for the door, the sound of her footsteps lost in the deep pile of the carpet. She was on her way out the door when he picked up the phone from the nightstand and glanced up to see her leaving. She slammed the door and ran, offering a prayer of thanks that the elevator was standing open at the end of the hall.

"Wait, please," she called as the doors began to close before she could reach them.

"Jiggs, damn it! Come back here!"

The doors slid silently together, shutting out Matt's face, red with fury, and Jiggs leaned against the wall for support, ignoring the speculative stares of the couple occupying the elevator.

As she walked from the hotel into the bright light of day, merging quickly with the crowd of uninterested pedestrians, it occurred to her that she would never see Matt again. Instead of being relieved, the thought unaccountably saddened her.

# Two

Jiggs pushed through the sparkling glass doors of the new SPC Building, paused to get her bearings, then headed for the reception desk in the center of a forest of potted plants. At the direction of an efficient blonde, she took the elevator to the tenth floor, praying to the gods who govern such things that her interview would be successful. She didn't think she could stand another six months of photographing catalog items for McNabb's Pipe Company. Maybe it indicated a deficiency in her character, but couplings and cast iron elbows just didn't seem to inspire her.

On the tenth floor, Jiggs swiftly found Suite 1020 and after confirming her appointment, was asked to be seated by a plump, motherly brunette. The office was tastefully furnished in a quietly modern style, the cool blue and green color scheme soothing to Jiggs's frayed nerves. Through the glass wall she could see the sprawling city of Dallas with the familiar outline of Reunion Tower in the distance to her left.

Will I ever be able to look at that building without feeling embarrassment? she wondered, her thoughts returning for the umpteenth time to the events of five days ago. Jiggs deeply regretted the childish way she had handled her encounter with Matt. Running away solved nothing. She had not given him a chance to understand. He had, for the most part, seemed a reasonable man. He had also seemed an irresistible man, her good sense reminded her. No matter how much willpower she possessed, if he had set his mind on seducing her, his expertise and her weakened condition would have guaranteed his success. On the other hand, he might have understood her strong objection to casual affairs—if she had stayed long enough to explain.

Jiggs sighed deeply in exasperation. The same arguments had been swirling around in her head for nearly a week. It was no use crying over spilled milk—she would never see him again, so she might as well forget the whole episode. If you can, an unbidden thought silently mocked.

"Miss O'Malley."

"Yes?" Jiggs slid forward in the seat and looked at the secretary expectantly.

"Mr. Timms will see you now."

Jiggs stood, smoothing down her white pleated skirt and straightening her peach blazer before proceeding with outward confidence into the adjoining office.

She liked Samuel Timms on sight. He was short and bald and reminded her of the stuffed panda that had been her best friend at age five. Apologizing for keeping her waiting, he motioned for her to be seated.

As he went over the details of her resume, now

and then asking pertinent questions, he seemed gratifyingly impressed and Jiggs mentally crossed her fingers for luck.

"Miss O'Malley . . . may I call you Jiggs?" At her nod, he continued. "Jiggs, your photographic background is excellent." He paused to clear his throat, then excused himself to pour a glass of water. Apparently he was unaware of her growing tension. She sensed an imminent "however" and prepared herself for disappointment.

"As I was saying, I'm very impressed by your photographic background and although I'm not an expert, even I can see your pen and ink drawings are remarkably good. However . . ."

Aha! she thought, here it comes!

". . . as you know, there is one other requirement. This one has given us considerable difficulty. That is, it has eliminated quite a few otherwise excellent candidates." He eyed her with regret, as though mentally crossing her off the list. "I'm referring to the geologic background which we specified as a requirement for the position. I see that you had two years of geology in college. Have you had any practical experience?" He asked as though it would be more likely that she had been to the moon.

"If you mean, have I drilled any oil wells—then the answer is no. I spent three summers in the field with my paleontology professor, if that's any help." She forced herself to remain calm. Experience had taught her that it was bad strategy to appear overanxious.

"You've studied paleontology, also?"

"Yes. Under Professor Ian McKenzie—perhaps you've heard of him?" His enthusiastic nod of recognition gave her new hope. "I've done some drawings for the professor. If you would like to call him, I'm sure he would give you any information you need regarding my work." She leaned back in her chair and watched as he sat in deep thought, occasionally tapping his forehead with a pencil.

"It might work," he muttered, reaching for the telephone. "I hadn't dared hope for a paleontological background. Yes, it just might work." He seemed suddenly to recall her presence, for he replaced the phone and swung his chair around to face her.

"I'm very hopeful, Jiggs. But of course, you realize that mine is not the final decision." Her puzzled expression gave him his answer and he explained. "You will be working for Mr. Brady. That is, if he agrees, you'll be working for him and he will, naturally, have the final say. I'm Mr. Brady's assistant and it is my job to simplify things for him. It's a difficult job sometimes, Jiggs." He sighed deeply, then as if fearing he had been disloyal, he hurried to add, "Mr. Brady is a wonderful man to work for and I hold him in the highest esteem. However, at times, he tends to be what we used to call 'persnickity.' "

And obviously still do, Jiggs thought, suppressing a giggle and becoming more and more enamored of this man's gentle pomposity. But Mr. Brady sounded like an old grouch and she had to swallow her disappointment at not working for Mr. Timms.

"And Mr. Brady is? . . ." she asked.

"Why, he is the president of Southwest Products Corporation." His astonishment could not have been greater had she asked "Who is Ronald Reagan?"

"Mr. Brady is a geologist?"

"He *was* a paleontologist. He had barely begun his career when his father died, leaving him in charge of SPC."

"How could his father leave him the presidency

of a company?" Jiggs was becoming more and more confused. Corporate structure was just not her milieu.

"It's very simple," he replied. "His father was also the major stockholder."

"I see," she said, not seeing at all, but deeming further pursuit of the subject fruitless. "Mr. Timms, could you give me an idea of what's involved in this position? Mrs. Overby, from the employment agency, merely said an artist-photographer with a geologic background was required. She didn't go into it in any depth."

"Certainly, certainly," he agreed. "Mr. Brady is writing a book—or to be more accurate—recording a history. I know nothing of fossils, but according to experts, he has one of the finest private collections of trilobites in the country. You're familiar with this type of fossil?" She gave an affirmative nod and he continued. "During his years of collecting these fossils, he also collected some, as I understand, rather interesting theories on the evolution of the trilobite. His book will be a compilation of the evidence to prove these theories."

As he spoke, Mr. Timms's smoothly rounded face beamed with proud approval. If he inspired such emotions in this kindly man, Jiggs mused, maybe Mr. Brady wasn't all bad and, grouch or no grouch, the details of his work had her champing at the bit. She would give her eyeteeth to work on this project.

"I'll just give Mr. Brady a call and find out when it would be convenient for him to see you," Mr. Timms said, reaching for the telephone. He spoke briefly into the white instrument before asking Jiggs if three o'clock met with her approval. She nodded, trying to conceal her joy, and he concluded the arrangements, sending her on her way with his best wishes and an encouraging thumbs-up gesture.

As Jiggs left the building, she checked her watch and saw she had almost three hours to kill—plenty of time for lunch and browsing through the downtown shops, a treat she didn't often enjoy since McNabb's was located on the outskirts of town. She decided to browse first and wait until the rush was over to have lunch.

By one-thirty, as she stored her purchases in the trunk of her car, her stomach was rumbling in protest. She was only a block away from Jake's Grille, the tiny bar and grill that was a favorite of her photographer friends, so she headed for it, thinking longingly of Jake's frittata.

Inside she was greeted by several of her friends, urging her to join them at the curved wooden bar. Spying Max in the far corner of the room, she waved her regrets to her friends and headed purposefully for his booth.

"Jiggs, honey!" he exclaimed with delight as she halted beside him. "Where have you been? I haven't seen you since . . ."

"Since last Friday night, Max," she completed for him, annoyed accusation evident in her tone. "At your celebration party. I'd like to ask you a few questions about that party, Max."

"Sure, honey, sure," he replied, all affability. "Ask away."

Jiggs wasn't taken in by his agreeable manner. Behind Max's blond good looks lurked the heart of a fiend. He knew she was gunning for him and hoped to bluff his way out of it. "I'm not going to say anything about your prolific toasting on Friday night, Max. I figure I'm old enough to watch out for myself. However . . ." She gave a stern look. ". . . I do want to know how I got separated from the rest of the party."

"You mean you don't remember?" His innocent expression was ruined by the grin he was struggling to suppress. "What's the matter, Jiggs, did you drink too much?"

"You know damn well I did, you traitor. Now tell me what happened." She couldn't stay angry with Max. Her sober image had been a challenge he simply couldn't resist and he had had no way of knowing what the consequences of her drinking on an empty stomach would be.

"What's the last thing you remember, sugar?" he asked, realizing she was serious in her request.

"I seem to recall being stuffed in a car on top of an octopus, but the whole thing is very fuzzy."

"That was George. You know he's always fancied you," he explained. His blue eyes sparkled and he was no longer trying to hide his grin.

"George!" Her outraged expression was almost comical. "You know I can't stand George—why did you let me sit in his lap?" The thought of that middleaged Romeo's hands on her body made her shudder in revulsion.

"And how was I supposed to stop you, Ms. Independence?"

"You might have tried using a sledge hammer on George," she muttered darkly. "Okay, I know—you didn't take me to raise, but after practically pouring your cheap champagne down my throat, you could have at least kept George away from me."

"I resent your insinuations about the quality of my champagne." He looked at her with injured dignity. "Do you think I would serve my friends anything but the best? That was vintage stuff."

"I don't care if it was *Dom Perignon*. It gave me a headache that lasted three days—*three days*, Max!" Her green eyes flared as he tried unsuccessfully to hide a gleeful grin. "It also left a big, black hole where Friday is supposed to be." She pinned him with a determined gaze. "Now tell why I was in a car in the first place. Where were we going?"

Max appeared not at all upset by her tirade. He settled back on the black vinyl bench seat, stretching his long, thin legs out in front of him with an air of calm deliberation. "We ran out of champagne," he explained, as if it were an obvious conclusion.

Jiggs closed her eyes in frustration. "For heaven's sake, Max. How many people does it take to fetch champagne?"

"We decided it would be better if we moved the party to a place where there was an adequate supply of booze—so we went to the Miranda Room."

Resigned comprehension dawned in her pale green eyes. "Isn't the Miranda Room in—"

"The Beresford House?" he interrupted, his sharp gaze spotting her discomfort. He drew himself upright and looked at her intently. "Yes, it is. Why?"

Jiggs knew she would have to act for all she was worth in order to throw Max off the scent. His enjoyment of her adventures while under the influence would be magnified a hundredfold if he found out about her night in Matt's bed. Jiggs had a reputation for being numb from the neck down and Max would take wicked delight in debunking that myth publicly.

She mentally girded her loins and looked straight into his suspicious blue eyes. "I just can't recall ever having been there," she said casually. "When did I leave the party, Max?"

He stared at her as though trying to divine her thoughts, then shrugged. "I noticed you were missing around midnight. George said you had gone to the ladies' room. I figured you had given him the slip and gone home."

The arrival of the waitress halted further conversation, much to Jiggs's relief. She wasn't prepared to answer any questions about how and when she got home.

After they had placed their orders, Max excused himself to talk with friends on the other side of the room, leaving her alone with her thoughts. Her presence in the Beresford House was no longer a mystery. But why had she gone to Matt's room? And how did that ridiculous memory of Abraham Lincoln fit into the puzzle? It seemed more than likely that she would never find out. Oh, well, she thought, some people see pink elephants—I see Honest Abe. This rationalization helped to restore her sense of humor, but did nothing to satisfy her curiosity.

After lunch, Jiggs told Max about her interview with Mr. Timms and of the coming interview with Mr. Brady. Max knew of her passion for fossils and responded with optimistic enthusiasm. He could be a genuinely nice man—when his weird sense of humor wasn't leading him astray.

He finished his coffee and stubbed out his cigarette, his sharp eyes searching her face quizzically. "I could never understand why you took that stupid job in the first place. I mean, really, sugar— McNabb's Pipe Company?" He looked as if the words left a bad taste in his mouth. "You might just as well have taken a job as counter clerk at the local dry cleaner's."

While secretly agreeing with his statement, she felt compelled to defend her choice. "It hasn't been a bad job, Max. I work with some very nice people."

"Nice people! Lord love us, Jiggs," he said, disgust evident in his tone. "Honey, you've got a talent that most people would give their right arm for. And you sit there mouthing platitudes about the 'nice people' you work with—at a pipe factory! It's a damned waste."

Max was on his soapbox with a vengeance, the muscles in his thin, angular face contracting in determination. The subject was a familiar point of contention between them. Her refusal to see things his way infuriated and frustrated him. His eyes were beaming wrathful fury as he continued to rail. "It's more than that—it's a sin, Jiggs." As usual, Max worked his way around anger and tried wheedling. "Look, sweetheart, why don't you let me arrange a showing of your watercolors? I told Barney about them and he said he would look them over as a favor to me." The kindling fire in her now jade green eyes warned Max to back off. "Come on, Jiggs, I know you told me you didn't want a showing. But are you being fair to yourself? To the world?"

Jiggs clamped down on her fury and managed to speak with near civility. "You had no business discussing those watercolors with anyone, Max. You wouldn't have known about them if you hadn't been snooping. Now, for the last time—listen carefully—I . . . do . . . not . . . want . . . a . . . showing." She said the words through clenched teeth. "I know the loss of my talent will be a devastating blow to the world, but believe me, the world will survive."

A quick glance at her watch confirmed that it was time for her to leave. "Max, let's not argue. I appreciate your concern and I'm glad you have faith in my ability—I value your opinion." His snort of disbelief brought a sympathetic smile to her lovely face. "Someday I'll paint a room full of watercolors and dedicate them all to you. But I'm simply not ready to expose my work to the public and even if I were, I wouldn't let you blackmail your friend into showing my work at his gallery. I have to make it on my own." Her eyes pleaded with him to understand and forgive her stubbornness. "Won't you wish me luck with the 'persnickity' Mr. Brady?"

"Sugar, eyes like yours should be available only with a prescription." He stared at her in bemusement, his voice soft, his crooked smile self-mocking. "Of course I wish you luck." He shook off his oddly wistful expression as he watched her rise to leave. "Speaking of Brady—did you get to the Mathew Brady exhibit at the museum? I looked for you on Saturday, but I must have missed you."

"I couldn't make it on Saturday. I was indisposed." Her green eyes dared him to comment. "I'm going to try to catch it next week on my lunch break. I hope it's not crowded." Jiggs had arranged to see a showing of the works of the famous Civil War photographer with a group of friends on the day after the party, but she had needed time to recover from her hangover—not to mention her encounter with Matt.

"It couldn't be more crowded than it was on Saturday. The bourgeoisie was there *en masse*," he informed her cynically, then hurriedly said goodbye when he was hailed by a very sexy blonde entering the room.

Jiggs was still pondering the intricacy of Max's character as she made her way back to the SPC Building. He delighted in teasing her, even embarrassing her. Yet on several occasions Max had tried to change their casually warm friendship into a more intimate one. And although she admired his talent and was very fond of him, Jiggs had never felt the curious tug of desire that was necessary for a physical relationship. Her engagement to Roger had taught her that much. When a red-faced Roger had stutteringly announced that he had fallen in love with his sister's best friend, Jiggs's only reaction, after a moment of pique, had been relief. The fact that she had felt no pain underlined how wrong the engagement had been. Roger couldn't hurt her because he had never touched her heart. She wondered now if she hadn't chosen him for that very fact. She knew he would never expose her vulnerability. Nice, safe Roger. She would never enter into that type of relationship again. In a way, she had used Roger. She had used him to stave off loneliness. Jiggs had considered his infrequent sexual demands as the price she had to pay for companionship. But Max was too much a man to settle for that type of lukewarm affair. He would demand more of Jiggs and perhaps she wasn't capable of more.

Unbidden, the memory of the overpowering desire she had felt while in Matt's arms filled her mind and raced through her body, chasing away all thought of Max and Roger, and effectively contradicting her doubts about her own sensuality. She was momentarily consumed by a yearning for something entirely beyond her ken. Consequently, she spent the remainder of her walk lecturing herself on the adolescence of daydreaming about a man she would never see again.

This time she was directed by the beautiful blonde in the potted forest to the twenty-first floor. That gave her eleven additional floors in which to mentally prepare herself for the coming interview.

It was two forty-five when she walked into the quietly elegant outer office of the president of SPC. Although she was early, the brisk, efficient secretary informed her that Mr. Brady was ready to see her.

The inner office appeared to be empty and Jiggs looked around in confusion. A moment later, her gaze was caught and held by the tall figure sitting on a brown leather couch, in the shadows, against one wall.

"Hello, Jiggs." The voice was deep. The voice was amused. The voice was Matt's.

# *Three*

Jiggs leaned against the closed door, squeezed her eyes shut, and slowly exhaled the breath she had drawn in sharply on hearing Matt's voice.

"I should have known," she muttered under her breath. "First Otis decided to have my new Italian sandals for breakfast, then that awful lady at the sale—I swear I've seen her on Saturday Night Wrestling—attacked me because I picked up the hat she wanted for herself." She sighed fatalistically. "Of course, it's you. It had to be either you or the lady wrestler."

"Who is Otis?"

Jiggs opened her eyes to find Matt standing directly in front of her, staring with the awed fascination of a man discovering a heretofore unknown species. She let her eyes range over his full length. He was tall. When she wore heels, the added inches brought her eye level with most men, yet he seemed to tower over her.

"Otis is my neighbor's cat. I'm cat-sitting while

she's on vacation." Her close proximity to the man who had lately disrupted her thoughts with disturbing regularity caused Jiggs's heart to pound in her chest, the movement visible under the thin silk of her blouse, and she began to babble nervously. "The cat has problems—serious mental problems—but being catless myself, I'm in no position to give Joanie advice on cat-rearing." *Jiggs, you're making an absolute ass of yourself,* she silently berated, unable to stop the flow of words. "Joanie's my next door neighbor. She's a wonderful person, but so protective of Otis. She thinks he's perfect, but, let me tell you, that is one disturbed cat."

As she chattered inanely, one hand crept behind her back and searched frantically for the doorknob. "Well, Matt, it's been really lovely seeing you again." Her fingers grasped the elusive knob and turned it surreptitiously. "I guess I had better be going now. You must be terribly busy and—"

"Jiggs."

"I don't want to take up any more of your time, so—"

"Jiggs!"

"Yes, Matt," she sighed in resignation, seeing her chance of escaping humiliation go down the drain.

"I thought you wanted a job?" He asked the question seriously, but with an irritating twinkle in his gray eyes.

She stared at him dubiously. "You don't mean you would actually hire me?" She snorted inelegantly in self-disgust. "People don't hire raving maniacs. Haven't you been listening to me in the last few minutes?"

"Yes, I have. But I've also seen your drawings." He eyed her hopefully. "Do you . . . uh . . . *talk* while you're working?"

She suppressed a smile at his tactfully understated question. "Never."

"Well, then there's no problem." He sighed thankfully, motioned toward a chair, and walked to his own chair behind the gleaming mahogany desk. "Why don't you have a seat and we'll discuss the job."

He isn't going to mention it, she thought in amazement. He was apparently going to ignore their misadventure of the previous weekend and calmly discuss business. From the moment she had recognized his voice, she had been unconsciously preparing for battle, her slender body tensing in anticipation of the confrontation. And now he seemed to be willing to forget the way she had childishly run from his hotel room. After instantaneous, knee-weakening relief came a moment of pique. He was obviously no longer interested in her personally. That's fine, she told herself, lifting her chin with a hint of belligerence. That's exactly the way I want it.

"Just one question before we get started, Jiggs." Matt was shuffling through some papers on his desk and spoke casually.

"Yes, of course," she said in her most businesslike voice.

He looked up and grinned, turning Jiggs's insides to gelatin. "Who got the hat?"

She stared at him blankly for a moment, then laughed. "She did, of course. Do I look stupid?" His curiosity put her at ease. "Besides, I don't wear hats. I was just browsing."

"I guess that's as good a way as any to excuse your cowardice." He was laughing with her, leaning back comfortably in his leather chair. Rays from the afternoon sun streamed through the glass wall behind him and gleamed along his craggy cheekbones, giving his tanned skin the look of sculptured bronze.

"Believe me, if you had seen this lady, you would have considered discretion the better part of valor, too."

"I believe you. Women at a sale scare the hell out of me." Matt paused and leaned forward to pick up a typewritten sheet of paper from his desk, then looked at her searchingly. "I've been looking through your resume, Jiggs, and I've spoken with Ian McKenzie about you. Ian's an old friend and I trust his judgment," he explained. "He absolutely sang your praises. He not only recommended your drawings, but also your dedication and reliability." He seemed puzzled by something, his stare causing her to shift uncomfortably. "You're now employed by McNabb's Pipe Company?"

"Yes, that's right."

"Why?"

"I beg your pardon?"

"Why are you doing work that uses none of the talent that you obviously possess?"

Twice in one day was too much for Jiggs. She was tired of defending the way she ran her life. She took a deep breath and answered angrily, her narrowed eyes sparking green fire and her sensuous lower lip protruding slightly with aggression. "Because I have this real nasty habit that I have to support. It's called eating. And the way I choose to support that habit is my own business. If you object, I suggest you hire me, then we'll both be satisfied."

"My, my. We're touchy, aren't we?"

"Yes, I'm touchy," she admitted. "But be fair. I didn't come in here criticizing you for running this place when you clearly would rather be digging for fossils." Her own audacity took her breath away, but she refused to back down.

"Okay, I give. You're absolutely right, it's none of my business. But just to set the record straight—I wasn't criticizing, I was curious." He smiled at her and asked, "Pax?"

I wonder if he's aware of the effect that smile has on women, she thought, then realized a man of his obvious experience would have to be aware and, most likely, would use it for his own purposes.

She saw that he was still waiting for her answer and hastily said, "Yes, of course. Matt—I'm sorry—Mr. Brady, have you definitely decided to hire me?"

"Matt's fine, Jiggs. And, yes, I've definitely decided. After talking with Sam Timms and Ian, then looking through your resume and drawings, there was no question about it."

The certainty in his voice sent pride racing through her veins like adrenaline. "Thank you," she murmured, inordinately pleased by the unexpected praise. "Could you tell me something about your work, Matt? From the little that Mr. Timms told me, it sounds fascinating."

Matt evidently sensed her enthusiasm was genuine for he began to speak of his work as one devotee to another. As he explained how he became interested in the fossil arthropods and his subsequent search for the cause of their evolution and eventual extinction, Jiggs felt she could listen to his beautifully timbred voice forever. He seemed to have accumulated an unending supply of anecdotes from his years as a working paleontologist. The foibles and frailties, including his own, of scientists on a dig delighted her and his sensitive recounting of the courage and kindness of the people he had met on his travels, brought a sheen of unshed tears to her eyes. She interrupted occasionally with what she hoped were intelligent questions, and Matt answered in depth, taking her knowledge of the subject for granted.

Finally, he sighed with regret as he consulted his watch. "I'm afraid I have another appointment in fifteen minutes and we haven't discussed the details of your work yet." He paused for a moment, then, as though coming to a decision, continued, inexplicably avoiding her eyes, "Would you like to see my collection?"

"Oh, yes, Matt!" she answered breathlessly. "When?"

"Now—I keep it on the top floor." He stood up, still looking carefully beyond her. "You can look at the fossils, read my notes, then when I finish here we'll straighten out all the details. Okay?"

"That sounds fine," she said quietly, his strange behavior bewildering her.

In the hall, Matt bypassed the public elevator to usher her into another which was ominously marked PRIVATE in large, bold letters. His curious silence was beginning to make Jiggs uneasy. The elevator opened onto an elegantly modern hallway. It looked like no laboratory or workroom that Jiggs had ever seen. It looked like . . .

She turned accusing eyes to Matt who was whistling nonchalantly as he picked up a stack of mail from a narrow ebony table set against the wall, and began to sift through it, confirming her suspicions. "Matt!"

"Be with you in just a second, Jiggs," he said, casually ignoring her indignation. "I've been waiting for this letter." He looked at her with assumed innocence and said kindly, "Why don't you go on into the living room while I take care of this."

She gritted her teeth, but went as directed through the wide archway. If I didn't want this job so badly, she fumed silently, I would tell Mr.

Matthew Brady to stuff it. Does he honestly think that I'm naïve enough to fall for that old etchings trick? She paused in her thoughts to chuckle as she realized she *had* fallen for it.

She glanced around, then stopped in her tracks. She stared, mesmerized by the spacious, light-filled room. It was artistically perfect. Everything in it was arranged for a precise balance of space and color. But the room was dead. She couldn't believe people were allowed to be human in it. How could you argue, cry, laugh, or simply be bone tired in a room that forbade it? She carefully examined the space to discover a cause for the curious sterility. As she ran her eyes over the plush, silver-gray carpet, the stark white walls, relieved only by the splashes of color in the geometric wall hangings, and the clean lines of the white, gray, and rust upholstered furniture, she came to the conclusion that it wasn't the fault of the decor. The room was perfect—too perfect. There was not even a plant in it to spoil the perfection by dropping an occasional dead leaf.

"Awful, isn't it?"

Jiggs was startled from her analysis by Matt's voice close behind her. She turned to see him eyeing the room with distaste. "No, it's not awful. It's just—just . . ."

"Awful," he finished for her.

She laughed, charmed by the frankness of his humor. "Yes, I guess it is pretty awful. Do you live here?"

"Only when I have to," he replied. "My real home is on the Brazos River west of here. I'll tell you about it later." He glanced at his watch. "Right now I'm late for an appointment, so let me show you where I keep my work."

She followed him down the hall and through a door at the end.

"It's all here." He indicated several work tables loaded with labeled fossils. "Make yourself at home and I'll be back around five-thirty to finish our discussion." He said these last words on his way out the door, giving Jiggs no chance to reply.

Obviously he's not going to hang around to seduce me, she thought, disgruntled, then hurriedly reassured herself that, of course, that's the way she wanted it.

She looked around the untidy room, wondering where to begin. Besides the tables, there were dozens of boxes stacked around the room. Picking up first one specimen, then another, she was soon totally absorbed in his work. Some of the fossils were rough, barely discernible in the rock that surrounded them, but many had been meticulously cleaned. The samples she examined ranged in size from less than an inch to eighteen inches and the variation in the features of each showed a similar wide range. As she picked up one piece of fossilized trilobite after another, she found no two alike. She recognized some of the types from her geology and paleontology classes. Most, however, were unfamiliar to her and she read the reports, which were filed under the label number, with an almost hungry relish. Time passed unnoticed as she pored over detailed, sometimes highly technical reports. Although she didn't understand all she read, enough of it was clear to make it fascinating for her.

She paused to stretch aching muscles, then stiffened as she felt a sudden tingling sensation on the back of her neck. Glancing hesitantly over her shoulder, she saw Matt leaning against the doorjamb. He had discarded his jacket and tie, his shirt lay open at the throat. His eyes dwelt an inordinate length of time on her mouth, narrowing briefly as she moistened her lips with her tongue in a quick, nervous gesture.

He moved into the room, breaking the tense silence as he spoke. "Well, what do you think . . . about my work?" He added the last words to answer her puzzled expression.

Jiggs gave a short, self-denigrating laugh. "That's like asking a three-year-old child with a crayon what she thinks of Picasso's paintings. From the parts that I was able to understand, I would say it's brilliant. And I'm thrilled to have even a small part in the project."

At her words, he shoved his hands in his pockets and glanced quickly out the window across the room. She was baffled by his behavior until it slowly dawned on her that he was actually embarrassed by her praise. He looked like a small boy who had just been kissed in front of a group of his friends—pleased, but trying desperately to hide that pleasure lest he be teased. The humanness of his reaction was endearing.

He shifted his position, giving her a wry look. "I wouldn't put you in the same class as a kid with a crayon, but thank you anyway for the kind words. I hope my colleagues agree with you."

He sounded as if there were a very small chance of that happening and Jiggs, knowing how slow the scientific community generally was in accepting any new theory, feared he was right.

She rose to replace the page she had been reading in his file, then turned as he said, "Come on, darlin', let's find a drink," and disappeared through the door. He moved with the restless grace of a caged lion. When she entered the large room seconds later, he was draining his glass. Judging by the bottle, he was showing great disrespect for a very fine Irish whiskey.

He caught her astonished look as he lowered

his glass and laughed heartily. "Don't look so dis-approving. I'm not a lush. I was just trying to wash away the taste of a phony, self-made, back-stabbing, good-ole-boy millionaire," he explained. " 'We'll make us a killin', I guaran-damn-tee ya', boy!' "

His mimicry was perfect and she burst out laughing. "Do you have to deal with many of them?"

"No, thank God. Sam handles most of them. This one was particularly persistent, but I'd go partners with a rattlesnake before I'd do business with him. He wasn't too pleased when I brought out a file showing the shady deals he's been in-volved in for the last ten years," Matt said mali-ciously, a reminiscent smile curving his well-shaped lips.

"Enjoyed it, did you?"

"Loved it. It was one of the highlights of my career as president of SPC. It almost made the whole thing worthwhile." A faint look of regret came into his gray eyes, then he shook it off and looked at her apologetically. "I haven't offered you a drink. What would you like?"

"Ginger ale is fine."

He grinned at her as she asked for the non-alcoholic drink. "Chicken?"

"Definitely," she admitted, accepting the glass from him. "I learned my lesson. Apparently my metabolism is not compatible with alcohol." Now that he had finally brought up that fatal evening, their relationship had progressed to the point where she could discuss it naturally, without embarrassment. She mentally applauded his di-plomacy.

Matt poured himself another drink and motioned her to the couch, then stretched out in the chair opposite with a relaxed sigh. "I'm sorry I was so late in getting back. I tried to get rid of Jackson early, but Lord, he was a tenacious bastard."

Jiggs glanced at her watch as he spoke and realized she had been so enthralled by his research she had failed to notice his tardiness. It was almost six-thirty. "I didn't mind. If you hadn't returned when you did, I probably would have stayed until hunger forced me out," she told him and smiled.

"Speaking of hunger, I skipped lunch today and I'm starving. I've asked Ruth to set another plate, so we can discuss your job over dinner." He moved to rise, but Jiggs's startled look stopped him.

"Ruth?"

"My housekeeper."

"Has she been here all afternoon?"

"Yes, she said she looked in on you once to see if you needed anything, but you were so absorbed in my notes she hated to interrupt you."

She couldn't believe that she hadn't heard the housekeeper. She had felt Matt's presence the moment he had walked into the room. For some reason, this fact disturbed her.

"Shall we go in to dinner now, Jiggs?"

"I really should get home, Matt. Couldn't you just outline what you need from me, then we could go into the details later?"

"I'd rather get it out of the way now," he insisted. "That way you can be thinking of the techniques you'll use and the materials you'll need."

His logic was hard to fight, but Jiggs felt a vague sense of uneasiness at the thought of spending the evening with Matt. "I understand, but I had made tentative plans for this evening," she lied.

"If they're tentative, then no one will be upset if you cancel, right?" How smoothly he rationalized. His damned logic was beginning to irritate her and from his smug look, Matt recognized her irritation. She fumed silently and was about to insist on leaving when his words startled her from her purpose. "I'm sorry, what did you say?"

"I asked if you wanted to know how you came to be in my room on Friday night?" The expression on his face held all the assurance—and satisfaction—of a poker player who has just laid down a winning hand.

# Four

"You know how I got to your room?" she asked, her eyes widening with surprise at the bomb he had casually dropped.

"Yep. I sure do." He stood and replaced his glass on the sideboard, then walked toward the archway.

Scrambling to her feet, she hastily placed her glass beside his and followed him out the door. "How, Matt? How did I get in your room? I talked to Max and he told me how I got to the hotel, but no one saw me after midnight. How did I—oh!"

Her words halted as she ran into Matt's broad back. He had stopped abruptly and now turned to face her. "It's a long story, Jiggs, and I'll tell you all about it *after* dinner," he said, smiling triumphantly.

"That's pure, unmitigated blackmail," she fumed.

"Yeah. Sharp move on my part, don't you think?"

"Do you really want to know what I think?" she asked, her eyes daring him to answer in the affirmative.

"No," he stated unequivocally, grabbing her hand and pulling her behind him into a small dining room. Her pleated skirt flared in protest of his abrupt movement, momentarily exposing long, shapely legs. "Now sit down and I'll tell you what you're going to be doing for the next six months."

Before she could question his high-handed treatment, he introduced her to Ruth, his thin, plain-faced housekeeper, who was bringing in steaming bowls of delicious, homemade vegetable soup. Matt then began to tell Jiggs of the problems involved in the work she would be doing for him.

He talked steadily through the meal, pausing occasionally to concentrate on his food or to answer one of her many questions. His vitality seemed to fill the room, breathing life into the magazine-perfect setting.

"So, you see, you'll not only have to re-create each specimen, often from a very small piece of the actual creature, you'll also have to re-create an entire environment—the world as it existed when the creature lived," he summed up. "I want to show each developmentally important type of trilobite in its natural surroundings. I want the reader to see the influences that were at work hundreds of millions of years ago, during the time that each type lived. You'll have to show what the weather was, what predators were prevalent, and what types of food were available during each time period."

Matt placed his wine glass on the table with a sigh of repletion, then looked at her inquiringly. "How much notice do you have to give at McNabb's?"

"Two weeks is standard."

"That's perfect. That gives me enough time to arrange things on my end," he said, more to himself than to Jiggs. She could almost hear the gears in his brain shifting to high speed. "Moving the collection won't take long. I'll get someone on it first thing tomorrow. In two weeks I should have everything arranged so that Sam can take over SPC."

"We won't be working here?" she asked in puzzled apprehension.

"I'm sorry," he apologized, seeming to recall her presence. "I didn't tell you about the move, did I? We would never be able to get anything done here. I would be too convenient in a crisis. So I've decided to move everything to my home on the Brazos. It's just west of Mineral Wells, isolated enough to guarantee no interruptions, but close enough to civilization for Ruth to do her shopping."

"Ruth will be there, too?" she asked, trying, but failing miserably, to hide her relief. The rapport that she sensed between them was not enough to make her feel comfortable about spending six months in isolation with Matt. Ruth, taciturn though she might be, would keep the situation from seeming too intimate.

"Of course," he said, surprised. "Neither of us will have time for cooking or cleaning. Besides, if we had to depend on my cooking for sustenance, I'm afraid we'd both come down with ptomaine or botulism or something equally unpleasant. How about you?"

"I don't think anyone has actually died from my cooking, but I wouldn't guarantee it," she replied, echoing his grin. "I have a few special dishes that I do well, but you can live only so long on a diet of dill weed dip and strawberry mousse."

The laughter they shared at their own inadequacies filled Jiggs with a warmth she hadn't known since she was a child. If anyone had told her she would feel this empathy, this oneness, with a man she barely knew, she would have accused him of fantasizing. Jiggs had been on her own for a long time—since her parents died when she was eighteen—yet she had never before come across this particular phenomenon. Not that she didn't have friends. She did. Good, close friends. Friends she would trust with her life. But with Matt it was different. There was an indefinable quality in their relationship. A quality she had been too confused to recognize at their first meeting. Maybe it was the sense of humor, present in each, that was always ready, almost eager, to surface at any moment.

"You'll love my home, Jiggs." His words recalled her to the present. "Have you ever been in that area of Texas?"

"I've driven through Mineral Wells on my way to the Guadalupe Mountains, but I don't remember much about it except that the countryside was hilly—and very beautiful."

"I'm glad you think so. It's a rough sort of beauty that not everyone appreciates." He looked at her thoughtfully. "It won't inconvenience you to leave Dallas, will it? I'm afraid I just took it for granted that you knew we wouldn't be working here." His tone was apologetic.

"It won't be inconvenient," she assured him. Apparently he was unaware of what a prize this job was. Jiggs would pick up and move to the Transylvanian Alps if it meant working on his project. "As soon as Joanie comes back from vacation next week and takes custody of her neurotic cat, I'll be totally free of responsibilities."

"Good. That's settled then." His face showed pleased eagerness, as if he too were anxious to begin working on the project. He rose from the table in a swift, concise movement she was beginning to recognize as characteristic of all his actions, mental and physical. "I've asked Ruth to leave our coffee in the living room. I believe we have one other matter to discuss."

The mischievous gleam in his eyes reminded her of his promise to fill in the details that were missing from her memory of that night in his hotel room. As she preceded him, she was astonished that she could have forgotten it. His eloquence at dinner had held her spellbound, driven every other thought from her mind.

The drapes in the large room had been drawn against the darkness outside. Soft, subtle lighting and subdued background music gave the room an intimacy that had been lacking earlier.

Now that he had reminded her of his promise, curiosity and the memory of acute embarrassment warred within her breast, with curiosity gaining ground each passing second. She sat on the long couch, as she had before, and fidgeted impatiently as she waited for him to begin.

"How do you like your coffee, Jiggs?" he asked from his position at the sideboard as he poured two cups from a tall, sleek, silver coffee pot.

"Black, please." She paused. "Matt?"

"Surely you're not on a diet?"

"No, I just prefer it black," she answered patiently, then tried again. "Matt, you said—"

"Good," he interrupted—again. "Your figure's perfect just the way it is." He let his gaze drift slowly over her slim body. The intimate inspection couldn't have taken more than a few seconds, yet she felt stripped by the penetrating look. There was a gleam of remembrance in his gray eyes and she could feel a telltale warmth stealing into her cheeks. With his words and his actions he had effectively destroyed the camaraderie that had been steadily growing between them throughout the evening. She felt a curious anger at the loss.

Disconcerted, she rose swiftly from the couch and walked to stand before a painting she had missed in her earlier examination of the room. "This is . . . interesting. Did you choose it?"

"You've got to be kidding." He had followed her silently and was standing directly behind her when he answered. "The entire place was done by an up-and-coming young decorator. He was recommended by a friend."

She shifted slightly to escape his suffocating closeness, then leaned forward, tilting her head to look at the splotches of orange and black on the canvas. "What do you think the artist was trying to convey?"

"I think he was trying to convey incompetence," he replied with dry cynicism. "And he succeeded beautifully."

Jiggs's peal of laughter echoed through the large room. Once again his humor had, purposefully it seemed, put her at ease and she went willingly as he drew her to the couch, sitting beside her and indicating her cup on the glass coffee table.

"Why do you live here if you dislike it so much?" she asked, genuinely interested. A man of his means should be surrounded with things that pleased him.

"You've got to admit, it's convenient," he replied. "If this place were important to me, I would have chosen a decorator myself. But I use it only for entertaining and for sleeping. It goes with the job. And as I said, my real home is on the Brazos. It's a home, not a reasonable facsimile."

"I see," she said doubtfully, knowing that if she had the means at her fingertips, as he obviously did, she would not be able to rest until she had brought some life to this plastic palace.

He leaned forward to pick up his coffee cup and Jiggs decided, now that the wall of sexual tension was no longer stretched between them, that she would jump right in and force him to make good on his promise. She looked at him sternly, her set face demanding his full attention. "Matt?"

After a quick glance at her expression, he replaced his cup on the low table and replied with comically overdone docility, "Yes, Jiggs."

She chuckled at his absurdity, but refused to be diverted from her purpose. "*Now* will you explain about that night?"

"Of course, why didn't you ask sooner?" His innocent expression didn't fool her for a minute. He grinned at her mock-glare and continued, "Let me tell you a story, Jiggs." He leaned back and extended his long, muscular legs, the fabric of his charcoal gray slacks stretching tightly across his thighs. "Once upon a time in a faraway land called Dallas, there lived a handsome prince." Jiggs giggled delightedly, as he modestly fluttered his eyelashes. "The prince was going through some very hard times. He was being set upon by dragons and trolls and wicked—but eager—interior decorators. Forced to flee his castle by dropcloths and fabric swatches, he finally found a place to rest his weary head. It was a modest little country inn called the Beresford House."

"So that's why you were there!" she exclaimed, then at his quelling glance, she murmured, "Sorry."

"As I was saying before I was so rudely interrupted, the prince decided to take refuge at the Beresford. After a couple of days, he grew lonely and decided to ask a friend to join him in exile. The friend he had in mind was known by the prince for her deftness in soothing an aching brow. She was also known for her beauty and . . ." he paused dramatically, ". . . her flaming red hair."

"The visitor you were expecting when you returned and found me instead," she exclaimed.

"Brilliant deduction, Watson," he congratulated her sarcastically. "And her arrival, or rather her non-arrival, is the key to the whole mystery."

"Tell me," she begged impatiently.

"I was expecting Barbie at eleven-thirty, but had to go out at the last minute."

*"Barbie?"* she repeated, one arched eyebrow raised in malicious inquiry. "And you're her Ken?" she asked sweetly.

"Stop interrupting, cat. On my way out, I tipped the night clerk to watch for Barbie, take her to my room, and unlock the door for her. Now we come to the intriguing part. Enter Princess Jiggs O'Malley." He paused for effect, then resumed his tale. "The night clerk was waiting for a beautiful redhead to ask for my room number. When he saw a beautiful, but totally smashed, redhead standing in the lobby looking very confused, he assumed you were the correct redhead and let you into my room instead."

"You mean I just went meekly along to your room without asking any questions?" she asked in disbelief. "Even if I were a *little tipsy,*" she said, ignoring his raised eyebrow, "I would never go willingly to a strange man's hotel room."

"That's the weird part. Let me tell you exactly what the night clerk told me, then maybe you can make some kind of sense out of it."

"Yes, by all means, let's try to make sense, because frankly I don't believe a word of it," she muttered under her breath.

"He said he saw you standing in the lobby looking 'confused' and he rolled his eyes eloquently as he said it, so I assume he meant you were . . . uh . . . tipsy. He walked up to you and asked if you were going to see Mr. Brady, to which you replied with great perspicuity, 'Do what?' He said you looked at him as if he had a lot of gall to even speak to you. Of course, he said it in a much more picturesque way. 'Looked at me like I was a dead skunk' was the way he put it." He paused, then said admiringly, "The man truly had a way with words."

"Matt!"

"Be patient, I'm getting there. Anyway, he said he wasn't offended by your attitude because, even though you were looking down your adorable nose—my adjective, not his—at him, it reminded him of his daughter when she gets on her 'high horse.' So he repeated, 'Matthew Brady. Are you going to see Matthew Brady?' After a few minutes of deep thought, during which you stood there 'kinda wobblin',' you said, apparently very pleased with yourself for having found an answer to his question, 'Yes, I am. But that's tomorrow.' "

Matt looked at her inquiringly. "Did you plan on seeing someone named Brady on Saturday?"

"No, of course not," she denied emphatically. "The only thing I had planned for Saturday was to go to the museum with some friends. We were going to see the—" She stopped, struck, and whispered, "No. I don't believe it. It's too much."

"What? Come on, don't keep me in suspense. It's my mystery, too."

"We were going to see the Mathew Brady exhibit at the museum," she said in resignation.

Matt stared at her, puzzled, then after a moment of thoughtful silence, threw back his head and roared with laughter, ignoring Jiggs's sour look. She couldn't see that it was all that amusing. He was holding his sides, gasping for breath. When he finally calmed down, she was staring at him with an expression that would have been familiar to the night clerk at the Beresford.

"What's so damnably funny?" she asked in an icy voice.

He quickly smothered a lingering chuckle and said, "You won't believe it, Jiggs. You simply won't believe it."

"Try me."

"After you told the night clerk that you were going to see Mathew Brady on Saturday, he said, 'Mr. Brady wants to see you *now*.' He couldn't understand why you were so surprised!" Matt could no longer contain his laughter. His words were barely audible as his body shook with mirth. "Then you said—you said, 'Mathew Brady is *here*? In this hotel? And he wants to see *me*?' "

Jiggs's lips began to twitch uncontrollably and she burst out in delighted, unrestrained laughter. "I—I was in your room—" She spoke between gasps, holding her aching sides. "—I was in your room waiting to see a man who died in—in 1897!"

The look on her face set Matt off again. He pulled her into his arms and they rocked back and forth, tears streaming down Jiggs's face. "Not only that," he choked out. "You apparently expected Abraham Lincoln to be there, too!"

She let out another whoop of laughter. "Remember I told you I recalled something about Mr. Lincoln."

Matt leaned back against the couch, pulling her with him, bringing his laughter under control with difficulty. "The night clerk said you got 'real thoughty' in the elevator, then sort of wondered aloud if Mr. Lincoln would be there, too. He said you seemed 'kinda anxious' about it, so he assured you that if Mr. Lincoln was supposed to be there, he would be there. He gave me a very nasty look when I had to admit that you didn't get to meet Mr. Lincoln, after all. He was so concerned about you I didn't have the heart to tell him that you were referring to Abraham Lincoln."

"Oh, no!" She laughed. "I always associate

Mathew Brady with the portrait he did of Lincoln. That poor night clerk!"

"Poor night clerk, indeed! He accused me of luring you to my room with false promises." Matt's injured air didn't quite come off. "I'll never be able to set foot in that hotel again."

She looked into Matt's face. Tears of laughter had brought to her green eyes a sheen that evoked dew-covered grass, sparkling in the sun. "I'm sorry, Matt," she said contritely. "I feel like a fool. Are you sure you want to work with me?"

He seemed to make an effort to come back from someplace deep in her eyes and gave her a crooked grin. "Don't be ridiculous. Of course I do. And don't worry about my reputation. It will survive." He brought one finger to the tip of her nose in a soft, playful tap. "You saved me from boredom that night, because, if you remember, I was stood up."

Oh, yes, she thought, the brow-soothing Barbie. For some reason, Jiggs didn't want to dwell on her beautiful doppelganger's relationship with Matt. Her own relationship with him was baffling enough. He had merely looked at her earlier and her blood pressure had jumped sky high. Now, here she was, sitting cozily in the shelter of his arms, as much at ease as if she had known him—and his touch—for years. Apparently he could turn that sensually electrifying current off and on at will. A very convenient talent to have. A potentially dangerous talent as far as Jiggs was concerned. It could make living with him very uncomfortable, like living on the edge of a maelstrom, always wondering if today would be the day you'd be pulled into the strange vortex. Thank God for Ruth.

"Jiggs, darlin', am I boring you?"

His amused voice brought her out of her reverie

and she looked at him apologetically. "I'm sorry, Matt. What were you saying?"

"I asked if you ever managed to see the Brady exhibit?"

"No, I haven't yet. I'll probably go next week," she said. "Have you seen it?"

"Not this one. I saw the one at the Smithsonian a couple of weeks ago."

"The Smithsonian! Then this one will seem like small potatoes to you. I've read that there are more than fifteen thousand photographs in that collection. I'd love to see it." She sighed regretfully, then gave him an inquiring look. "Are you a photography buff?"

"No, not really. But since we do have a name in common, I naturally know a bit more about Brady and his works than the average person."

His hand, which had been resting loosely on her shoulder, moved beneath her hair and began a subtle caress on the nape of her neck. She could almost feel him pull the switch and release that exciting, slightly terrifying, current. He whispered words she couldn't hear as he lowered his head and placed soft, nibbling kisses on her earlobes, then her neck. The caressing hand stopped to push her long, auburn hair aside and he began to rain soft butterfly kisses on the nape of her neck.

Suddenly, her entire body seemed supersensitized—the soft lighting blinded her with its brilliance, the gentle strains of Chopin throbbed in her eardrums, and her clothes seemed strangely intrusive on her skin. Shock widened the pupils of her dazed eyes as her heart strove for a more conventional rate. With tenacious will she fought her way back to sanity. She blinked in confusion and tried to hear Matt's softly spoken words.

"Why did you run out on me, Jiggs?" He drew

back and, framing her face with his big, rough hands, looked into her troubled eyes. "Why?"

Jiggs's gaze dropped uncomfortably to the floor, then lifted to meet his puzzled look. "I'm sorry, Matt. It was childish of me." She murmured her apology earnestly. "I don't have a logical explanation. I simply couldn't cope. My resistance was low that morning and you were very . . . persuasive." She paused. "Running seemed the only solution at the time." His doubtful look forced her to continue. "I regretted it later. I wished that I had stayed and tried to explain how I felt."

"Explain now," he urged. "I want to know." He gave a short, harsh laugh. "Haven't you ever heard of the fragility of the male ego? I've struck out before, but I've never had anyone actually run from me. All week I've been wondering if there was something my best friends hadn't told me." He looked at her, his eyes commanding honesty, and asked again, "Why, Jiggs? I thought you felt the same attraction I felt."

"I did," she assured him, struggling to find the words to express her feelings. "I don't know how to explain without sounding like Goody Two-Shoes, but I'll try. I've been on my own for a long time, Matt. And I've been exposed to quite a bit of the so-called freedom that both sexes now enjoy. I made the singles' scene when I went through a depressingly typical stage of trying to be 'with it.' I've got to say it, Matt." She glanced at him quickly from the corner of her eye. "The truth is the whole thing stinks. When I went to those places with soft lights and loud music and wall-to-wall bodies on the make, I saw loneliness. A loneliness deeper and more desperate than any I ever felt sitting at home alone. I knew then—I guess I really always knew—that I wasn't the type to indulge in casual affairs. So many of the people I've met—not just in clubs, but at work, at parties, and even in grocery stores—seemed to be looking for something more than sex. They seemed, in some strange way, to be looking for themselves. It was as if they had to have someone near to confirm their own existence. Maybe it's some kind of big city syndrome. Whatever it is, I don't need it and I don't want it. I know I exist. I don't need that confirmed by anyone."

Matt leaned back, keeping his eyes on her face, listening to her words with deep concentration.

"I know what happened between us is not in the same category as a casual pick-up," she continued to explain. "We were victims of circumstance who happened to be attracted to each other. But, Matt . . ." She covered the hand that was resting on his thigh with her own. "If we had continued, it would have ended the same."

He turned his hand and captured her fingers. "What about your relationship with your ex-fiancé? Was it 'meaningful'?" His words didn't mock. He sounded as if he truly wanted to know.

"No. You were right about that." She stared thoughtfully at their entwined hands. "Roger was a sweet man, but I felt nothing for him physically. That was part of the lesson I've learned. I now know what I'm looking for. And someday I'll find it."

"And that is?" he asked, intercepting her gaze with a quizzical look as he brought her fingers to his lips in a gentle, non-threatening caress.

"I want a relationship that doesn't swamp my individuality. I don't want to be absorbed by any man. But then, I had that with Roger. So I know now that I also need to be attracted physically." She shifted sideways to face him as she warmed to her subject. "But even that's not enough. What I want is a man I truly like, that I feel comfortable with, but that I'm attracted to. I guess what I'm trying to say is that I want a loving friendship."

"Friendship? Is that really what you're looking for?"

"Yes. Don't you think that would be the ideal affair? I wouldn't have to worry if my hair frizzed or wonder if he thought my birthmark was ugly. Don't you see? He would be my friend, so he would care about the me inside the available body. I wouldn't hate myself the morning after and, best of all, he wouldn't tie my emotions up in knots because we would just be friends." She looked at Matt eagerly, wanting him to understand.

"Oh, I see all right." He laughed as if enjoying the antics of a child. "I'm afraid you're the one who doesn't see." He kissed the tip of her nose that had wrinkled in bewilderment at his statement. "Although you don't realize it, darlin', you just gave a pretty good description of love." He stifled her protest with a finger against her lips. "Oh, yes. Think about it a minute. You want someone who respects you enough to let you be yourself. Someone you enjoy being with, that you can laugh with. Someone who turns you on physically and who is turned on by you. And . . . you want someone that you can trust not to hurt you." He gave her a consoling grin. "That sounds suspiciously like love to me."

His words sank in and spread a numbness in her brain. Love? No, that wasn't what she wanted. She had miscalculated somewhere—or he had—but love was definitely not what she wanted! "No, you're wrong, Matt. There has to be some other way." Her words were urgent, almost pleading. "Surely a loving friendship is possible. I mean, sure, it's a kind of love, but not the 'till death do us part' kind. Right?"

"Hey, calm down. I was just teasing you." He pulled her against the comfort of his broad, hard chest. "Listen, baby, if that's what you want, then of course it's possible. There's nothing to be frightened of."

He tilted her chin so she was forced to look into his eyes. "What are you afraid of, Jiggs?" he asked in a gentle whisper, his voice gruff as if he were affected against his will by her fear.

A blush spread across her face as she realized how foolish her reaction had been. "I'm not afraid—not really. Your conclusion just took me by surprise, that's all. I thought I had the equation worked out so brilliantly. Then you came up with an entirely different solution." She looked at him in frustration. "It just threw me for a minute."

His look was frankly skeptical. "What have you got against love? I know some very nice people who are in love." He wasn't going to let it go and she silently cursed the way she had overreacted.

"Matt, don't be ridiculous. I don't have anything against love," she denied. "I fully intend to fall in love, and get married, and even have children—someday. I'm just not ready yet."

"Then why were you so emphatic about finding someone who wouldn't tie you down, wouldn't mess around with your emotions?"

"Because that kind of affair is sloppy! I lead a well-ordered life and that's the way I want to keep it," she defended heatedly. "The women I work with—married and single—come to work as if they are living on an emotional seesaw. One day they're euphoric because their love life is going well and the next day they're suicidal because it isn't."

"But haven't you ever wondered how that euphoria feels, Jiggs?" As she began an emphatic denial he interrupted her, leaning closer until she felt his breath, warm and smelling faintly of coffee, stirring the baby-fine curls at her temple. "I'm not talking about being in love, Jiggs, I'm talking about making love. Not the Milquetoast affair you had with Roger, but the kind of thing that makes you forget about your well-ordered life and simply feel."

He leisurely tilted her chin with one crooked finger and gently, slowly touched his lips to hers. The kiss was warm and soft and coffee-flavored. It didn't threaten. It didn't plead. It was a simple salute to her lips that brought with it a snug, sitting-in-front-of-an-open-fire coziness.

Matt withdrew slowly, smiling as he gazed at the pleasure evident in her face. Her echoing smile seemed to answer his unspoken question, for he returned his mouth to her lips, this time with a subtle pressure, a vaguely sensual interrogation. His strong, long-fingered hands framed her face, the calloused thumbs softly stroking the smooth skin of her cheeks.

The roughness of his large hands caused Jiggs to ask silent questions of her own. Questions that would have shocked her sensible mind at any other time. How would it feel to have those calloused hands on her breasts, her thighs? She drew in a breath sharply at the shaft of desire brought by her erotic thoughts. The breath she inhaled was Matt's and the intimacy of the action sent wildfire searing through her limbs.

Her parted lips were an invitation to plunder. An invitation Matt obviously had no intention of refusing. His hands moved to support the back of her head, his fingers becoming entangled in the rich silk of her auburn hair, as his coaxing tongue traced the outline of her lips, then slid with moist sweetness along the inner softness of her mouth.

Somehow all her nerve ends had become concentrated in her lips. They seemed alive with tingling sensation. His subtle exploration was a languid assault on her senses, a drugging adagio movement. Their bodies were not touching, yet she knew she was being seduced. She knew, but she no longer cared.

"You feel it now, don't you, Jiggs?" His whisper was simply an added caress, as was the male scent of him that invaded her nostrils.

She looked at his strong face with dazed eyes, knowing he had asked a question, yet unable to concentrate enough energy on her vocal cords to form the words to answer.

"God! You look drunk," he groaned huskily, triumphantly. "I knew it was there, inside you. And I want it, Jiggs. I want it all." He closed her eyelids over dilated pupils with urgent kisses.

Frustrated by his wandering kisses, she clasped his head fiercely between her hands and guided him to the aching throb of her lips. But the kiss was torturously short. She moaned in desperation as he pulled back from her lips.

"Is this what you need?" he rasped harshly, giving her another brief, hard kiss.

He was driving her mad. She was in a frenzy of longing for his lips. He had built a rapacious hunger inside her. Restless tremors shook her body as she pleaded, "Matt, please!"

"Oh God, yes!" His voice was unrecognizable, as if he were driven by the same demons that had taken over Jiggs's body—and her mind. He clasped her savagely to his chest, plunging his tongue deep into the ambrosial cavern of her mouth in an act as intimate, as possessive as the ultimate act of love.

The current flowing between them was intensified, surging and kindling a pulsating pressure in the center of her desire. In a convulsive movement entirely beyond her control, her agitated body arched against his, trying to assuage the paroxysms of desire.

In one swift, decisive movement, he removed her jacket, then eased her back until she lay beneath him on the couch. The feel of the hard, male body pressed against hers forced a groan of pure pagan delight from her throat.

Never had she received such pleasure from a man's body, felt such voluptuous satisfaction in simply being a woman. She felt a desperate need to celebrate her intoxicating discovery. She wanted to explore the cause of this tumultuous joy.

Cautiously, she removed her restless fingers from his neck and began light, searching strokes across his shoulders and, as he moved to give her adventurous hands free rein, over the muscles of his heaving chest. She could feel the intense heat of his body through his soft cotton shirt, but somehow it wasn't enough.

Jiggs lifted her eyes and found Matt avidly watching the hunger in her flushed features. As he captured her gaze, he began to unbutton her blouse in deliberately, maddeningly, slow movements. His eyes never left hers and his hand never faltered, even though the thin silk of her blouse was rising and falling with the increased rate of her breathing.

She closed her eyes and a tiny whimpering sound came from the back of her throat as he reverently touched her exposed flesh. She could feel her nipples hardening beneath the lace bra that was the only barrier between her and rapturously new sensations.

Matt's harshly drawn breath forced her eyes open. The wonder, the awe she saw etched in his craggy, tough face as he stared at her taut, erect nipples was a mirror image of her own. She gazed, hypnotized, as he released the front of her bra.

"Sweet, sweet Jiggs. This is what I ached for that night I held you in my arms." His voice was hoarse, raspy—a grating whisper, as he molded one full breast with his hand, cupping it to facilitate his greedy, sucking mouth. He drew the hardened tip deep within his mouth, his tongue taking and giving heady, sensual delight.

Her head thrashed from side to side, her hips arching against his throbbing maleness, and, from deep within her came a cry so barbaric, so basic, a saner Jiggs would have been appalled.

With the swiftness of lightning, Matt moved to capture the sound of her arousal with his mouth. The raging fury of the kiss did nothing to assuage their tormented desire.

In reckless haste, her wanton fingers unbuttoned his shirt and pushed it aside. Matt released her slowly from his frenzied kiss to watch her glazed eyes devour the rough beauty of his broad chest with its tight, hard male nipples. Jiggs was mesmerized, totally fascinated, and as though drawn by the force of a powerful magnet, she raised her head and, in a trance, slowly extended her tongue to caress the erect tip.

Suddenly, Matt was a madman. He threw back his head, his strong, masculine nostrils flaring, his breathing labored. He seized her to his heaving chest in a bone-crushing embrace. The mat of curling hair was an eagerly welcomed roughness against her erotically sensitized breasts. Her frenzied hands explored the rock hardness of his curved buttocks, his powerful thighs. She reveled in the feel of his strength, the wonderful maleness of him. She wanted to feel that strength, that masculinity against her bare skin.

His own hands had not been idle during her exquisitely tactile exploration. She felt long fingers spread on her nylon-covered buttocks, cupping them and pressing her aching loins to the matching ache in his. His hands were kneading, molding, pushing down the offending pantyhose, to feast on the rounded softness.

The movement of Jiggs's clumsy fingers searching for the buckle of Matt's belt brought her out of her drugged state as effectively as ice water thrown in her face. "My God!" she gasped, horrified. "What on earth am I doing?"

She shivered spasmodically as shock spread through her body. She had become a creature unrecognizable to her sane, logical mind.

"What's wrong, sweetheart?" Matt looked at her, concern in his sensually glazed eyes. "What is it, Jiggs?"

How could she tell him? How could she come this far and stop? "Oh, Matt," she moaned. "You're going to hate me. And I don't blame you, I hate myself." She sat up in disgust. "I'm no better than a pubescent teenage tease. I don't know what came over me. After all my fine talk about being *above* casual sex, I practically ravage you on the couch—a man I barely know! And then back out at the last minute!" As she spoke, she furiously jerked her clothing together, clasping her bra and buttoning her blouse with savage gestures. "God! I'm so ashamed of myself. Of all the stupid, adolescent tricks. I'm supposed to be a mature adult and I acted like an emotionally disturbed virgin!"

She slumped against the couch, her irrational behavior defeating her, holding back tears that would be the final humiliation. Staring at her nervously entwined fingers, she whispered miserably, "Aren't you going to say anything? Aren't you going to yell at me? Throw something?"

"Well, to tell you the truth, darlín' . . ." Amazingly, his voice sounded almost . . . amused. "I'm still recuperating from the shock. But don't let me stop you. You were doing a real fine job of yelling at yourself."

She lifted her gaze to confirm his mood. She was right. The now familiar twinkle was in his gray eyes, the crooked grin curving his strong lips.

"Matt," she said, bewildered. "How can you take what I did so lightly? It was unforgivable of me."

He put his arm around her in a reassuring hug and looked into her confused eyes. "Don't whip yourself, Jiggs. I was here on the couch with you. You didn't do anything alone. If anyone has to take the blame, then I should. I knew how you felt about it." He ran long fingers through his unruly hair and gave her a wry look. "To tell you the truth, I wasn't doing much thinking at the time. Things just got out of hand, darlin'. Can't we just leave it at that?"

"Yes, of course," she agreed slowly. "But even if you forgive me, I can't. I should have had more control. I can't understand what happened."

He chuckled devilishly. "Speaking as a totally unbiased observer—I was delighted with the way you lost control."

His delight was obvious—and expected, but Jiggs was definitely not delighted. On her second meeting with Matt, she had almost cast aside her hardearned reason, the well-ordered structure of her life. What was going to happen when they were thrown together for six months in the isolation of his Brazos home? She had depended on Ruth to counter the potential intimacy of the situation, but apparently the quiet housekeeper wasn't going to magically appear when Jiggs needed her.

"Don't worry about it, Jiggs."

Startled, she looked at him inquiringly and he explained, "You were worried about the next six months, weren't you? There's no need, sweet. I won't press you."

Her doubts about the future wouldn't be banished that easily and they showed in her expressive features.

"Look, Jiggs, remember what you said about wanting a loving friendship?" She nodded hesitantly, uneasily comprehending his train of thought. "Well, I think we've got the basis for that sort of relationship. But first, we've got to work on building a good, solid friendship." He chuckled wickedly. "I don't think we'll have much trouble with the loving part. We make magic together, darlin'."

Her face went beet red at his audacious observation. She struggled against her embarrassment and the fear that unreasonably overtook her at the thought of an intimate relationship with him. She needed time to think, time to make a rational decision about her future. Her recent brush with the sensual side of Matt had frightened her. Her logic, her sanity, had disappeared in his arms. Could she take a chance on being totally engulfed by an affair with him?

"Matt, do you really think it would work?" she asked doubtfully. "Earlier, you didn't seem too impressed with my formula for an ideal affair. Do you honestly think that type of relationship is possible?"

A strange, tender look came into his eyes. "As I said before—anything's possible if you want it badly enough." His smile was curiously determined as he repeated, almost to himself, *"Anything."*

He seemed to shake free of his odd spell and rose with her from the couch, helping her into her jacket. He turned her to face him, tilting her chin to smile into her still doubtful eyes. "Whatever happens in the future, darlin', I can promise you one thing. Our association will definitely be . . . interesting."

# *Five*

---

Jiggs stepped from the small bathtub onto the white tiled floor under the inscrutable stare of a large brown cat and began to towel herself dry. Matt was due to arrive in thirty minutes, which didn't leave her much time for dawdling. He had insisted on taking her to the Mathew Brady exhibit and although she was still wary of the swiftness with which their relationship seemed to be progressing, she was too intrigued by the man and the way their personalities meshed to refuse his invitation.

"Well, Otis," she said, addressing the twitching leaves of a large fern on the floor which was the cat's observation post, "for good or for ill, I'm committed to working for the man. As for the rest, I've got two weeks to decide whether or not it's going to go any further."

Last night in Matt's penthouse when he had held her in his arms, she had lost the logic of which she was so proud—too proud according to some people. But the people who said that were usually men who were irritated because she had failed to fall in a heap at their feet. No, her logic and reasoning power were definitely not admired by men who were looking for an easy conquest!

But Matt had not been irritated by her reasoning. In fact, he had agreed to develop the relationship according to her rules. His attitude was a completely unknown quantity to Jiggs and the unknown was always a little frightening.

She was just stepping into the cocoa brown shoes which matched her moiré silk dress when she heard the doorbell ring, announcing Matt's arrival. Trying to slip on the remaining shoe, she hurried awkwardly across the room, tripping several times over Otis who was trying to claim another pair of shoes as his own.

"Otis! This pair is mine." Ignoring his hurt look, she opened the door to find Matt about to push the bell again.

She smiled, motioning for him to enter, but he wasn't looking at her. He was staring with wary fascination at the thirty pounds of fur disappearing beneath the loveseat.

"What in blazes was that?"

"*That* was Otis. It's one of his James Bond days. He's pretty harmless when he's playing spy," she assured him drily. "Just be glad you didn't come on one of his Bruce Lee days. I'm sure he thinks he's the reincarnation of that martial arts master. Anyway, his paws ought to be registered as lethal weapons."

"Aren't you afraid he'll pounce on you in your sleep some night?" he chuckled, watching the sinister twitching of the flounce around the bottom of the loveseat.

"Oh, he's done that already." She laughed. "I very nearly smothered to death before I got him off. Since then I've slept with my bedroom door locked."

Matt walked into the living room, looking around as he talked. "Locked? Surely closing it would be enough."

"You don't know Otis," she said ruefully. "Closed doors are child's play to him. I don't know how he does it, but I can put him out of the apartment so that he can play with dandelions or whatever it is that cats do for recreation and five minutes later he'll jump out of the closet at me. It's downright spooky, not to mention unnerving. The blasted cat has me so jumpy I've started knocking on the closet door before I open it."

"At least he's not dull." Matt laughed, then lifted her chin with one finger so that he could look into her eyes. "Hi, darlin'."

Watch it, Jiggs, she silently warned herself. It's a very bad sign when two softly spoken words can turn your insides to mush. "Hello, Matt," she replied in the same soft tone. "Are you sure you want to go to this exhibit? Won't it seem a little small townish after the one in Washington?"

"I wouldn't have asked you if I hadn't wanted to go," he assured her. "It may be smaller than the one at the Smithsonian, but that isn't necessarily bad. A small exhibit gives you more time to study each photograph."

"Yes, I suppose you're right. I would hate to rush through it, but I wouldn't want to miss anything either." She looked at him inquiringly, slightly ill at ease. "Would you like anything to drink before we leave? I don't have much, but I'm sure I could find something besides cooking sherry."

"No, thank you. I'm ready to leave if you are." He smiled indulgently at her nervousness and, calling a cheerful goodnight to the still-twitching fur, escorted her out the door.

On the drive to the small college museum, Matt spoke quietly about the Brady exhibit in Washington. His friendly, impersonal manner overcame Jiggs's attack of nerves and by the time they arrived she was once again looking forward to the evening.

On an easel in the lobby was a reproduction of the famous Brady photograph of Lincoln that was housed at the Library of Congress. It was a beautifully sensitive portrait that Jiggs couldn't view without a twinge of emotion.

She stared at the familiar portrait, feeling, as millions of others before her had, that she knew this man. The sensitive homeliness of his face, the hint of sadness in his eyes, brought an emotion closely resembling pain—a curious sense of loss.

"You really admire him, don't you?" Matt said, sounding surprised and a little touched.

"He was a great man," she said quietly.

"That depends on which history book you read," he said. "According to some experts he was an ordinary man who was made great by the unavoidable events which were taking place in the world around him. And some have even gone so far as to state that he badly mismanaged quite a few affairs while he was in office."

"I don't want to hear it," she protested. "Maybe I'm being naïve and unrealistic, but I don't want to hear that my heroes had feet of clay. I don't want to know if George Washington was fooling around on Martha. Or that Cleopatra was an ugly little broad with squinty eyes and bad teeth. Or that Abraham Lincoln was an ordinary man." She pointed to the portrait and said vehemently, "Look at that face. That is not the face of an ordinary man."

"Okay, okay," he said, laughing at her belligerent defense. "I don't know if I should be jealous of the man or grateful to him."

"Grateful?" she asked, smiling as she realized he had been teasing her.

"You went to my room last Friday night expecting to meet Abraham Lincoln," he explained, grinning. "You might not have gone if you hadn't been so impressed by him." He drew her arm through his and they walked into the first room of the exhibit. "I guess that makes me the only man alive today who's had Abe Lincoln fix him up with a date."

For the next two hours they were both absorbed by the photographs. Some were portraits of people who, though obscure today, had been the elite of that era. Some were poignant studies of soldiers in ill-fitting uniforms—heartbreakingly young men with confused eyes and rough, older men with sad eyes.

Matt seemed to sense when she needed silence to study a lonely soldier or when she needed to discuss a particularly interesting detail. She found his opinions and knowledge of history and photography as enthralling as she had found his anecdotes on paleontology. He was astonishingly well-informed on the events of the Civil War and they debated that tragic period as though it were a recent event.

When they left the exhibit they drove to a small neighborhood restaurant where their debates continued through dinner. Their enthusiastic discussion, which was interrupted periodically by their bursts of unrestrained laughter, drew indulgent looks from the other diners. But Matt and Jiggs were unaware of the presence of strangers. They were totally absorbed in each other. As much as she loved photography Jiggs knew that Matt would stand out in her memories of this evening.

They drove home in a comfortable silence, replete with good food and their own good company. How amazingly well their minds meshed! Although there were many things on which they disagreed, each sparked new ideas, fresh thought in the other.

Jiggs gazed out the window at the passing shadows, nervous anticipation building inside her. She couldn't let him leave without offering to make coffee and once inside, then what? Disappointment seeped into her mind as she felt the warm, comfortable companionship disappear, leaving tension in its place.

Why did she always anticipate problems? Why couldn't she take things as they came instead of making herself a nervous wreck over what *might* happen?

"You're mad about the cake, right?"

His voice breaking the silence brought her head around to look at him inquiringly. Feeling very foolish, she realized that they were parked in front of her apartment and he was studying her face intently. She laughed nervously and said, "I wasn't thinking about the cake, but if I had been thinking about it, I definitely would have been mad. It was outright thievery."

He stared at her tense features for a moment, then replied to her teasing words, overlooking her nervous tone. "I did it for you, darlin'. That cake was obviously too much for you to handle. You probably would have been sick if you had eaten it all." He looked at her, dramatically earnest. "So, with no thought of my personal safety, I finished yours as well as mine. You can see that I acted with the best of intentions."

Jiggs laughed softly, the tension draining from her body. "Your only intention was to stuff your face, Matt Brady," she said in mock indignation. "So you can cut the blarney."

He was still chuckling when he came around to open the door for her. "Being with you seems to improve my appetite for food . . ." He gave her a devilish glance as they walked up the stairs. ". . . As well."

When they reached her door she forced herself to sound casual when she turned to him and asked, "How about a cup of coffee, Matt?"

He gazed down at her, a crooked smile playing about his lips, and the silence stretched unbearably. Finally he chuckled softly. "No thank you, Jiggs. I'd better be going."

She stared at his face in the dim light, puzzled and a little chagrined by his refusal. Before she could frame a question he touched her cheek softly and said, "We're going to get to know each other, remember? It was very obvious that you were worrying about things going too far tonight and I'm afraid if I came in with you, you really might have something to worry about. There's a lot of electricity sparking between us, sweet, but I want you to feel right about it before we go any further. I decided last night to back off until you feel you're ready for the next step."

My God, she thought in astonishment. He can't be real. Nobody was that understanding. She was overwhelmed by his thoughtfulness. But how did one respond to that kind of generosity?

"Well?" he said, staring at her expectantly. At her quizzical look, he continued. "Aren't you going to save me from myself and talk me out of such a stupid decision?"

"No." She laughed, kissing his tanned cheek.

"I'm not and thank you for your understanding, Matt. You're a very unusual man."

"I'm going to take that as a compliment." He smiled ruefully. "Now before I go we need to talk about tomorrow."

"Tomorrow?"

"There's an open-air concert at Fair Park tomorrow night. How do you feel about Schubert?"

She hesitated for only a moment. "I love Schubert and I'd be happy to go with you."

He beamed his pleasure at her acceptance, reminding her again of a small boy, which was ridiculous considering his size. "That's great," he said enthusiastically. "I'll pick you up at seven and we'll grab a bite first."

"Why don't I fix something here?" she offered. "I have some TV dinners that I swear will fool you into thinking they're real food."

"You're on," he laughingly replied, then tilted her head and kissed her softly. "Shall I bring champagne, Jiggs? I have a terrible craving to see you the way you were last Friday night. So soft and cuddly in my bed."

A tingling warmth spread through her body at his soft words. "Maybe we had better go out to eat after all, Matt," she whispered. "I think it may be a while before I'm up to tackling either you or champagne."

Giving her hand a quick, hard squeeze he smiled gently and said, "I'll behave, I promise." He gave her a sly look. "Although the thought of you tackling me is definitely intriguing." With another fleeting kiss, he was gone.

She stayed outside her open door until she could no longer hear his softly whistled melody. It didn't strike her until later as she lay in bed that the tune he had been whistling was "Anticipation." Chuckling softly in the dark, she hugged her pillow, an inexplicable joy growing inside her.

The feeling stayed with her through her working day, bringing a smile to her lips at frequent, sometimes inappropriate times. She would suddenly find herself humming his softly whistled message as she worked.

On her way home from work she stopped by the supermarket to pick up the ingredients for a never-fail Mexican casserole, arriving at her apartment to find Joanie on her doorstep, eagerly waiting to claim Otis. Jiggs unlocked the door, juggling her groceries and trying to field Joanie's anxious questions.

"But did he eat enough, Jiggs?" the petite blonde asked, following her into the kitchen.

"Joanie, you worry too much about Otis. That cat is a survivor if I ever saw one," she drily assured her friend. "He ate all the cat food you left for him and two pairs of leather shoes. That should be enough to keep any cat healthy."

"Oh! Did he ruin your shoes? I thought I told you that you have to hide your shoes."

"No, you didn't mention it," Jiggs said, chuckling at Joanie's flustered look. "But even if you had it probably wouldn't have done any good. I'm convinced Otis would have found them wherever I hid them."

"He is awfully intelligent, isn't he?" Joanie said, lovingly indulgent. "Where is he, Jiggs? He usually comes when he hears my voice."

"Try the closet," Jiggs said, putting away her groceries. "But be careful, according to my calculations it's time for a Bruce Lee number. He hasn't been into martial arts for several days."

Moments later as she poured herself a glass of soda, she heard a faint voice from the bedroom.

"Jiggs, you weren't really partial to the green sandals, were you?"

Jiggs rolled her eyes in amused resignation. "No, Joanie. They were only an old pair. I had intended to throw them out anyway," she lied, then walked to the bedroom to watch the loving reunion—and guard her remaining shoes.

After Joanie had told Otis and Jiggs all about her trip to Canada, Jiggs reciprocated with a resume of recent events—leaving out the developing relationship between Matt and herself. Joanie was properly enthusiastic and promised to water her plants and watch for burglars while she was out of town.

Although she adored Joanie, she could see the minutes ticking away and was afraid that she was going to have to ask her outright to leave. Subtle hints went completely over Joanie's head, but as it turned out, there was no need because Joanie decided she couldn't wait a minute longer to give Otis the gifts she had bought for him in Canada.

Jiggs saw them out with a sigh of relief, then rushed around the kitchen, combining the casserole ingredients. When it was safely in the oven she quickly showered and slipped into forest green slacks and a cream silk blouse. She arranged her hair in a loose knot on top of her head, finally leaving the curls around her face and neck that were hard to be tamed. In a dim light, she decided she might pass for casually elegant.

The doorbell rang just as she finished tossing the salad. She ripped off her apron, trying futilely to smooth her hair as she walked across the living room. She was already opening the door when she realized she had forgotten her shoes.

Matt entered carrying a large bottle in a paper sack and Jiggs looked at him suspiciously. "Matt," she accused.

He grinned at her reaction and pulled the bottle out of the sack to show her the label. "Ginger ale," he said. "Now aren't you ashamed of yourself? Didn't I promise to behave?"

"Yes, you promised and no, I'm not ashamed. I don't trust you when you have that look in your eyes."

"Jiggs! I'm hurt." He sniffed the air, then followed the aroma into the small kitchen. "You're going to have to tell me what kind of TV dinner that is. It smells gorgeous."

"Actually," she confessed, "I was exaggerating slightly when I said I couldn't cook. If I have very detailed instructions and can throw out my first few attempts at a recipe, I eventually manage to produce something edible."

"How many times have you tried this one?" he asked cautiously.

She laughed, tempted to lie. "I've used it for years and no matter how I try I can't seem to mess it up. It always turns out great." Grabbing two potholders she took the casserole from the oven, carrying it carefully into the dining room with Matt trailing behind bringing the salad.

During dinner they talked about their respective days and as Jiggs listened to Matt's deep, beautiful voice, she found herself wishing they could skip the concert and remain where they were. But she knew that eventually the talk would dwindle and then that sizzling electric force would return to throw her into turmoil. So when Matt suggested it was time to leave she didn't demur.

The concert took place in the band shell at Fair Park and was exquisitely performed. They sat on the wooden seats, holding hands and letting the beauty of Schubert surround them. Afterward they walked through the park to his car, Matt's arm around Jiggs's waist and her head resting on his shoulder in contentment.

The following days were filled with excitement and laughter—and Matt. They explored obscure little art galleries and back street antique shops. Although they joined Matt's friends for an occasional evening, more often it was just the two of them. He seemed to take it for granted that they would spend every evening together and Jiggs was enjoying herself too much to object.

Toward the latter part of the second week Matt had to go out of town on business. Since he would be gone for several days they arranged to meet at his house on the Brazos and he gave her detailed instructions on how to get there. The evening of the day he left dragged on interminably for Jiggs. By nine o'clock she could stand it no longer and fled the too quiet apartment for the home of an artist friend.

As she rang the doorbell, the sound of loud music and voices filtered out to her. Jason, her friend, opened the door and Jiggs was hit full force by blasts of music, laughter and smoke-filled air.

"Jiggs! You're just in time. The party's in full swing now," he shouted cheerfully, then left her on her own as someone shouted for more food.

Although a mob scene wasn't what she had had in mind when she left her apartment, at least she was no longer alone with her thoughts. Across the room she spotted Max holding court and waved a greeting. She found a vacant corner when she saw him headed in her direction. He threaded his way slowly through the boisterous crowd, stopping every few minutes to give his opinion on whatever topic was under discussion in each cluster of people. He started a heated debate at each stop. Jiggs smiled. How Max loved stirring things up! He felt it was his duty to take a viewpoint that was in direct opposition to the one expressed. Consequently you never knew what real views he held.

He finally reached her side, leaning gracefully against the wall next to her. "Did you come to send me off on my adventure?"

"Is that what this is all about?" she asked, trying to make herself heard over the ear-splitting noise. "Jason left a message for me with Joanie yesterday, but she was so vague I couldn't make sense of it. I thought you had already had your celebration party. I dimly remember attending it," she added drily.

"I gave that one because I was happy to be going," he explained. "My friends are giving this one because they're happy to be rid of me."

She laughed softly at his cynicism, wondering briefly how much of it was real. "Who was the dark-haired beauty who was clinging to your arm with such fervor when I arrived?"

"Mandy?" he asked, after a moment's thought. "Mandy has been crossed in love. She gave her all—including the balance in her savings account—to her dearly beloved and he took a powder. Now she's seeking sympathy from anyone who cares to listen."

Jiggs grimaced in distaste. The idea of telling the world of one's humiliation was incomprehensible to her. How did supposedly intelligent women manage to land themselves in such ridiculous situations? Of course, she thought, there were no warning notices posted in advance that proclaimed a relationship might turn out badly. More than likely it started innocently and grew into something else. It could even start out as Jiggs and Matt's relationship had. How did she knew that she wouldn't be at a party sometime in the future, crying on the nearest shoulder?

Jiggs shuddered, horrified at the thought, then realized Max was watching her changing expression closely. He was the most unnerving man. . . . One always had the feeling that he was delving into private territory as he intently observed the world's antics.

"I think I'll go now, Max. If I don't see you before you leave, good luck and bon voyage," she said, hiding her disruptive thoughts as she stood on tiptoe to kiss his cheek.

He returned her friendly salute, holding her hand for a moment. "You take care, Jiggs. And if you ever need me, call my agent. He'll know where I am at any time."

She chuckled. "I can just see you flying back from Europe next time I lock my keys in the car."

"For that you can call a locksmith, but if you ever need a friend, you can call me."

But having a friend was what was causing all kinds of problems now, she thought as she drove home. What if her relationship with Matt turned into a sticky mess like that poor woman's? She was already very fond of Matt. How would she feel in six months?

The next few days were filled with turmoil, the nights filled with tossing and turning sleeplessness. She wanted to be with Matt and she wanted to be a part of his project, but she couldn't face the thought of their carefree friendship turning into something sordid and sloppy.


Headed west on Highway 80, Jiggs inhaled deeply. The first taste of fall was in the air, giving an added exhilaration to the drive. The breath-stealing heat of summer was beginning to fade, leaving a freshness that was all the more precious because spring and fall were so brief in Texas she sometimes felt she had imagined those mild seasons.

The change of seasons seemed to be echoed in the shifting tenor of Jiggs's life. She had almost driven herself crazy in the past few days, trying to decide what she wanted out of her relationship with Matt. Her only possible course of action had become clear late last night. Her friendship with Matt had to develop in its own way—in its own time. She was mature enough to handle whatever happened in the future and she had enough control over her emotions to keep from making a fool of herself.

As she drove through the gently rolling countryside, she congratulated herself on conquering her fear of an unknown situation. Reason and logic win again, she told herself smugly, forgetting all the doubts she had felt the last time she was with Matt.

Immediately to the east of Mineral Wells she entered rougher terrain—outlaw country of a century ago. The mesquite and gnarled cedar that grew in abundance appeared to challenge the right of the larger, more aristocratic oaks to grow in their territory. At one point, the road was cut through a hill of solid rock. The steep, weathered roadcut seemed to be a monument to the courage and determination of the people who had settled this ruggedly beautiful area.

Jiggs stopped for gas just inside the sprawling town and to reconfirm the directions Matt had given her. Then she continued west, passing over the winding Brazos River, and finally turned north onto a road of crushed sandstone which ran beside an ancient gas station made of native rock.

The crazy jigsaw pattern in the walls of the small structure was a reoccurring sight in this part of the country, along with piles and piles of cedar posts used in barbed wire fences.

She slowed her Pinto down to a snail's pace to cut down the clouds of choking dust that flew up from the narrow, rocky lane. Just as she began to think she was headed for nowhere, the road curved west and she began to catch glimpses of the river. Huge boulders shared the banks with towering cottonwood trees and the sparkling turquoise of the water was broken occasionally by a startlingly white sandbank. She couldn't imagine a more perfect place to spend the next few months. She would be right on hand when the leaves began to change color. Fresh air and the smell of burning wood would replace the gas fumes and pollution to which she was accustomed. My lungs probably will stop from shock, she thought.

She caught her breath sharply as she rounded another curve and was faced with the most enchanting house she had ever seen. It didn't jar the eye with startling beauty. It seemed a part of its surroundings—a brother to the very ground on which it stood. Made of the native Palo Pinto rock and weather-silvered cedar, the house appeared to have sprung from the earth, complete, without benefit of man's labor.

Jiggs pulled into the gravel drive, stepped from her car, and stood in silence. In the past, whenever she had tried to imagine the perfect house, only vague images had come to mind, yet she knew she would recognize that perfection if she ever saw it. And this was it. The kind of house that she instantly felt a part of. She let her eyes drift lovingly over the clean lines of the structure. It belonged to no architectural style that she recognized, but was in a class all its own.

Her gaze followed the deck around the corner of the house, then stopped suddenly as she saw Matt leaning against the rail watching her. He looked different. It didn't seem possible, but he looked bigger. She knew he was tall, but now he seemed a giant of a man, as if changing from a suit and tie to jeans and chambray shirt had given extra breadth to his shoulders, added iron to his thighs. An unexpected shiver shook her as he pushed away from the rail and moved toward her.

"Well, how do you like it?"

For one heartstopping moment she thought he was referring to her close examination of his body, then she realized he had meant the house. "Matt, it's lovely. It's the most perfect thing I've ever seen."

Jiggs almost laughed aloud at the apprehension she had felt in the last few days whenever she had thought of this man. How can you be afraid of a man who grins like an idiot when you compliment his house?

"I knew you'd like it," he said, his grin spreading, making deep grooves in his rough-hewn face. "Come on, let me show you around the inside. Then I want you to see the woods and the stretch of land along the river." As he talked, he grabbed her hand and pulled her behind him up the stairs to the deck, then through a beautifully carved door.

"Matt, wait." Sooner or later she was going to have to speak to him about his habit of pulling her around—preferably sooner before one arm became noticeably longer than the other. "Matt," she repeated as he continued walking, "what about my luggage? I'd like to change my clothes."

"Saul will take care of the luggage and what you're wearing is fine," he answered.

"Matt!"

He stopped and turned to face her. "Jiggs, I want to show you my home. You can change later." He looked at her quizzically. "Don't you want to see it?"

"Of course, I do. But first I'd like to freshen up." She wiggled her eyebrows at him to try and get the point across. "You know—*freshen up.*"

He stared at her eyebrows in confusion for a moment, then comprehension broke through. "Damn, I'm sorry, Jiggs. I did it again, didn't I? Just like at the hotel. I'm a terrible host. Come on, I'll show you your room first, okay?"

She sighed in relief and followed him into a large bedroom. The late afternoon sun, pouring through the windows, gave it a welcoming glow. It was a pale-blue gem of a room. The old-fashioned four-poster bed was covered with an exquisite crocheted bedspread. And a beautifully simple Quaker bench was placed beside a rocking chair in front of one large, blue-curtained window.

"It's beautiful, Matt. I can see why you're so proud of your home."

"You ain't seen nothin' yet," he boasted with a cocky grin. "I'll wait for you in the living room, Jiggs." He strode out the door saying, "Hurry. There's so much I want to show you."

Jiggs stood for a moment thinking about the complexity of Matt's nature. She had seen so many different facets to his character—shy and enthusiastic little boy, experienced lover, efficient businessman, dedicated scientist, and, briefly, totally enraged male. But she somehow felt she had yet to discover the real Matt. The driving force behind all his different faces. Did she really want to discover that Matt? If she found a vulnerability beneath his self-assured facade, wouldn't her own vulnerability respond?

She shook away the disconcerting thought and

went into the adjoining bath. When she reentered the bedroom, a very small, very old man was setting her suitcases beside the bed.

"You must be Saul," she said, remembering Matt's words.

"Yes, ma'am. Least I was last time I looked." He chuckled irresistibly at his own humor and Jiggs had to join him.

"I'm pleased to meet you, Saul. I'm Jiggs." She extended her hand to have it grasped in a gnarled, brown fist.

"Same here, Jiggs. You here to help Matthew with his book?" His voice was gravelly—the audible counterpart of his weathered face.

"I'll be doing the drawings and some photographs," she explained. "I'm really looking forward to working on the project."

"And so you should be. Matthew's a smart kid. I taught him everythin' he knows." The grizzled old man seemed to grow two feet taller in his pride.

"You taught him?"

"Sure did. Leastways, I taught him the important things. He went to college to learn about them giant bugs he's so crazy 'bout, but I taught him how to be a man. Did a damn good job, too." His faded blue eyes drifted around the room. "This house here—me and him built this house with our own hands and we didn't use no store-bought stuff either. We cut ever' stick of cedar and dug up ever' piece of rock that's in this place."

His eyes seemed to grow brighter as he pinned her with his gaze. "He coulda' lived in that fancy house in Dallas that his daddy left him when he passed on, but he didn't. He wanted a place that was his own. And this place—well, this place *is* Matthew. When you look at the rough rock in the fireplace and the weathered timber in the walls, you're lookin' at Matthew. Ain't no frills to that boy. He's rough, but he's natural. Ya' get my drift?"

Saul seemed to be giving her a warning of some sort, but why? Did he think she wanted artifice? She thought of Matt as he had looked when she arrived, leaning against the rail, wearing worn, comfortable clothes, and she could see that Saul was right. Matt had seemed a part of the house. She had seen him in a polished environment and, though he had looked polished also, there had been no pretensions about him. "Yes, Saul, I think I see what you mean," she murmured thoughtfully.

He grinned at her, showing a mouthful of surprisingly white teeth. "Good girl. Now you better scoot. Matthew's in there pacin' around like a caged-up bobcat." He chuckled. "Never could teach the boy patience."

She felt as though she had just passed some kind of test. But why should Saul feel it necessary to inspect her? Maybe he thought she would be a bad influence on "the boy." She giggled at the thought of Matt—forty at least, judging by the gray hair she had seen threading through the brown, and a six-foot mountain of a man—being called a boy. She certainly wasn't brave enough to try calling him that.

Jiggs quickly changed into a pair of jeans and a short-sleeved, green sweatshirt with "Frodo Lives" emblazoned across the front, then left to find Matt. He was standing in the large, open doorway of the living room, impatiently watching her traverse the hall.

"Come on, darlin'. Time's a'wastin'." He pulled her into the large living room, motioning about him with one hand as though introducing her to the room.

It was an airy, high-ceilinged room with one wall of that crazy jigsaw-patterned rock. In the center of the rock wall was the most enormous fireplace she had ever seen. It seemed to have stepped out of some medieval castle. Earthenware pottery containing plants and flowers was scattered about the room and the color scheme was taken from the huge Navajo rug in front of the hearth, with navy blue and burnt umber predominating. The room was more than homey, you could almost taste the welcome in it.

"I'm afraid my adjectives are limited, Matt," she apologized. "I can't keep saying 'It's beautiful. It's perfect,' but that's the way I feel."

He gave her a quick, enthusiastic hug and led her back into the hall saying, "I know what you mean. That's exactly how I feel every time I come home."

In the kitchen, Ruth was busy preparing dinner, so they only stayed long enough to glance around the large, efficient room with its gleaming white cabinets and huge wooden table that looked as though it had seen many years of use.

Matt led Jiggs through the screened back door and down the wooden steps. The area adjacent to the road had been partially cleared, but here wilderness reigned. It was cool and green and unrestrained. As they walked, Matt pointed out plants that were edible, including several types of wild berry, plants that were medicinal, plants that were poisonous, and some that were simply incredibly beautiful. His knowledge reminded Jiggs of Saul's words earlier.

"Matt, who is Saul?"

He leaned against an ancient pecan tree and nibbled thoughtfully on a stem of Johnson grass. "Saul? He's just Saul. There's no one word to identify him. He's friend, teacher, father, confidant, comrade-at-arms. He raised me and now he's my right arm. He's like this tree." He looked up into the huge, spreading branches. "He's always been here and he always will be."

Matt put his arm around her shoulders and they began to walk in silence. There were so many things she wanted to know. Why had Saul raised Matt instead of his parents? And why, if his father had owned a "fancy" house in Dallas, had Matt spent his boyhood here in the wilderness? But from Matt's silence, she gathered the subject was closed, so she turned her mind to the appreciation of her surroundings.

Suddenly, without any warning, they were standing on the edge of a cliff overlooking the river. In the distance to her right, she could see a massive sandbank parting the shallow, blue-green water, but directly below them it was deep and took on a darker, more mysterious hue.

For a moment neither spoke as they stood bound by awe of the natural beauty before them. Then Matt's voice broke the spell.

"How do you like my kingdom, Jiggs?"

She looked at the water, deep and dark beneath them, and, across the way, sparkling in the setting sun. "Anything I could say would seem inadequate, Matt. I don't see how you can bear to leave it for that plastic perfection in the SPC Building."

He hugged her to him, brushing the top of her head in a rough feline caress. "It gets harder and harder each time I have to, darlin'. One of these days I'm going to chuck it all and turn hermit." He tilted her head with one hand. "How about staying with me and being my hermitess?"

Although she knew he was teasing, Jiggs felt a shiver of yearning course through her body. Disconcerted, she broke the loose embrace and turned back the way they had come. "Shouldn't we be starting back? Ruth will want to serve dinner soon."

He followed close behind her, apparently accepting her abrupt change of subject. As they crossed a patch of rocky, open land, something scuttled across the dusty ground in front of Jiggs.

"My God! What was that?" she exclaimed, startled.

"It was just a little horny toad."

She looked at him in skeptical surprise. "I beg your pardon?"

Matt threw back his head and roared with laughter, the sound echoing through the surrounding trees. "I'm sorry. It's a horned toad," he chuckled. "We called them horny toads when we were kids—before we knew the word had another meaning. Actually it's not a toad at all. It's a lizard of the family Iguanidae."

"I don't care if it's a Rockefeller, it scared the hell out of me," she muttered darkly. "It looked like a Lilliputian dinosaur."

"You can rest easy—it only eats insects. They have never been known to attack lady artists—even terribly green lady artists. And even if one did attack, I would slay the fiend with my trusty sword. So stop worrying."

"Okay, Saint George," Jiggs answered, then suddenly began to giggle. "I can just see you with a huge sword, fighting that four-inch monstrosity. He would have to be a fire-breather to make it a fair fight."

"Well, he doesn't breath flames, but he does squirt blood if he's annoyed."

"Come on. I may be green, but I'm not that gullible."

"No, honest, he does. It's a kind of built-in protection, like a skunk's scent."

"That's grotesque!"

"Not really," he objected. "Every living creature has evolved some kind of protection. Sometimes it's obvious, like a porcupine's quills. Sometimes it's hidden, like the scent of a skunk or the blood of the horned toad. And sometimes it's a very subtle form of protection." He paused and looked into the woods behind them toward the spot where they had stood moments before. "Like the shell a human animal builds to keep from being hurt."

They walked the rest of the way in silence, each pursuing his own thoughts. Jiggs wondered if the easygoing charm that came so easily to Matt was a shell behind which he hid a more uncertain, less confident self. It didn't seem possible. He was always in control. Even when she had been carried away by passion, he had been in control of his emotions within moments of her withdrawal. Did he hide his deep feelings or did he have none? Somehow, remembering his boyish pride in his home and his work, she felt sure it was the former.

During dinner she watched him closely, trying to detect a crack, a flaw, in his attractive facade. As they sat in the dining room, which extended off the large living room, the shadows deepened in the woods and the moon rose, striking silver fire on the river as it wound around the wooded area behind the house, gently curving in to a sandy bank not a hundred yards from the glass wall through which they watched it. They talked softly of Matt's book and the plans Jiggs had made for her drawings and photographs.

It seemed to Jiggs that she had stepped into another world. It was not only the difference in the scenery or the freshness of the air. She felt as though she had somehow undergone a personal metamorphosis. She couldn't equate the way she felt now with the person she knew herself to be. She seemed to have left her orderly self behind, along with the heat and crowds of the city. The change made her uneasy. The tranquillity and contentment she felt here, with Matt, were an illusion that would disappear in six months when her job was finished. She had to remain objective and not fall any deeper under the spell of his magical kingdom. Her future sanity could very well depend on the amount of control she had over her emotions now.

"Have you come to a decision?"

His words broke through her intense concentration, startling her into awareness of his watching presence. "I'm sorry, Matt. What did you say?"

"I just wondered if you had reached a decision."

"About what?"

"I have no idea, but judging from your expressions, it must have been a serious one. For a while you seemed puzzled, then almost scared, then you got the most adorably pugnacious look on your face as though you had just decided on a course of action." He looked at her inquiringly. "You're not having second thoughts about leaving the bright lights and glamour of the big city behind, are you?"

"Bright lights keep me awake," she assured him, "and somehow glamour never decided to visit the side of town where I worked and lived. No, I'm not having second thoughts about that."

"About what then?"

"No second thoughts at all really. It just seems to me that it would be very easy to lose yourself, your goals, in this place. Things that were important yesterday don't seem as important today."

He looked at her thoughtfully. "Yes, you're right, but what you see as a threat, I see as a blessing," he murmured softly, almost to himself; then, in a swift change of mood, rose, pulling her to her feet. "Don't worry, darlin'. Jiggs O'Malley would be impossible to lose and if your goals are the right ones for you, they wouldn't stay lost for long."

Out on the wide deck, they had coffee in the moonlight and listened for a while to the frogs as they sang lovesongs in the night. The warm softness of the air enveloped Jiggs in a cocoon of sensual feeling. Oh, Lord, she silently moaned, I'm in trouble if the very air can seduce me. She felt as though her senses were being bombarded from all directions, bringing a fresh awareness, a rebirth. She had shed her old skin and this new skin was sensitive to every movement around her, every sound—the tiniest flutter of a leaf caused an echoing vibration to ripple through her body. She was in tune with the earth.

My God! she thought in horror, if he touches me now, I'll probably drag him off to my bedroom.

"Are you ready, Jiggs?"

Her face, mercifully obscured by the darkness, flamed and she sank lower in the wooden lounge chair. "I beg . . ." Her voice was a croaking mimicry of the frogs below. "I beg your pardon?"

"Now don't tell me you've forgotten. We're working on our friendship. Remember?" His voice held a warm amusement, as though he had somehow discerned her thoughts.

"Oh, yes," she sighed in relief. "Of course I remember."

"Good. A lot of it will come naturally since we'll be staying in the same house for the next few months, but to speed up the process, we'll play I love—I hate."

"I love—I hate? I've never heard of it."

"That's because I just made it up. Now be quiet while I explain. We each take turns listing the things we love, then the things we hate. And we can't include any big, universal loves or hates. We all hate hunger, war, and warts, so they don't count. Right?"

"Oh, I don't know about that. A well-placed wart is an inspiring thing. Can you imagine the Wicked Witch of the West without her warts? She would have been totally ineffective."

"Okay, I'll give you the warts, but you get my general drift." His appreciative grin added to the warmth of the evening. "You go first."

She sat thinking for a moment, then began. "I love Cary Grant and Jimmy Stewart movies; Walt Disney's animation; the smell of cottonwood trees; backpacking; English situation comedies; one-man-bands; cold buttermilk; John Philip Sousa and Johann Strauss—Junior and Senior; skiing; omelets in any way, shape, or form; bathing babies; chamber music; the Dallas skyline; old-fashioned hymns; and books—not just reading them, but the shape and feel of them. Now it's your turn."

"I love Texas at dawn; African sunsets; all music; murder mysteries; the smell of coffee perking; the sound of children—of any nationality—playing; Robert Burns's poetry; Saul's hands; Ruth's home-made peach cobbler—and watching you sleep."

"Disqualified!" she objected. "That last was a universal thing. My beauty while sleeping is leg-endary. It's only when I'm awake that people flee in horror."

"I'll concede your legendary beauty, but not the rest!" He chuckled. "Now your hates."

"I hate bubble gum, people who say 'You know what's wrong with you?;' flavored lipstick; jogging; frilly clothes; depressingly realistic novels; hamburger patties that you can see through; men who patronize; women who apologize for being women; arty movies; and mud wrestling." She looked at him inquiringly, enjoying the game.

"I hate the gritty taste of sand in dehydrated

eggs; people who tap you on the shoulder to make a point; wine snobbery; quiche; women who cry on cue; men who bully; people who ask 'What's your sign?;' and cold oatmeal."

"Apparently," she laughed, "you're a nicer person than I am. Your list of hates was shorter than mine." She glanced at him out of the corner of her eye. "By the way, what *is* your sign?"

"Slippery when wet," he replied. "What's yours?"

"Personally I've always fancied 'Piano for sale by owner with mahogany legs.' " she answered in the same serious tone.

"Now that we've gotten our signs out of the way, let's see what we've learned. I know that I must never tell you what I think is wrong with you and . . ."

"And I know never to tap you with my finger to help get a point across."

"And I promise," he vowed earnestly, "never to wear flavored lipstick or chew bubble gum when I kiss you."

"Right." She laughed, then sobered. "I do see what you're trying to do, Matt. But surely these are surface things. Do they really help us to get to know each other?"

"It's a start, darlin', and didn't you notice how many things we had in common?"

"Like what?"

"We both mentioned children, music, and literature as things we like. We both detest artificial, pushy people and we both like being outdoors."

"And I think I would have to agree with you on the cold oatmeal," she added.

"Wonderful! What a pair we make!"

"Matt?"

"Yes."

"Have you ever met anyone who actually *liked* cold oatmeal?"

"Sure," he answered, grinning. "My roommate in college loved it."

"Okay, you win," she laughingly conceded. "So we make a great pair. Now what?"

"Now we take it as it comes—go with the flow—do whatever comes naturally. I just want you to feel comfortable with me, darlin'."

"I want that, too, Matt. But you won't be angry if the other—the sexual relationship—doesn't evolve, will you?"

"Angry! Me?" he exclaimed, offended. "Upset . . . depressed . . . suicidal? Yes. But angry? Never."

"Oh, Matt," she reached across to where he sat and squeezed his hand, "I do like you."

He turned his hand, capturing her fingers, and stood, pulling her to her feet. With his hands resting softly on her hips, he pulled her forward to receive a gentle kiss. "Oh, Jiggs," he mimicked. "I do like you, too. Very much."

Later as she lay in bed, the warmth, the comfort of his kiss was still present and she prayed that if a loving friendship was indeed possible, she would find it with this man. She had kept such a tight rein on her emotions, she had forgotten what a wonderful thing true friendship was. It was a sharing that went beyond companionship. She hugged herself with the thought of, tomorrow, being able to explore Matt's kingdom and Matt's mind.

"What was I so worried about?" she asked aloud, laughing defiantly as the words echoed with a vaguely ominous hollowness throughout the darkened room.

# *Six*

In the following days, Jiggs threw herself whole-heartedly into her job—and into her new-found friendship with Matt. In her enthusiasm she extended that friendship to include Saul and Ruth. Saul had sage advice and earthy witticisms to fit any occasion from brushing teeth to bearing children.

And Ruth's bland face hid a motherly soul that usually found expression in non-stop criticism. But even when she was scolding, neither scowl nor wrinkle marred her plain face. Her total lack of expression was a challenge Jiggs simply couldn't resist. Every time Ruth served a meal or passed her in the hall Jiggs had to restrain herself from making funny faces.

Finally she could hold back no longer. After Ruth had finished serving breakfast, Jiggs laid a hand on her thin arm to stop her from leaving. "Ruth, what do ducks who live beside nuclear laboratories say?"

Ruth looked at her for a moment, then said, "Well, Jiggs, I can't rightly tell, as I've never heard a duck actually 'say' anything, but I suppose that ducks being ducks wherever they live, would most likely make the same racket that God planned for all ducks to make. Of course, Mr. Johnson, my neighbor back home, had a duck that had been bit in the throat by a dog and it did make a kind of croaking sound. And some said it was talking, but the ones who said that were just as addled as that duck. Specially that old crone that lived down the road a piece. I remember the time that she—"

"Ruth," Jiggs interrupted, "this is a joke." She looked at the housekeeper in amused exasperation. "You're supposed to ask me what they say."

"Well, why didn't you say so, girl? I like a good joke as well as the next person. What do the ducks say?"

"Quark, quark." She looked at Ruth expectantly, but the older woman simply shook her head as if in pity and left the room mumbling about addled people. Jiggs stared after her in frustration, then turned to catch Matt looking insufferably smug.

"I could have told you that it wouldn't work," he chuckled. "Saul and I have been trying to get her to laugh, or even smile, for years. It can't be done."

"Well, you and Saul must not have been using the right ammunition," she said, more determined than ever. "That joke was probably too technical. Next time I'll try something more basic."

In the next few days Jiggs went from basic to downright corny. She popped out every time Ruth passed her studio, following the housekeeper down the hall with what was turning out to be a very bad monologue. To make matters worse, every time she tried, either Matt or Saul was lurking in the background to give her a superior "I told you so" look.

Finally, after the failure of her fail-proof gorilla imitation, Jiggs was forced to admit defeat. As consolation, Saul assured her that her gorilla act was one of the best he had ever seen and had certainly cracked him up. Although his words of comfort were appreciated, they couldn't drown out the sound of Matt's laughter as he leaned help-lessly against his study door.

Saul looked at her, his expression serious, his eyes twinkling suspiciously. "And of course, you can see that the boy enjoyed it. He's sharp enough to spot real talent when he sees it."

After a few choice words about "the boy's" men-tality, Jiggs returned to her studio, followed by their combined laughter. Alone with her drawings, she permitted a small chuckle to escape. She must have looked like a full-fledged, card-carrying idiot, chasing Ruth down the hall. She smothered her laughter with her hand as she recalled the way Ruth had hurried away as though the devil him-self were at her heels.

She settled down to her work with a contented sigh. Never had she laughed as much as she had in the few short weeks that she had known Matt. He was always there to share in the warmth which surrounded her in his house, but he had never once pressed her for a more intimate relationship. He was giving her a chance to adjust at her own pace. Jiggs had never met anyone like him. The attraction she felt for him would have made it simple for him to seduce her, but by waiting he was showing her that he valued their friendship as much as she did. This was not the casual, when-it's-convenient friendship that Jiggs had found in the past. This was the old-fashioned, lasting kind. And she was coming to rely on his gentle understanding as well as the all-enveloping warmth that she felt in his presence. Matt seemed to be interested in every aspect of her life and she, in turn, devoured every bit of information about his life that came her way.

Saul occasionally joined them for dinner and it was through him that Jiggs learned of Matt's childhood. Matt's parents had been so caught up in the Texas political scene that they had had little time for their only child. Saul, at that time the caretaker of the exclusive boys' camp where Matt spent his summers, had unofficially adopted Matt as his own. The gruff recluse and the repressed little boy had become constant companions, and Saul had introduced Matt to the wonders of the magical kingdom he would later claim as his own.

When Matt and Saul spoke of their early days together, Jiggs could detect no resentment, no regret in Matt's memories of his parents, yet she knew that those years must have played a part in making him the man he was today.

As they sat together in front of the first fire of the season, she once again questioned him about his past, hoping to find a clue to his present character.

"When did you build this house, Matt?"

"Saul and I built it the summer and fall of the year I turned twenty—nineteen years ago." He joined her on the rug and leaned against the couch, pulling her with him. "I had gotten my B.S. that spring and Dad was pushing me to join him in the business, with an eye to a political career for me in the future. I refused point blank and he, in turn, refused to pay for the rest of my education." He stroked her hair unconsciously as he spoke. "He had a perfect right to spend his money as he saw fit, but there was a rather nasty argument, so I walked out.

"That was when I got the brilliant idea of hitching to California." He chuckled.

"Why California?"

"Why not?" Because it was there I guess. Anyway the trip out was a snap. I got lucky and hit the coast in only two days. The trip back was a different proposition entirely. I spent three days trying to get out of the damned desert. It finally got to the point that I was so desperate to hear the sound of another human voice, I started to throw rocks at passing cars, hoping that someone would stop, if only to punch me in the mouth."

"Matt, you didn't!" She laughed.

"Oh yes I did. It worked, too. I didn't get punched, but I did get a ride back to Texas. When I got back to Saul, I figured the time had come for me to make my own way in the world. So after a night of hard drinking, Saul and I pooled our resources, bought this land, and started clearing it."

"Saul got drunk, too?" she asked, unable to picture the tiny man inebriated.

"Did he ever! As he would put it, he was 'drunker than Cooter Brown.' He said a true friend shares everything—even tying one on."

"I like Saul, Matt." She smiled broadly. "He's the strangest man I've ever met, but he has a way of saying things that makes you really stop and think."

Matt hugged her briefly, as though she had pleased him, and they sat in companionable silence, watching the flickering fire. With her head on Matt's shoulder, Jiggs grew drowsy, hypnotized by the motion of the flames and the warmth of his body.

"Matt?" she murmured sleepily.

"Um," he answered, as though he too were in a semi-trance.

"Who's Cooter Brown?"

"What?" He shook himself awake and looked at her as if he had not heard her correctly.

"All my life I've heard of people being 'drunker than Cooter Brown,' but nobody has ever been able to tell me who he was. Apparently he was a Texas phenomenon, because people from out of state don't know what I'm talking abut. Do you know who he was?"

He rubbed his jaw thoughtfully. "No, now that you mention it, I can't say that I do. In fact . . ." his expression was a cross between suppressed laughter and accusation, ". . . you're the first person who's ever asked me the question."

"Oh, well," she sighed regretfully. "It's not really important. I just wondered. He must have been a powerful drinker to have everyone in the state of Texas talking about him."

"I suppose so," Matt agreed, settling back in their former comfortable position.

Several times in the next hour Jiggs attempted to make conversation, but Matt seemed preoccupied. She began to wonder if he had grown tired of waiting for their relationship to develop and had lost interest in her. If he's lost interest this quickly, she thought, it can't have meant much in the first place. She realized she was working herself into a fine state of annoyance, so she decided to go to bed before she made a fool of herself.

"Matt, I think I'll turn in now if you don't mind," she said, pulling away from him.

He looked at her thoughtfully, not seeing her, and, after a moment, said, "I'll bet Ian could find out."

"What? Matt, what are you talking about?" she asked, totally confused.

"Ian McKenzie knows every anthropologist in the state of Texas. One of them is bound to know who Cooter Brown was," he answered, enthusiastically.

"You idiot," she laughed, framing his face with her hands and kissing him soundly. "You're wonderful!"

"Are you just now discovering that?" he asked, bewildered but obviously pleased.

He smiled into her eyes and suddenly the air between them was electrified. With the gentlest of pressure he drew her closer. Jiggs didn't even try to resist. She knew she wanted, needed to be held by him. Slowly, never taking his eyes from her face, he lowered his head. Then when his lips were so close she could feel his warm breath, he stiffened and abruptly withdrew.

She could almost see him switch off the force that had drawn them irresistibly together. It seemed as though he had willfully destroyed the sensual empathy which had vibrated between them moments before.

"Matt?" she inquired hesitantly.

"You know, Jiggs," he said in a curiously edgy tone, "I've been thinking about that Pennsylvanian drawing. I think that instead of dividing the scene into part underwater and part shoreline you should do two separate drawings. It would give the reader a more accurate idea of the type of foliage that grew during that time period. And, of course, aesthetically it couldn't hurt to have more of the lushness that was typical of that climate."

Jiggs had to make a visible effort to keep her mouth from dropping open in astonishment. One minute they were on the verge of making love and the next they were discussing business. As much as she loved her work, this just didn't seem the time or place to iron out the details.

Why was he shutting her out like this? He had said more than once that he wanted their friendship to progress as quickly as possible, so why this abrupt about-face?

She tried to quiet her confused thoughts and concentrate on what he was saying, but as he talked on and on about the project in an oddly stilted voice she simply became more confused. He was going over procedures they had already discussed. The only possible reason he could have for bringing them up now was to establish a less intimate climate in the room.

Bewildered, she searched his face, hoping for a clue to his strange behavior, but he assiduously avoided her eyes, eventually rising to his feet and absentmindedly helping her to hers.

"You said something about being ready for bed, didn't you?" he asked. His casual manner seemed forced. "I don't want to keep you up. I know the work you're doing now is particularly delicate."

"Yes, I suppose it is," she agreed hesitantly. "Well, I—I'll see you tomorrow." Jiggs walked slowly to her room, confusion plaguing her thoughts. Surely a physical relationship was part of what they had each hoped for? Why had he pulled away at the last minute? It was almost a replay of their encounter in his penthouse. Only this time *he* had withdrawn. Was it some subtle form of torture he had devised to get even? If that was his plan, then it had worked beautifully. She was a mass of frustrated longing.

Frustration was to be her constant companion in the days to come. Every time she seemed to be getting close to Matt, he would back off abruptly. She had never chased a man in her life, but she definitely felt that Matt was running from her. His weird behavior was driving her crazy, the inner turmoil making it difficult for her to concentrate on her work, and sleep was impossible. She lay awake nights, torturing herself with memories of Matt's touch.

One day as she was filling in a particularly detailed section of an underwater scene, he appeared in the doorway of the studio he had furnished for her use. She looked up at him inquiringly.

"How would you like to play hooky?" he whispered conspiratorially.

Laying aside her brush, she regarded him suspiciously. "What did you have in mind?"

"Look outside, darlin'. It's a picnic kind of day." He pulled her to her feet and urged her to the window. "You see? That sunshine out there is just aching to shine on us. It would be a crime against nature to waste it. How about it, darlin'? It may be our last chance to swim this year."

His eagerness was irresistible. She was making very slow progress with her work, anyway. And a swim in that beautiful water sounded sinfully delicious. Matt was watching her with a pleading little boy look, waiting for her answer.

"Sure," she acquiesced. "I'd love it." The next moment she had to laugh as the little boy look disappeared and the efficient businessman took over.

"Great!" he said, pulling her out the door. "Go change into your swim suit and I'll ask Ruth to pack us a lunch."

After dragging her to her bedroom, and leaving her with a stern admonition not to dawdle, Matt continued on to the kitchen to confer with Ruth. Jiggs looked carefully at her slender arms in the bathroom mirror. "I don't think he's even aware of the way he pulls me around," she told her image in surprise. "There's probably some deep, psychological reason for this overwhelming need he has to see one of my arms longer than the other. Oh, well," she sighed, turning away to step out of her clothes. "It's not such a big thing. Everyone has a quirk or two—there's no need for me to mention it." She pulled on the bottom of her tiny black bikini, then turned again to address the sympathetic mirror with a thoughtful expression. "Of course, when I can scratch my knee without bending, I may say *something*."

Before she had finished fastening the top of her suit, she heard Matt pounding impatiently on the door and soon found herself trailing behind him, shrugging philosophically as he pulled her through the woods to the river.

They swam in the pool he had shown her that first day, diving from one of the monolithic boulders that appeared to be guarding the river. When Jiggs finally pleaded exhaustion they relaxed in the water, letting the current push them to the sandy bank where they had left their lunch. Ruth had packed enough for the proverbial army, but after their strenuous exercise it tasted absolutely ambrosial and they had no trouble doing full justice to it. Afterward they lay on a blanket, giving the sun a chance to do its thing on their drowsy bodies.

Jiggs awoke sometime later to the sound of gently splashing water and raised herself slightly to watch Matt emerge from the pool. His muscular, tanned body gleamed bronze in the sun. He was a mountain of a man. It didn't seem possible that he had been born of mere flesh and blood. His rough features and enormous strength looked as though they had been carved by the elements from virgin stone. This sort of natural beauty should have taken centuries to produce, not a paltry thirty-nine years. She watched, mesmerized, as a trickle of water blazed a trail through the curling hair of his chest, down his flat stomach, to be absorbed by his cut-off jeans which rode low on his hips. She caught her breath sharply as a piercing streak of desire hit her forcibly in the lower part of her body. Her vivid imagination spurred by pure lust had her following the water's course in her mind.

Scarlet flooded her face as she realized what she was doing and she jerked her eyes away from forbidden territory to find Matt watching her with a wide, pleased grin. He knew! The grinning idiot knew she was aching to touch him.

Jiggs responded to his knowledge in the only truly dignified way open to her. Rising to her feet, she pushed him—with dignity—into the river. The ensuing war was punctuated with cries for mercy— from Jiggs—and victorious laughter—from Matt. It ended with her ignominiously begging for a truce as he flung her to the rumpled blanket.

Straddling her body on his knees, he held her arms above her laughter-weakened form. "Now, me proud beauty, you'll pay for that bit of treachery," he said, leering evilly at her prostrate body.

"No, please, sir. Not that," she pleaded, breathless with laughter. "I'm saving myself for Burt Reynolds."

"I'm afraid Burt is doomed to disappointment," he murmured, lowering his head to tease her smiling lips.

The taste of him, the feel of him had filled every moment of her time—waking and sleeping—for what seemed like centuries and the first tentative touch of his lips triggered a wildly explosive response. She pulled her hands free to clasp his head, fearing he would once again withdraw, and hungrily searched the warm moistness of his mouth with her eager tongue.

She felt him gasp with surprise at her response, then he groaned as if in agony and rolled sideways, drawing her body to his in an exquisitely intimate, thoroughly possessive embrace.

"God, sweet! I've been going crazy these last few days." His laugh was rough and self-mocking. "If you had known the thoughts that have been running through my mind while I watched you paint, and watched you eat, and watched you curling up beside me like a trusting little kitten—you would have run in terror."

"You want to make a bet on that?" she whispered, sucking delicately on his earlobe. "Your acting ability—or my stupidity—is frightening, Matt. I thought you had changed your mind about wanting me."

He laughed shortly, pulling her closer in a bone-crushing bear hug. "You've got to be kidding. I thought I was being very obvious. Saul certainly noticed. Every time I see him lately he starts laughing, the wicked old goat."

"Well, why didn't you say something?" she said, punching him in the shoulder, then kissing the same spot as tears began to form in her green eyes. All that frustrated longing could have been avoided if she had only known.

He gently tilted her face, forcing her to expose the depth of her hunger. "Was it bad, baby?" he whispered, stroking the side of her face with his rough giant's hand, wiping away the tears with a calloused thumb.

"Oh, Matt," she sighed, digging her fingers urgently into his shoulders. "It's been hell."

He captured the sound of her pain with greedy lips, bringing a moan of pleasure from deep within her. Lifting his lips from hers, he sought the sun-warmed skin of her throat. A quivering tension was building inside her. By the time his thirsty mouth reached the rounded tops of her breasts, she was breathing in frantic gasps.

His trembling hands sought the clasp of her bikini in urgent, fumbling movements. "Sweetheart," he moaned, "I thought I could do this kind of thing blindfolded, but I think you're going to have to help me." He kissed the top of one full breast, his mouth seeking the treasure that was just out of reach. "And hurry, please, Jiggs, or I may rip the damn thing off." His intense words were muffled against her softness.

She reached behind her back to help with the clasp, exultant at the depth of his desire for her. Together they managed to undo the stubborn fastening and he impatiently pulled the flimsy covering from her eager, tumescent breasts.

With a sharply indrawn breath, he closed his eyes and gently touched first one, then the other taut, erect nipple. He seemed to be concentrating all his senses in the tips of his fingers, reveling in the feel of her obvious desire. The earthy, pagan pleasure visible in his strong face was the most erotic thing she had ever seen. She arched to his touch as a cat arches to the touch of its owner.

No longer able to sustain the slow, gentle movement, Matt clutched her roughly to his body. The feel of his hair-roughened chest and thighs against her softness was an exquisitely tactile delight and she clung violently, arching her hips convulsively, entwining her legs with his as though she would pull him into her body.

The frenzy of their movements brought a sheen

of perspiration to their writhing bodies. Matt clasped her buttocks with his large hands and began to blaze a fiery path down her body, trying frantically to quench an unquenchable thirst. He drank deeply from her heaving breasts, bringing moans of pleasure from her throat that increased the hunger of his searching mouth. He explored her ribs and the sensitive area of her navel, then slipped lower to the soft inner part of her thighs. Jiggs caught her breath in a tremulous gasp as he moved his head and suddenly, through the soft fabric of her bikini, she could feel his heated breath on that most vulnerable place, merging with the heat he had already kindled, the flame spreading like wildfire throughout her body.

Sounds began to penetrate her fevered mind. Strange whimpering sounds. And, from somewhere on a different level, she realized that Jiggs the strong, Jiggs the independent was whimpering in sheer, unadulterated pleasure. She was astounded that anyone could provoke such an unrestrained response from her. The incredible feeling of being immersed in sensation was too great to contain. She needed to show her joy in action. She wanted to share her pleasure, give measure for measure.

Jiggs slowly urged Matt's head up and, under his glazed, watchful eyes, began a reciprocal exploration of his body. The feel of the short, curling hair on his chest against her face was glorious. She tasted the damp saltiness of his skin, inhaled the scent of his masculinity. Her tongue on his hard, male nipples sent shudders of pleasure rippling through his body, an aphrodisiacal tremor to her seeking hands. His fingers were threaded through her disheveled auburn hair, not guiding, but a gentle affirmation of his pleasure in her wandering tongue. As she reached the top of his low-riding cut-offs, she felt him take a sharp, rasping breath.

"God, yes, sweetheart. Touch me," he groaned, his voice hoarse and urgent.

She moved her hand from his rock hard buttock slowly across his firm hip, caressing her way to his throbbing shaft of desire, then exhaled a soft, moaning breath as she found his pulsating strength.

The effect of her touch on Matt was explosive. He moved with swift urgency and suddenly she was beneath him feeling the hard, wonderful length of his body against the receptive softness of hers. His frantic mouth devoured her lips, his tongue plunging deep into the seductive depths of her mouth, then his lips moved to her vulnerable neck in search of more sweet sustenance.

In the dim reality of her mind, faint, intrusive noises—voices in the distance—began to penetrate. She lifted her leaden eyelids to look at Matt. "Matt?" she whispered hoarsely.

He raised his head to look at her lips as she spoke. His eyes had a wild, fiery gleam like a man possessed. "Yes, sweet."

That ragged voice couldn't belong to Matt. The wonder of his being so consumed by desire and the burning intensity of his stare put her intended question back where it belonged—in the realm of the real world that had no part of their tactile fantasia. A slight pressure brought his mouth back to her hungry lips where it belonged.

But the real world would not stay out for long. As Matt slid her legs apart to mold her more completely to him, the voices intruded again, this time louder and more difficult to ignore. He raised his head to look questioningly into her sensation-drugged eyes. "I don't think we're alone, darlin'," he whispered.

"Oh?" she replied lethargically. His lower lip suddenly seemed the most fascinating thing she had ever seen. She lifted her hand lazily from its resting place on his neck to trace the shape of it with one trembling finger. "You're a very dangerous man, Matt."

He gave a short, oddly tremulous laugh. "Where you're concerned, sweet witch, I'm a great, hulking bowl of jello."

Her hands moved to his broad shoulders, feeling his strength, denying his statement. She raised her head from the blanket to kiss the warm, tanned flesh. "Did you say something about our not being alone?" she asked with complete indifference, moving her hands down his back to his firm buttocks, exploring the rounded flesh thoroughly.

"I can't remember," he whispered huskily.

She arched her body against his in pleasure as his lips found the sensitive spot at the base of her neck and his hand stroked her thigh and hip, sending an erotic message to her impassioned body.

Turning on his side, he slid his hand inside her bikini and, with gentle tugs, was beginning to ease it off when a loud squeal of laughter disrupted their sensuous idyll. He sighed deeply and stroked her cheek with his calloused hand. "I'm afraid we can't ignore them any longer, darlin'." His wistful tone was comical and, at the same time, strangely moving.

He rolled onto his back abruptly, his body hitting the blanket with a disgusted thud. He lifted his eyes to the blue, cloudless sky and muttered in frustration, "Why me?"

Jiggs giggled helplessly at his exaggerated sigh, scrambling to find her bikini top and refasten it before they were face to face with the noisy group which seemed to be getting rapidly closer. The hook was hopelessly tangled and she broke into fresh laughter as she thought of how much trouble they'd had unfastening it.

"Matt," she cried, beginning to panic. "It won't hook."

He pushed her hands aside to try his luck with the recalcitrant hook. "Good Lord, darlin'. What did you do to it? It's twisted all around." He fumbled impatiently, jerking her backwards in his fight to the death. "What in the hell happened to buttons?"

"Matt!" she squealed as she twisted to look over her shoulder, trying to see what he was doing. "I refuse to go home wearing your shirt!"

"Stop wiggling or I'll never get it done," he demanded. "And if I can't get it fastened, you'll either wear the blanket or leaves because, if you'll remember, I didn't wear a shirt."

Jiggs heard a muffled sound from behind her and, ignoring his order, turned to look over her shoulder. "Matthew Brady, you're laughing!"

"I can't help it, darlin'. I was imagining Saul and Ruth's faces if you returned to the house wearing leaves." His laughter was no longer muffled. It rang across the river in a deep, rich peal.

After a few seconds of indignant silence, the mellow sound of his laughter wove a spell of pleasure around her and she joined him, leaning on his bare shoulder when he had finally triumphed over the demon hook. When they heard another shout from just around the bend they began to pack away the remains of the picnic. As they folded the blanket, they saw a fully-loaded canoe come around the bend.

"Canoes," Matt said, his tone disgusted. "As much as I love canoeing, I don't think I'll ever be able to see another one without flinching." He stood, hands on hips, watching the boat come nearer. "Look at those idiots throwing beer cans into the river," he said as though it were the last straw. "They can't be experienced canoeists."

As Jiggs watched Matt, a devilish gleam appeared in his eyes.

"Matt! What are you planning?" she asked suspiciously. His mischievous grin boded no good for the unsuspecting intruders.

"Who, me?" The halo surrounding his angelically innocent face was slightly crooked.

"Matt," she repeated sternly.

"I was just thinking, darlin'. There's a place about two hundred yards downriver from here, right around the next bend, where the rocks sometimes give inexperienced canoeists a rough time."

She looked at him in alarm.

"Oh, nothing serious," he reassured her. "Just a little, bitty chunk of white water. They'll only get wet."

He reached for her and swung her surprised form around in a joyously wide circle. "Let's go watch them tip over, darlin'. I deserve that much for the frustration they've caused. They should have known I was loving my Jiggs on this part of the river. Please, darlin,' " he coaxed, his little boy look firmly in place. "Besides, we can pull them out if they're too drunk to swim."

The belated addition of righteousness helped to sway her and they ran like children, with clasped hands, to the spot downriver. By the time they arrived the first canoe had already floundered on the small rapids and they rushed to help its passengers rescue their possessions.

As she worked, Jiggs recalled Matt's words. "My Jiggs," he had said. Why didn't the implied possessiveness of those words bother her? Why did she melt a little inside when she remembered? She didn't want to be anyone's possession and the fact that his words didn't bother her, bothered her.

After Matt, having had his revenge, sent the dampened party on its way, the two of them walked back to pick up their things.

On the way home, Matt whistled cheerfully, pausing at frequent intervals to kiss Jiggs's slightly swollen lips. As much as she enjoyed being kissed by him, this delightful occupation couldn't stop the doubts from reverberating inside her brain. She knew he was expecting to take up where they had left off as soon as they were alone. And it was what she wanted also, wasn't it? All week she had been aching to be in Matt's arms, in Matt's bed. Why did her stupid brain have to get in her way now?

As she showered and changed, the doubts kept returning. He hadn't shown any signs of wanting anything more from her than a friendly affair, so why did she hesitate? His words by the river had meant nothing. If they made love it would only deepen their friendship. She could handle that.

"Well, I can," she belligerently told the doubtful face in her mirror. "So you can keep your opinion to yourself!"

All through dinner she felt Matt watching her—and Saul watching Matt watch her. She could see the questioning concern in Matt's eyes and made a determined effort to join in the conversation, but it was no use. The doubts that were swirling around in her head would not let her relax.

After what seemed like hours, Saul stood and bade them goodnight, his faded blue eyes twinkling with hidden merriment. He resembled an old elf enjoying the antics of a couple of frail human creatures.

Left alone with Matt, Jiggs decided finally and for all that she would not hesitate when he took her in his arms. It was what she wanted, she told herself, and she'd be damned if she would let her stubborn brain spoil her first night with him. A loving friendship was what she wanted and that was what he was offering her. She felt comfortable with Matt. She laughed with Matt. She lusted after Matt.

The miracle of his freely given friendship was unmatched by anything else in her·life. A total acceptance of her as she really was. He asked nothing from her except that she allow the friendship to grow and develop in other ways. He had expressed no desire to tie her down or absorb her personality. What they shared was so new and so precious she found herself wanting to protect it from any harmful influence. Even if that harmful influence was herself. It was the most wonderfully exciting thing that had ever happened to her and she wasn't going to let a little matter of semantics— those words "*my* Jiggs"—ruin it.

Having made up her mind, she waited impatiently for Matt to make his move. She glanced at him from the corner of her eye as he sat beside her on the couch. He seemed preoccupied as he watched the fire.

Maybe she should make a move. Her affair with Roger had been brief and uninspiring, teaching her none of the man-woman games people supposedly played, but surely she had enough feminine intuition, however atrophied, to carry off a simple seduction. Women throughout the centuries had been beguiling men with provocative looks and seductive poses. But Jiggs had the horrible suspicion that if she tried these artful measures, she wouldn't look seductive, she would look sick!

Oh, help! she silently pleaded. What in the world did she do now? Should she grab him and start kissing? No, definitely too crude. Maybe a subtle hand on his thigh? Oh, yes, touching his thigh would be nice, but was it the right move? Wasn't there some kind of signal that a woman gave a man when she was ready?

Lord, why hadn't she ever read any of those books all her friends had read? She bet none of them had a problem making a pass at a man.

"Jiggs, darlin', are you all right?"

She jumped guiltily at the sound of his voice. He was watching her closely, a strangely wistful smile playing about his firm lips.

"Yes, of course," she hastily assured him, trying to hide her chaotic thoughts. "Why do you ask?"

"The most intriguing expressions have been flitting across your face," he explained. "If I didn't know for a fact you didn't touch your dinner, I'd swear you had indigestion."

He pulled her into his arms and she snuggled closer. Returning his gaze to the flickering flames, he asked, "What's bothering you, Jiggs?"

"Nothing, really, Matt," she prevaricated. "I guess I just wanted you to hold me."

"Is that why you didn't eat any dinner?" He turned his head to look into her eyes. "It couldn't be because you were having second thoughts about this afternoon, could it?"

"No, of course—"

"Jiggs," he reprimanded. "The truth."

"Well, maybe a few tiny second thoughts," she admitted. "But they went away, honest."

"Tell me about it."

She looked thoughtfully into the fire, hesitant to discuss the subject since she had already decided to ignore her doubts. However, knowing Matt, he wouldn't rest until she had told him.

"It's not any one definite thing, Matt. I think part of it has to do with our friendship. I don't want you to think I'm saying 'poor, poor pitiful me,' but, as an adult, I've never had a real friend—not until I met you. And I value that friendship, Matt. *It's the most precious thing I've found in my life.* I don't want to jeopardize it. What would happen if we had an affair and then one of us wanted to call it off? Wouldn't that be the end of our friendship?" She looked him in the eyes and said candidly, "You're the most physically exciting man I've ever met, Matt. And I want you desperately, but from what I've heard desire doesn't always last very long. Should we take a chance on ruining a lasting friendship for the sake of a brief affair?" she asked earnestly.

For a while he simply stared into her face, then he sighed deeply. "So we have to choose between the two?" he asked. "I don't think you know either of us too well, darlin'. Personally, I think it would take more than a dead affair to ruin our friendship. There's something between us, Jiggs. I knew it the minute you opened your eyes that first morning. Something that won't go away no matter what happens." He sighed again, sounding tired for the first time since she had known him. "But that's not the real problem, is it, Jiggs? That's not the reason you were having second thoughts." His eyes were fixed intently on hers, demanding the truth.

"I said it was only part of the reason," she defended. "The rest is really too nebulous for me to put into words. It's just a vague feeling I had today on the riverbank. I felt as though things were going beyond my control. You know how I feel about sloppily emotional relationships. All my life, beginning with my own mother and father, I've seen what a man can do to a woman emotionally, if he chooses. It's not pleasant to watch, believe me." She shuddered in reminiscent horror. "A man can degrade and destroy a woman more quickly, through her emotions, than anything else on earth. I want no part of that sort of thing."

"So your parents had a bad marriage," he said scornfully. "Darlin', my parents forgot they even had a son until they wanted something from me, but I stopped letting that hurt me a long time ago. I can understand how your parents could have affected your view of life. But, Jiggs, you can't let that scare you into retreating from life. Someday you'll find something that's worth risking a little of that sloppy emotion on."

He stood abruptly and helped her to her feet, making no move to touch her, his features closed, almost cold. "But not tonight, darlin'. When you feel like making love to me is worth a little risk, you let me know."

As she undressed in her darkened room, Jiggs saw his face again in her mind. She had never seen Matt so forbidding. Was he angry at her reluctance? If she lost his friendship she didn't know what she would do. Maybe she should go to him, tell him that she was wrong, ask him to make love to her.

Her hand was on the doorknob before she came to her senses. She couldn't go to him like this, begging for his friendship. Matt wouldn't want her on those terms. She had to work things out in her own way. If he got tired of waiting, then the relationship wasn't as strong as it should be.

She walked to the window and stared into the moonlit night. She had a crushing feeling that it was going to be a very long night.

Suddenly Matt appeared on the deck, the moonlight glancing off his roughly chiseled features. She watched in silence as he leaned against the railing. He seemed deep in thought and—she drew in a harsh, pained breath—so terribly, terribly alone.

# Seven

Jiggs sat staring at the preliminary sketch with disgust. It was simply awful. It looked stiff and amateurish. She ripped the offending sketch from her pad, crumpling it with suppressed violence. Nothing was going right and it was all Matt's fault. He had been away on business for three miserably long days.

At least he *said* it was business. He's probably visiting that little old brow-soother Barbie, she thought maliciously. He's probably playing doll house with her right now.

"What on earth is wrong with me?" she asked, revolted by her unreasonable bitchiness. She stood and walked to the window, remembering the way Matt had acted before he left. The coldness she had seen in his face on that disastrous night had been missing the next day. But so had the affectionate warmth she had come to count on. He had been polite, and interested in her welfare, the perfect host in fact. And all the while he had been holding himself from her. He had erected barriers that Jiggs couldn't penetrate. They had no longer laughed together. Finally in desperation, she had sought the company of Saul and even the stone-faced Ruth, rather than spend agonizing evenings with a stranger with Matt's face.

She had thought nothing could be worse than her deteriorating relationship with Matt. She was wrong. Being without him was worse, much worse. No matter how hard Saul and Ruth worked at trying to cheer her, the house seemed empty and curiously dead without Matt's vitality. Just knowing he was in the house, even if she weren't with him, made all the difference in the world. Saul was right. Matt was a part of the house—he was its heart. And without him the house was no longer alive.

She shook away the morbid thoughts and returned to her work. Not that she expected to accomplish anything, for her work had suffered dreadfully in Matt's absence. She couldn't seem to concentrate on what she was doing. She ripped page after ruined page from her drawing pad, finally laying her pencil aside in exasperation. It was useless to continue. She might as well take up needlepoint until Matt returned. She was so preoccupied with her aching feelings of loss of Matt that the notion she was coming to depend on him too much could only nibble at the edge of her mind.

"Do you want me to bring your dinner in here again, Jiggs?"

She looked up to see Ruth standing in the doorway and smiled ruefully. "I don't think I want anything tonight. Thank you, anyway, Ruth." Her appetite had been dwindling to the point of non-existence.

"Girl, you're going to be nothing but skin and

bones when Matt gets back if you keep this up," Ruth scolded. "You only picked at your lunch and toast is no kind of breakfast at all." Her tone was rich with disgust.

"I know, Ruth, and I'm sorry. I just don't seem to have much appetite," she apologized.

"Be that as it may, a body's got to have nourishment," she said pragmatically. "Now how about a nice bowl of soup?"

"Soup would be fine, Ruth," she acquiesced, knowing the woman's bland face hid a stubborn determination that was difficult to fight. "And I'll have it in here, please." The other rooms in the house were too evocative of Matt's absence.

As she watched Ruth leave, she wondered again what emotions lurked behind her expressionless face. Jiggs knew her lack of expression did not indicate a lack of intelligence or a lack of sensitivity, for she had come to know Ruth well and found she had a sharp mind. And although she could see no evidence of emotion in her face, Jiggs could feel warmth emanating from the older woman. She wondered what kind of childhood Ruth had had to cause that curious stone-featured facade. She would have to ask Matt when he returned.

Matt. It hadn't taken long for her thoughts to return to him. If only she had been able to hide her doubts from him, all this turmoil could have been avoided. But was that fair? Surely a good relationship deserved honesty? Yet she had been honest with him and what had it gotten her? He had forced the truth from her and then used that same truth against her. He was the one who wasn't being fair. He should have tried to understand. And how long was he supposed to go on understanding? she asked herself ruefully. At the rate she was going he could reach the age of eighty still asking, "Now, Jiggs?" She giggled at the thought of Matt, an old man with a cane, chasing her around a rocking chair.

For Pete's sake, give it up, Jiggs, she told herself. Don't think about it any more tonight. Excellent advice, but its effects barely lasted through dinner, dissipating entirely as she showered before going to bed.

The warm water caressing her exhausted body brought back memories of a rougher, more substantial caress. As she lathered her body, the sensations she had felt while in his arms, lying beneath his hard, male body, welled up with such strength that she cried out in anguish at her loss. After turning the cold water on full force, in a vain attempt to banish her erotic thoughts, she dried herself vigorously, each movement a chastisement for her errant body. She chose her nightgown carefully, avoiding the sensual silks, opting instead for a plain cotton shift. The warmth of her overheated body had not dissipated under the cold water and she paced the floor before flinging herself on the bed in disgust.

Twenty minutes later she knew she would not sleep tonight. She switched on the bedside lamp and picked up the book from the nightstand. Although she normally relished Goethe's every word, she was very much afraid this attempt at diversion would end like the others. She couldn't pull her thoughts away from Matt long enough to concentrate. Tonight she could see herself as Mephistopheles—a living spirit of negation. She had always considered herself to be optimistic in the extreme, but was she really? Wasn't she expecting the worst in her relationship with Matt? People who look for the worst, she told herself, always find it. Do I have so little faith in myself that I run from a situation because it could possibly be beyond my ken? So what if it turns out badly? Then I'll learn from it and next time I'll do better.

"I refuse to be Mephistopheles," she said aloud, slamming the book down on the nightstand. Scrambling from the bed, she grabbed her lightweight robe and stalked down the hall to the kitchen. She had never tasted warm milk, but if ever there was a time to try the repulsive sounding stuff, it was now. Anything was better than lying there, driving herself insane with thoughts of Matt.

She searched the cabinets for a small saucepan, poured in a cup of milk, then stood watching it, waiting for it to heat.

"How warm is it supposed to be, I wonder?" she mused aloud. "Why do I always read the wrong books? Betty Crocker or Julia Child would have been able to tell me how to heat milk," she muttered darkly. Since meeting Matt she had felt more inadequate about more things than she ever had before in her life.

*I can't cook. I can't make up my mind. I can't even make a decent pass at a man,* she thought in disgust. *But I've got lots of good qualities,* she mentally defended. *I'm a good artist. No . . . I'm a damned good artist. I'm an adequate photographer. I'm a friend in need. I don't make noise when I eat jello. I look presentable—when I make the effort. And . . . and I'm cosmopolitan. I know enough Italian to sing along with Rossini, enough German to sing along with Lehar, enough French to order the right soup, and enough Spanish to get me out of El Paso.*

"What more could I ask of myself?" she said aloud, then screeched in panic as milk boiled over the sides of the saucepan, pouring onto the stove.

"Damn, damn, *damn!*" She turned off the burner and grabbed a dish towel, wiping furiously at the revolting mess. "I can't even heat a simple cup of milk," she wailed, as though answering her earlier question.

Defeated, she laid aside the sopping wet towel and sat looking into space, silent tears streaming down her troubled face.

Look at me, she thought. This is the woman who didn't want to live life on a seesaw? No mental turmoil. No sloppy emotions. Ha! This is just about as sloppy as you can get. No matter what happens with Matt, things couldn't possibly be worse! I've got all the turmoil and none of the pleasure. It's not fair!

As she cleaned the stove she prayed for Matt's swift return. She plotted ways to show him she could handle an affair, but finally decided simply to tell him in plain English that she wanted him.

She walked into the hall, turning out the kitchen light as she left, then stopped for a moment, allowing her eyes to adjust to the darkness. As the furniture in the hall became distinguishable, something else became clear. Matt was standing in the hall not two feet away from her.

He stood, not speaking, looking so tired, she ached for him. His shirt was open at the neck and he had thrown his jacket over one strong shoulder. The need to move, to touch him was agonizing, but his silence held her still—until she looked at his tired face. A lock of brown hair had fallen forward on his forehead, lying neglected as though he were too weary to push it back. Slowly she extended her hand, gently smoothing the thick hair into place.

Her movement seemed to work as a catalyst, for with a deep groan, Matt pulled her into his arms and held her tightly as though he were afraid she would disappear. She cradled his head with her hands, stroking his face softly, murmuring words of comfort to soothe away his hurt.

"Oh God, baby," he moaned. "I need you." He didn't loosen his tight hold and made no move to kiss or caress her. He simply held her, trying to meld her body with his.

"I know, darling," she murmured. "I know. It'll be all right, you'll see. I'll make it all right for you." She whispered the words as though she were comforting an injured child, stroking his hair and neck, trying to make the hurt all better.

He laughed. A short, self-mocking sound in the darkness. "Jiggs, you idiot," he whispered, caressing her face with his own. "I'm not a child. I'm a man and my hurt won't go away with a band-aid or even a kiss—although a kiss might help."

"I know that, Matt," she answered solemnly. "I know how you hurt because I hurt in the same way."

He pulled away a fraction of an inch and looked into her eyes. "Sweetheart, I kept telling myself I would give you all the time you needed to make up your mind. That I wouldn't rush you." He closed his eyes and sighed deeply. "But I don't want to wait any longer. I'm not saying I won't, but I sure as hell don't want to. I need you tonight, Jiggs."

Cradling his face with her hands, she smoothed the troubled lines from his brow with gentle hands and softly whispered a will-o'-the-wisp kiss across his well-shaped lips. "Yes, please, Matt," she murmured. The words were finally out and a mixture of relief and nervous anticipation spread tremors throughout her body.

For a long moment Matt simply looked at her, feeling the trembling of her slender body. "You're sure? Jiggs, please be certain this is what you want." He brushed his lips across the top of her head. "I hope it is, sweetheart, because I don't think I can stop this time."

The look on his face was one Jiggs had never seen before, in fact she was quite sure it was an expression very few people had ever seen. Matt—as strong and self-confident as any man she had ever known—looked vulnerable. She had been so busy protecting her own vulnerability she had never considered the possibility that he too could be susceptible to hurt. That look of uncertainty stilled the trembling of her body and when he lifted her into his arms she sighed in pure joy, all doubt, all fear wiped away. She knew in that moment that whatever happened in the future, being in Matt's arms was indisputably, unequivocally right.

He carried her with swift, sure strides up to his bedroom and placed her on the outrageously large bed. He hesitated beside the bed as though unsure of his next move.

"Damn it, Jiggs. What kind of witch are you?" he muttered, raking his fingers through his thick hair. "I feel as nervous as a kid on his first parking date. What in the hell do I do now?"

A loving smile playing about her lips, she rose from the bed and drew a caressing hand across the hard muscles of his chest. "I'll bet if you really put your mind to it," she murmured in vampish tones, "it'll all come back to you."

"Imp!" He chuckled, grabbing her and pulling her to him abruptly, forcing the air from her lungs as her body made contact with his. "What am I going to do with you, you sweet idiot?"

"You mean you still don't remember?" she asked in disappointment.

She moved away and looked at him, intending to tease, but suddenly the air was fraught with electricity. The moonlight was streaming through the open windows and as she looked at him it seemed to her that his body was the most beautiful, the most perfect thing she had ever seen. She wanted—needed—to see him standing there in the moonlight, naked.

It never occurred to her to ask his permission. Compelled by a force beyond her control, she raised her hands and began to unbutton his shirt. His sharply indrawn breath didn't penetrate her intense concentration. Although she felt a deep urgency to see him unclothed, her movements were deliberately slow. She wanted to prolong the exquisite anticipation, reap the full benefits of the moment.

She spread his unbuttoned shirt wide across his chest, delighting in the feel of his warm skin and dark, curling hair. Kneading and stroking the muscles of his shoulders, she pushed his shirt aside. A gentle tug pulled the cotton shirt loose and it was discarded carelessly as she reveled in the sight of his bare upper torso. Caressing the now heaving chest with one hand, the other went willfully to his belt. She fumbled momentarily, bringing the other hand down to assist.

With a deep, shuddering groan, Matt took over from her groping hands and she moved back, the better to see him. In seconds he was free of the remaining garments. He moved toward her silently, then stopped as he took in the awe on her lovely face.

This was no Greek god she saw before her. This was all nature's rough beauty portrayed in vital, living flesh. No gentle lines and sleek form—he was pure, unadulterated male animal. Staring at his moon-glazed form, she knew she was seeing a basic truth, an honesty that had always escaped her.

"I was right," he whispered, wonder and something elusive in his tone, "you are a witch." He moved to stand before her, breaking the spell his hard, male beauty had cast upon her. He looked into her eyes as he touched her face softly and murmured, "You simply look at me and I feel things I've never felt before."

Jiggs turned her face into his large, calloused hand, kissing his palm. She felt a slight movement at her waist, on her shoulders, then her belted robe fell to the floor, lying at her feet like a discarded inhibition. He drew the cotton gown over her head, softly brushing her curves with his hand as he went, then stood, drinking in the subtly rounded softness of her slender shape. Her body shone, illuminated by an ethereal lunar spotlight. Later it would occur to her that she felt no embarrassment as he stared at her naked form. Matt seemed to be trying to memorize every part of her, his gaze lingering on her breasts, her thighs, the triangle of curling hair that spoke of her femininity.

When he picked her up and gently laid her on the bed, it seemed the most natural thing in the world. There was no hesitancy now for either of them. They were where they were destined to be—in each other's arms.

Resting on one elbow, he began to touch her face, exploring her high cheekbones, the softness of her eyelids, her sensitive lips. She lay motionless, eyes closed, as his hands moved lower to her body, absorbing his subtly erotic movements through every pore. It was a languid, drugging seduction of the senses. His hands were reaffirming the beauty his eyes had discovered before. As though still unconvinced, he followed the same path with his lips. The rate of his breathing increased, whispering a heated foretelling of each searching kiss.

As his hot breath and moist tongue gently teased her taut nipples, Jiggs felt a moan begin deep within her, shuddering its way to the surface, disrupting her motionless state.

Her quaking response was greeted by a short, triumphant sound from Matt and he cupped her now trembling breast, taking the erect tip deep within his mouth, then moved his hands to revel in the undulating softness of her hips.

Jiggs felt a burning ache in her loins—an agonizing urgency she had never experienced before. Her breathing accelerated to short, desperate gasps. "Matt," she moaned, pleading. "Please."

"Easy, sweet," he soothed, his voice raspy and strange. "Not yet. Just a little longer."

She groaned in frustration, grasping his thighs, his hard buttocks, trying to pull him closer. She gasped at the pleasure she felt at his uncontrollable shudder. To know her touch affected him so deeply was an unbelievable high.

"God, sweet!" he grated, as she grasped him boldly. His caressing hand moved to seek the heated moistness guarded by the curling triangle of hair. "So warm, so sweet. And it's all for me, isn't it, Jiggs?"

She trembled violently, making indistinguishable sounds in her throat as his fingers teased her to a frenzy. "Matt, damn it! Now!" she rasped harshly.

"Yes, by God! Now." And he raised above her, her eager hands guiding him to the source of her agony.

She moaned her pleasure as his hard shaft filled her. The feel of his manhood inside her was deliciously strange, yet unexplainably familiar. The slow, sensual strokes stoked the fiery tension inside her unbearably. He suddenly increased the pace of his lovemaking, carrying her away on a fantastic voyage with rhythmically orchestrated movements of exultation.

Her fingers dug sharply into his shoulders as she felt an intolerable pressure, a flaming hunger in her loins. She writhed in agony, her head thrashing wildly on the pillow. "Matt," she gasped, frightened by the intensity of the unfamiliar sensations. Then, "Matt!" in astonishment and wonder as she soared, leaving all earthly trappings behind. She rose to overwhelming heights before shuddering softly back to earth.

"Matt." This time the word was a sigh of loving gratitude—a gentle whisper of the pleasure still with her. She would have been terrified had she seen the adoration shining out of her eyes.

She wrapped her long legs around him, watching in fascination as he threw back his head, his rugged face contorted with the intensity of his pleasure. She rode out his storm with a warm feeling of *déjà vu*, cradling his gasping body as he reached his shuddering release.

They lay quietly for long, luxurious moments, bound together by exhaustion and the warm afterglow of love, then he propped his head in his hand, touching her swollen lips with one finger. "Well, darlin'," he whispered, smiling into her shining eyes, "didn't I tell you it was there inside you, waiting just for *me*." His voice was softly exultant—and a little smug.

"You're a conceited man, Matthew Brady." She laughed indulgently, kissing the tip of his finger, then stretched her body in a languorous, feline movement, bringing her arms to rest around his neck. "But I'll overlook it this time because you, my dear," she punctuated her words with tiny kisses on and around his mouth, ". . . are an amazing . . . example of . . . masculine . . . pulchritude." She laughed again, a delighted, exuberant sound of pure joy.

"Happy, sweet?"

"Happy! That doesn't come near describing it." She hugged him tightly, bursting with the incredible discovery she had made in his arms. "It's the most unbelievably intoxicating thing I've ever felt! I'm twenty-nine years old and I've just stumbled onto what it's all about." Genuine amazement was evident in her expressive features.

"Not stumbled, sweet," he whispered quietly, his face showing a momentary trace of guilt. "I'm afraid it was more a case of pushed."

Caught up in her own enthusiasm, Jiggs missed his barely audible words. "Why on earth didn't you tell me what it was like, Matt?"

He looked at her excited face for a moment, then laid his head on the pillow, cuddling her close with her head on his shoulder. "Would you have believed me? It's something you have to feel to believe!" He laughed softly. "And to tell you the truth, I wouldn't have been able to describe what just happened because it's something I've never felt before either."

His words brought a soft, warm glow to her body and she snuggled comfortably against him. They whispered and giggled like disobedient children far into the night, halting occasionally to speak with their bodies, and eventually dropping off into the deep, peaceful sleep of sated lovers.

# *Eight*

Jiggs grunted disagreeably as bright sunshine inconsiderately struck her full in the face. With tightly closed eyes, she reached down to pull the cover over her head. Instead of a blanket, her fumbling fingers encountered a large, hairy object lying across her breasts.

"Matt," she sighed in sleepy satisfaction. Memories of the night before flooded her body, bringing a secret smile to her lips. She opened her eyes and looked at his sleeping form. Last night in the moonlight he had seemed unreal, unfamiliar to her unawakened senses. Today she knew every inch of him. She knew the scar on the back of one hard thigh, acquired while climbing—or rather falling from—a tree when he was ten. She knew the slight crook in one big toe—a gift from a disobliging cow at a dig in Africa. She was on speaking terms with the incredible strength in his arms, the ticklish spot on his back, and the errant curl at the nape of his neck. She knew his body better than she knew her own. And familiarity definitely did not breed contempt in this case. Her fingers itched to touch him again—to visit well-loved places—but the pleasure of watching him sleep held her back. She wanted to taste the full range of emotions in this loving friendship.

He had been so unbelievably gentle last night, so warmly affectionate. And then at times she had sensed a strange desperation in his loving, as though he needed to store up her warmth against hard times. But however he made love to her—gently or with a raging hunger—she reveled in it. And greedily she wanted more.

Matt stirred slightly, the movement causing the blanket to slip low on his hips. God! she thought, drawing in a small, sharp breath, his was the most erotic centerfold pose she had ever seen. The blanket was draped with almost purposeful discretion, showing his lean, dark hips and the flat plane of his stomach, but enticing the mind to imagine the rest.

Only I don't have to imagine, she thought, closing her eyes and smiling smugly. I have first-hand knowledge of how beautifully all his parts match.

"My, my," a drowsy, amused voice reached her ears. "You look like you've just discovered that Mrs. Reagan buys her clothes off the rack."

"Better," she murmured, opening her eyes to see his face smiling down at her. "Much, much better." She looked him over in mock surprise. "Haven't we met before? I seem to recall waking once before to find a man who looked just like you in the bed."

"And I remember waking, feeling more frustrated than I ever had in my life." He chuckled. "But of course, at the time I didn't know what was in store for me. I've learned that what I felt that night was mild compared to what I've felt since."

He shook her shoulder in gentle reproof. "You certainly believe in trial by fire."

He rolled onto his back, pulling her on top of him. "But for what you gave me last night, darlin', I would gladly suffer all that and more."

"My pleasure, I'm sure," she said demurely, earning a sharp, vaguely erotic slap on the derrière.

Suddenly she rolled off him and sat up. "Oh Lord, Matt!" She looked at him in horror. "What time is it?"

He glanced at the alarm clock on the nightstand. "It's ten. Why?" he asked, surprised at her abrupt actions.

"Ruth, Matt! Ruth!" She shook his shoulders to make him understand. "She brings my coffee every morning at seven. She must know by now that I didn't sleep in my room last night."

"I'm sure she does," he said matter-of-factly. "Because, you see, darlin'," he grinned irritatingly at her agitation, ". . . she brings *my* coffee every morning at six-thirty." He gestured to two cups sitting on the nightstand. Two cups!

"Oh, no," she moaned, sliding down in the bed and pulling the sheet over her head in misery.

He listened patiently to the unintelligible mumbles coming from beneath the sheet, then gently pulled it aside.

"Sweetheart, I can't understand a word you're saying. You'll have to take the sheet out of your mouth if you want to tell me about it." He gave her a stern look. "Now—slowly—tell me what's bothering you. I know you're not ashamed of sleeping with me because you didn't mind Saul knowing how we felt."

"Of course I'm not ashamed of it!" she repudiated indignantly. "But Ruth is different, Matt. She's—she's—American Gothic! I like her and I don't want her to think I'm a—a hussy."

Matt laughed in sheer delight. "But you are. A thoroughly brazen hussy," he said, hugging her to him. "Jiggs, you baby, haven't you seen the looks Ruth and Saul have been giving us ever since you arrived?"

"No," she said thoughtfully, trying to remember anything unusual in the way the older couple had looked at her, then finally admitted, "I guess I was thinking about . . . um . . . other things."

"Well, if you had been looking around, you would have seen that they both knew what was going on and what's more, my adorable blockhead, they probably think we were crazy to wait so long."

"Do you really think so?" she asked hopefully.

"Of course. Now stop worrying and kiss me, woman," he ordered, then as she stared at him in haughty inquiry, he added meekly, "Please."

"That's better." She looked at him in thoughtful consideration. "I suppose after all the strain you put on your decrepit body for me, you deserve a reward. Pucker up."

She squeaked in mock terror as he moved swiftly and moments later had pinned her laughing form beneath his giant frame. "Decrepit? Is that what you said, Jiggs?"

"I think you must have mistaken my words, darling," she said, gasping for breath beneath him. She felt his chuckle shaking her body and looked at him in bewilderment. "Were you this heavy last night?"

The chuckle grew into a laugh, rocking her violently. "Matt! For heaven's sake, stop laughing before I'm permanently disabled!"

"Am I heavy, sweet?" he asked considerately.

"Yes," she muttered with what felt like her last breath, squirming beneath him. "And you're not my brother either."

"Thank God," he breathed sincerely.

His voice sounded strange and Jiggs started to question the cause, but stopped at the look in his eyes. She caught her breath and, miraculously, his body no longer felt heavy. It felt exactly right.

"Matt," she murmured softly, "shouldn't we go have breakfast or something?"

"We'll have the 'something' now, sweet witch. Breakfast can wait." And it did.

As they sat down for breakfast at three o'clock that afternoon, they listened contentedly to Ruth scolding them for neglecting their food. She served them plates heaping with eggs, potatoes, and steak, then stood and watched as they fell on it voraciously.

"Well, it's about time. You, young lady, haven't eaten enough to keep body and soul together since Matt left." She looked at Jiggs as she scolded, her expressionless face giving the words a curiously mechanical sound. "And now you don't eat breakfast 'til it's nearly time for dinner. What's gotten into you, girl?"

It was definitely the wrong question to ask. Startled, Jiggs and Matt looked at each other, faces red with suppressed laughter, then, together, slowly they turned to face Ruth.

She looked at them for a moment with her usual non-expression, then an incredible sound split the silence.

When Ruth left the room, Jiggs looked at Matt, shock holding her face rigid. "Matt, was that—"

"I don't believe it," he said, shaking his head in bewilderment. "A smile would have been a shock. But, Jiggs . . ." he looked at her, his face comical with astonishment, ". . . that was an honest to God *guffaw*!"

It was some time before they could control their laughter enough to eat. Every time Jiggs thought of the look on Matt's face she broke up again.

When he left the table to consult with Saul, she sat quietly thinking how the world seemed to be smiling at them today. Ruth's incredible laugh was only a part of the magic. The house seemed to be laughing in delighted approval of their union.

In Matt Jiggs had someone with whom she could share all the incredible wonders, all the human comedy abounding in the world around them. This was truly the loving friendship she had sought. Never again would she have to suffer a deliciously funny incident in silence. Matt would never look at her in confusion and say, "What are you talking about?" He appreciated the subtleties and satire that occurred with astonishing regularity in day-to-day living.

Someone to laugh with. She now realized the importance of those words. She hadn't known what she was missing until she met Matt. There was a special communication between them. An invisible line that tied them mind to mind, soul to soul. When Matt saw or heard something that struck a chord within him, he simply glanced at her and she understood. Although their backgrounds were totally different, it was as though the basic ingredients of their separate personalities matched perfectly—a fact that seemed to amaze and delight Matt as much as it did her. He was constantly touching her. Not in a possessive, or even in a sensual way, but simply a gentle affirmation of her presence. His joy in their friendship kept her wrapped in a warm glow that made every moment with him different and special. Things that were nice before suddenly became poignant and wonderful in Matt's company. And things that were merely funny suddenly became hilarious.

And, at last, she understood what Saul had

been trying to say the day she arrived. There was nothing gaudy or flowery about Matt's friendship. It was basic and honest and real. The sort of thing that would stand when other more tenuous friendships fell. Saul had, in his own way, been warning her to value that honesty, but Jiggs needed no warning. She had seen enough artificial relationships to cherish the real thing when it came along. She would not take the risk of losing the special rapport that they shared.

She hugged herself with the thought of sharing with Matt. Last night she had discovered something wonderful in his arms and, like a child after its first taste of ice cream, ordinary fare would never again suffice. She was torn between the desire to hide away and relive each precious memory and the consuming need to make new ones.

This kind of affair—this loving friendship—was perfect. Her equation had worked after all. She would have all the highs, but none of the depressing lows of what was popularly known as love. She would be free of the ties and the helplessness that plagued those caught in the throes of that erratic emotion. A good solid friendship that would last a lifetime. And no worries about unfaithfulness or any of the other indignities constantly being perpetrated by lovers the world over. One is not unfaithful to a friend. The easy relationship eliminates the need for that type of devious behavior.

She leaned back in her chair with a contented sigh, totally satisfied with her life. She conveniently overlooked all the agony of the last few days as she thought smugly: No possessiveness. No jealousy. No emotional tangles that constantly need unraveling. Just warmth and laughter and companionship in their wonderfully uncomplicated friendship.

"What are you thinking about with such deep concentration?" He had entered her studio silently and was noisily nuzzling her neck as he spoke.

"Matt, stop," she laughed. "You sound like a pig, rooting around on my neck."

"Come on, darlin'," he said, giving her neck one last snorting kiss, then pulling her to her feet. "There's a beautiful day waiting for us." He grinned cockily. "At least, what's left of it is waiting for us."

"I hate to interject any vulgar practicality, but shouldn't we be working?" she asked, smiling at his enthusiasm.

"Now you're thinking like a mortal," he admonished. "If you want to fly on my cloud, you're going to have to make some radical changes."

"What model is your cloud?" she asked suspiciously.

"Well, actually it's a Jeep Wagoneer, but it'll have to do until I can check into the price of a used cumulus." He chuckled.

Oh Lord, here we go again, she thought, rolling her eyes as he pulled her through the front door and halted beside the large square vehicle. "Matt, darling, where are we going?" she asked with sweet patience, surreptitiously checking the length of her right arm against her left.

"It's fall, Jiggs," he said, gesturing around them. "And Palo Pinto County is all dressed up in her Sunday best. We're going to pay homage to a glorious season. Revel in the splendiferous beauty of nature."

"Does that mean we're going for a drive in the country?" she asked guilelessly.

"Philistine," he said, chuckling as she climbed into the high seat.

They drove through the country, stopping occasionally to enjoy a particularly beautiful setting.

They followed narrow side roads to their ends—usually at the front yards of tiny, white frame houses. Jiggs was seeing the world with new eyes. The riotous colors of autumn had never seemed so brilliant. The air was crisp and clean. She wasn't only seeing the world, she was tasting it—absorbing it into her body until she was a part of it.

They returned home for a very late dinner, hurrying guiltily at Ruth's muttered reproaches.

After dinner they strolled arm in arm to Saul's campfire by the river. The wizened old man watched them approach, his eyes twinkling in the firelight.

"You two look like it just rained after a long dry spell," he chuckled. " 'Bout time, too. I've seen dumb in my day, but you kids take the cake."

Matt hugged Jiggs tightly, whispering "I told you so" softly in her ear. She punched him sharply in the ribs and turned to Saul. "Are you from around here, Saul?" she asked, anxious to change the subject.

"Born and raised 'bout five miles from here," he confirmed proudly. "And my daddy 'fore me and his daddy 'fore him."

"You love it, don't you?" she asked softly.

He looked at her sternly. "I *know* it. My family's always been farmers and this land made 'em old 'fore their time. It's hard country. If the drought or flood don't get you, a tornado will. But look at it, girl." He looked like a miniature Merlin, casting spells in the firelight, as he motioned to the trees and the river, then whispered reverently, "Lord, it's beautiful."

Jiggs stood silently in the warm circle of Matt's arms, contentment filling her to the brim, as he and Saul quietly discussed the way the fish were biting.

In the days that followed, her contentment grew. At Matt's insistence, they postponed their work until they could get the strength to force their feet to touch ground. They spent long, lazy days exploring the woods and long, lazy nights exploring each other. They made love in the warm glow of the fire and on the soft, fallen leaves in the woods. They were on a whirling carousel that kept them dizzy with delight.

And always—day or night, laughing or loving—Matt watched her, a strange, waiting look in his eyes.

Two weeks passed unnoticed before Jiggs insisted they spend a part of each day working. She felt guilty about keeping Matt from his book and she also needed to express some of her overflowing joy in her painting. She threw herself into her work with an unequaled fervor, feeling that she had never painted so well. Fantastic, long-dead worlds sprang from her brush; exotic creatures took life under her flying pencil.

She giggled as she erased a knowing wink from the eye of an enormous prehistoric fish, then stretched her stiff back and want in search of Matt. She hadn't seen him in three hours and she missed him.

She met him in the hall on his way to find her. He pulled her into his arms and breathed a husky sigh in her ear. "I think I'm having withdrawal symptoms, sweet," he whispered softly. "I haven't kissed you in three hours."

"So long," she sympathized, playing with the wayward curl at the nape of his neck. "Are you sure your lips aren't atrophied?"

He drew his lips slowly across her cheek in a sensuous, tingling caress and paused before tracing the outline of her sensitive mouth with his tongue. Nipping gently at her lower lip, he teased her until she was giddy with desire, then began an erotic exploration of the inner sweetness in a deep, breathless kiss.

Jiggs leaned against him weakly as they walked to sit before the fire. "They're fine, Matt," she told him with lethargic complacency.

"Who's fine?" He pulled her into his lap and began to toy with the top button of her silk blouse.

"Your lips," she explained, leaning against his shoulder. "I just thought you'd like to know. They're fine. Not a sign of atrophy."

"Minx." He chuckled, undoing the button and moving to the next.

Jiggs looked into his beautiful, rough face and sighed. He was so perfect. At times she felt inadequate beside his perfection. But he didn't seem to mind her many imperfections. He loved the strawberry birthmark on her derrière and gloried in the riotous curls of her auburn hair when damp weather made it frizz.

"I was right and you were wrong," she told him smugly, remembering.

"About what?" He looked at her in exaggerated disbelief.

"About the loving friendship. You said I had it figured all wrong. But I was right and you were wrong. So admit it."

For a moment Jiggs saw a look of such deep sadness—almost pain—in his dark eyes, it alarmed her. "Matt, what is it?"

He closed his eyes tightly, leaning his head on the couch, then when he opened them again, it was gone. "Nothing, Jiggs. Just a case of incipient stupidity," he muttered obscurely, then at her questioning look, "It was nothing really, darlin', and as to your observation, I believe *I* was the one who said anything's possible, remember?"

"You only said that to make me feel better," she replied indignantly.

"No," he said with a crooked, self-mocking smile. "I really believed it—then."

As she began to question his ambiguity, he covered her mouth with his hand. "Jiggs, are we or are we not having an affair?"

She removed his hand and smiled lovingly. "We are."

"Then please be quiet so we can get on with it. You don't seem to be taking this seriously, darlin'. A successful affair takes practice, practice, and more practice. Understand?"

"Yes, sir," she said meekly, then sighed as they "got on with it."

Later that same night, Jiggs awoke to find the bed beside her empty. For a moment she felt an unreasonable panic take over—until she saw Matt standing by the window, looking out at the still, moonlit night. "Matt?" she murmured, still not fully awake.

He turned to see her sitting up in bed. "Go back to sleep, sweet," he said softly. "I'll be there in a minute."

His face held the same expression that it had the first time she had seen him in the moonlight. The night that—unaware of her observation—he had leaned against the rail, looking so desperately alone. Why should he feel a loneliness that deep? She thought she knew him so well. But was there something about him, something in his background, that he had hidden from her? Or was it something he needed that she was unable to supply? As his friend—his *best* friend, she corrected her thought—he should be able to talk to her about anything that was bothering him. Maybe she had been so busy thinking about how well he satisfied her needs, that she had not been sensitive to his. She had been so thrilled to find someone to share her laughter, but maybe Matt needed someone to share his tears.

She rose silently from the bed, drawing on her robe, and walked to stand beside him, laying a hand on his shoulder. "Matt," she said quietly. "I haven't been a very good friend, have I?"

He laid his cheek on her hand, rubbing it gently. "What makes you ask that, sweet?"

"I've been so wrapped up in my own pleasure that I completely missed the fact that something is bothering you." She turned his head slightly so that she could see his face. "Can't you tell me about it, Matt?"

"It's nothing, Jiggs," he denied, then as she was about to protest, "Honest. I was just thinking."

"About what?"

"Oh—about cabbages and kings and sealing wax—and the fact that a man can live a perfectly content life for years, then one day, something happens that turns everything around and makes those years seem wasted and empty." His voice was quiet and, strangely, a little lost.

"Are you regretting your past, Matt?"

"Not regretting." He put his arm around her and walked her to the bed. "Just an observation. And now, young lady, let's go back to bed and get some sleep or you'll have bags under those lovely eyes."

She paused before getting into bed. "Matt, do you need some time alone? Would you like me to sleep in my bed tonight?"

"*This* is your bed, sweetheart. So don't talk about leaving me alone." He hugged her to him tightly when they were both in the large bed. "This is where you belong, isn't it, Jiggs?" His voice sounded odd, as though he were painfully in need of reassurance.

She murmured soft, loving words in his ear and stroked his body until his doubts were forgotten and he took her with a ravenous hunger.

The next morning she watched him closely, but saw no signs of last night's strange mood. Everyone is entitled to a little moodiness now and then, she thought. Just wait until he sees me after one of my sinus headaches.

After breakfast she worked on a sketch of one of the rarer, more intricate trilobites. One particular detail kept giving her trouble, so she finally laid it aside and went in search of Matt, hoping he could clear up her confusion.

She stopped outside his study as she heard his voice.

"No, Barbie, of course not."

Barbie! Jiggs had completely forgotten about the beautiful redhead. Why was Matt talking to her? She stepped closer to hear what he was saying. Jiggs, she scolded herself, you're eavesdropping. No, I'm not, she defended, I'm simply waiting until he's through so that I can speak to him.

"Barbie, I told you before that I wasn't angry. I understand completely, sugar. There was nothing else you could do."

It was no use. No matter how much she rationalized it, it was eavesdropping. She walked slowly back to her studio, turning her head occasionally to glare at the open door of his study.

Barbie, she thought again, nonplussed. Who was Barbie anyway? And what did she mean to Matt? What had he said about her that night? He had called her a friend—"a brow soothing friend." And what else did she soothe? They had obviously had an affair, for he had asked Barbie to stay at the hotel with him. Was it a long-standing affair?

An off again—on again thing? Maybe Jiggs had met Matt during one of the off again times.

Damn him! He had no business carrying on with two women at the same time. It wasn't fair and it wasn't neat and it wasn't . . . kosher! How could he make love to Barbie when he belonged to—

Oh my God! She buried her face in her hands as she completed the thought. He belongs to me. Possessiveness. Jealousy. All the things she swore she would avoid. Things she now realized she had been feeling since she first met Matt.

I love him, she thought in horror. Sloppily, emotionally, possessively—I love him.

What in the hell am I going to do? She didn't want to be in love. Her mother had been in love and look what it had gotten her. A lifetime of degradation. And those silly women at work— crying in the ladies' room, unable to do their jobs. She was one of those silly women now and she hated the thought, hated Matt for making her feel this way. She had simply wanted a nice, friendly affair. Where did she go wrong? Why did it have to be love?

Lord, I'm so stupid, she thought in disgust. Any idiot would have seen what was happening. I couldn't keep my hands off him—or my mind. And every time I thought of him I could feel that silly, simple-minded grin on my face. Of course, I love Matt. Anyone could see that. Anyone except me.

Matt! How on earth was she going to face him? After all her fine talk about no emotional tangles she had to go and fall in love with him—and he would know! She could never hide what she was feeling from him. He seemed to be able to read her mind.

She stood and began to pace back and forth,

kicking the chair viciously as it got in her way. She couldn't let Matt find out! They had agreed to have an affair—a loving friendship. He would be embarrassed when he realized she had fallen in love with him. The thought of Matt pitying her made her shudder. They had always met as equals, but his pity would diminish her in his eyes—and her own. Pity was the only emotion she knew that was more destructive than love and a relationship that contained both elements could only humiliate the people involved.

She had to get away. She couldn't face Matt right now. She would go back to her apartment for a few days and think things through alone. Maybe in time she would think of a way without losing her self-respect to tell him why she must end their affair. It would mean giving up her job also, for she would never be able to work with Matt without touching him . . . loving him.

She hurried to their room for her purse, praying he wouldn't come out of his study before she got safely away. She had to leave a note for him and she hesitated briefly, trying to find the right words, but it was impossible. Nothing would explain adequately her running away. In the end, she decided to keep it simple and avoid fabrication. She wrote that she had decided to go away for a few days and would call him later to explain. It was woefully insufficient, but it was the best she could do in the circumstances.

She felt like a thief, creeping silently down the hall and out the front door, but she knew she would dissolve ignominiously in tears if Matt caught her. She stood in the shadows inside the garage and fumbled nervously for her keys.

"Going somewhere?"

Jiggs jumped and whirled in absolute terror at the sound of the voice behind her, then sighed in relief as she realized the voice and tiny form couldn't possibly belong to Matt.

"Oh, Saul," she said, "you scared me."

"You got a guilty conscience, girl?" The little man looked at her suspiciously.

"I'm not making off with the family silver, if that's what you mean. I just decided to get away for a few days."

"You tell Matt?"

She looked away from him, avoiding his eyes. "I left a note."

"A note?" He snorted in disbelief. "You coulda' hollered as you went out the door if you're in a hurry. He's right there in the house."

Jiggs closed her eyes, desperation to be on her way building unbearably, then looked at Saul with a sigh of resignation. "I just can't talk to Matt right now." Her eyes pleaded with him to understand. "I've got to get away for a while, Saul."

His keen eyes pierced her, searching her face. "I guess you do at that, girl. Go on, Jiggs. And be careful—it's comin' on to rain."

It would hurt to lose this man's friendship, too. Jiggs shuddered in sudden loneliness, then bent down to kiss his weathered cheek. "Thank you, Saul."

He stood in the yard and watched her back out of the drive. She gave the house one last, longing look, then headed east.

# Nine

The rain that followed Jiggs all the way to Dallas was the perfect setting for her black mood. She turned her radio up to an ear-splitting volume, trying to drown her thoughts, but she only succeeded in making her head ache as well as her heart.

Even though the rain had slowed her down, she still beat the afternoon rush and by four o'clock she was pulling into the covered parking space in front of her apartment. The driving rain turned her blouse into a transparent second skin and she shivered uncontrollably as she reached her door and inserted the key.

She was home. Home. This empty apartment wasn't home. Home was warm and welcoming. Home was love and laughter. Home was Matt.

The tears streaming unheeded down her face mingled with the raindrops as she stood in the middle of the large, lonely room, looking for all the world like a lost child. And she felt lost. She felt as though she had been cast out of paradise. Somewhere east of Eden, she thought with a choking, sardonic laugh.

She moved slowly, wearily toward the bedroom, intending to change her clothes, then halted in her tracks as the ringing of the telephone broke the stillness.

Matt!

She couldn't talk to him. She moved in panic toward the bedroom, but the insistent ring drew her back. I've got nowhere else to run to, she thought. The terrible weariness had completely sapped her strength and the fight drained out of her, leaving her empty of emotion.

She walked to the phone, an unnatural calm showing in her face.

"Hello?"

"Jiggs! Is that you?"

It was Max. Relief buckled her knees and she sat down heavily in a high-backed armchair.

"Yes. It's me." There was a slight tremor in her voice and she ran a shaking hand over her damp face, trying to pull herself together.

"You sound strange. Are you all right?" His voice held concern.

"I'm fine, Max."

"You don't sound fine. You sound sick. And you haven't asked why I'm in town. I'm supposed to be in Europe, remember?"

"Oh, Max, I'm sorry. Of course, you are. I forgot." She tried to think. What should she say now? Obviously, words were expected from her, but which words? She was very much afraid anything she said would come out complete nonsense.

"Jiggs!" Now his voice held more than concern— it held a distinct uneasiness. "Stay right where you are!" he commanded anxiously. "I'll be right over."

"No, Max . . ." But the connection was broken. He was already on his way.

She stared at the phone in her hand for a moment, then replaced it lethargically. She felt she should move. Maybe change into dry clothes or brush her hair, but by the time she had definitely decided to do *something*, she heard Max's knock on the door.

"Jiggs! Jiggs, you're wet!" he exclaimed as she opened the door.

"I know," she said, looking down at her clothes which had begun to dry on her body. "I meant to change, Max, but—"

"I know, you forgot," he finished for her. "First we're going to get you into a hot tub, then—we talk."

He brushed aside her halfhearted protests, steering her to the bathroom. She leaned against the door and watched as he filled the tub, testing the water carefully and adding scented bathsalts.

"Now hop in and don't take too long or I'll come in and get you," he warned.

She removed her uncomfortably damp clothes, sighing in pleasure as she stepped into the steaming water. She relaxed for long moments, letting the warmth soak in and soothe away the cold tiredness. When she returned to the living room, she could face Max with a semblance of normalcy.

He rose to watch her closely as she crossed the room to stand before him. "Now, let's talk." His voice was uncompromising, warning her not to prevaricate. "What happened?"

She sat beside him on the loveseat and looked at his thin face. She felt she was truly seeing him for the first time. "You know, Max, I was wrong. I did have a friend. At least I could have had one if I had just opened my eyes." She touched his face, surprised at how much she liked this man. It seemed that loving Matt had pulled a dark veil from her eyes and her mind. She would never be able to hide from emotion again. The realization made her shiver in apprehension. She looked up to find Max watching her through narrowed, piercing eyes. "You really are a nice man, Max. I should have been a better friend to you."

Max sighed, a thin hissing sound. "I always knew it would happen, sugar. And now that it has, I don't know whether to be thankful for your sake or sorry for mine." His tone was wry and perhaps a shade cynical.

"What are you talking about?"

"Well, sugar, you've either joined one of those encounter groups or you're in love."

She looked at him in amazement. "My God, Max! Is it written in 'Marks-a-Lot' on my forehead? Am I really that obvious?"

"No, not obvious," he reassured her. "But I've spent quite a bit of time studying you, Jiggs. I take my role as scorekeeper for the human race very seriously, you know." He allowed a touch of his usual mocking humor to show. "And you, Toots, make one interesting subject. You always held yourself away from life, as though you were on a different plane from us lesser mortals." When she looked at him in alarm he added, "I don't mean snobbish, Jiggs. You didn't think you were better than us, just different. You were interested in everything and everyone around you, but you didn't participate. You were a spectator. And that's fine for football, but not in life."          •

She could see the truth in his words—now. And she could also see how much she had missed. No matter what he said, her attitude had been a form of snobbishness. She had felt unutterably smug at not being subject to the emotions that others felt. Now she simply felt sadness for the time she had wasted.

"I knew that if you ever found someone who could make you feel love, it would open the floodgates for all the other emotions."

"Was I so unfeeling, Max?" she asked, concerned. "I know I felt an unforgivable pride in what I considered my strength, but was that all? I guess it's pride again, but I hate to think of myself as an automaton."

He put a comforting arm around her shoulder. "You were a sucker for every hard luck story and you know it," he reassured her. "But there were times when you were, shall we say, unsympathetic to those who were slaves to their emotions. I didn't really blame you. They get on my nerves, too, but it worried me because you're so soft-hearted, you should have felt something for the poor slobs. Then I realized that you felt nothing for them because you had locked away the part of you that would have recognized love and passion."

"Whew!" she said, laughing ruefully. "I didn't realize I was in such bad shape."

"Your shape is great," he said, leering. "It's the emotional part of your mind that's screwed up."

"Thanks a lot," she muttered drily. "Since you were so concerned about me before, I guess it pleases you that I have unlocked all the doors and joined the human race."

"It's healthier, Jiggs. Even if it hurts like hell now." He paused, looking at the floor, then said quietly, "Do you want to tell me about it?"

His gentle understanding brought a sheen of tears to her green eyes. "I don't think I can right now, Max. But—" She hesitated momentarily, then plunged into unknown territory. "—If you'll hold the thought until your assignment is finished,

I—I think I would like to tell you. And maybe by then I'll be able to." She looked at him shyly, feeling incredibly vulnerable.

He accepted her gift, recognizing its true value. "Anytime, Jiggs. All you have to do is call."

She kissed his cheek softly, overwhelmingly relieved that he had understood her gesture of friendship. Suddenly she looked at him in surprise. "Max! What are you doing in Dallas? You're supposed to be in Europe!"

He chuckled, squeezing her shoulder affectionately. "You're a little slow, kid. But I'll overlook it this time because what you lack in mental ability, you make up for in physical splendor."

Overlooking his comment on her body as she usually did, she looked at him in concern. "Nothing went wrong with the assignment, did it?" She knew how much the series meant to Max. If it fell through now, it would be a terrible disappointment.

"Nothing that I can't handle," he said arrogantly. "I was getting a little flack about the way I was treating the articles so I decided to drop out and let them sweat for a while. They're beginning to come around to my way of thinking," he said smugly. "I've only been here two days and they've already passed anger and gone on to glorious panic." He grinned maliciously.

"But I thought the format was all set when you took the assignment?"

"They had an idea and a basic territory for me to cover, but the way I tied the articles together was up to me. At least I thought it was. All of a sudden they decided my pieces were too sensational, too depressing for a peace series. What they meant was they were too real. If they had wanted fairy tales they should have hired the Brothers Grimm," he finished in disgust.

"They won't try to get someone else, will they, Max? You know there are plenty of writers around who will give them just exactly what they want."

"I'm not worrying, Jiggs, so don't you either."

Max had a confidence in his own worth that she wished she had. As he talked quietly of the things he had seen in the tiny villages and crowded cities of the European countries he had visited, she realized what an enormously attractive man he was.

Why couldn't I have had an affair with Max instead of Matt? she wondered. They would have had a calmer, saner relationship and Max would have gentled her into the more disturbing human emotions, avoiding the drastic shock to her system that she had experienced with Matt.

Suddenly a curious thought struck her. Perhaps what she felt for Matt wasn't love after all. Perhaps possessiveness was a natural part of an affair of that intensity. Wouldn't she have felt the same about anyone who had given her the mind-boggling pleasure that Matt had?

But *could* anyone else have given her that much ecstasy? The thought came unbidden, adding to her confusion. Did she care for him because he gave her pleasure or did he give her pleasure because she cared for him? It was a tangle and she simply didn't have enough experience to know the answer.

Experience. She looked at Max out of the corner of her eye, seeing him only as a member of the opposite sex for the moment. Max was very attractive, sexy even. And—judging by the women she had seen wrapped around him at regular intervals during their association—very experienced. Would she feel desire if she kissed Max? Had her encounter with Matt unlocked her emotions enough for her to feel passion with someone else?

If it had, then it would mean that Matt had simply been a catalyst, releasing the passion she had suppressed for so long, and—having accomplished the release—he was no longer needed.

In hopeful desperation, she looked at Max's long, lean body. He was thin, but he looked very strong. He seemed a little pale, too. But maybe that was just his natural fairness. All in all, he wasn't bad—he just wasn't . . .

"Jiggs! Where the hell are you?"

She glanced up from his thin hands, so different from brown, rough, giant's hands, to see him staring at her with a genuinely puzzled look on his face. "I'm sorry, Max. I guess I was thinking of something else." As she apologized, her face went scarlet.

"I'd like to know what it was. You looked as though you were about to take some extremely nasty medicine."

"No, not nasty," she denied hastily, then realized how much she had admitted. "What I mean is . . . Oh, Max, I don't know what I mean. I'm so confused."

"Can I help?" he asked sincerely.

"That's what I'm asking myself and I just don't know." At his inquiring glance she continued, before she lost her nerve. "Max, I know you're always talking about my great body, but when you look at me, do you feel . . . well . . . lust?" She looked at him anxiously, waiting for his answer.

"Sugar, no man, no matter how old or infirm, could look at your body without feeling a little lust." He chuckled deeply and looked at her in amusement. "And I think I know where your tiny little mind is leading."

She glared at him, annoyed by his attitude. "Well, if you know so much, then why don't you help me out instead of letting me make a fool of myself?"

"Because it's your show, sugar. If I try to seduce you and fail, then I'll look like an ass. And if one of us has to look like an ass, I'd rather it were you."

"Some friend you are," she muttered indignantly, watching as he stretched out his legs comfortably, waiting. She moved her head slowly, wishing he would close his eyes or at least look away from her face. When she was an inch away from his lips, she jerked back, rising to pace the floor in agitation.

"I can't do it, Max." She shook her head in a violently negative movement. "I feel I'm being unfaithful. As though I'm breaking vows." Her voice rose in indignation. "Vows that I didn't make in the first place. I didn't promise anything, so why do I feel that I'm going back on my word?" She broke the rhythm of her stride to say in misery, "He probably doesn't care what I do, so why do I?"

Max looked at her for long moments with that strange analytical curiosity that she had seen in the past. When he spoke, his voice was quiet, thoughtful. "So you're still fighting it. I thought you had decided to stop running away."

"Damn it, Max! I admitted it was time for me to get my feet wet, but do I have to drown? Isn't there a happy medium?"

"No, Jiggs, there's not. You're either alive or you're dead. With no in-between. You were dead before and now you're alive. You can't choose the degree of emotion that you feel like you choose the shade of your lipstick. At least people as sensitive as you can't. You either feel with every bit of you or you don't feel at all. And until you realize that, Jiggs, and go with the current instead of fighting against it, you're going to make yourself a mountain of misery."

She flopped down beside him in disgust. "What am I going to do, Max? Do I just drop a lifetime of beliefs and go mindlessly where my emotions lead? That sounds so—so disorganized."

"Things are not always cut and dried, Jiggs. There are some things that are neither black nor white," he cautioned.

Max rose to his feet, his tall, lean figure casting a nebulous shadow in the dim light. He picked up the jacket he had discarded earlier and looked at the confusion written on her lovely face. "Only one more piece of advice from the old sage and then I'll leave. If you can never bring about a reconciliation between your slightly befuddled brain and your heart, go with the heart, honey. No hell on earth is worse than regretting a lost opportunity." He touched her softly on the cheek. "Just trust yourself, Jiggs. You're a very strong, very intelligent lady. You'll figure out what's right for you."

Jiggs walked to the door to see him out, a thousand thoughts ricocheting around inside her head. She didn't want Max to leave. He was familiar and comfortable and non-threatening. But she watched him walk to his car in silence. He had left her with new insights. More knots in the tangle. But he trusted her to untie those knots and she respected him enough at least to try.

As he drove away, she turned and reentered the late-afternoon gloom that filled the apartment. Staring at the shadows, his parting words returned to haunt her. What *was* right for her? She hated the thought of allowing her emotions to rule her mind. Everything she had seen in her observations of human relationships had reinforced the initial impression she had gained from her parents.

Thoughts of her parents flooded her mind. She

had always avoided thinking of her gentle, ineffective mother and her boisterous, untrustworthy father because with their images came the memory of pain.

Jiggs quickly crossed the living room and entered her bedroom, throwing off the bright caftan she was wearing and pulling on linen slacks and a light sweater. This was one thing she would stop hiding from right now. She hadn't been to visit her parents' graves in months and this time the visit would be more than a guilt-soothing duty trip. It was time she let go of the past, no matter how painful it was. Maybe then she could deal with the future.

As she laid the bunch of yellow and rust chrysanthemums between the two graves, she thought of her charming, deceiving father. He had such charm and he used it with a cunning that took one's breath away. Although he was third-generation Irish, he would lapse into a thick, strictly manufactured brogue in order to obtain what he wanted. It was usually a woman or a contract for his construction company that caused him to display his plumage, but occasionally he would turn on the brogue—and that charm—for Jiggs.

And she would always fall for it, a fact that had made her feel a traitor. But no matter how much she despised him for humiliating her mother, she had consistently succumbed. Later, of course, she had realized that he had needed his infrequent act as loving father to boost his ego. Everyone had to love Sean O'Malley.

And everyone had—including Jiggs. She had been just as hopelessly infatuated as her gentle mother. Only her mother had never seen, or she had pretended not to see, the dark side of Sean O'Malley. Jiggs had made one frustrating attempt to tell her of his affairs and of the way he ridiculed his adoring wife behind her back, but her mother had looked at her with those gentle, uncomprehending eyes and blithely ignored her warnings.

When Jiggs was seventeen her father had died in an automobile accident, leaving her with the double burden of caring for her distraught mother and coping with her own grief. She had watched her petite mother wither away—first mentally, then physically. Jiggs had known the grief-stricken woman was committing suicide in her own quiet way, but there had been nothing she could do to stop her. Her mother had died in her sleep eight heartbreakingly short months later.

Standing between the two graves, unaware of the soft, drizzling rain that was beginning to penetrate her clothing, Jiggs realized that not only had she never forgiven her father for *his* weakness, she had never forgiven her mother for hers. The contempt she had always felt for women who allowed men to ruin their lives had begun with her mother.

How could she have been so judgmental? What right did she have to think she was wise and to condemn others as wrong? She had been a child, seeing her parents with a child's eyes, understanding them with a child's reasoning. All these years she had avoided thinking about her parents, thinking about them as an adult. Although her parents' relationship had not been what she considered a healthy one, it was right for them. And they were the ones who mattered. They each had made a conscious choice. The depth of Jiggs's feelings for Matt had given her new insights into what motivated her gentle mother. Sean O'Malley had been the one person in the world who made her mother's life worthwhile. Imperfect as he was, he had given her happiness, had made her whole.

Jiggs straightened her back in determination. Silently, lovingly, she made her peace with the past and walked slowly to her parked car. While she was relieved that she could think now without bitterness of the two people who had given her life, her belief in her ideals—her judgment—had received another shattering blow. But at least she had taken a first step toward straightening out her tangled emotions. Perhaps the next step would be easier. She suddenly doubted it, though, because the next step was, of course, Matt. And she wasn't quite ready to think about Matt. She simply wanted to crawl into a dark hole and pray that when she crawled out again things would be back to normal—if she could call her life before Matt normal. Life before Matt. The words sounded like a historical marker. Life before electricity. Life before the smashing of the atom. Life before Matt.

Dear God, what was she going to do about Matt? She would have to call him tonight and explain, but what could she say that would sound rational? I'm sorry, Matt, but due to a sudden drop in the temperature of my feet, I won't be able to continue our affair? Or maybe—I can't see you again because I love you and it scares the hell out of me?

She recalled his reaction the last time she had shown doubts. He had been cold and distant and it would be much worse this time. Of course, that would make the ending of it much more final. And ending the affair was exactly what she wanted—wasn't it? So why was the thought tearing her apart?

What had he said that night? "Someday you'll find something that's worth risking a little of that sloppy emotion on." Sloppy was right. She felt like stopping the car and howling in pure misery.

But it was ridiculous to wallow in self-pity. It accomplished nothing. She needed to look at the situation logically.

Was loving Matt worth the risk? If she chose to end the affair she would be able to return to her uncomplicated, orderly life. Or would she? Even if she managed to cut the memory of Matt from her heart, hadn't she already seen how her eyes and mind had been opened to the world around her? No, there was no going back. Her life would be different. She would make friends—true friends like Max. She would have a fuller life because of Matt, but she wouldn't have Matt.

If she chose to continue the affair there was no guarantee that Matt wouldn't tire of her in a few months and drop her completely. Or that he wouldn't decide to try one of her father's tricks and juggle his women. She could be letting herself in for a lot of agony, but she would have Matt.

And that about summed it up. She could choose a better-rounded, fuller life without Matt—or a life that could possibly lead to even more misery with Matt.

Logically there was only one choice, but she simply couldn't bring herself to make it. Matt had given her more than any other human being and she couldn't forget that. Nor could she forget the love and laughter that existed for her only with Matt. She didn't want to end their affair. It was as simple as that. She wanted to live in his sunshine for as long as he would let her.

So finally the decision was made. Illogically, unreasonably. She would take what she could get from him for as long as she could get it. And if it included pain, she would take that too.

Positive that she had never made a more insane decision in her life, but totally unconcerned by the fact, she pulled into her parking space, then began to climb the stairs, wondering if she should drive back tonight or wait until tomorrow.

Tonight, she thought. I won't be able to sleep, so I might as well drive. But what am I going to say to him? After running out on him again how *can* I face Matt, she wondered, as she turned the corner to find herself facing Matt.

# *Ten*

He stood still and straight in the middle of the railed walkway. Gone were the casual clothes she had come to accept as natural to him. His tan cord slacks and brown blazer accentuated his masculinity, but hid his enormous strength.

Jiggs stared hungrily at his face, devouring his craggy features with her eyes. She felt she had been separated from him for years. She wanted to touch him, reassure herself that he was real, but the look on his face held her back. It was a look totally different from any she had ever seen. This was much, much worse than she had anticipated. She had expected the cold, distant Matt—but not this total stranger.

She waited in silence for him to speak. Would Matt's voice come from this stranger's lips? Or would that be changed also? Apparently he wasn't going to give her a chance to find out, for the taut silence continued, stretching Jiggs's nerves to the breaking point.

Desperate to break the tension, she moved to unlock the door, her trembling fingers botching the simple procedure. She walked inside and fumbled for the light switch, watching anxiously as he entered the room behind her and glanced around.

His gaze touched on every piece of furniture, every painting, in the room as though seeing it all for the first time. Then his eyes returned to her and he began the same detached, but intimate, examination of her body.

His impersonal inspection seemed an obscene mockery of the affectionate looks she was used to receiving from him and it hurt unbearably. Had she thrown away the special relationship they had shared by giving rein to her insecurities? Had she destroyed whatever affection he had for her with her ridiculous doubts? The aching emptiness that followed the question caused her to shiver uncontrollably.

"Go change your clothes before you catch pneumonia."

It was his voice, yet it wasn't. There was no emotion in it. Not hurt nor hate. And certainly not affection. It was indescribably chilling. He was standing before one of her pen and ink drawings and had turned his head to look over his shoulder as he spoke. Looking again at the drawing, he seemed not to care whether or not she followed his curt advice.

Jiggs walked slowly to her bedroom, feeling a strange, debilitating weakness invade her body. Inside she leaned against the door, pain piercing her to the core. No sunshine for her now. He was so solemn, so strange.

A deep shuddering sigh shook her body, then she walked into the bathroom to change her clothes. She was through with running. She had vowed to take what she could get from him and if this was all he had to offer her, she would take it. She had had a chance for more and she had hesitated. Most people never find what she had rejected. She deserved her punishment.

She stripped off her damp clothes and toweled her hair dry as she walked naked back into the bedroom, wondering how she was going to endure his continued silence. It was all very well to say she deserved his treatment, but she was very much afraid she would scream in frustration if it lasted much longer.

She felt Matt's presence, announced by that electrified current, moments before she saw him. He was standing in the shadows of her bedroom, staring at her body as she stood in the light streaming from the bathroom door. His inspection was even more intimate than the one that had taken place earlier—and this time his gaze was not detached. He searched out each vulnerable part of her body, lingering with narrow-eyed greed on her breasts, her flat stomach, the lush, gold, curling triangle of hair that his hands and lips and body had sought so much in the past days.

Memories of those moments flooded her body, causing her nipples to harden into tight, firm buds and her body to quiver in anticipation. She ached with an all-consuming need—a burning, frantic desire that caused her breath to come in short, tremulous gasps.

Then he shifted slightly into the light and she saw the expression in those narrowed eyes. Her body had reacted to the loving memories, for there was no loving affection in his look. There was stark desire, but nothing of the gentleness remained.

Frantic with fear, Jiggs searched the room desperately for an escape route—a place to hide her vulnerability from his terrible eyes. She grabbed up the caftan she had discarded earlier and held it in front of her shivering nakedness.

As panicky thoughts ripped through her mind, she heard a strange sound—an ancient sound. The cry of an injured animal. Her head jerked up in alarm and saw his face seconds before he turned toward the door. Incredibly there had been a sheen of tears in his eyes and on his face was a look of ragged, undisguised pain.

"Matt!" she cried, halting his hurried steps. She walked softly to stand beside him, dropping the caftan to the floor. He turned his head slightly, not looking at her, but giving a subtle acknowledgement of her presence. "Matt," she said again, her voice gentle, loving.

Her tone released the breath he had been holding in a deep, shuddering sigh. He reached out to pull her body to his in a bruisingly tight embrace. Grasping her hair with one hand, he pulled her head from his shoulder painfully and crushed her lips in a kiss that devoured.

He was totally out of control, his movements demanding, as he pulled her across the room to the bed and discarded his clothes. Pushing her back onto the bed, he threw himself on her, his need critical. The fierceness with which he touched her body contained an unconcealed desperation, which was transmitted to Jiggs and her responses took on an urgent insistence. This was no gentle loving. This was burning, compelling necessity. A rough kind of magic that took them quickly to an explosive, shuddering release.

Afterward, she had no idea whether she had lost consciousness or if she had simply fallen asleep from exhaustion. When she awoke she was in the bed alone and she lay quietly in the dark, thinking of the wild mating that had just taken place.

She could feel the bruises on her body and knew her nails had left deep scratches on his back. The barely contained violence of his lovemaking held no terrors for her. She could meet his needs with needs of her own. But the desperation behind it baffled her. It was as though he had needed the violence to imprint their lovemaking indelibly in his mind—as though it were the last time!

She jumped from the bed, pulled on the caftan and ran from the room, terrified at the thought which became stronger with each passing moment. She had to find him and reassure herself that her impression had been wrong.

The living room and kitchen were empty. She leaned her head against the front door and felt the strength drain from her body, in despair. It was several long minutes later before the faint sounds of movement in her studio penetrated her misery.

She flew down the hall, wiping the tears from her face, and opened the door. She stopped just inside as he turned his head away from his quiet contemplation of the watercolors, which covered every inch of wall space.

"You have a great talent, Jiggs." His voice was quiet, unutterably weary.

"Thank you." What could she say to him? How could she break through the barriers he had erected? "Matt, I'd like to explain."

"Why do you hide them in here?"

He was not going to let her explain or apologize for running away. She lifted her head in determination. If he wouldn't let her explain in her own way, then she would go along with him. But one way or another she would get her point across.

"I told myself that I wasn't ready for a showing. I told myself that I couldn't let strangers see the inside of my head by looking at my paintings. I told myself everything except the truth. I was afraid, Matt. Afraid to take a chance on failing."

She walked to stand beside him and looked at the painting on the wall before him. "This one was painted just after my mother's death," she explained quietly.

"I thought watercolors were supposed to be gentle and soft," he mused. "How did you manage to express such violence with so few strokes?"

"All my anger and frustration went into that painting," she recalled. "I thought at the time it expressed a kind of civilized rage, but I see now that it was merely repressed like all my other emotions." She looked at his face, but he continued to stare at the painting and with a sigh of resignation she continued. "I watched my mother die, Matt. She slowly, intentionally gave up her life right before my eyes and no matter how I tried, I couldn't do a damn thing to stop her. I failed. That was when I began to live my life so that failure of that magnitude could never touch me again."

At last, Matt turned to face her. "I'm sorry, Jiggs. About your mother, but also for what just happened." He closed his eyes as though in terrible pain. "God, baby, I'm so sorry. That was not why I followed you here. God knows I needed it, but I never meant to hurt you." He looked at her closely, then gently touched the bruise on the side of her neck. "And I did hurt you, didn't I?"

Before she could deny his words, he continued to speak. "I came here to apologize. I didn't mean to compound my guilt by practically raping you." He ignored her protest. "Jiggs, I saw the terror in your eyes in there. I never thought I'd see that look in your eyes. Anger or disgust maybe, but not terror."

He paused, walking a few feet away, before turning abruptly to face her. "I came here to tell you that the whole mess was my fault. I knew you would feel guilty for running away again, but I wanted you to know that I understood." He took a deep breath, as though he had to force himself to continue. "Jiggs, I cheated. I knew you had doubts about our relationship, but I ignored them and pushed you—blackmailed you—into going to bed with me."

She stared at him in confusion. What was he talking about? He was carrying an enormous load of guilt over something. "But, Matt—"

"Jiggs, wait. Let's go sit down so that I can explain it to you. I want you to know the truth."

She followed him into the living room and sat on the loveseat, facing him solemnly as he took the large armchair. He stared for a while into space as though gathering his words and, incredibly, it seemed, his courage.

"Do you remember the night you told me how important my friendship was to you?" She nodded, waiting. "I believed you. I could see that you honestly valued my friendship. And I took advantage of that fact. I hoped that you would fight to keep it. So," he sighed deeply and looked straight into her eyes, "I deliberately withheld my friendship in order to force you into a decision that you weren't ready to make."

"Matt, please listen to me," Jiggs said earnestly, hating the self-blame she saw in his eyes. "There was one reason and one reason only why I slept with you that first night—pure, unadulterated lust. I'll admit that I considered coming to you after you turned cold and distant, but that night—that glorious night, Matt! That had nothing to do with friendship. Later, of course, the two were inextricably intertwined, but the night I met you in the hall I wasn't looking for friendship. I had been

unable to sleep because I needed you so badly."
She looked at him with smiling indulgence. "And
don't tell me you arranged that because I won't
believe you."

"Of course, I didn't. I had been thinking of nothing but you for three days straight. When you
appeared in the hall it was as though my need
had conjured you up. I was afraid if I moved you
would disappear," he murmured, caught up in
the memory. Then he leaned forward and said
urgently, "But, Jiggs, don't you understand?
Even if you didn't realize it, even if it made no
difference—I cheated on our agreement."

She couldn't allow him to continue feeling guilt
over what she considered a very human error. He
had worked to bring about something that was
important to him—by slightly devious means it
was true, but he meant no mental or physical
harm to her. He was not a man to sit back and
wait for things to happen. He took the bull by the
horns and *made* them happen.

She looked at him sternly. "So Mr. Perfect finally made a mistake," she scoffed gently. "Big
dumb deal. It simply means I don't have to worry
so much about all the mistakes I make. I don't
know if I've mentioned it," she said in a confiden-
tial tone, "but I can't heat milk."

Matt stared at her silently, his strong face
thoughtful, then began to chuckle. "I guess that
means you forgive me." He looked at the loving
amusement showing in her face. "I don't deserve
it, Jiggs, especially after tonight, but thank you."

She stood and moved across to his chair, kneel-
ing before him, feeling the need to touch him.
There was one more ghost that she had to lay to
rest before they moved on to other, more pleasant,
diversions. "About tonight, Matt." She held his
face with one hand to keep him from turning

away in self-disgust and looked deeply into his dark eyes. "Listen to me, love. You're not looking logically at what we shared tonight. And I did say *shared*, Matt. If you'll check your back you'll see that I'm not the ravaged—I was the ravager, too. Yes, I did quite a bit of ravaging myself. I have never in my life experienced anything like that. You pulled something from deep inside me that I didn't even know existed. It was something so exciting and so special, I'll never forget it as long as I live." She caressed his face softly, trying to find the right words. "The circumstances that brought about what happened tonight will never occur again . . . I hope. Which means the consequences—that special joining, that intensity, that depth of feeling we shared—was a once in a lifetime event. And that makes it even more precious. Something to pull out of my store of memories on a cold night. What I'm trying to say in my own clumsy way is—I loved it, Matt. Every glorious minute of it."

His eyes were shining suspiciously as he turned his head to give her hand a soft, almost worshipful kiss, then he said simply, "Thank you."

"You're very welcome, believe me. Now not another word about it," she ordered. As she was struck by a thought, she laughed in mischievous amusement, earning an inquiring glance from Matt. "Darling, Max would have a field day analyzing you."

He raised his gentle giant's hand to her head, stroking her auburn hair and sighing in contentment as she rested her head on his knee. Then with quiet curiosity, "What made you think of Max?"

"Max loves what he calls 'people watching.' He picks us mortals to pieces with his fiendish little brain, never satisfied until he finds out what makes us tick. Then he puts us into convenient categories. I bet he would have to invent a new category for you." She chuckled. "I remember thinking when he was here this afternoon that—"

"He was here? In your apartment?" His voice sounded curiously stiff. "I thought he was in Europe."

Jiggs looked at him sharply, perplexed by his disgruntled tone. "Yes, he was, but he came back because—Matt, what's wrong?"

He stood abruptly and her derrière met the floor with a hard thud. She rose slowly, rubbing her injured posterior, and watched totally bewildered, as he paced back and forth in agitation.

"Why in the hell did he come here, Jiggs?" He looked at her, accusation in his eyes. "He's a friend, too, isn't he, Jiggs? I asked you once the first day I met you and I'll ask you again—how good a friend is he?"

"Now wait just a minute, Matt. You have no right to question me in that tone." She glared at him furiously. "You have no right to question me at all!"

"I'll question you at any time, in any tone I damn well please!" he shouted, grabbing her arm. His face was red with rage. "Now you had better tell me what happened here this afternoon before I give you the shaking of your life. You were upset and your *good friend*, Max, just happened to show up," he fumed. "So then what happened?"

"You great, hulking oaf! You'll shake me with the help of the Marines!" She jerked her arm from his grasp. "Nothing happened!"

Never in her life had she been so furious. The absolute nerve of the man! As if she would—

She stopped rubbing her arm, suddenly remembering. She had tried to see if Max could help her forget Matt. And although she couldn't bring herself to touch him, she *had* tried.

"Jiggs," he said, his voice suspicious. "Jiggs, I see guilt in your face."

She turned to walk away from him, but he pulled her back. "Jiggs, that's guilt and don't you deny it!"

She sighed and faced him in resignation. "Matt, it was nothing really. I simply wanted to see if he could—" She stopped abruptly, her eyes widening in wonder. "Matt, you're *jealous*!"

"Jiggs," he warned through clenched teeth. "Don't you dare try to change the subject. You wanted to see if Max could do what, for heaven's sake?"

"Forget Max for a minute," she said in urgent excitement. "Today I was trying to figure something out. I haven't had enough experience to know, but you have. If you feel jealous and possessive, does that mean you're in love?"

He closed his eyes in frustration, then opened them to look at her as he quietly answered her question. "Those things alone don't mean love, but when they're added to—to loving friendship, then, yes, it does mean you're in love." He framed her face gently with his large hands. "And if you're trying to ask if all that shouting means I love you, then—even though it's a very poor way of showing it—I do. More than I ever thought possible, Jiggs." His hands tightened on her face. "Now, please, *please*, finish that damned sentence. You wanted to see if Max could *what*?"

She put her arms around his waist and squeezed him in exuberant joy. "You darling, darling man! I wanted to see if Max could help me forget you. But, Matt," she continued as she felt his body jerk. "I couldn't touch him. I looked him over and decided he was very sexy, but he wasn't you." She laughed, delighted at her good taste. "I couldn't go through with it because I love you. I felt I was being unfaithful even to try."

"And you were right!" he said huffily. "Sexy! What in hell's that supposed to mean?"

His voice was filled with disgust, causing Jiggs to chuckle in indulgent amusement. She backed away to look at his face, loving every rugged, annoyed line. Then his face froze and moments later he jerked her to his chest, her breath leaving her lungs in a soft whoosh as she made hard contact with his chest.

"Jiggs! You said you love me," he whispered, his voice trembling slightly with emotion.

"Yes, darling," she gasped, her voice weak and restricted from the tight embrace. "And if you'll let me breathe," she panted, "I'll show you how much."

"God, sweetheart! I'm sorry," he apologized, loosening his grip and watching as she took a deep breath. "Jiggs, your face is bright red." His voice held puzzled concern.

"Yes, darling," she said, patting his arm. "That's what happens when you cut off a person's oxygen. But don't worry about it. I had planned on cutting down anyway." She touched his bemused face in wonder. "Besides I know exactly how you feel. I want to shout or run or *something!*"

He laughed delightedly, throwing back his head and whirling her around in a movement of pure joy. He dropped into the chair with Jiggs in his arms. "That's how I felt when you woke up that very first morning. I didn't recognize it as love then, but I knew I wanted you—a stranger—more than I had ever wanted anything in my life. There was something special between us from that first moment. When you ran out I thought it was some evil fate working—letting me have a glimpse of happiness, then taking it away." He closed his eyes, remembering. "When Sam showed me your application, I couldn't believe my luck. Yours was too unusual a name for it to be coincidence, but I checked with Sam to be sure." He chuckled softly. "You were lost before you ever set foot in my office, darlin'. I was determined not to let you get away a second time. It wasn't until I saw you in my home that I knew I really loved you. You looked so right there. It was as though I had unconsciously designed the house with you in mind." He shuddered as a painful memory flitted through his mind. "I thought I had lost you through my own stupidity. You kept talking about friendship when I desperately wanted your love. I was afraid I had rushed you into something you weren't ready for and as a result you ran." He looked at her with sharp, narrowed eyes. "Why did you run, Jiggs?"

She opened her mouth to put him off, but stopped in time. She owed him the truth. "I found out I was jealous, Matt. Agonizingly, possessively jealous. I heard you talking to Barbie on the phone and I wanted to rip that phone right out of your hand! The power of my emotions scared me—then."

He stared at her in amazement. "Barbie? Why should you be jealous of Barbie?"

"Why should you be jealous of Max?" she countered.

"Oh, I see what you mean. But, darlin', I haven't seen Barbie since long before the night I met you."

"Matt, you don't have to explain," she said, meaning every word. "I trust you."

"But I want to. Barbie's a nice lady and we owe her a lot. If she hadn't had a migraine and stood me up—and if you hadn't had a crush on Lincoln—you and I would probably never have met." His hold tightened at the thought. "Barbie and I were lovers, Jiggs. Lovers who decided to be friends instead. It's as simple as that. Nobody could ever give me what you do, Jiggs. Don't ever doubt that."

She looked into his beautiful face, love shining from her eyes. "I won't, Matt. No more doubts— ever. I made my choice once and for all today." She kissed him gently, quivering as she felt his blazing response.

Drawing away slowly from the kiss, he whispered huskily, "It's been a long day, sweet. Don't you think it's time for bed?"

She smiled contentedly and laid her head on his shoulder. "Matthew Brady, you've got a one-track mind." She closed her eyes with a smug sigh. "Isn't it wonderful that mine runs on the same track?"

Laughing as he stood with her in his arms, he said, "and you, Jiggs O'Malley . . ." He paused, looking down at her. "Darlin', what in the hell is your real name?"

"Jiggs O'Malley," she said innocently.

"Jiggs," he reproved. "That isn't your real name and you know it. Your job application showed the initials 'J.I.' in parentheses."

"You don't need to know." Her face was set in stubborn lines.

"You hard-headed mule, they'll want to know when we apply for a marriage license."

"Oh." She looked at him, startled. "Are we get- ting married, Matt? That's wonderful!"

He sighed in exasperation. "Darlin', sometimes you're so dense. Of course we're getting married." He looked at her sharply. "That is what you want, isn't it?"

"Oh yes, Matt! More than anything—now that I think about it. I hadn't planned that far ahead. I had only thought as far as loving you," she explained.

"Well, hold that thought!" He laughed. "But right now I want to know your real name."

"All right, all right," she muttered, then set her jaw, her eyes daring him to laugh. "Jessamine Iona O'Malley."

She watched as he struggled to control his features. He swallowed loudly, took a deep breath and said, "I think it's time for bed, *Jiggs*."

Her laughter echoed behind them as he carried her into the bedroom and slammed the door shut with his foot.


Two months later Jiggs and Matt were driving along a dusty road, catching glimpses of a winding river through bare trees, headed for home. As glorious as their sunshine-filled honeymoon had been, they were both anxious to return to the warmth of home for Christmas.

Matt, deliberately teasing, slowed the car just before they rounded the bend that would give them their first view of the house.

"You fiend," she cried, laughing.

"Anyone who sings 'Kill da' wabbit' to the music of 'The Ride of the Valkyries,' for *two hundred miles*," he said righteously, "deserves all the punishment she can get."

"Can I help it if I'm addicted to Bugs Bunny cartoons?" she asked, fluttering her eyelashes. "Besides if you didn't like it you should have put on a different tape. Now drive faster."

Chuckling in delight at her excited anticipation, he drove faster and minutes later they pulled into the drive. They sat for quiet moments, staring contentedly. Then Matt turned and kissed her gently. "Welcome home, darlin'."

He had said the same words two months earlier as he held her tightly in the darkened bedroom of her apartment. Now the words had a different, but equally loving, meaning. Her smile echoed his pleasure in their return.

"Come on, Mrs. Brady. I want to see Saul and Ruth," he said, grabbing her hand and pulling her across the seat.

She rolled her eyes and sighed as she was hauled from the car. "Matt, darling, there's something I've been meaning to talk to you about."

He stopped and turned to look at her. "What is it, Jiggs?"

But she didn't get the chance to make the complaint, for Ruth and Saul emerged from the house at that moment. Oh, well, she mused silently, giving Matt a lovingly indulgent look, he'll probably realize the effect of all that pulling when my left hand begins to drag on the ground. She turned to embrace the laughing pair and followed them into the house.

As they sat in front of the crackling fire later that evening, the twinkling lights of the huge Christmas tree made their homecoming perfect. They had added their gifts for Ruth and Saul to the pile already under the tree, but Jiggs had her gifts for Matt hidden away. She refused to let him open them before Christmas and she had already caught him tampering with them once. She had wanted to buy him everything in sight; however she kept her purchases simple. Her favorite was of her own making—a watercolor she had done on their honeymoon. It showed a figure, vaguely resembling herself, trapped in a dark forest of dead trees with gnarled, grasping branches. On the left side of the painting, glorious sunlight was streaming through the trees as the figure stared at it with wondrous longing.

She suddenly wished she had not been so stubborn about waiting until Christmas morning to open the gifts. She wanted to give the watercolor to Matt now. She wanted to see his face when he understood what she was telling him. And she didn't doubt for a minute that he would understand. She knew him too well.

Saul entered the room and gave Matt a very mysterious nod. Matt smiled broadly at the conspiratorial signal, turning to her to echo her wish.

"Jiggs, I've got a gift for you in the bedroom and I don't want to wait until Christmas to give it to you. We can call it a welcome home gift."

She looked at him, puzzled by his suppressed excitement and unmistakable amusement. What was he planning? She didn't trust him when he got that look in his eyes. "Matt, what are you up to? If you've got something outrageous in the bedroom, you'd better tell me now or, so help me, you'll be sorry."

"Darlin'!" he said in an injured tone. "Would I do that to you?"

"Yes, you would," she stated unequivocally.

"I promise it's nothing outrageous—just a little portrait."

She looked at him suspiciously. "A portrait of whom?"

"Patience, darlin'," he said grinning. "Come and see."

Curiosity piqued, she followed closely as he left the room. Outside their bedroom door he stopped and demanded she close her eyes.

"Matt, is that absolutely necessary?"

"Humor me. Come on, Jiggs. I don't want you to see it until you're standing in front of it."

She closed her eyes impatiently and let him lead her into the room. He pulled her to a halt, positioning her while she grumbled irritably, then said, "Okay, open them."

She carefully opened her eyes to look at the

portrait before her. For a few seconds she simply stared in open-mouthed surprise. Then as she took in the lean cheeks, familiar beard, and famous stovepipe hat of the man in the portrait, her delighted peal of laughter filled the room.

"Oh, Matt," she gasped. "It's perfect."

He pulled her into his arms and whispered, "*It's* appropriate. *You're* perfect."

His kiss was a tribute to their joy in each other and as it deepened, the eyes of the great man in the portrait on the wall seemed to twinkle in approval of their loving union.

# *A Very Reluctant Knight*

(Previously published as Loveswept #16)

To Nancy—the diminutive dynamo who
threatened, cajoled, and frog-marched me
into believing in myself.

# *Chapter One*

Maggie will do it.

The familiar words reverberated in her mind, mocking her as she bent to pour the dry dog food into the first of six containers. Sure, she thought in disgust; if no one else wants the job, ask Maggie. She'll do it. Good-hearted, reliable Maggie.

"All right, all right," Maggie muttered in her soft, husky voice as six widely assorted dogs tried noisily to eat from one dish. "I'm going as fast as I can."

The neat, white-fenced yard seemed too small to accommodate the mob of eager dogs. She had never understood how Uncle Charles could have acquired six dogs. Aunt Sarah said he was too soft-hearted to turn away a stray, but then, Aunt Sarah always managed to make everything her husband did sound wonderfully humane, remarkably thoughtful. Maggie couldn't imagine her uncle doing anything that wasn't practical.

One simply never knew what motivated others, she thought with a shrug, looking at the proof of his impracticality. She managed to fill four of the containers before being knocked off her feet by an excitable Great Dane. Pulling her five-foot frame upright, she brushed the dirt from her khaki shorts and glared belligerently at the offending animal.

"You want to try that one again, buster?" She took a menacing step forward, and the huge dog licked her hand, humbly begging her pardon with a soft "whoof." "Yes, that's all well and good, but just see that it doesn't happen again."

She struggled among the unruly dogs, pushing them aside to fill the remaining dishes, then looked at the dark clouds building overhead. The sultry, threatening weather suited her mood perfectly. She had been waiting for weeks for Dave to ask her out, and when he finally did, she had been "previously committed"—to babysitting a menagerie of mongrels, for heaven's sake!

Perspiration ran down her chest and was absorbed by the blouse she had tied loosely under her small, rounded breasts, as she pulled a grossly fat dog away from the bowl of a small cocker spaniel. How do I get myself into these situations? she moaned silently. She should have known when Aunt Sarah asked if she had plans for the weekend that it would lead to something like this. It always did.

"I'm a sucker," she told the clamoring dogs. "No." Her gold-tipped brown curls bounced emphatically as she shook her head in a woeful denial of their barked comments. "No, I'm not exaggerating. I tell you, when people see me coming, they don't say, 'Here comes Maggie Simms, the brilliant sales consultant,' or 'Here comes Maggie Simms, the beautiful, vivacious divorcee,' or even 'Here comes Maggie Simms, one heck of a good sport.' No, they say, 'Here comes Maggie Simms—the chump.' "

Framing the friendly Great Dane's head with her small hands, she gazed into his sympathetic brown eyes and said, "Don't you understand? I could have been with Dave this weekend!" She laughed ruefully as a large, wet tongue licked her face consolingly. "Thanks, pal, but I'm afraid it's just not the same."

Minutes later, as the greedy dogs snuffled noisily around in the empty bowls, Maggie leaned against the porch rail of the white frame house, feeling stifled by the heaviness of the air and the futility of her thoughts. She had always enjoyed visiting Aunt Sarah and Uncle Charles in their small East Texas home. The scent of pine in the clean, fresh air was a refreshing change from the heat and exhaust fumes of Dallas. But this weekend was different. If she hadn't promised to watch their beloved brood, she could have been with the only man she had found interesting since her divorce.

Dave was the new man at the office. The company had transferred him from Houston to replace Maggie's retiring supervisor. Dave's shy smile and slender, but good looking frame had attracted her immediately. She had watched as he had put her coworkers at ease, demonstrating his authority with thoughtfulness and diplomacy, avoiding office politics. His quiet intelligence had a way of calming even the most troubled waters, and he had already gained the respect of his superiors.

Recently divorced, he was the target of a lot of

lively speculation and gossip, but so far he had not paid noticeable attention to any of the attractive women in the building. Several times, however, Maggie had turned to find him watching her with a gleam of interest in his pale blue eyes.

Then, on Thursday, in the middle of a casual conversation, he had asked her to attend a concert with him. She had had to force a refusal from her lips. After all the overconfident males Maggie had met since her divorce, Dave's shyness was like a breath of fresh air. And, best of all, he was only seven inches taller than she. Her neck had a permanent crick from looking up at her previous dates.

Maggie sighed in regret and looked around her at the beautiful country setting. If there were any justice at all, she would be preparing for her date with Dave instead of watching a storm build.

The dark clouds now hung low over the open fields behind the house, convincing her that it was time to start securing the windows. She pushed away from the rail just as a large silver Mercedes passed the house, throwing up a choking cloud of dust from the dirt road.

"Thanks," she muttered darkly. "That's all I need. Add that to all my perspiration and it makes a real nice layer of mud." She glared impotently after the disappearing vehicle, then stared in surprise as it pulled to a stop and began to back up. When it reached the front gate set in the white picket fence, it stopped. The man inside turned off the ignition and got out of the car.

Speaking of king-sized—the man was Brobdingnagian, one of those giants straight out of *Gulliver's Travels*. Several inches over six feet, he moved with the agile grace of a sleek greyhound.

His handsome, lightly tanned face held a casual, almost bored expression, but there was nothing dilatory in his movements. Even from a distance Maggie recognized the dynamic energy vibrating from his lean, hard body. His superbly cut suit, which he wore with the careless ease of one used to such things, looked out of place in this homey setting, his dark-blond hair and refined features giving him the aristocratic look of Scandinavian nobility.

A Norse god in the flesh, she thought impudently as he swung open the gate and walked toward her. "Hello." She smiled her welcome with the courtesy that was a deeply ingrained part of her nature. Although she very much resented the way he eyed her bare midriff and shapely tanned legs, she kept the polite smile glued firmly in place. "Is there something I can do for you?"

"I certainly hope so," he said silkily.

His voice was deep and refined, and a practiced smile played about his perfectly sculptured lips. His steady examination of her face made her tingle in discomfort as she waited for him to continue.

"I thought perhaps you could tell me if this road will take me to the Kingman Lodge," he asked smoothly.

Is that the best you can do? she scoffed silently. There were signs every five hundred feet that led straight to the lodge, which was located on a small, privately owned lake several miles west of her uncle's home—a fact that this Lothario knew full well. And what was more, judging by the amused gleam in his unusual silver-gray eyes, he knew she was aware of his knowledge. Wonderful, she mused sarcastically. With all my problems, I have to run across a full-fledged nut with a kinky yen for sweaty, dust-covered country bumpkins.

Refusing to comment on the transparency of his gambit, she sighed deeply, then answered politely. "Yes, it will."

He looked at her face for a long moment, then dropped his gaze to her breasts. Maggie caught her breath sharply at the caressing quality of his look. Here it comes, she thought, mentally preparing to parry his advances.

"Thank you," he said quietly; then, incredibly, turned to walk back toward the gate.

The oversized idiot was leaving! He had actually stopped to confirm his directions, she thought in amazement, watching his lithe figure as he strode across the yard and out the gate.

On the other side of the Mercedes he halted, looking at her across the silver top with an amused twinkle in his strange eyes. "By the way," he remarked casually, "while you were rolling around in the dirt, your shirt came unbuttoned." His smile broadened audaciously as he heard her gasp and saw her hand fly up to cover her partially exposed breasts. "Very nice. Compact, but nice," he added in a soft murmur, then opened the door and folded his tall frame into the driver's seat.

"Insufferable man," she muttered as the car disappeared in a cloud of dust. He could at least have refrained from mentioning it. Turning abruptly, she walked indignantly into the house.

Two hours later, a shower and clean clothing had restored her, mentally as well as physically. As she rocked gently in the porch swing, she decided with a good-humored grin that she had deserved that man's parting shot. She had begun making ridiculous assumptions about him the minute he stepped from his car. While she still thought his reason for stopping was highly suspect, there had been no excuse for prejudging him.

Maggie looked into the gathering darkness and admitted that mentally she had been punishing the man simply because he wasn't Dave. Dave would never in a million years have had that superior, knowing look in his eyes. He was gentle and sensible and honorable. And after her disastrous six years with Barry, she appreciated those three qualities as she never had before.

Barry had seemed like a charming child. Tall and beautifully formed, he had taken what the world—including Maggie—had handed him as though it were his due.

Born to middle-class parents, Barry had been outrageously spoiled by his mother. She had deprived her other children of luxuries so that her last-born could have whatever took his fancy, and Barry had come to expect that kind of sacrifice.

Stunned by his physical beauty and charming, boyish facade, Maggie had taken over from Barry's mother, willing, even eager to do whatever she could to make him happy. She soon found that money was necessary to keep Barry in the manner to which he had become accustomed, so she had worked long hours babying their small printing business along until it was at last a financial success. Perhaps she had worked too hard. Somewhere along the line the urge to please Barry— which had proven an impossible task anyway—had been superceded by a personal need for success. And a wife who was absent for most of the time and dead tired when she was home couldn't have been very pleasant. But Maggie had been the practical one in their marriage. A doer tied to a dreamer. Slowly she had come to realize that Barry resented the very thing that had drawn him to her in the beginning—her strength and her drive.

She stood in agitation as the thoughts she had carefully kept buried for two years crept into her mind. Henry, her Great Dane friend, joined her on the porch nuzzling her hand in a vain attempt to comfort.

If only I could have given more of the responsibility to Barry, she thought. If Maggie had been weaker, perhaps he would have been stronger. But she had seen early in their marriage that Barry was simply not capable of handling responsibility. Every time she had encouraged him to take part in the operation of their budding business, he had botched the simplest tasks.

As she paced back and forth across the porch, her slender figure tense, the huge black dog matched her steps, looking up occasionally with sympathetic eyes.

"I tried, Henry," she told the friendly beast, her soft, husky voice sounding vaguely regretful. "I tried to be what he wanted, but I simply can't be weak and brainless."

When Barry had finally admitted he had been having an affair for over six months, Maggie had felt like an utter fool. It had never occurred to her that he would be unfaithful. An oddity in this supposedly enlightened age of disposable relationships, she'd believed that marriage was forever. "Till death do us part," she thought cynically . . . or at least until he didn't need me any more.

But as faulty as their marriage had been, Maggie had fought tooth and nail for its survival—until she realized that Barry's new love had a weapon that beat anything in Maggie's arsenal. Barry felt sorry for the woman.

She had more problems than any ten women I know, Maggie sighed mournfully. And on top of all her physical and financial woes, her apartment was overrun with bugs. During the many arguments that marked the end of their marriage, Barry had always returned to that fact as an example of how much his intended needed him.

"Lord, Henry." Maggie stopped pacing and looked into the soulful brown eyes that watched her closely. "If I had known he wanted bugs, I would have had them shipped in!"

But she couldn't pretend to be other than she really was, so she had given in, and she counted the divorce a personal failure. She knew she had either failed in her choice of a life partner or she had failed as a woman. Either one was a devastating blow to her self-esteem.

Weakened emotionally by doubt and self-blame, she had not fought Barry's claim to their printing business. So at the age of twenty-nine she had found herself without a husband and without the business for which she had worked so hard. Although she didn't regret breaking her ties with the past by turning over the shop to Barry and his new wife, seeing it die slowly through mismanagement had broken her heart, and she had learned to avoid the small side street where it was located.

Her job as sales consultant with Howard Electronics had been a lifesaver. Throwing herself into her job, she had adapted quickly to her new life style, and the friends she had made at work kept her too busy for idle speculation about the past.

Now, two years later, she had at last met a man

9

she felt she could trust. Dave had none of Barry's showy male beauty. He was attractive in a quiet, understated way. He was thoughtful and interested in the people around him, whereas Barry had been interested only in what benefited Barry.

Maggie shook free of her depressing thoughts of the past and looked again into the darkening afternoon around her, this time with a hint of bewilderment. It was only four o'clock. It shouldn't be this dark for another three hours. The air had an eerie blue cast, and there was not a breath of wind, the strange stillness somehow menacing.

As she stood and walked into the yard to survey the surrounding dark clouds, she heard a car approaching. The silver gleam was recognizable even in the blue-tinted shadows. The arrogant stranger had obviously finished whatever business had taken him to the isolated lodge. The lodge and lake were frequently rented for company parties or for tired executives to enjoy a weekend of quiet, undisturbed fishing. But somehow Maggie couldn't visualize that particular man doing anything as mundane as arranging a rental. His car slowed to a crawl as it passed the house, and she resisted a childish urge to poke out her tongue as she saw his head turn to take in her jean-clad—and, thankfully, clean—form. Suddenly the car screeched to a halt and he was hurtling through the gate to grab her roughly by the shoulders.

"What in the hell are you doing?" she squeaked, slapping ineffectually at the hands that were digging painfully into her skin.

"Look!" he commanded urgently, turning her body to face the fields behind the house.

The low clouds were rolling and swirling furiously. And three fields away a slender, snaking tail hung down from the angry mass, taking terrifying shape before her eyes.

"My God," she breathed in awe. "A tornado. It's spectacular." Her whispered words were barely audible. "Grim, but somehow magnificent and elemental."

"Look, love," he said drily, "unless you want to get your camera and take pictures, I think it's time we made our move."

"The cellar!" she exclaimed, pulling her eyes away from the mesmerizing force of the gray funnel.

She grabbed his hand and began to run. Behind the house, Maggie headed for a mound of grass-covered earth. As he swung the metal door wide on its hinges and began to push her inside, she recalled the reason for her stay. "The dogs! I've got to get the dogs!"

"There's no time," he shouted impatiently, shoving her into the cellar before him, then pulling the heavy door shut with a loud thud.

The sound of her own breathing seemed unnaturally loud in the sudden silence as Maggie moved cautiously down the wooden steps. At the bottom she stood stock still, paralyzed by the engulfing darkness around her, the musty smell of damp earth invading her nostrils. "There's a light pull somewhere," she said nervously, shuddering at the thought of the snakes that continually sought refuge in the cellar.

She stumbled forward with a startled squeak as the tall figure behind her bumped into her, then caught her breath in a gasp of pure terror as something soft and slithery brushed her face. Breathing an audible sigh of relief, she realized it was the string of the elusive light pull and grasped it firmly, turning on the dim bulb in the ceiling of the small room.

Maggie hadn't been in the cellar since she was a child, and as she looked around, a variety of childhood memories came flooding back. Memories of long, lazy summers. Of playing tag with her cousin Chuck. Of helping Aunt Sarah can fruit and vegetables in a steaming hot kitchen, then storing the labeled jars on the shelves of this wonderfully cool place.

"We might as well be comfortable while we await the tempest," the man said in a lazy, amused voice.

Maggie had completely forgotten the stranger. He had moved a stack of burlap bags from a wide bench to the floor and was removing his jacket, hanging it neatly on a peg on the wall. He must have taken off his tie earlier, for his white shirt was opened wide at the neck.

"How long do you think it will be?" she asked, joining him hesitantly on the bench. "It looked awfully close."

"Most tornadoes move about ten miles per hour, I believe." His voice sounded casual, almost uninterested. "I should say the whole thing will be over in a few minutes."

"I wish I could have gotten the dogs. Uncle Charles will kill me if anything happens to them," she said anxiously.

He leaned comfortably against the wall, stretching out his long legs, and looked around the cellar. "The dogs will be fine."

Maggie shifted uneasily when he stopped his examination of the room to look her up and down as though she were a slave he was thinking seriously about purchasing, his curious gray eyes glinting in amusement at her discomfort.

"Dogs have the uncanny ability of sensing natural danger," he continued, sounding unutterably bored with the subject. "They'll take cover until all danger has passed. Besides, I can't really see us cooped up in this tiny place with all those dogs. It would be total chaos."

And they might rumple your suit, she thought sarcastically. You pompous ass! I'd rather have the dogs for company.

Suddenly the quiet was broken by a thundering crash that shook the cement floor beneath them. The Furies had pursued them into the underworld. Maggie shrieked in terror as their dim light was extinguished and jars leaped from the shelves to shatter on the floor all around them. She felt herself being jerked abruptly from her cowering position on the bench; then she was lying on the floor under the bench, held in a fierce grip by the man who now represented security in their underground world gone mad.

She shook in fright for what seemed like hours, hugging him tightly around the waist as he held her wedged between his body and the wall. Quiet reined for some time before she was calm enough to loosen her hold and whisper softly, "Do you think it's over now?"

His face was buried in her short brown curls, and she felt his husky whisper on her sensitive scalp. "You've never been in a tornado before?"

"No, thank God," came her heartfelt reply.

"There is sometimes a lull like this before the worst part." He sounded serious and concerned—almost too much so—and there was a strange undertone of something—amusement, perhaps?

—in his deep voice. "Just to make sure, we had better stay where we are for a while." He pulled her closer, shaping her tiny frame to his long, hard body.

"How . . ." Her voice was a thin imitation of its natural soft huskiness. She cleared her throat to begin again. "How long?"

"That's difficult to say." His mouth had moved closer, a hair's-breadth away from her tingling ear. "It could be as much as an hour. But believe me, I'll know when it's time to leave." His long-fingered hand moved to rest just below one small breast. "Don't you think it's time we introduced ourselves? My name is Mark Wilding."

"How do you do? I'm . . . I'm . . . What are you doing with your hand?" she gasped as his hand moved a fraction of an inch higher.

"Just checking your body temperature and pulse, love," he explained smoothly. That curious undertone in his voice was stronger now. "I want to be sure you're not in shock."

"I'm perfectly fine, thank you, so you can move your hand," she said stiffly. "And my name is Maggie Simms."

"Maggie. Is that a diminutive of Margaret?" he asked politely as his hand moved over the smooth line of her trim hip.

Maggie shivered in unbidden pleasure as she felt the warmth of his palm through the denim of her jeans. Steeling herself against his insidious touch, she pulled his hand to her waist. "No, it's just plain Maggie," she stated firmly, determined to win the battle of wills.

He moved one hard thigh until it rested on hers, slipping his hand around to stroke her back beneath her loose cotton top. "Were you named

14

for your mother?" he whispered, his lips moving against her ear.

Her small hand dug into his thigh as she shoved it away, then with her elbow she pushed down on his arm until it rested again on her waist. "No, my parents simply liked the name," she said through clenched teeth.

But the roving hand didn't stop for long at her waist. After a barely perceptible pause, it continued down to mold one firm buttock, and his knee moved suggestively against her leg. "I believe one of my maternal great-aunts was named Maggie," he murmured huskily.

Reaching behind her back, she dug her nails into the strong hand and forcibly shoved it back around to his chest, her tennis shoe connecting with his shin at the same moment. "It's very possible. The name is not uncommon," she panted, out of breath.

An imperceptible movement brought the back of his hand against her breast, where it gently brushed one sensitive nipple through the soft fabric. "It's a very pleasant-sounding name, with practical, even earthy, connotations." He took the lobe of her ear between his teeth in a soft, erotic nip.

"It serves its purpose," she gasped, tilting her head to avoid his persistent lips, then pulling his hand away from the hardening tip of her breast to hold it firmly between both of hers.

"Yes, I'm sure it does." His lips moved to her exposed neck as though she had offered it purposely for his pleasure. He brought her hands to his chest, pushing one inside the open neck of his shirt.

The sensual feel of his warm, hair-roughened

chest beneath her small hand was the last straw, and Maggie groaned in defeat, bringing her free hand up to grasp his neck as he sought her sensitive lips with his own. In a swift sideways movement he half-covered her soft body with his lean, hard frame.

His firm mouth gently teased her delicate lips, taking immediate advantage of their hesitant parting to caress the inner softness with his seeking tongue. His strong fingers lightly stroked the bare skin of her back under her shirt. As his hand moved slowly under her arm and across her rib cage, his lips left the pliant softness of hers to skim lightly down her throat to the rounded tops of her small, firm breasts.

In a harmony of subtle movements his lips pushed aside her blouse, and he brought his hand up to cup her breast. "Beautiful," he sighed against her velvety skin. "Just as I said—compact, but nice. There's nothing ostentatious about you, princess. Your body is perfectly formed. A goddess in miniature."

Maggie moved her head to kiss the side of his tanned neck. "You know I don't like you, don't you?" she whispered, breathless from his touch, then tasted his warm skin with the tip of her tongue.

He groaned at the sensual caress and murmured huskily, "Yes, I know, love," then found the taut tip of her breast with his stroking thumb. "God, I love that husky little voice of yours."

He moved his head to reclaim her lips, and Maggie went under for the third time. She brought her hands to his neck, smoothing the taut sinews. His bold tongue caressed the moist sweetness of hers, discovering and memorizing the depths of pleasure to shake her slender body.

"As soon as we're able to leave," he murmured against her tender lips, "shall we continue this charming enterprise in more comfortable surroundings?"

The softly spoken words filtered temptingly into her brain, then brought her to the surface with a shuddering jolt. She was letting the arrogant fool make love to her! "No!" she gasped, her voice weak. She pulled away as far as the wall behind her would permit.

"I told you before, Mr. Wilding, I don't like you." Her voice was firmer now. Her eyes had adjusted to the dark, and she looked at his face as she spoke. "And I don't like the idea of your taking advantage of the situation to try to amuse yourself." She straightened her blouse with a jerk. "Just because my body is small doesn't mean my brain is undersized as well. I may have gotten a little carried away—it's been a very tense evening—but don't think I'm stupid enough to play along with a supercilious playboy who's out for a roll in the hay with a local peasant just to pass the time!"

"You're absolutely adorable!" He chuckled in delight, reaching out to pull her close again.

"But you've got a tile loose," she muttered under her breath, pushing against the solid wall of his chest.

"You look like a little Bantam hen with its feathers all ruffled," he laughed, trying to still her struggling body.

"Huh!" she snorted inelegantly. "Bantam hen, my foot. I'll bet my Aunt Martha's teeth you've never even seen a Banty."

"You know," he said in surprise, "I believe you're

right. I haven't. That just shows you should feel sorry for me. I had a deprived childhood."

"I'm sure the only things you were deprived of were spankings," she said maliciously. "Now, let me go, you insensitive clod!" She shoved her small fist into his stomach with as much force as her confined circumstances allowed.

"But, love," he objected, wheezing slightly from the blow, "can't we discuss this?" Suddenly he jerked upright, banging his head on the bench as a blood-curdling howl filtered through the door and echoed eerily around their miniature cavern.

"My Lord!" he exclaimed, rubbing the top of his injured head. "The keening of the hounds of the Baskervilles, no doubt."

"Henry!" Maggie said, recognizing the howl of her sympathetic friend. She scrambled over Mark's prone figure and stood upright. "That must mean it's safe to go out."

"Watch the broken glass, for heaven's sake," he warned irritably. "Those flimsy sneakers you're wearing aren't much protection. Just stay where you are. I'll go open the door and show the miserable beast that you're still alive."

Maggie stifled a snicker at his disgruntled tone, relieved to be rescued from what was turning out to be a very awkward situation. She waited patiently at the foot of the stairs, listening with a satisfied smile to the duet of his grumbling, unintelligible comments and the piercing howls of the Great Dane. She heard a muffled thud as Mark shoved against the door with his shoulder. Seconds later he swore viciously and she heard louder, more forceful thuds.

"What's wrong?" she asked anxiously as the unmistakable sound of his descending footsteps reached her ears. When he was standing before her she could see surprise etched on his handsome features.

He rubbed his jaw thoughtfully. "I'm sorry, Maggie, but it appears we'll be here for a while. His voice was guarded, and he watched her closely as he continued. "The door seems to be blocked from the outside."

## Chapter Two

"Blocked? What do you mean, blocked?" she asked, confused. "How can it be blocked?"

"By blocked I mean obstructed or barricaded," he explained with irritating patience, a grin of genuine amusement taking the place of his practiced smile. He placed his foot on the bench beside her, resting his forearm leisurely on his knee, and looked her up and down, a speculative gleam showing in his clear gray eyes. "And as to how it came to be blocked, I'd put my money on the tree that was growing several yards from the cellar door."

"Aunt Sarah's magnolia tree!" she gasped in horror. "But she loved that tree. She planted it the year she and Uncle Charles were married."

"Although your aunt has my deepest sympathy," he said, "I'm afraid the demise of her tree is the least of our worries right now. Apparently it's fallen across the door, and"—he paused dramatically, then dropped his voice to a whisper, watching her face as he spoke to see if his words were sinking in—"we are trapped . . . together . . . alone . . . in a very small, very dark cellar. *Capisci?*"

"Oh, no," she moaned, eyeing him warily, at last grasping the full import of his words. She backed slowly away from him and his smug, knowing grin.

"Oh, yes, love. It should be interesting, to say the least." He chuckled in satisfaction. "Now, where were we before we were so rudely interrupted?"

"Hen-ry!" she screeched, her voice rising on the last syllable. Then, turning sharply, Maggie raced through the broken glass and up the stairs as surefooted as though each step were planned in advance instead of being the result of blind panic. She pressed urgently against the door with her shoulder. When it refused to budge, she kicked it viciously, yelping—more in annoyance than in pain—when she bruised her foot. Then, in a frustrated fit of pique, she beat against the metal door with her fists, all to the accompaniment of Henry's excited barks.

At last, realizing she was accomplishing nothing except perhaps to make herself look foolish, she leaned her head against the door and took deep, steadying breaths. The sound of crunching glass brought her head up sharply, and she peered over her shoulder into the darkness below. She could barely make out his tall shape at the foot of the stairs as his disgruntled reprimand floated softly up to her ears.

"All that energy wasted on a *door.*"

Oh, Lord, she moaned silently. She was trapped underground with an overbred, oversexed octopus, and there was nothing she could do about it. At least, she thought, squaring her shoulders, there is nothing I can do about escaping, but I'll be damned if I'll let that arrogant behemoth chase me around the cellar until my aunt and uncle return on Sunday.

Standing straight, and as tall as one can when one is five feet nothing, she marched down the stairs, moving Mark abruptly to one side, and said briskly, "There was always a kerosene lamp on one of these shelves. I'm sure my aunt and uncle haven't changed their habits and keep the lamp primed for an emergency like this. But the first thing to do is clean up this mess so that we can move without stepping on glass." If it did come down to playing tag, Maggie at least wanted a clear running field. "If you'll look to your immediate right you should find it along with the matches."

She held her breath, waiting for his reaction, then gave a sigh of relief as she heard him strike a match and saw the lamp in the faint glow. Thank heaven it hadn't been destroyed in the turbulence earlier.

Mark lit the lamp and placed it on a shelf beside the bench, whistling cheerfully as he moved, then turned to face her in the dim light, saluting smartly. "What now, Captain?" he asked briskly, grinning devilishly at her obvious irritation.

"Oh, for heaven's sake," she muttered, "just sit on the bench and stay out of my way until I finish."

"But I wouldn't dream of letting you do all the work," he argued. "Hand me the broom and I'll have it clear in no time at all."

"I doubt very seriously you would know what to

do with a broom. And besides," she added maliciously, "you might get your hands dirty."

"No!" he exclaimed in mock horror. "In that case perhaps you had better do it yourself. Judging from the first time I saw you, you're particularly fond of dirt, and I wouldn't want to deprive you of the pleasure."

As Maggie sputtered indignantly, he turned and walked to the bench. After clearing it of a few fragments of glass, he sat down, his arms folded, then leaned back against the wall, watching her closely, a waiting look in his gray eyes.

Clearing her throat nervously, she turned her back on his disconcerting stare, lifted the push broom from the corner, and began to shove vigorously at the broken glass, thankful that most of the filled jars had stayed on the shelves. As she worked she glanced frequently over her shoulder at him, waiting for she knew not what. Each time he would merely smile inquiringly, occasionally stifling a bored yawn, but never once taking his eyes from her.

When she had done all she could, she slowly replaced the broom, then stood facing the wall, feeling a perfect imbecile. Now what? she thought desperately. If he had shown signs of aggression she could have handled it, but his silent waiting was driving her crazy.

Careful, Maggie, she told herself, you're letting him get to you. She turned abruptly to face him. He was leaning against the wall, still watching, still waiting. As she stared he moved his arm to pat the bench beside him, suppressed laughter sparkling in his eyes.

The elegant jackass is teasing me! she thought, feeling momentary relief. Then fury began to seep into her veins. As if being trapped weren't bad enough! No, she had to be trapped with a damned comedian. She glared at him coldly, but the only effect was a broadening of his smile.

"Come and sit down, Maggie," he said softly. "You must be tired after all that work."

"No, thank you," she replied icily. "I'd rather stand."

"For two days?" he queried in disbelief. "Your aunt and uncle aren't due back until Sunday evening, so we might as well resign ourselves to a long wait."

Astonishment froze her features. "How did you know?" she whispered, staring at his handsome face as if he were the devil himself.

"Jake told me," he replied, as though it were obvious.

"Jake? Jake? Why should he tell you about my aunt and uncle?" she asked in confusion. Jake owned the Kingman Lodge and was Uncle Charles's best friend. Maggie had known him all her life, and she would have bet anything that he was not the kind of man who discussed other people's business with strangers.

"Because I asked," he said simply, "And perhaps because I'm his favorite nephew."

"Jake is your uncle? I don't believe it," she stated flatly. "That sweet old man couldn't possibly have a nephew like you."

"He does, I assure you." Her astonishment seemed to add to his amusement.

"Then why has he never mentioned you?" she asked suspiciously.

Mark rose to his feet, casually stretching his lean frame, and walked toward her as he spoke. "Would you call Jake a garrulous man?"

Backing up a step, she eyed his advancing form warily. "No, I would not. Which makes it even stranger that he should suddenly become so talkative with you." Her words came out as an unequivocal accusation.

"That was different—I asked," he said reasonably, still walking casually in her direction. "I'm sure if you had asked, he would have been glad to tell you all about his attractive, talented nephew."

"And just exactly what made you ask about my aunt and uncle?" Her cautious retreat was halted abruptly as she backed into the shelves lining the wall.

"Actually, I didn't mention either of those worthy people." He was only steps away now, giving every appearance of enjoying himself immensely. "I asked about a beautiful but haughty featherweight with gold-tipped brown hair and gold-flecked brown eyes." There was a subtle difference in his voice, and the softly murmured words were like invisible caresses that lingered in the air and on her sensitive skin long after he finished speaking. Staring intently at the fluttering movement of her small breasts as the rate of her breathing increased sharply, he added in a husky whisper, "I knew what it would be like to hold you the moment I saw you. But I underestimated the feeling. It was incredibly right, Maggie."

Mesmerized, her eyes followed his slow movement forward as a cobra follows the movement of a snake charmer's flute. He was a step away, lifting his arms to enfold her, when she shook free of his spell. Searching frantically for something stronger than her will to hold him off, she found only the jars on the shelves that were pressing uncomfortably into her back. Grasping the largest jar she saw, she held it threateningly high.

"Stay back," she warned. "Take one more step and I'll hit you with this jar of"—she glanced at the jar—"chow-chow."

He stood abruptly still, shock spreading across his perfect face. Then, incredibly, he began to laugh. His laughter grew, echoing richly in the small room, until he was holding his sides weakly. Just as he was beginning to control it, he glanced at Maggie's features, and the perplexed astonishment in her features set him off once again.

"Foiled by a jar of chow-chow," he gasped, finally settling down to a chuckle. "Maggie, you're wonderful! But tell me, sweetheart, what exactly is chow-chow?"

His laughter was so natural, so irresistible, she found herself grinning too. "It's a relish made of . . ." Maggie paused as he moved oh, so casually closer to her, ostensibly to examine the jar. "It doesn't really matter, does it? What does matter, Mr. Wilding, is the fact that I don't want you to make love to me. So would you please cut out the playboy stuff? It's very wearing on the nerves." As she spoke she realized she was addressing him as an equal for the first time and felt vaguely ashamed of herself.

"Of course," he replied matter-of-factly. "I wouldn't dream of pushing in where I'm not wanted." His innocent expression was just a shade overdone. "But tell me, *Ms. Simms*, just exactly what is it about me that you don't like?"

His curiosity seemed genuine, causing Maggie to search for solid reasons to explain her dislike. However, nothing that came to mind seemed an adequate explanation for the instant antagonism she had felt. Feeling defensive, which was probably what he had intended all along, she blurted out, "You're too tall."

"So I'll slump," he said agreeably, making his actions suit his words. "Anything else?"

"Is this necessary? Can't we just put it down to chemistry?" The wicked gleam that appeared in his eyes at the last word reminded her of the sensual sparks that had flown between them earlier. She cleared her throat nervously. "Oh, very well. I've never cared for fair men, and your attitude toward life is the antithesis of mine."

"You're very sharp," he observed lazily, "to have interpreted my attitude toward life in the space of"—he glanced at his watch—"two hours and fifteen minutes." He paused and watched her shift uncomfortably. "What you're trying to say is that I remind you of your ex-husband, right?"

"How did you? . . . Of course. Jake told you about Barry, too." She moved past him in annoyance. "Jake talks too damn much."

He watched her irritated pacing for a moment. "I'm sorry, Maggie. Forget I said that. Come sit down and relax." When she threw him a doubtful look over her shoulder, he added, "We'll simply talk—I swear."

Maggie shrugged wearily, tired of running and tired of the way the past kept popping up this evening. That was all behind her, and she wanted to forget it. She sat on the bench, glancing at him warily but not protesting when he settled her comfortably against his shoulder.

"You poor baby. You're all worn out, aren't you?" he asked softly. "I'm sorry I gave you such a hard time. I suppose I acted from habit. Although that's not an adequate excuse, it's the only one I have—

unless you count a stupendous craving for your body."

"Do you realize what you're saying?" she murmured sleepily, pointedly ignoring his last comment. "You've just admitted that you normally view women as sex objects. Didn't you know that the male chauvinist is on his way out?" She chuckled lazily. "If you're not careful, you'll find yourself in the same fix as the dinosaur."

"I'm sorry to disillusion you, love," he murmured drily, "but there are some women who can be viewed in no other way. Perhaps it's different in your world, but so many of the people I meet— male and female—are only too eager to trade their integrity for filthy lucre—or its equivalent."

The amused cynicism in his voice brought her eyes to his face in curiosity. But there was something besides cynicism in his silver eyes. Something that Maggie didn't want to recognize, for it made him too human. A sadness, perhaps even loneliness, that didn't show in his lazily drawled words. She buried the thought quickly, saying in a casual voice, "I suppose everyone has wondered at one time or another what it would be like to be one of the beautiful people, but to tell you the truth, I never felt I would enjoy that kind of life. It seems to me that it would be the most boring thing in the world. If you could have anything you wanted, you would have to search continually for a new and different high. It seems that it would breed a terrible kind of desperation."

Mark looked at her thoughtfully for a moment with something resembling respect in his eyes. "Amazing," he murmured, then smiled wryly. "You're right, of course. Not that it's that way for everyone. Some are lucky enough to find something solid to anchor them—their work or, more rarely, a special person to love. But too often the person who has everything has nothing."

Just as she was—reluctantly—beginning to be moved by what he seemed to be admitting, his face was transformed by a mischievous grin, and he said, "Didn't I tell you that you should pity me?"

"You're incorrigible," she said, exasperated. "I think I would be wasting my time feeling sorry for you. I also think that wealth is wasted on the wealthy. If I had money I think I'd be a full-time student. There's so much to learn," she explained thoughtfully. "Or maybe I would be a part-time student and spend the rest of the time seeing the world."

"Have you done much traveling?" he asked, smiling, his mood of moments before seeming a figment of her imagination.

"If you count trips to Oklahoma to see Aunt Martha, I guess the answer would still be no," she laughingly admitted.

"But you would like to?"

"Who wouldn't?" she asked, puzzled by the strange light appearing in his eyes.

"How would you like to go to St. Thomas?" At her baffled look, he continued. "I have to fly to Charlotte Amalie next weekend on business. Come with me."

"Mark," she reproved. "I thought you were going to behave!"

"Maggie, you'll love the Virgin Islands," he said, ignoring her reprimand. "Even though they're over-run with tourists, they're still the most charming islands you could imagine. My business wouldn't take long, and we would have plenty of time to explore. How about it?" he coaxed.

"Mark, you're impossible! You were just speaking of people who trade their integrity for the things money can buy. Now you're trying to make me one of them." She looked at him sternly. "Unless you want me to believe that you mean for the trip to be strictly platonic."

He chuckled. "I may be a little warped, love, but I'm not masochistic. I can't imagine you and me having a platonic relationship."

"And I can't imagine our having any kind of relationship at all," she stated firmly. "Once we're out of here, we'll never see each other again. We don't move in the same circles. You're name brand and I'm generic, and never the twain shall meet. *Capisci*?" Her tone mimicked his polished accent.

"Maggie, Maggie." He laughed. "I may be name brand, but I defy anyone to label you. You, love, are strictly one of a kind. Which is why I don't intend to let you disappear out of my life." He hugged her briefly, then said, "Tell me about your ex-husband. I get the feeling I'm taking some of his blows, so perhaps I had better know more about him."

"There's not really much to tell." She sighed, wondering wryly why the past would not die gracefully instead of popping up when she least expected it. "Barry was charming and extremely good-looking. He was also greedy and self-centered. I think it's something that he had no control over. In any situation that arose, his first thought was how it would affect him. He simply wasn't able to consider anyone else's feelings." She paused, thoughtfully considering her next remarks. "There was something lacking in his character, and that lack stunted his emotional growth. It was sad, actually. He missed so much by constantly looking inward." Sighing regretfully, she continued. "At first I hoped Elise, his current wife, would bring out some latent caring in Barry, but now I doubt it. He's caring when it suits his purpose or when it's convenient." Suddenly finding herself feeling the frustration of those years, she asked, "Why are we talking about this? It's not my idea of a pleasant topic."

"I thought perhaps if I understood your relationship with Barry, I might find the chink in your armor." He gave her an exaggerated leer. "Which would make it easier to seduce you."

Maggie chuckled, not feeling threatened by his teasing. "I have no chinks in my armor, and now that you mention it, I had no relationship with Barry. I thought I did at the time, but it was all in my mind." She smiled in reminiscence. "Dr. Ames forced me to admit that I had fought the divorce not because I wanted Barry, but because I didn't want to admit my marriage was a failure. He finally convinced me that even I—Maggie Perfect— am allowed to fail occasionally."

"He sounds like a wise man. Who is he?"

"He's the psychiatrist at the clinic that I entered after . . ." She grinned impishly as she remembered the events that led up to her stay at the clinic.

"After what?" he asked, his curiosity aroused.

"When Barry didn't come home one night, I called Elise, and of course, he was there. I told him I had changed my mind. He could have the divorce and our printing business. Then I took all his beautiful, expensive suits that I broke my back to buy, put them into the bathtub, and doused them with his lovely—and also expensive—cognac."

"And then?" he asked, grinning widely as he anticipated her next words.

"Then I threw in a lighted match and *then* I admitted myself to the mental clinic."

"Why, for heaven's sake?"

"I had never lost my temper to that extent," she explained. "I didn't consider my actions rational. It took Dr. Ames two weeks to convince me that I had handled my anger in a way that was harmful to no one. He said if I had doused *Barry* with the cognac and set him alight, then he might consider treating me, but under the circumstances, he needed the bed space."

"I was right," Mark murmured softly. "You are one of a kind. As tough as an army sergeant and as vulnerable as a baby sparrow."

"No, not vulnerable," she denied, shaking her head, her gold-tipped curls catching the soft lamplight. "Not any more."

"You think not?" he whispered, smiling as though she had issued a challenge. "Come with me to St. Thomas and we'll see who's right." His hand cradling her shoulder suddenly became electrified, causing the skin beneath it to tingle in the most peculiar way. A gentle movement of his long fingers spread the sensation across her upper body, and she shivered in a dangerously sensual response.

"Mark," she whispered huskily. Her voice held a vaguely pleading note, and for a moment she wasn't sure whether she was pleading for him to stop or to continue. "Mark," she said, her voice firmer, "I've already told you that I won't go with you. Can we please drop the subject? And I thought we had decided earlier that there would be no more hanky-panky."

"Hanky-panky?" He chuckled. "Where on earth do you pick up words like that? And for the record, love, you decided. I was coerced into agreeing." He laughed softly. "Perhaps I'd better warn you that I've been known to lie to get what I want."

"You're admitting that you would stoop to a lie just to get your own way?" she asked in astonished disbelief.

"Admirably honest of me, don't you think?" he asked with an audacious smile of satisfaction.

Maggie drew back and looked at his complacent features. "I think, Mr. Mark Wilding," she said with grudging admiration, "that you are totally untrustworthy, and I wouldn't be surprised if you were lying about lying."

"Oh, no. I'm absolutely serious," he vowed. "My one character defect is not handling defeat well—so I simply avoid it, then at the very least I retain the appearance of perfection."

"All that and humility, too," she said and laughed.

"Of course. Now you're getting a glimmer of what you're passing up by not going with me."

"I'm sure I'll hate myself for not jumping at the chance," she said, beginning to enjoy his offbeat sense of humor. "But I guess I'm just too dim-witted to recognize the opportunity of a lifetime."

He patted her consolingly on the shoulder. "Don't worry about it, love. I have occasionally run across someone who doesn't appreciate my true worth, but I eventually manage to convince even the most stubborn skeptic."

"I'll just bet you do," she muttered, stifling a sleepy yawn. "And it appears you'll have plenty of

*33*

time to convert me." She looked around the cellar. "Two days, in fact. Mark, what are we going to do about a place to sleep? This floor is concrete."

"Don't worry, princess. While you were playing janitor I was scouting the territory . . ." He intercepted her indignant glance, as she recalled the way he had watched her so intently, and added quickly, with injured innocence, ". . . for sleeping accommodations."

"Uh-huh," she agreed skeptically. "And what did you find?"

He stood and moved to where he had stacked the burlap bags earlier. "The burlap will do for a mattress." He picked up a canvas tarpaulin. "And here we have milady's eiderdown comforter." He looked strangely as though he were enjoying himself. "Not exactly the Connaught, but it will suffice, don't you think?"

She smiled inwardly at his enthusiasm. It wasn't what she had been expecting from him. "I'm speechless with admiration. I didn't think you had it in you to be practical."

"Well, as you can see, I'm not just another pretty face," he said, beginning to arrange the bags on the floor in front of the bench. "I have brains as well as beauty."

"And we've already established your modesty." She chuckled.

"Quite," he agreed, absorbed in his task.

She watched as he vigorously fluffed the burlap bags, then spread the canvas neatly over the makeshift bed. "Mark," she asked curiously, "are you part British or something? I've never heard anyone say 'quite' like that—except maybe Cary Grant."

He stopped working for a moment and looked at her with an amazingly boyish grin. "I did spend several years in London, but"—his voice dropped to a confiding whisper as he glanced around in an exaggeratedly conspiratorial fashion—"if you want to know the truth, ninety percent is pure affectation." As she laughed in delight, he added hopefully, "If it would help I'll start saying 'y'all' and wear cowboy boots and chew tobacco."

"Good Lord, no!"

"Oh, well," he said, unable to keep the relief out of his voice. "Perhaps it's best. The vernacular and boots I could manage, but I'm afraid the chewing tobacco would prove more difficult."

"I can imagine." She smiled.

"I can't," he muttered, grimacing in distaste. "Now, if you're ready, your bed awaits."

Maggie looked from the pallet to Mark, then back to the pallet. "Mark," she said hesitantly, "you wouldn't . . . I mean, tonight while I'm asleep, you won't . . ."

"Maggie," he chided, shaking his head, "how can you even ask? I may have a few eccentricities, but necrophilia is definitely not one of them. You can go to sleep and dream the sweet dreams of the righteous without fear. I promise I won't touch you. At least," he added with a wicked grin, "not until you're awake."

"Mark!"

"Just teasing, love. Now, come to bed." His smile became curiously wistful. "That sounds nice, doesn't it. Come to bed, Maggie."

What a complex man, she thought as she removed her shoes, shifting her eyes to the floor when he began unbuttoning his shirt. She could never tell when he was acting and when he was serious—that is, if he ever *were* serious. Maggie had the feeling that sobriety was one of those eccentricities to which he didn't subscribe.

Minutes later, as she drifted off to sleep, enveloped in the warmth of his lean body beside her, Maggie thought how strange it was that she had never felt this comfortable and secure sleeping beside Barry. Then, in one of those brilliant flashes that come on the threshold of sleep and are never remembered afterward, she thought how wonderfully right it felt.


"No!"

Maggie jerked awake as the sound that had been gradually incorporating itself into her dream finally separated into reality. She felt Mark twisting beside her, moaning softly in his sleep. Peering at her watch in the darkness to confirm that it was indeed morning, she wondered anxiously if she should wake him from what was obviously a nightmare or let him sleep through it and wake naturally.

She looked closely at his beautifully shaped features. The confident, almost arrogant look that seemed natural to him was gone, and in its place was a look of such anguish, she simply could not let it continue. She gently touched his face, finding it damp with perspiration.

"Mark?" she whispered softly in his ear.

Jerking his head away from her hand, he mumbled unintelligible, urgent words. Then her hand gently shaking his shoulder seemed to penetrate his dark world, for his eyes flew open suddenly. "Maggie?" he whispered hoarsely, searching her face avidly in the dimness.

"Oh, God!" He groaned, closing his eyes and

pulling her abruptly into his arms, holding her so tightly she could scarcely breathe. Burying his face in her neck, he pressed her lower body close, as though he were trying to absorb her.

Maggie was so caught up in his intensity, the desperation evident in his urgent movements, it never occurred to her to protest. He needed help, and she could provide it. But what started as comfort gradually changed into something far more self-serving. His lips on her neck and face, his hands moving on her body, started tremors of feeling that grew in intensity until her urgency matched his.

She touched his smooth, bare chest with trembling fingers, feeling she was about to make an important discovery. How could simply touching and being touched cause such acute sensation? It was as though all her senses had been veiled. Now, suddenly, the veil was lifted, and she was giddy with the heightened awareness.

He moved his impatient lips to the vulnerable, tingling skin behind her ear, and she arched her neck to the side, helpless against the tantalizing spell of his touch. His long fingers explored her back—caressing and smoothing, and neglecting not one inch of the velvety-soft skin.

His lips moved slowly across her cheek, tasting the warmth. She moved her head toward the magnetic attraction of his mouth, and their lips met explosively, bringing a whimpering moan of pleasure from her, a startlingly earthy groan of satisfaction from Mark. She brought her fingers up to clasp his neck, guarding her pleasure with eager hands, as he caressed the sweet inner parts of her lips with short, thrusting strokes of his tongue.

From somewhere in the midst of the sensual

mist surrounding her, she acknowledged his fingers on the buttons of her blouse and gave a delicious shudder of anticipation. Searching his face as he drew back from their kiss, she found his eyes trained with consuming hunger on the treasure his fingers were revealing.

He finished the last button and slowly drew her blouse open, catching his breath sharply as though discovering something wondrous and rare. The aching intensity in his glazed eyes was the most erotically stimulating thing she had ever experienced. His eyes slid over her swollen breasts, with their provocatively taut tips, his face tense with impatient greed, sending a thrill of longing surging through Maggie's veins. She moaned deep in her throat as his eyes devoured her body, affecting her as more substantial caresses had failed to do in the past.

"God, Maggie," he breathed, his voice rough with desire. "You're beautiful." He seemed crazed, driven by unseen spirits as he lowered his head to her breasts. "So perfect . . . so precious."

He cupped one small, firm breast with his large hand, bringing it to meet his rapacious lips, and sucked the erect nipple deep into his mouth, sending a burst of incredible sensation coursing through her body. Closing her eyes, she threw back her head in exultant delirium. Her body's reactions were suddenly taken out of her control. She was a quivering puppet, sensually arching her hips, digging frantic fingers into Mark's shoulders as an invisible puppet master pulled erotic strings.

He moved to share the bounty of his enthusiastic lips with the other envious breast, removing her blouse with skillful tugs. When she was free at last of the restraining garment, he drew her with slow, deliberate movements to his strong, muscular chest, and the feel of warm, naked skin merging was so blindingly beautiful, so breathtakingly exquisite, she wanted to clasp the sensation to her and hold it close forever.

Sliding her hand irresistibly across his shoulders and down his back, she reveled in the feel of his smooth, strong flesh. She continued her downward path to his lower back, following the ridge of his spine to his lean, hard buttocks, stroking and molding the rounded flesh through the soft material of his slacks.

Her exploring touch brought a deeper, harsher groan from Mark. He sounded strangely as though he were in pain, as he pushed her pliant body urgently to the pallet. He began to kiss the silken softness of her shoulders and neck. Then, moving lower, he teased each tumescent breast with catlike strokes of the moist, warm tip of his tongue, concentrating on the hypersensitive peaks standing sensually erect.

Maggie moaned in disappointment as his mouth left her breasts, then in the same moment gasped with pleasure as he brought his unflaggingly delightful caresses to her navel, his hands on either side of her small waist holding her a willing captive.

With a minimum effort his agile fingers released the fastener on her jeans and slid the zipper down, parting the fabric as he stroked the warm flesh beneath. When the seeking fingers encountered the lace top of her bikini panties, they slid under the sheer fabric without a pause and moved across her slim hips to grasp her warm, rounded buttocks.

His mouth then followed the path his fingers

had blazed. He buried his face in the soft, satiny skin of her stomach while his hand cupped and molded the smooth flesh of her derriere, pressing her closer to his demanding lips.

Maggie's fingers sought his thick blond hair without waiting for a conscious command from her dazed brain. She pressed his head ever closer, her body writhing in unbearable need. She felt she would burst if the incredible mounting tension in her lower body were not assuaged.

"Mark!" she gasped frantically. "Please."

He moved swiftly, rising above her, then lowered his head to absorb the sound of her desire with his hungry mouth. Her tongue sought his, darting eagerly until he mastered the sensuous duel and plunged his tongue intimately into the honeyed depths of her mouth, an erotic mime of the act they were both craving.

Her anguished moan brought his head back so that he could search her bewitched features. "Yes, Maggie?" he asked, seeking permission to continue in a harsh, urgent whisper. His hand rested on her partially bared hip, awaiting a sign of affirmation.

"Oh, yes. Please, Mark," she murmured hoarsely. Then, as he drew in a deep breath and his long fingers began to slide the fabric down, her innate honesty forced her to add, "Mark, you know I don't—"

"I know, princess," he interrupted gently. "You don't like me. Don't worry about it." He looked into her dazed eyes. "Don't you see? It doesn't matter. Right now there are no labels between us. There is only this." He moved to kiss her swollen lips—soft, slow, drugging kisses—leaving her weak with desire, unable to think sanely.

Gradually a combination of sounds crept into their dark haven, disturbing their sensual wonderland. Mark lifted his head lethargically in a distracted acknowledgment of the intruding noise, and at the same time Maggie recognized Henry's excited barks. But there was more—a heavy scratching on the cellar door.

"Civilization intrudes, princess," Mark whispered hoarsely, kissing her lips in a punishingly rough caress.

"What is it?" she whispered, still floating somewhere beyond reality.

Mark sat up, sighing deeply as he clasped his arms around his knees, and looked at her regretfully. "Someone is moving the tree. And as much as I hate to say it," he said ruefully, "the troglodytes must emerge." He picked up her discarded blouse, helping her into it, then buttoning it deftly after a last, lingering touch on her breasts. "Whether we want it or not, love, we are about to be rescued."

He stood, muttering a stifled groan of exasperation as he watched her fasten her jeans and slip into her shoes. Then he moved swiftly to put on his shirt. By the time the light from the opening door flooded the cellar, they were at least physically composed, and the pallet that had been their entire world moments before was once again a stack of burlap bags and a folded canvas tarpaulin.

"Mr. Wilding?" inquired a timid male voice.

Maggie stood still, allowing her eyes to adjust to the bright morning sun, as Mark stepped forward to meet their rescuer.

"Yes, John, I'm here," he replied, evidently recognizing the voice. "What on earth are you doing here?"

"It's your father, sir. He called from Ireland last night and wanted to speak to you immediately."

Maggie followed behind Mark, climbing the stairs slowly, confusion pressing in on her from all sides. Things seemed to be happening so fast. It was just beginning to dawn on her what had almost happened in the cellar, but her brain was too foggy to cope with the thought now.

The back yard seemed to be full of people, but as she watched she realized that there were actually only four men besides Mark's friend. She recognized one as Jake's caretaker, deciding the other three must be neighbors. As Mark conferred with the short, dapper little man he had called John, Maggie stood in the doorway of the cellar, looking around the back yard to assess the damage. Miraculously, except for the magnolia tree and a torn screen, everything was just as she had left it. She had heard of the freakish quality of the winds of tornadoes and was glad this particular twister had decided to leave her aunt and uncle's house standing. She had expected to see nothing but wreckage.

"Hello, Henry," she greeted the joyful dog as he shoved her against the doorjamb in his exuberance. "Yes I'm glad to see you, too, but back off a little and let me breathe." She gave the huge dog a shove. "Where are the others, Henry?" she asked, looking around. But she didn't have to look far. At that moment the whole brood came trooping around the corner of the house, and she breathed a sigh of relief that she wouldn't have to face Uncle Charles with the news of the loss of one of his pets.

Now all she had to worry about was Mark. After what had happened in the cellar, how could she possibly convince him that she wasn't interested in having an affair with him? Her response had been explosive, so there was no way she could say she was not attracted to him. Of course, she thought hopefully, his interest could have been a case of any port in a storm. Now that they were out of isolation, he would probably want to go on to his more sophisticated pursuits.

Maggie turned slowly to find Mark watching her, and the look in his eyes effectively canceled her doubts concerning his continued interest. He said something in a low voice to the man beside him, then walked to where she was standing.

"Well, love," he said, regarding her tense features closely, "it seems our subterranean idyll is at an end." She flinched inwardly at his reminder, looking away as he continued. "John is my father's assistant. When Dad called, trying to get in touch with me, John took it as his sworn duty to find me. Knowing Dad, he was calling to let me know that the trout were biting, but that's not important. What matters is that John got in touch with Jake and, finding that I had left the lodge yesterday afternoon, decided to track me down. After he found my car, the rest was easy. Your leviathan friend"—Mark turned and scowled menacingly at Henry—"led him right to us." He lifted a hand to touch her cheek softly. "The only thing worse than a conscientious assistant is a devoted dog. Next time I promise there'll be no interruptions."

"Mark," she began hesitantly, uncertain of how to begin.

"I have a terrible feeling," he said, "that you're about to say something I don't want to hear. Remember what I told you, Maggie. I don't handle defeat well."

"I'm sorry if I gave you the wrong impression, Mark," she began despite his protests. "Down there in the cellar, nothing was real. It was like you said—no labels . . . just the moment. But now we're back in the real world and I have to remember who and what I am. And what I'm not. I'm simply not the kind of person who can pick up and fly off with a stranger. It goes against everything I believe in." She looked at him, an unconsciously wistful expression in her eyes. "It will be easy for you to find someone else to go with you to St. Thomas, but if I went, it wouldn't be easy for me to forget that I wasn't strong enough to do what I believe is right."

He was silent for a moment, his expression thoughtful, as though he were assimilating her words. "Is it the trip and the fact that I would be paying that's bothering you? Or is it me?"

Maggie hesitated momentarily, then closed her eyes and plunged in. "It's both, Mark. I'm my own person and I pay my own way, yet even if there were no trip involved, I would still say no. You're a very attractive man and it would be too easy to become physically involved with you, but we're so different. We don't think the same way. Our lives are too different, and an affair between us would be a dead-end street."

"What you're trying to say," he said with dry humor, "is that if we slept together, you wouldn't respect me in the morning. I suppose it's no use my telling you that your respect is not my major concern here?"

"Maybe not," she replied, wishing desperately that he would stop dragging it out and simply leave. "But my respect for myself is *my* major concern."

"And making love with me would cause you to lose your self-respect?" he queried softly. For a brief moment something curiously like hurt appeared in his eyes, but before she could grasp its importance, it was gone and the playful twinkle was back. "You may be right, love, but after a night in my arms, I guarantee self-respect would be number two on your list of priorities."

"Mark!" she gasped, unable to suppress a smile at his audacity.

"Okay, Maggie, I'll concede defeat." He paused, a wicked grin appearing on his handsome face, then added, "For the moment."

He turned to pull her toward the group of men, ignoring her attempts to question his last statement. After he had introduced her to John Lowe, who turned out to be an absentminded but sweetly gallant man, Mark turned to speak to the other men. Maggie watched curiously as he joked with them about the tornado. Mark was irrepressible. He seemed totally unaffected by her rejection.

Is that what I wanted? she asked herself reflectively. Did I want to see him touched by my actions? Maggie didn't care for the idea at all. She had said no because it was the right thing to do, not because she wanted to test his feeling for her—which was the proper way to have acted, for evidently Mark had no really deep feelings. He was a self-admitted pleasure-seeker, the total opposite of Maggie's more Calvinistic attitudes.

The men suddenly started to disperse, and minutes later Maggie was standing in the front yard surrounded by six boisterous dogs, watching Mark and Mr. Lowe preparing to leave. As the latter waved before stepping into his small car, Mark approached her again. He pulled a card from his breast pocket, holding it between two long fingers when he stood before her.

"Just in case you have a sudden change of heart, love," he explained, extending the card. "All you have to do is whistle, and I'll be there." His deep voice was confident and amused. As she hesitantly reached for it, he grinned and slipped it inside her blouse, his warm fingers touching the rounded tops of her small breasts. He released the card, stepping back, and they both watched as it fluttered to the ground.

Mark laughed in delight as Maggie raised her eyes to heaven, praying for divine intervention. Then he said in a confiding whisper, "Just as I said—compact, but nice." He stooped to retrieve the card, this time placing it in the pocket of her blouse, then turned and walked to his car, whistling cheerfully and never once looking back to see that she watched until he was out of sight.

# Chapter Three

"Maggie! You're doing it again."

Maggie looked up from the ivy that had held her mesmerized, to see Carrel hanging over the side of her cubicle. This month Carrel had decided to be a redhead, and, although the color should have clashed unmercifully with her bright wardrobe, she looked as exotically striking as always.

Maggie carefully measured the exasperation in Carrel's face. Her friend had been watching her strangely all week, as though puzzled by something. "Doing what again?"

"You keep going off into some weird kind of trance." Her blue eyes brightened with curiosity. "What's up, sweetie? That's an 'I've just met an exciting new man' look if I ever saw one. And I see one almost every time I look in the mirror, so I should know," she added with a wicked smile.

"Don't be silly, Carrel," Maggie said, her voice

heavy with scorn. "I was just trying to remember when I last watered Sophronia."

"Sophronia is a ridiculous name for an ivy plant. It should be something . . . something leafier," she complained, momentarily distracted from her interrogation.

"Maybe," Maggie said, chuckling. "But she's used to it now. How would you like it if someone told you your name didn't suit your looks? Would you change it?"

"Oh, no, Maggie," Carrel said, looking at her friend in accusation. "You're not throwing me off the scent that easily. Now, why have you been brooding all week? What happened last weekend?"

"I haven't been brooding," she said firmly, then saw the stubborn set of Carrel's elegantly molded jaw. "Oh, very well. I spent the weekend with a gorgeous, wealthy man who begged me to fly away with him to exciting foreign cities. Now are you satisfied?"

"Well, at least your fantasies have improved. You used to dream about being president of the company."

Maggie laughed. "You mean you don't believe me?" she asked, fluttering her lashes in artless surprise.

"No," her friend replied unequivocally. "It's sad to say, but you're simply too practical for something as delicious as that. Now, tell me what's bugging you. It can't be Dave, for heaven's sake."

Maggie regarded Carrel's face curiously. "Why couldn't it be Dave?"

"Be reasonable, Maggie, the man wears argyle socks!"

"Oh, no!" Maggie laughed in mock revulsion. "The kiss of death."

"Laugh if you like, sweetie, but it definitely shows something lacking in his character—like good taste. I would be afraid for a man who chose argyle socks to choose me, too." Carrel leaned closer over the cubicle wall, her expression earnest. "You see what I mean?"

"No, Carrel, I don't. And that's the way I want it. Somehow, the thought of understanding the intricacies of your twisted brain scares the hell out of me."

Smiling at her friend's rueful expression, Carrel walked around the low wall and sat casually on Maggie's desk, crossing her long legs. "Enough of this drivel, Maggie. Tell me what happened last weekend. You went to babysit with your uncle's mutts and then . . ."

Maggie sighed heavily, leaning back in her padded chair, staring at the pencil in her hand. "Actually, it happened exactly as I told you." She paused, hesitating momentarily, then said in a rush, "A storm came up, and I was trapped in the cellar overnight with a strange man."

"Maggie!" Carrel shrieked, causing several heads to turn in their direction. "That's marvelous! And was he really rich and handsome?"

"Oh, yes," Maggie said emphatically. "You would have flipped over him."

"Meaning you didn't?"

"Of course not," she said, then felt crimson flood her face as Carrel looked at her dubiously.

"My God," Carrel whispered in awe. "Maggie, you're blushing! I've never seen you blush before."

"That's because I don't blush," Maggie said drily, fanning her face with a magazine.

"But you are," Carrel pointed out, her voice puzzled. "What happened, Maggie? I didn't think any man could affect you that much. Your immunity worries me sometimes, but I'd rather see you uninterested than take a chance on getting in over your head. I would hate for some slick white knight to come along and hurt you."

"There is absolutely no chance of that happening, Carrel," Maggie assured her friend. "Mark may have been slick, but he was definitely no white knight. He was the most . . . frivolous, superficial man I've ever met." She paused as she remembered the look of agony that had contorted his beautiful sleeping face, then murmured softly, "At least he was most of the time." She shook her head to clear it of the disturbing memory. "Anyway, I'll never see him again, so there's nothing to worry about."

"Mark who?"

"According to his card it's Marcus Wilding the Fourth. Do you believe that? I've met a few Juniors, but never a Fourth."

"Mark Wilding!" Carrel closed her eyes weakly. "Maggie, you idiot! Do you realize who he is?"

"Is he somebody?" Maggie asked, casually curious.

"Is he . . ." Carrel sputtered. "Do you have any idea how many women would kill to spend the night with Mark Wilding?"

"I told you he was attractive—in an arrogant kind of way."

"Attractive? Dear Lord, give me strength." She looked at Maggie with pity in her eyes. "The man is only gorgeous. And famous. Not just in Texas— I mean *internationally* famous. Mark Wilding doesn't go where the jet-setters go. He goes where the mood takes him, and they follow. He has been linked with practically every movie star and debutante you could name. Don't you ever read the newspaper?"

"Sure, I do," Maggie said, overwhelmed by her friend's outburst. "But I read it for news, not for that garbage. I'm sure if he had contributed something worthwhile to mankind, I would have heard about it sooner or later." She looked at Carrel's exasperated face. "I realize what you're saying, Carrel. And of course I'm flattered that he asked me to go to St. Thomas with him. It's very good for my ego. But even you, moonstruck as you are, must surely see that it wouldn't work."

"St. Thomas," Carrel murmured in a strangled monotone. "He asked you to go to St. Thomas with him."

"Are you all right?"

"Yes," Carrel replied, dazed. "Just let me get the blood flowing again." She shook her head, the long auburn hair swirling around her face, then drew in a deep breath. "You're right, of course, Maggie. Any kind of relationship between the two of you would be disaster. But"—she leaned closer— "a fling, sweetie? Couldn't you have a casual weekend with him?"

"I don't even like the man, Carrel," Maggie said in frustration.

"Maybe not, but you feel something, and don't say you don't. I haven't asked what happened in that cellar, because it's none of my business." She smiled and shrugged as Maggie raised her brows in doubt and surprise. "I have to draw the line somewhere. Anyway, it's not necessary. In the two years that I've known you, you haven't had one single affair—you haven't even been strongly attracted to anyone—and before that, there was the adorable Barry. You've never said so, but I always got the feeling that Barry was no great shakes in bed."

"Carrel!"

"Well, it stands to reason. He was selfish in everything else. Why should he be any different where sex was concerned?" Although Carrel had met her ex-husband only once, it had been enough to convince her that Maggie had had a lucky escape.

And of course Carrel was right about the sex. Maggie's years with Barry had been miserably frustrating ones. But Maggie never allowed herself even to think of the barrenness, much less speak of it. She looked calmly at Carrel's intent expression. "And your point is?"

"I know you were a virgin when you married— you did say that much. Which means that you are thirty-one years old and have never had a satisfying sexual relationship," Carrel said in a purposeful whisper.

"Oh, horrors!" Maggie gasped teasingly, and laughed. "Do you suppose it's warped my personality?"

"Maggie, be serious. The chance of a lifetime has just been dropped into your lap. It doesn't matter that he's not the white knight. I'll bet knights are lousy in bed anyway. The man turns you on. Don't deny it," she said firmly as Maggie began to protest. "And he's very experienced. Just look at all the women he's managed to please. You'd be a fool to pass him up."

Maggie looked at her friend's earnest face and sighed. "I'm sorry, Carrel. I can't do it. I'm simply not the kind of person who can just pick up and fly away with a man I barely know. The whole idea seems irrational—and totally impractical."

"For heaven's sake, where has being practical got you? Maggie, can't you see . . ."

Before Carrel could finish her argument, Dave walked into the office, and his presence sent her swaying back to her own cubicle, but not before she had sent Maggie a look that promised more to come.

Maggie surreptitiously watched Dave walk across the room to speak with a visiting consultant. Carrel's derogatory comments about his choice of clothing meant nothing to Maggie, but she had to admit that something had changed in the way she felt about him. Before, his bland expression had seemed calm and quietly dignified. Now it simply looked dull.

She shook her head, irritated at her thoughts, and turned back to work on her latest account, but the doubts kept pulling her away from her work. Why should a man who had been ideal last week suddenly seem so ordinary?

It didn't take a genius to figure out that it had something to do with Mark. Admittedly Mark was enough to make any man seem ordinary, but Maggie wasn't the type to be attracted by surface glamour, especially not after Barry. It must have something to do with the way she responded when Mark touched her. She had never felt anything close to the sensations that being in his arms produced.

And what if I never feel that way again? she asked herself, shivering as she was shaken by an aching sense of loss. Maggie! she reproved herself, you're turning into a sybarite. Think of all of Dave's good qualities. His sensibility, his forthrightness, his . . . his . . . *dullness*, she admitted reluctantly.

Biting her lip in exasperation, Maggie pushed the thoughts away.

As the day wore on she kept running into Dave. Each time she studied him carefully. His quiet smile and soft voice didn't seem signs of dullness. He really was an exceptionally nice man. Always considerate of others' feelings. Always ready to help when help was needed. Maggie finally decided that she would be a fool to let someone as artificial as Mark blind her to Dave's good qualities.

At five o'clock she saw Dave again across the room. He smiled at her shyly as she stood talking to Marcie, a beautiful blonde who was relatively new to the office. Maggie said goodbye to Marcie and turned back to her desk, pleased that she had come to her senses regarding Dave. As she turned, she saw Carrel watching her once again over the cubicle wall.

"What was Little Miss Muffet after?"

"I don't know why you don't like Marcie," Maggie said. "She's really very sweet."

"She's a dumb blonde, Maggie. And she's too dumb to realize that dumb blondes are extinct." Carrel's tone was rich with disgust. "She acts so helpless. It makes me sick to see someone like her set equality back fifty years."

"Why on earth should you think that?" Maggie asked, astonished at her vehemence.

"Haven't you ever seen her go into her frail little woman act? And she's always so blasted sweet. She agrees with everything I say—with everything anyone says."

"I think you're overreacting. I thought what we all want—male and female—is the right to be ourselves, whatever that may be. Maybe Marcie is just being herself."

"She's as phony as my hair," Carrel insisted, unaffected by Maggie's logic. "Why was she over here?"

Maggie hesitated, unwilling to bring Carrel's wrath down upon her head. "She was so excited, Carrel. She has a very important date tonight and—"

"Don't tell me she stuck you with the Lawrence account!" her friend fumed. "Maggie, for God's sake, why do you let people do that to you?"

"Calm down," Maggie said. "I didn't have anything planned for tonight, so why shouldn't I finish up for her?"

"I simply hate to see you let people take advantage of you. Especially that over-the-hill cheerleader."

"You're just jealous because she's the only other woman in the office who can make the male contingent look up when she walks by." Before Carrel could voice her indignation, Maggie continued. "Carrel, I'm an adult. Sometimes I feel that just because I'm small you feel you have to watch me constantly in case I burn my fingers or something." Her attractive friend shifted uncomfortably. "I appreciate that you care, but honestly, I know what I'm doing. If people take advantage of me, it's only because I let them, and it's something I'll have to work out by myself."

Carrel looked at her thoughtfully. "It's not your size, Maggie. You're just so damned naive." At Maggie's astonished look, she continued. "Maybe naive is not the right word. Maybe it's just that you're too genuine and nice for your own good. I know you can be tough when you want to be. Like last week when Jerry made that snide remark about your needing extra time on the Reynolds account because you're female, you laid him out flat with your sharp tongue. But that same afternoon you loaned him ten dollars, when everyone knows he's the biggest mooch in the office and never pays his debts."

"I know." Maggie sighed. "I've been giving it a lot of thought lately. The obvious answer is that I'm trying to buy friendship by being so amenable, but I don't think that's it. I only allow people to take advantage of me when it concerns something that doesn't matter to me—like the ten dollars or the time it will take me to finish this work. Surely that's harmless."

"But doesn't it make you mad when you find out you've been had?" Carrel asked curiously.

"That's the point. I know beforehand what's happening. It just doesn't matter to me—at least, not usually."

Shaking her head in exasperation, Carrel said, "I was wrong. You're not naive—you're just plain stupid!"

Maggie chuckled as she watched the tall woman gather her things together, muttering to herself in disgust as she prepared to leave for the day. Maggie knew that she was lucky to have a friend who cared so much, but there were some things that she and Carrel would never see eye to eye on. There was a subtle cynicism about her friend that would never find its way into Maggie's easygoing personality.

Feeling the need to stretch her legs before continuing her work, she decided to walk with Carrel as far as the elevator. In the hall she suddenly found herself being hauled behind a massive potted plant, and she looked at Carrel in amused inquiry as her friend indicated the need for silence with a finger to her lips.

"Your sweet, shy ingenue is about to devour Mr. Wonderful," Carrel hissed, pointing to a spot out of Maggie's range of vision.

"Carrel," she began in protest.

"Hush!"

Feeling like an absolute idiot hiding in the anemic shrubbery, Maggie stood silently and watched as Dave and Marcie walked by, their conversation low and intimate.

"I think you'll like it, Marcie," Dave said softly, his voice unnaturally eager. "They have the best food in Dallas, and the band is great."

"I'm sure I will, Dave," Marcie replied in her shy, sweet voice. "I'm just glad I didn't have to stay late on that Lawrence account. It's so complicated, it would have taken me hours."

"I told you Maggie would do it," Dave said smugly, his voice just reaching them before the elevator doors closed. "She really is a good scout. And so reliable."

Maggie leaned against the bright turquoise wall, closing her eyes as the words seemed to echo in the empty hall.

"Maggie?" Carrel inquired hesitantly. "Are you mad?"

"Now, what on earth gives you that idea?" she asked through clenched teeth.

Carrel didn't answer for a moment, then she said slowly, "I know it sounds crazy, but I swear I can see steam coming from your ears."

Maggie opened her blazing eyes and glared at her friend. "Very funny."

"Maggie! I've never seen you so furious," Carrel exclaimed, obviously pleased. "It's wonderful."

"I'm always glad to entertain my friends," Maggie said, turning abruptly to march back into the office with Carrel following close at her heels. "I mean, being such a good scout and all." She walked to her desk, opened her purse, and pulled out Mark's card.

"Maggie, what are you doing?" Carrel hovered over her friend in excitement as Maggie picked up the telephone. "Maggie, answer me!"

"The next thing you hear, Carrel," she said, suddenly feeling exhilaration flood her veins, "will be the sound of an image shattering."

"You're calling Mark!" Carrel crowed triumphantly.

"Quite," she confirmed, grinning as the memory of his deep voice saying the same word floated through her mind.

The phone was picked up on its second ring, and a soft feminine voice said, "Mr. Wilding's office."

"Is Mr. Wilding in?"

"No, I'm sorry, he's not. May I take a message?"

Maggie hesitated. As much as she hated the fact, she had always believed in signs, and this seemed a definite indication that what she was doing was wrong. "No . . . no, thank you. No message." She started to replace the phone but felt it being jerked from her hand by Carrel.

"Tell him Maggie Simms called," Carrel said, then hung up looking at Maggie with a satisfied smile. "Did you really think I'd let you chicken out at the last minute? It's about time you did something that was strictly for Maggie Simms."

"It was a nice thought," Maggie said. "But I'm afraid your gesture was wasted. You see," she looked at Carrel wryly, "he doesn't know where I live or where I work."

"Then let's call back and leave the information with his secretary."

"No," she stated firmly. "If it had been the right move, he would have been there."

"Maggie, that's dumb."

"Maybe, but that's the way I feel." She smiled at her friend. "Don't worry. I've learned my lesson. From now on—no more Mr. Nice Guy."

Concern showing in her blue eyes, Carrel asked quietly, "Are you very upset about Dave?"

Maggie sighed deeply. "Not really. It's just the idea of everyone regarding me as a patsy."

Later, after Carrel had reluctantly departed, Maggie finished Marcie's work quickly, then sat thinking in the quiet building. She thought she had made such giant strides after the divorce, but now she found that she was making the same mistake, only in bigger proportions. Before, it had been only Barry she was trying to carry on her shoulders. Now she was trying to carry all her coworkers.

Carrel was right. It was time for her to change. Her amenability didn't indicate an easygoing nature. It indicated an inability to say no to pushy people.

Maggie had always thought of herself as a strong, practical person. And in some ways she was, but it was neither strong nor practical to let people use her. It showed a weakness of character that was suddenly very clear. And definitely not attractive.

She glanced moodily at her watch, to find it was already six-thirty—time for her to leave before she was locked in. She straightened her desk, grabbed her purse, and walked out of the office to the elevator, still wondering what her first step should be in overcoming her "reliable patsy" image. Something drastic, surely. Maybe she should take a week off, leaving her work for someone else. She was certainly due a vacation.

Maggie walked out the front door of the building, completely absorbed in her thoughts. Whatever she did would have to be totally self-serving. Something that would simply give her pleasure. Something frivolous and superficial. Something . . .

"You whistled, love?" drawled a deep, lazy voice from close behind her.

# *Chapter Four*

Startled, Maggie whirled around to see Mark leaning indolently against the building she had just left. "Mark! How on earth did you find out where I work?" she gasped, confounded by his unexpected appearance. "Don't tell me Jake told you that, too?"

He pushed away from the wall and looked at her astonished face, a smile making his handsome features even more attractive. "As a matter of fact, Jake didn't know where you lived or worked," he said, his lazy, polished tones sounding unaccountably pleasing to her ears. "I had to telephone your Aunt Sarah for that information."

"Aunt Sarah?" She stared in open-mouthed surprise. "Do you mean she tells anyone who asks where I work?"

"Of course not," he chided, his gray eyes sparkling with amusement. "We talked for quite a while before she told me. Being Jake's nephew got my foot in the door, but I think what turned the tide was the fact that I'm young, handsome, and gainfully employed." He grinned as Maggie closed her eyes in embarrassment.

"What you mean," she said, sighing in resignation, "is that Aunt Sarah has been matchmaking again." She didn't wait for a confirmation—she knew her aunt too well to doubt it. "And you just volunteered the information about your being young, handsome, et cetera?"

"It simply happened to come up in the course of our conversation," he said with feigned innocence. "After it did, she seemed only too eager to give me your place of employment. And so, my darling La Fayette—I am here." He looked amazingly pleased with himself, standing before her expectantly as though waiting for her to praise his ingenuity.

"Why?" Maggie asked, shaking her head in bewilderment. "Why on earth would you go to so much trouble?"

"It was no trouble. I enjoyed talking to your aunt," he said, stubbornly hedging.

"But it doesn't make sense. From what my friend Carrel tells me, you have to beat women off with a stick. Why me?"

He moved closer, putting his hand earnestly to his heart, and said in a soft Southern drawl, "Why, 'cuz Ah fancy you, Miss Maggie." Then, with raised brow, his eyes sparkling with curiosity, he added, "You discussed me with your friend—that's an excellent sign. What did you tell her?"

"I told her you were the most impossible, exasperating man I had ever encountered," she muttered through clenched teeth. "Please be serious for one minute and tell me what this is all about."

"I have to protect my reputation, love. If word got out that you had turned me down, I wouldn't be able to hold up my head in the country-club locker room." His exaggerated hangdog look made her want to hit him. He sighed deeply and continued. "Everyone would say: 'Poor Wilding—he's past it now. Just a pitiful shell of a man. A shadow of his former self.' "

"You're crazy!" she exclaimed, torn between laughter and exasperation. "Why can't you give me a straight answer?"

He looked at her thoughtfully, his playful expression fading. "Perhaps because there is no simple answer," he said, his expression serious and, strangely, revealing slight confusion. "If I told you why it's important to me, Maggie, you really would think I'm crazy. Can't we just say that I had a hunch—a hunch that came in a dream—and I need to find out if it means anything."

"I don't think I understand, Mark." His solemn expression made her a bit uncomfortable.

"Neither do I, princess, but I've got to find out," he repeated, almost to himself. Then suddenly the strange mood was gone and he continued in his normal lighthearted manner. "You called me. Does that mean you couldn't withstand my charms— which, of course, are too numerous to mention— and have decided to go with me to St. Thomas?"

"You egotistical . . ." she sputtered, about to deny his assumption, then remembered her earlier decision. Under his curious eyes, she stiffened her resolve, took a deep breath, and said in a rush, "As a matter of fact, I have. When do we leave?"

"That's wonderful," he said, looking honestly

pleased and, to her surprise, a little relieved. "Come. We'll have dinner and make our plans."

Before she could blink twice, Maggie was being ushered to the silver Mercedes he had been driving the day of the tornado. She leaned back against the black leather seat, wondering giddily what she had gotten herself into. Whatever was in store for her, Mark was certainly not giving her time to change her mind.

After settling his lean frame behind the wheel, he started the engine, then turned to her. "Where's your car?"

"It's in the shop," she replied vaguely, still dazed by her actions. "I rode the bus today."

"Perfect. Then we don't have to worry about getting it home. Where would you like to eat? Do you fancy French . . . Italian . . . Mexican . . . Greek? . . ." He continued the list, waiting for her to interrupt when he reached the right one. "German . . . Hungarian . . . McDonald's? . . ."

"You choose, Mark," she said helplessly, unwilling to make another decision so soon. Her last one still loomed enormous on her mental horizon.

Thirty minutes later Maggie knew she had been wise to leave the choice to Mark, for the tiny café they entered was charming. It specialized in expertly prepared salads of every conceivable kind. Pots of herbs hung from the ceiling, filling the room with a piquantly fresh aroma. The tables of dark, heavy wood and the waitresses—dressed as eighteenth-century English servants—gave the room an informal yet exciting atmosphere.

During dinner Maggie gave herself up to the enjoyment of the evening as Mark kept her entertained with a running commentary on the places all over the world where he had dined. His opinions of what he drily described as "the gauche, the gaudy, and the godawful," were outrageous, and her unrestrained laughter attracted the indulgent attention of the other diners. Before they had finished their salads the people from the surrounding tables had joined them in a hilarious game of "Can-You-Top-This?"

The time flew by, and the wine seemed to go as quickly. As they sipped coffee laced with cognac, Maggie felt deliciously light-headed, and showed an alarming tendency to giggle at inappropriate moments. But she wasn't bothered by her giddiness. Nothing bothered her tonight. She was enjoying herself more than she had in years. She didn't have the time or inclination to think of anything beyond the present, postponing all thoughts of St. Thomas and her proposed fling until a more sober moment.

In her enchanted state, the drive to Maggie's suburban apartment was a magic carpet ride. The wind that whipped her hair into frothy curls did nothing to blow away the cozy mist that enveloped her brain.

The vague, careless directions she had given Mark as they drove must have been adequate, for they arrived in what seemed like record time at her apartment. As he helped her from the car, Mark smiled down at her with a gentle indulgence that escaped her completely as she leaned against his shoulder, feeling a delicious sense of camaraderie.

At her door, Maggie fumbled through her oversized purse for her keys, but they seemed to take on a life of their own, scrambling out of reach each time she thought she had them in her grasp. She held the bag open wide, peering myopically into its depths, then looked at Mark, who was waiting patiently beside her. "They refuse to come out, Mark. What shall I do?"

Chuckling quietly, he took the purse from her and said, "You're not stern enough, love. You simply can't let yourself be browbeaten by a set of keys." He reached into the bag and pulled out an enormous key ring, which held a miniature flashlight, an antique brass police whistle, an all-purpose screwdriver, a wooden plaque proclaiming "GREEN PEACE," and three keys. Looking at the bulky assemblage he muttered, "Of course, I can see how this key ring could easily intimidate one, but you'll simply have to show it who's boss." Immediately selecting the right key, he opened the door and ushered her inside.

"Won't you come in?" Maggie murmured in cheerful unconcern as she watched him disappear into her small kitchen. Turning, she softly hummed a half-remembered melody under her breath while she removed her jacket, then sat on the long yellow sofa, relaxing against the back with a contented sigh.

She couldn't quite recall what it was she had disliked about Mark. "I suppose it will come to me tomorrow," she murmured, her eyes closing irresistibly with the thought. Whatever it was, it couldn't have been very important. He had given her the most delightful evening she had known in a long time. She wasn't certain if it was the wine or Mark that had inspired the carefree flavor of the night, but she couldn't find it in her to be concerned about it one way or the other. Possibly it was a combination of the two. Whatever the cause, she had become more deeply enthralled with each word he had spoken. He was the most spellbinding man she had ever been with. As a raconteur, Mark was worth his weight in gold.

Maggie heard the object of her thoughts moving quietly into the room, and opened one eye to find him standing above her, holding a cup in one long-fingered hand. "What do you actually *do*, Mark?" she asked.

"I'm charming," he replied succinctly, setting the cup on the low white table.

"Oh," she murmured, finding nothing strange in his answer. She opened both eyes and regarded his tall frame as he moved to sit beside her. "You're very good at your job, aren't you?"

"Naturally." He smiled lazily. "I'm successful at everything I undertake." Picking up the cup, he held it to her lips.

Maggie obediently sipped the strong black coffee, gazing quizzically at his smiling face. "Does nothing ever bother you, Mark? Doesn't anything ever ruffle your feathers?"

"My dear Maggie," he said, raising one elegant eyebrow. "If one could stretch one's imagination so far as to picture me with something as ordinary as feathers, they would definitely be well-groomed feathers."

Maggie stared in open-mouthed awe, then expelled an appreciative breath. "I guess that's what I admire most about you," she murmured, almost to herself.

"Are you saying you actually admire something about me?" Mark asked, his eyes widening in surprise. "Evidently my campaign is beginning to pay off. Didn't I tell you I would eventually bring you around to my way of thinking?" He looked at her inquisitively. "Which of my many virtues do you find admirable? The perfection of my appearance? My remarkably even-tempered nature?"

"Your diction," she informed him enthusiastically. "You e-nun-ci-ate everything so clearly. It makes everything I say sound nasal and slurred in contrast." She sighed. "It's beautiful."

Mark looked at her blankly for a moment; then his surprised laughter erupted and filled the room with a deep, rich sound so contagious that Maggie joined him, not knowing or caring why they laughed.

Setting the cup on the coffee table, he pulled her into his arms in an exuberant hug. "You're priceless." He kissed the tip of her slightly retroussé nose. "Sometimes, Maggie, I want to fold you away in my wallet so that I can carry you next to my heart and take you out whenever I need a lift." He pushed the curls from her forehead in a gentle caress. "Having you admire my diction was not exactly what I had in mind, princess, but I suppose it will have to do for a start." His large hand slid down her face, exploring her delicately molded cheekbone, discovering the hint of obstinacy in her gently squared jaw, then slipped to her neck, ruffling the baby-fine curls that clung to her vulnerable nape.

Shielded from reality by a warm, alcoholic glow, Maggie snuggled closer in his arms, moving her face against his broad shoulder like a satisfied cat. A contented "M-m-m-m" was her only attempt to hold up her end of the conversation.

As though her murmur of pleasure were a signal, he launched a delightful series of soft, nibbling kisses, beginning on her forehead, then wandering down to her closed eyelids, across her cheek to the sensitive skin behind her ear, then to the corner of her slightly parted lips.

"Mark," she whispered, her husky voice sounding sensual even to her own ears. "Are you trying to seduce me?"

"Yes," he answered softly, without hesitation, his breath against her lips causing them to tingle in awareness. "Am I succeeding?"

Maggie chuckled lazily, lifting her heavy lids to look into his eyes and discovering they had turned several shades deeper, to a glinting steel gray. "You're a devious man, Marcus Wilding the Fourth," she murmured. "But I don't care, because"—she dropped her voice once again to a confiding whisper—"I'm a little tiddly." Bringing her hand to the back of his neck, she threaded her fingers through the thick, springy blond hair and, with the slightest pressure, urged him back to her lips.

But instead of continuing with the aforementioned seduction, Mark lifted his head and looked carefully at her languid features. "And if you weren't 'tiddly,' as you so quaintly put it, you *would* care?"

"Probably," she answered distractedly, staring at his lips in deep concentration as she stroked the muscles of his strong neck. When he remained silent, she raised her eyes to meet his. "Does it matter?"

After a momentary hesitation he said, "No . . . of course not," then lowered his head to kiss her waiting lips, gently at first, then with a growing urgency.

Maggie sighed deeply at the first touch of his warm mouth and allowed herself to be carried along on the sensuous tide. Then, just as she was tightening her hold on his neck, Mark lifted his head again.

"Damn," he muttered under his breath, drawing her head down to cradle it against his shoulder with one large hand. "I must be getting senile."

Maggie raised her head to look at him in puzzled inquiry. "What's wrong?"

"It seems," he said drily, "that at this late stage in my life I'm developing principles." His tone was rich with disgust.

"Oh, Mark," she commiserated, unable to suppress her laughter. "How awful for you."

"The understatement of the year," he muttered, then framed her face with his hands, outlining her lower lip with his thumb as he looked into her drowsy brown eyes. "But don't think this is the end of it, Maggie. Just because I want you sober and aware when we make love doesn't mean I've gone entirely soft in the head. Tomorrow night your tipple will be lemonade, and nothing short of cardiac arrest will stop me—understand?"

"Yes, Mark, I understand," she said, smiling in sympathy. "I'm sure this is just a temporary aberration. Tomorrow you'll probably be back to your old unscrupulous self."

Giving her a brief, hard squeeze, he laughed. 'You're just saying that to make me feel better." He stood, pulling her to her feet as well. "I'd better leave now, before I come to my senses."

At the door he turned to give her a last lingering kiss. "Just to hold me until tomorrow, love," he whispered, tipping her chin with one long finger. "I'll pick you up at three, and Maggie . . . ?"

"Yes?"

"You won't change your mind again, will you?"

His expression was unreadable as he waited for her answer.

"No . . ." She hesitated, then continued. "No, of course not."

He regarded her face for a moment as though trying to read her thoughts. Then, apparently finding what he sought, he nodded and turned to go.

Maggie watched Mark disappear into the darkness, then closed the door behind him, leaning against it to find that, although she was no longer under the influence of the excellent wine they had had with dinner, something more potent was moving in her bloodstream. Something more intoxicating than alcohol.

Before she could follow the disturbing train of thought and examine what was happening to her, the quiet was disrupted by the shrill sound of the telephone, and she moved quickly to stop its insistent ring.

"Hello." Her voice came out dreamy, with none of its usual briskness.

"Maggie, it's me," Carrel said. "I've been calling all evening. Where have you been?"

Maggie's face took on a hunted look at the sound of Carrel's voice. She was reluctant to discuss her evening until her mind was clearer, but she knew from experience that her friend would be difficult to put off. "I went out to dinner. You would love this place, Carrel. Their salads were out of this world and the decor was fantastic. They had hung little—"

"You're hiding something," Carrel said suspiciously. "That's a very sneaky voice you're wearing. Who were you with?"

"What makes you think I was with someone?"

"Come on, Mag, 'fess up."

"Carrel, why do you automatically assume that I owe you an explanation of my whereabouts?" Her voice was stilted in a last-ditch effort to evade her inquisitive friend.

"Boy," Carrel breathed. "This story must really be good. What did you do—knock Little Miss Muffet in the head with a tire tool and steal Mr. Wonderful?"

"Don't be ridiculous. Of course I didn't. I . . . I was with"—she dropped her voice to a barely intelligible mumble—"Mark. Now can I go to bed?" she added hurriedly.

"Did you say Mark?" her friend squealed. "But how? When . . . ?"

"Carrel," she interrupted. "I'm very tired and I'm not going to stay up all night to give you a blow-by-blow account of my evening. Just be satisfied with the fact that everything has turned out the way you wanted."

"You're going with him," she breathed in excitement. "When?"

"Tomorrow at three."

"You can't!" Carrel shrieked.

Maggie held the phone away from her ear, frowning in exasperation at her friend's about-face. "Please explain to me—and even though I'm probably permanently deaf I'll try to understand—why you've changed your mind. You were the one who said I needed this . . . this fling in order to aid my growth as a well-rounded human being. You are absolutely—"

"Your clothes," Carrel said urgently. "You have nothing but those too, too sedate business clothes. You're embarking on an adventure, Maggie. You've got to capture the spirit of the thing. No one, but no one can be adventurous in those things you wear. You always look so . . . so trustworthy."

"I do have other clothes."

"Yes, I've seen them," Carrel said in an offhand way, effectively dismissing Maggie's entire wardrobe. "What you need is an emergency shopping trip. I'll take tomorrow off and we'll see what we can do."

Maggie groaned, seeing herself being backed into a corner. "I'm old enough to choose my own clothes," she complained.

"Age has nothing to do with it. If I leave it to you, you'll end up buying tailored pajamas and a three-button, double-breasted, pin-striped bikini."

"Carrel," Maggie said through clenched teeth, her tone threatening.

"Don't try to thank me, Maggie. You'd do the same for me—if you weren't blessed with the taste of a turnip."

Before Maggie could utter the imprecations that leaped to mind, her enthusiastic friend informed her that she would pick her up at eight the next morning and Maggie not so gracefully gave in to Carrel's cheerful bulldozer tactics.

As she prepared for bed, Maggie was consumed by a feeling of helplessness—a feeling entirely new to her. She was accustomed to taking charge and getting things done on her own. Now she felt she was being shoved along a one-way path . . . a path that led straight to Mark.

## Chapter Five

At eight sharp the next morning, as Maggie was making the arrangements for her days off, she heard Carrel's knock on the door. Squaring her shoulders, she hung up the phone and walked slowly to admit her friend, the courageous resignation in her bearing reminiscent of a prisoner facing the firing squad. She opened the door to an explosion of enthusiasm that took her breath away.

For the next four hours she was shuffled from one shop to another, trying on mountains of clothes at each one. Carrel seemed to think Maggie would be changing clothes every hour on the hour. After her friend insisted she buy a microscopic sleep teddy in melon silk with sheer ecru lace and a matching floor-length peignoir, Maggie went into a state of blissful catatonia that insulated her against any further shock. She surfaced long enough to rebel against having her hair bleached platinum blond, but couldn't halt the army of eager experts who creamed, massaged, and manicured her into shape.

At twelve-thirty Maggie looked at her smiling friend across a small table in the tea room of yet another department store. Stunned astonishment filled her golden-brown eyes as she asked, "Do you do this every time you meet a new man?"

"I don't have to, sweetie. I treat my body like the finely tuned instrument it is—for which my men are eternally grateful," Carrel added with a grin. "I don't think you even know that you have a body."

"Oh, I know it, all right. I feed it and bathe it and clothe it. Is all the rest really necessary?"

"That's what I mean." Carrel's tone was exasperated. "You said yesterday that Marcie and I make all the men in the office look up when we walk by. Have you never noticed how they look when you walk by?"

"Me?" Maggie asked, surprised. "You're crazy. When I stand next to you or Marcie, I look like the boy next door."

"You're such a bozo! You think that just because you don't have bazooms that you have to carry around in a wheelbarrow, you're not sexy," Carrel said, raising her voice slightly in her indignation—to Maggie's extreme discomfort. "Maggie, if you dressed to emphasize your sexuality instead of hiding it, you would have men falling all over you. I've seen their reactions when they first hear that husky, bedroom voice of yours. Then they tune in to what you're saying and immediately tune out. They start out wondering what it would be like to undress you and end up wondering if you're a robot in drag—a robot with very dull taste in clothing, I might add."

Maggie listened in unbelieving silence, then shook her head skeptically. "That doesn't make sense, Carrel. If everyone is lusting after my body like you say, why did Dave ask me out once, then switch to Marcie? Was he put off by my business suits, too?"

"If any man is brave enough to get past your sober appearance, your sober brain stops them flat. You act like a damned computer." Carrel sipped her tea, looking at Maggie as though gauging her mood, then continued. "You're a business person first and a woman second. If you really wanted Dave, you would have gone all out to get him, and he knows that. You're the most reliable, efficient sales consultant in that office, Maggie. But when a man takes out a woman he wants someone who sees him as a man, not a business colleague."

"What you mean is a woman has to drool all over a man to keep him interested. I thought these were enlightened times. I thought men and women were eons past the game-playing stage."

"Maggie." Carrel sighed. "You've been out in the single world for two years and you're just now opening your eyes to look at it. Forget everything you've read about the new equality. This is reality. When it comes to men and women and their relationships, things don't change. The games you're so contemptuous of are a part of nature. Look at the peacocks. When a peacock spreads that beautiful plumage he's so very proud of, do you think he's going to look twice at the peahen who says, "Yeah, that's nice, but how are you at building nests?" Of course not. It's the peahen who flutters her lashes and goes weak with admiration that he'll follow."

Maggie toyed with her spoon for a minute, then looked at Carrel's serious face. "Do peahens have eyelashes?" After she laughingly dodged the redhead's napkin, Maggie smiled wistfully and said, "I see your point and I suppose it's valid, but it's still a little disappointing. It seems dishonest to me. If I sincerely admire a man, I want to be able to tell him so without artifice." Maggie crumbled the bread on her plate thoughtfully. "I've seen the eye games. You look a man over in a way that says he's something special and he responds in a similar fashion, but it's not sincere. It's all programmed."

"To you it may seem artificial, but to the people involved it's very real. I'm not suggesting you have to pretend to be brainless like Marcie, but there is a happy medium. It's simply a matter of compromise. You have to give men what they need, in order to get what you need. And like it or not, you live in this world, too. You're either going to have to play the game or sit waiting until you're gray for a man who thinks as you do." Pushing her plate aside, Carrel propped her elbows on the table and rested her chin in her hands. "And now that I've done my bit to straighten you out, tell me everything you left out yesterday."

Maggie began her tale hesitantly, slightly uncomfortable about discussing Mark. She had pushed him to the back of her mind and was afraid of what would happen if she took her doubts out to look at them. Carrel listened with narrow-eyed concentration, avidly drinking in every word as Maggie gave her a carefully expurgated version of the events of the past weekend.

Maggie gave the facts as objectively as possible, and as soon as she had filled her friend in on Mark's sudden appearance the night before, Carrel sighed deeply, envy and excitement sparkling in her clear blue eyes as she lit a cigarette, then said, "He's perfect, Mag. He's just exactly what you need. If anyone can get you to look at yourself as an attractive, sexy female, Mark Wilding can. It doesn't matter that he's not your type—he'll make your femininity blossom so that your knight on a white charger will at least recognize you as a woman when he eventually gets 'round to finding you."

Looking at her friend curiously, Maggie remarked, "That's the second time you've said something about a knight. Do I seem to be looking for something as chimerical as a knight?" She searched Carrel's face. "Do you think I'm being unrealistic about the things I expect in a man? I would hate to think I'm not capable of dealing with a real, live man."

"Damn it, Maggie!" Exasperation was evident in Carrel's voice and the abrupt way she stubbed out her cigarette. "When are you going to stop trying to be Miss Polly Perfect? For God's sake, allow yourself an occasional imperfection. Haven't you learned yet that a perfect person makes all us imperfect slobs uncomfortable? Slouch when you walk, or forget your mouthwash or *something*, but stop trying for sainthood."

Maggie sat in stunned silence, trying to assimilate her friend's forceful words. Do I make my friends uncomfortable? she wondered in shock. Because I want to be the best I can be, do I give the impression that I think I'm better than everyone else? Carrel's softly muttered curse interrupted her thoughts, and Maggie raised her eyes to catch her friend's rueful expression.

"Oh, Lord," Carrel said under breath. "Now I've given you something else to worry about. Maggie, forget what I said. You haven't got time to root out a fault today. It's one o'clock already and you still have to pack."

"Pack?" Maggie stared blankly at her friend; then the present overtook her in a rush, and she opened her eyes wide. "Pack! Oh, Lord, I've got to pack!"

She stood, grabbing her oversized purse, then stopped, perspiration springing out in the palms of her hands. "Carrel," she said slowly, her eyes lowered to the discreet gray carpet, "I've got to pack so that I can fly to a place I've never been to with a man I barely know." She looked at her friend in curiosity. "Are you sure this is me?" Maggie closed her dazed brown eyes for a moment, then opened them to add, "I feel so strange, as though it were all happening to someone else. Are you sure I'm doing the right thing?"

"Yes, I'm positive," Carrel said, grabbing her arm and walking purposefully toward the door. "And you are not going to back out at the last minute. Just pretend he's a dose of castor oil. You need him for your emotional health."

Unexpectedly Maggie began to giggle, relaxing in spite of herself as she thought of Mark's reaction to being compared to castor oil. "Okay, I promise I won't back out, but . . ." Maggie looked at her more experienced friend as they walked. "What if he's . . . I mean, what if he wants . . ."

"Maggie, you baby." Carrel laughed. "Don't tell me you're afraid he'll get you to St. Thomas and start sucking on your toes or something." Carrel shook her head in wonder. "You're so dumb. You spent the night in a dark cellar with the man. He had every opportunity to smear you with jam or any other weird thing that came to mind." She pulled Maggie to a stop and looked at her sternly. "Did he do anything that disgusted or worried you?"

Carrel's pointed question brought a vivid picture to Maggie's mind. A picture of herself lying in Mark's arms. She relived the gentleness of his touch, his delight in her body as he undressed her. She shook her head as a tingling warmth spread throughout her body. Her face was slightly flushed with the sensual memory as she answered softly. "No, of course he didn't. And you're right. I'm dumb."

"That's what I thought," Carrel said smugly, eyeing her glowing features. "Now, get moving or you'll be late."

Carrel's animated—and slightly irreverent—chatter kept Maggie occupied on the drive to her apartment. As they unloaded a trunk full of packages, Maggie wondered for the first time what she had bought. Other than the sleep teddy—which stood out vividly in her mind—she had no idea what the sacks and boxes contained.

"Carrel," she asked suspiciously as they dumped their load on the sofa, "exactly how much did I spend today?"

"Don't worry about it," Carrel said, shrugging with cheerful unconcern. "They were worth every penny. And anyway, I've heard that peanut butter is very healthy food."

"That much, huh?" Maggie gave a long-suffering sigh and muttered, "I just hope you bought something pawnable."

Leaving Carrel to sort out their purchases, she went to the hall closet to dig out her luggage. She carried the two pieces she would need into the bedroom and laid them on the bed. As she began removing a few odds and ends from the pale-blue suitcase, Carrel entered the room carrying a periwinkle-blue silk dress draped across her arm.

She stopped suddenly, looking dubiously at the open cases on the bed. "Maggie, that stuff is awful. It looks like surplus from World War II. If you had told me you needed new luggage, we could have bought some today."

"Thank heaven for small favors," Maggie grumbled. "There is nothing wrong with this. It's good, sturdy luggage. My parents gave it to me when I went away to college."

"That was thirteen years ago, stupid," Carrel said, shaking her head in exasperation. "It's banged up and scarred and it simply doesn't look like it's about to fly away on an exciting adventure. It looks like it's going on a Greyhound to visit Aunt Martha."

"Then it matches me. So if I can go, it can go," Maggie said thrusting her chin forward obstinately.

"Okay, don't get so huffy. I simply wanted you to have a touch of panache."

Maggie looked at her friend, a thoughtful expression on her face. "What if I can't handle panache? Maybe I'm supposed to be the reliable old slippers type. Maybe being a good scout is in my genes."

"That's unmitigated applesauce and you know it," Carrel argued. "Good scouts are not born that way. It takes years of practice. The rut you're in is simply habit, and now you're going to start forming new, less boring habits."

A strange expression crossed Carrel's striking face, and she walked to the window, nervously stroking the silk dress as she walked. She looked out into the courtyard, silent for a moment, then turned to face Maggie. "What I said in the tearoom— I didn't mean . . ."

"Don't apologize, Carey," Maggie interrupted, feeling her friend's embarrassment. "You know you can say anything to me."

"I know. But I wouldn't hurt you for anything in the world." She hesitated, moistening her lips. "It was a case of two neuroses meeting. You're always so careful to examine your motives, making sure everything you do is logical and right. I feel so damned inadequate, and every time you work out another fault, it seems to put me a rung lower on the ladder."

Maggie sat slowly on the bed, stopped in her tracks by Carrel's unexpected confession. "But you're the most secure person I've ever met—other than Mark, that is. You're beautiful and intelligent and witty. For heaven's sake, you absolutely exude self-confidence."

Carrel shrugged her elegant shoulders and sat beside Maggie on the bed. "It's all bluff. Something I began years ago. I figured if everyone thinks I'm sure of myself, maybe someday it'll take root and I really will be." She looked at Maggie as though struck by a sudden thought. "Maybe Mark is all bluff, too."

"No way," Maggie stated unequivocally. "There is no way his confidence is only skin deep. It goes all the way to the bone. He was born knowing exactly who and what he is. And if he occasionally forgets, I'm sure there are dozens of women just waiting to remind him. You'll see what I mean when you meet him."

Carrel stood, shaking away her reflective mood. "I suppose you're right. Anyway, we don't have time to analyze either Mark or me right now. Come on, old girl, let's get moving."

For the next thirty minutes they moved back in time and were teenagers preparing for their first date, giggling hysterically one moment, shrieking in anguish the next. Carrel hurriedly packed the new clothes while Maggie showered and dressed.

Maggie was slipping into honey-colored linen pants when the doorbell rang. All motion in the room was halted abruptly; then they turned slowly to look at each other.

"Do you want me to let him in for you?" Carrel asked, trying very hard to sound nonchalant.

Maggie nodded silently, wiping the palms of her damp hands on her slacks. She watched Carrel leave the room; then, as though in a trance, picked up the short, belted jacket and pulled it on. After slipping into her leather sandals, she moved to the door, pinned a brave smile on her face, and walked into the living room.

Mark was standing with his back to her, laughing softly at what Carrel called her party prattle. Was it only last night that he'd been here in this room making love to her? In her mind he was so separated from reality, she might have only dreamed him. But his tall, lean frame was too solid, too real to be a dream.

As though sensing her presence, Mark turned his head in her direction, regarding her silently. Then he held out one hand to her and the invisible puppet master once more pulled the strings to move her across the room and lay her hand in his.

"Hello, Maggie Simms."

His deep voice sent electric sparks shooting through her, concentrating in a tingling mass in her fingertips. "Hello." The soft huskiness of her voice gave the whispered word an intimacy Maggie had not intended. She wanted to take it back. She wanted to move away and give a new, casual tone to their meeting, but his eyes held her rooted to the spot. The silver sparks radiating from the irises seemed to catch fire while he gazed steadily at her until she felt the silver flame as a physical touch on her face.

Suddenly Maggie realized she had tightened her hold on his hand and was clutching it fiercely. She slid her hand from his in embarrassment, turning her head away just as Carrel's voice penetrated her spell.

"No, really," Carrel said to no one. "Begging won't help—I simply can't stay. I promised my neighbor I would pick up some denture cleaner for her, and it's a treat I've been looking forward to all day."

Laughing softly at her friend's idiocy, Maggie walked to the door and waited as Carrel said goodbye to Mark. She gazed at the pale-green carpet until Carrel was standing before her.

"Maggie," Carrel whispered as she walked out the door, "he's delicious. If I weren't positive he would notice the switch, I'd lock you in the closet and go in your place."

Maggie closed the door, took a deep breath, then turned quickly to lean against it. "Well," she said, intending to sound bright and breezy. Instead she sounded scared and squeaky, so she began again. "Well, Mark, what do we do now?"

Without giving him a chance to answer, she pushed away from the door and walked to the center of the room, talking nonstop. "This is all new . . . at least, the flying away part is new . . . I'm certainly not trying to say I'm a virgin . . . I was married for six years, for heaven's sake, and . . . well, anyway, what I mean is, I've never done this sort of thing before and . . ." Maggie clenched her fists and closed her eyes tightly. "God," she whispered, "please don't let me say, 'I'm not that kind of girl.' " She waited a moment, then opened her eyes, raising them heavenward to murmur, "Thank you," then lowered her gaze to Mark. "I'm ready," she said firmly.

Mark looked at her silently for a brief moment, then smiled a gentle, understanding smile and walked to her. As he enfolded her in his strong arms, she relaxed against him, snuggling into the comforting warmth of his body.

"You poor baby," he whispered against the top of her head. "Don't worry. It will be all right—I promise."

"Oh, Mark," she groaned. "I'm such an ass."

"Yes, love," he agreed soothingly. "But the loveliest ass I've ever seen." He tilted her chin, forcing her to look at him. "Feel better now?"

Smiling up at him, Maggie said, "Yes, thank you."

"Then let's go," he said, hugging her enthusiastically. "Blue skies and excitement are waiting just beyond the horizon, love."

"I don't think my nerves can stand any more excitement," she murmured helplessly as she moved past him to get her purse and the smaller case. Mark followed, chuckling as he lifted her other case, and Maggie thought what an attractive sound his laugh was. It was the last truly lucid thought she was to have for quite a while.

From that moment on things moved too quickly for thought. An enthusiastic young man drove them to the bustling regional airport, where enthusiastic young people behind the counter turned them over to enthusiastic young stewardesses. Maggie suffered their exuberance in silence, smiling indiscriminately and, she feared, somewhat vacuously, growing more and more nervous with each passing minute—all under the smilingly watchful gray eyes of her tall companion.

When, after take-off, the attractive attendant offered them a drink, Maggie's acceptance was comically grateful. "Yes, please. I'll have—" she began.

"Lemonade," Mark interrupted, his voice quiet but emphatic.

Maggie turned to look at him inquiringly. He was leaning back, resting his head against the high-back seat. Glancing at her from the corners of his eyes, his lips softened in a sensual smile, and he murmured, "Lemonade—remember?"

Maggie's eyes widened as she remembered his promise of the night before, and she swallowed audibly before haltingly requesting a soft drink.

"You seem a little nervous, love," Mark said, his tone concerned but his eyes twinkling with mirth. "Is something wrong?"

"No . . . no, of course not. It's just . . ." She felt hopelessly pressured—pressured by all the enthusiasm, by Mark's smiling eyes. "Everyone is so damnably cheerful," she complained unreasonably.

"I'm sorry," he said apologetically, subduing a

grin as her eyes narrowed suspiciously. "I could stand and make a speech on war or famine if it would make you feel better."

Maggie's rude comment on what he could do with his speech was mercifully obscured by loud laughter from the seats behind them, and she hurriedly excused herself to go to the ladies' room.

But the aluminum-walled bathroom did nothing to soothe Maggie's frayed nerves. She felt she had fallen down the White Rabbit's hole, encountering strange creatures in a strange land, with every one of them accusing *her* of being the odd one. It seemed like a well-planned conspiracy to make her feel that, even if she couldn't recognize it, everything happening to her was perfectly normal.

Maggie leaned weakly against the door, the fog that had surrounded her all day lifting at last. This is crazy, she moaned silently. Why am I here? Surely there must be a less traumatic way to break a bad habit. She could have started small and gradually worked her way up to this. A novice climber doesn't start with Mt. Everest, she told herself. He begins with tiny little hills and advances slowly to mountains.

So what do I do now? she asked herself frantically. My silver-eyed Mr. Everest is out there waiting for me to return to my seat, so it's a little late for second thoughts. After all, no one was going to offer to turn the plane around for her. Maybe if she offered to pay for her own ticket Mark would forget his plans for her. Pay for it with what? she thought contemptuously. After that shopping trip, I'll be lucky to have peanut-butter money for the next month.

Maybe I could talk my way out of it, she thought.

But that seemed vaguely dishonest, like breaking a promise or going back on her word. She shook her head, reluctantly rejecting the thought. That was not Maggie's way. So, she decided, breathing deeply in resignation, there's no help for it. I'll simply have to go through with it.

She wished suddenly that she and Mark were alone. When he was holding her everything seemed right. It was only when she left his arms that this affair seemed to go against her nature. This fling business was simply not her style. She had never been impetuous, and action without careful thought behind it was worrisome to her orderly mind.

However, according to Carrel, it wasn't her nature at all, but merely a habit she had acquired over the years. It was all academic anyway, and deciding between the two would accomplish nothing —except to delay the inevitable. She simply had to accept the situation and carry on from there. Having made the decision, Maggie's panic subsided somewhat. She was almost relieved to find no action was called for, as she made her way back to her seat before she could think of another futile argument with which to torment herself.

Mark seemed untroubled by her extended absence. He was still reclining comfortably in the seat with his eyes closed. Maggie quietly resumed her former position, being very careful not to disturb him. Breathing a sigh of relief, she leaned back in the seat, then turned her head to look at the cause of her turmoil.

In repose, his features were even more striking than usual. With a face like that he could have been an actor or model. She allowed her gaze to drift down his broad shoulders and chest. His silk suit fitted like a second skin, perfectly molded to his lean frame. Maggie couldn't imagine him in anything other than the expensive clothing he always wore. He probably wears a smoking jacket when he's relaxing, she thought, smiling inwardly.

"Was it too small?"

His softly spoken words brought her gaze back to his face. His eyes were open, an unfathomable smile causing the corners to crinkle slightly, and he was studying her face. Maggie stared at him, lines of puzzlement appearing on her forehead. "Was what too small?"

He lifted her hand from her lap, holding her outspread fingers against his. Staring at their two hands, he turned them first one way, then another, as though fascinated by the difference in size. Then, glancing up at her face, he said casually, "The window in the ladies' room. I thought perhaps you went in there to climb out the window and escape the ogre." He returned his gaze to their intertwined fingers. "Since you were gone so long, I was afraid you had tried it and gotten stuck. I was just about to ask the stewardess for a blowtorch, when you returned."

"There's no window in the—" she began, then caught sight of the merriment dancing in his eyes. "Very funny," she muttered, pulling her hand away and returning it to her lap.

A loud, cheerful argument broke out across the aisle, and Maggie glanced toward the sound, around at the other passengers, and then back to Mark. "I thought all you wealthy playboys owned your own jets," she said, her voice sweetly sarcastic.

"You're just chock-full of preconceived notions, aren't you?" he asked, looking at her with raised eyebrows. As she had the grace to shift her gaze uncomfortably, he chuckled and said, "Actually, I do own one tiny, little jet, but I didn't think it would impress you, so I let John use it for his trip to Austin. Was I wrong? Would you have been impressed?"

"No," she stated bluntly.

"Good. I'd hate to make a tactical error so early in our relationship."

Our relationship, Maggie echoed silently. Why did he have to say that? If he would just stop making those intimate comments and looking her over like a rib roast he had picked up for dinner, maybe she could at least get to the hotel before turning into a sniveling coward.

But he didn't take his eyes off her. Even when Maggie pretended to sleep, she could feel him watching her, feel that silver flame penetrating her flesh like the rays of the hot summer sun. Throughout the changeover in Miami, he watched —and smiled. When she chattered like a silly schoolgirl, he watched—and smiled. During the drive from the airport in Charlotte Amalie, he watched and—damn his silver eyes—he smiled.

The smile grew to menacing proportions in her frantic mind. In the backseat of the taxi, the evening darkness cast mysterious shadows around his tall figure, and the barely distinguishable movement of his lips as the smile widened sent tremors rippling through her exhausted body. She glanced hurriedly out the window, to find they were climbing steadily up a winding road, passing through what appeared to be a residential area.

"The hotel . . ." The words seemed to stick as her throat closed in a nervous spasm. "The hotel must have a nice view if it's on the top of this hill."

"Hotel?" he asked quietly.

"The hotel where we're . . ." She paused as a new and terrifying thought took hold. "We're not staying at a hotel," she murmured in defeat.

"No, we're not." His voice was almost a whisper.

Their arrival at their destination, the transfer of their luggage, and the departure of the taxi all took place in a blur of motion. Maggie stood dazed the whole time. What's happening? she thought in bewilderment. At her apartment, he had been charming, and so thoughtful of her feelings. Then suddenly he had turned into something out of a late-night horror movie.

She stood in the eerie shadows of the tiled entry hall, oblivious to her lush surroundings, and watched, a chill running down her spine, as Mark closed the enormous front door with a loud, echoing thud, then leaned against it.

"Maggie," he said quietly, his voice serious— deadly serious. "I want you to be comfortable here, but there is one thing I will not tolerate, so listen carefully." His voice dropped to an ominous whisper, and his polished accent became a startlingly good imitation of Bela Lugosi. "Don't ever go into the room at the end of the hall, my lovely. I keep ten of my wives chained in there."

Maggie closed her eyes, inhaling a deep, slow breath, then opened them to glare at him in narrow-eyed fury. "You low-down"—she whispered the words in venomous rage, her voice barely audible above Mark's laughter, as she searched the hall for something to throw—"conniving, misbegotten worm!" She picked up an empty vase and held it threateningly high as she advanced toward

Mark, who was leaning weakly against the door, his large frame shaking uncontrollably. "You did that on purpose. All that silent watching. And that evil smile!"

"Now, Maggie," he gasped, circling around her warily, still laughing. "Be reasonable, love. You looked as though you were about to enter Bluebeard's castle." He smiled at her beguilingly. "It was an irresistible impulse."

"Yes, of course," she said through clenched teeth, not pausing in her vengeful stalking. "That's perfectly reasonable. I understand all about irresistible impulses, you see, because I have one right now. To do you great bodily harm with this vase!"

"Not this vase," he said, stepping forward and effortlessly removing it from her grasp. "It's an antique. Let me find you something less valuable to bash me with." He looked around the room, ignoring Maggie's indignant gasp. "Paul must keep something around here especially for bashing."

"Paul?"

"The owner of this house," he explained, picking up a porcelain figurine, then shaking his head regretfully as he replaced it. "He lets me stay here when I have business in town. Although he rarely uses the house, I'm sure he would miss all of these things. Shall we go into the living room to search for something suitable? What you want is something solid enough to do me an injury, yet not too heavy to lift."

"Oh, shut up," she muttered irritably, the impetus of her anger dwindling, leaving her drained.

Mark looked into her tired eyes and frowned in concern. "You look exhausted, Maggie, and my ridiculous clowning didn't help matters. Would you like something to eat? Or perhaps a hot bath?"

The thought of lying in a hot tub was too tempting to resist. "A bath, please," she said, willing to forgive him anything for a chance to soak away her frazzled nerves.

Indicating a door down the hall, Mark followed her, carrying her bags. She opened the door onto a large, spacious bedroom. He flicked the light switch behind her, illuminating the room and, to her overactive imagination, spotlighting an enormous canopied bed. She glanced away quickly as Mark deposited her bags on the bed, then turned to face her.

"The bathroom is through there," he said, casually waving toward a door. "Paul has an excellent housekeeper, so it should be fully stocked."

Maggie moved to the bed to open her large case and remove her nightwear. She raised her eyes to find Mark leaning against the carved end post, and clutched the flimsy garments protectively to her chest. "I'm sure I'll find everything I need, Mark," she said, moistening her lips nervously. "You'll want to eat dinner now . . ." She paused, her voice fading away to nothing. "Or something."

"No, I'm not hungry either." He walked to the closet, pulling out a pale-gray robe. "I think I'll shower and then—" he stretched, covering an obviously feigned yawn with his hand, "then I think I'll turn in."

# Chapter Six

Maggie turned away in frustration, walking into the bathroom and locking the door behind her. Her time had run out, and there was no use trying to postpone the inevitable.

Moments later she stepped into the huge sunken tub, paying little attention to the elegant fixtures. One thing and one thing only occupied her mind— Mark. Mark leaning against the bedpost. Mark stretching his lean body, watching her intently.

Damn him! Why couldn't he have let her slide into it last night, when her doubts had been temporarily subdued? Why drag it out until her nerves were stretched to the breaking point? Why . . .?

Hold on a second, Maggie, she cautioned herself. It was grossly unfair to blame Mark for her troubles. Coming with him had been her own decision. It wasn't his fault that she had lost her nerve at the last moment. He had no idea what had motivated her decision to come. Not that the reason mattered now, she thought. She was here, and she was adult enough to accept the consequences of her actions—wasn't she?

Maggie stood and stepped purposefully from the tub wrapping a bath sheet around her dripping body. "Okay, girl," she muttered, briskly rubbing her skin dry, " 'If it were done when 'tis done, then 'twere well it were done quickly.' " Good grief, she thought with a brief return of her normal good humor, she had chosen the wrong play for a quotation. *The Comedy of Errors* would have been much more appropriate than *Macbeth*. She slipped into the skimpy teddy and shrugged on the matching peignoir, then turned slowly to look into the mirror lining one wall.

"Oh!" she gasped, sucking in her breath in horrified amazement and closing her eyes weakly against the reflection. That barely dressed female couldn't be Maggie Simms. Maggie was brushed nylon and cotton. She would never be able to carry off this masquerade. Opening one eye, she peeped hopefully at the image in the mirror—but it remained unchanged.

Flopping down on the satin-covered vanity stool, she nibbled thoughtfully at one neatly manicured nail, glancing occasionally over her shoulder to reconfirm her first impression. "Of course," she murmured quietly, "it doesn't really matter what I'm wearing. It will all come off soon enough anyway." But somehow the thought brought no comfort at all, and confused heat flooded her body. Why couldn't she have a figure like Carrel's? With a body like her friend's, maybe she could have carried it off. But her own was so . . . so inadequate.

"But then," she sighed, "he's already seen most of it. It's not like he's going to take one look at me and shudder in revulsion." Maggie leaned forward, propping her elbows on her knees and resting her chin in her palms. "But we haven't made love. What if nothing happens? What if I really am a cold fish?—uninspiring, Barry used to call me. What if . . . *hic*." She stopped abruptly, her eyes taking on a harried look as the hiccup shook her body. "Oh, no, please. Not *now*."

Since childhood Maggie had fought a losing battle against this humiliating affliction, and as a teenager she had suffered agonies over the frequent attacks. Later the spells diminished in frequency and she learned to anticipate the diaphragm spasms, controlling them somewhat with deep-breathing exercises. Today she had been too distracted to give a thought to the possible results. It had been years since her last attack, so that Maggie had been lulled into a false sense of security. Once the hiccups began, she knew she would have no relief for at least twenty-four hours. No remedy, no matter how drastic, had been able to help her after their actual onset.

"That's all I . . . need," she whispered despairingly. Out of self-defense she had taught herself to hide the effects of an attack, frequent pauses in her speech the only outward sign of her inward distress.

"Maggie, love." Mark's voice came through the locked door, causing her to jump skittishly. "Are you going to come out tonight or were you thinking of taking a lease on the bathroom?"

Maggie walked to the door and leaned her forehead against it weakly. "Mark?" she whispered hesitantly.

"Yes, love?"

"Mark, I'm scared."

"But there's nothing out here to frighten you, princess," he said gently. "Come out and we'll talk it over."

Maggie sighed heavily. "Mark?" she whispered again.

And again he replied, "Yes, love," this time with a hint of laughter in his voice.

"Will you . . . walk to the other side of the room before I . . . come out?

"Certainly," he replied. Moments later he added, his voice fainter, "You can come out now, Maggie."

Unlocking the door, she opened it and peered hesitantly into the now dimly lit bedroom. Mark was nowhere to be seen. Puzzled, she stepped into the room to look around, whirling in fright when she heard the door slam shut behind her.

"Mark!" she gasped. "You said you would stay . . . on the other side of the room."

He was standing with his back to the bathroom door, staring at her scantily clad body. "I lied," he stated offhandedly. "Lord, don't you look beautiful in that!"

"No," she stated bluntly. "I look like a floozie."

"You look beautiful," he repeated firmly. "Now, what's this all about?"

"Look, Mark, I've been thinking," she said in a rush, wrapping the loose robe around her waist. "I realize I've been unfair to you . . . and I'd like to explain. This whole thing is really rather silly." She smiled nervously, willing him to see the humor. "There is a man in my office . . . whom I was interested in, but he called me a good scout and took out the cheerleader instead . . . so you see, I'm really here because I got tired of my image.

You wouldn't . . . want me on those terms, would you?"

"Sure, I would," he replied without hesitation, moving toward her.

"Mark!" she squealed, backing away.

"I'm teasing, love," he assured her smilingly, his sparkling gaze again drifting down her petite body. "You don't have to do anything you don't want to do."

His admiring stare spoke louder than his words, and Maggie said irritably, "Would you stop looking at me like that? This is not me." She lifted the lace edge of the peignoir, exposing one shapely thigh. "These things are stupid. The robe doesn't even have a . . . tie. It serves no earthly purpose other than to incite a man's . . . lust."

"It certainly works," he murmured, his eyes fixed on the line of her slender leg. He chuckled softly when she whirled around and walked a few paces away from him. "You're looking at it wrong, Maggie. What use does a smile have? Nothing except to make you feel good when you wear it and to make others feel good when they see it. And do you ask a butterfly to explain itself?"

He walked to stand behind her, grasping her shoulders firmly and moving her to stand before a cheval mirror in the corner of the room. "Now, look at yourself." He moved his hands down her arms, loosening their hold on the robe. "Beauty needs no explanation, Maggie."

She looked at the dual reflections in the mirror but was so mesmerized by his image, she overlooked the beauty in her own. His blond hair was still damp from the shower, and the gray robe had fallen open at the throat, giving her a glimpse of his broad chest. This was beauty. A harsh, stimulating male beauty that his fine suits subdued.

Lifting her eyes from his chest, she met his blazing eyes in the mirror. "Yes," she whispered. "I see what you mean." Maggie also saw the desire that was raging in his now steel-gray eyes, and suddenly, instead of being intimidated by it, she was overcome by a strange calm. "Mark, I . . ." A particularly violent hiccup took her unawares, shaking her body with its force. Maggie closed her eyes in resignation as Mark, feeling the jolt, looked at her in puzzled surprise.

"Maggie?" he said, turning her to face him. "What in the hell. . . .?"

"It's these damn . . . hiccups," she railed, opening her eyes. "They are the most abominable things. I haven't had them . . . in years, and I had hoped I was cured." Miserable, she leaned her head forward to rest it on his chest. "I had them weekly when I was a . . . teenager. At my first dance, my date had to contend with . . . more . . . more than sweaty palms. I hiccuped in perfect three-quarter time . . . all evening. Every time I got nervous I got the hiccups. And knowing they . . . were coming only made me more nervous."

Mark wrapped his arms around her, pulling her closer to his lean frame, and brushed the curls from her forehead in a gentle gesture of comfort. "Poor little princess," he said, laughing softly. "Shedding your comfortable, well-ordered cocoon to come with me has brought it all back for you, hasn't it?" He lowered his head to kiss her on the cheek. "Don't worry so, love. Everything will be fine. I'll sleep in another bedroom, if you like."

"You would do that?" she asked, raising her head, her eyes widening in surprise.

"Yes, I will," he said, then grinned. "I won't like it, but if it will make you feel better, I'll do it."

"I can't believe it. You came down here expecting to . . . make love to a warm, willing woman and you're not even angry about . . . sleeping alone?"

Mark closed his eyes in frustration at the picture she painted and muttered drily, "Don't press your luck, Maggie. It's going to be tough enough without your reminding me of what I'm missing." He opened his eyes and looked down at her. "And if you don't move away from me soon, all my good intentions won't keep me from kissing you."

Maggie was suddenly conscious of his hard body pressing against her softness. She lowered her eyes and brought her hand up nervously to tease the curling hair on his chest. "I don't see what one little kiss could hurt," she mumbled perversely.

"Don't you?" His voice sounded oddly strained.

"Of course, if you'd rather not," she began. He moved swiftly, and her words were lost in a hard, searching kiss.

Mark raised his head a fraction to examine her stunned face. "Now do you see?"

"Yes," she whispered breathlessly, but stood motionless, unable to break the spell his lips had cast on her.

"The thought of making love with me has put you in a highly nervous state, Maggie," he murmured, caressing the side of her neck with gentle fingers; then he lowered his head to kiss the sensitive pulse point behind her ear. "We wouldn't want to do anything that might aggravate those nerves —right?"

Maggie moved her head to give him access to

the velvety line of her neck and agreed in a soft sigh. "Right."

Sliding his hands down her slim back, he caressed her round buttocks softly, pressing her subtly closer to his hardness. "So we'll have to stop now—right?"

She whispered tiny exploring kisses across his chest, nuzzling the V at the base of his neck. "Right," she murmured against his throat.

Drawing a deep, shuddering breath, Mark raised his hands to grasp her shoulders firmly, holding her away from him. "Maggie," he said firmly, "you're sober now—I made sure of that. So any decision you make will be a rational one." He looked deeply into her dazed eyes. "If you want me, I'll stay. If not, I have to know now, before this gets beyond my control." And with those words he threw the whole thing squarely in Maggie's lap.

But Maggie didn't want to make a rational decision. She wanted the delicious sensations to continue until her body took control of her actions without giving her a chance to think. He was forcing her to consider the situation sanely. And, unreasonably, she resented his interference.

Maggie shrugged off his hands and moved away from him to stand at the window. All right, she told herself, think. Study your alternatives. Confused, she leaned her head against the cool glass and suddenly, as though it were written there in the bright, star-filled sky, she knew there were no alternatives. She wanted Mark more than she had ever wanted anyone, had wanted him that way since the night in the cellar, but she had kept the knowledge from herself, shoving it away as foreign to her. She knew now, without a doubt, that with Mark she would come to know fullfillment for the first time. And, greedily, she was going to grasp that with both hands.

Drawing in a soft, shivery breath, she stepped away from the window and walked to the bedside table to switch off the lamp, throwing the room into soft, moonlit darkness. She heard Mark's sharply indrawn breath and felt his piercing stare as the silk robe fluttered to the floor.

She walked slowly across the room until she stood before him. A streak of moonlight fell across his face, casting soft shadows on his tense features. Stretching out her hands, she confidently loosened the tie of his robe, then spread her fingers on his chest, moving them slowly, deliberately upward to push the soft garment from his shoulders.

A groan from deep within his chest broke Mark's statuelike stillness, and he clasped her roughly to his naked chest, wrapping his long arms around her, his hands caressing her frantically, pressing her closer and ever closer. "My God," he rasped. "I thought I was going to have to get down on my knees and beg." He framed her face with his hands in a rough caress, holding her face to the faint light, forcing her to look into his eyes. "And I would have. Never doubt that, Maggie. After I kissed you, there was nothing on earth that could have gotten me out of this room tonight."

The intensity, the urgency in his voice was shockingly raw. This wasn't the lazily laughing Mark she had come to know. She would never have believed she would see such depth of emotion in him. Something was very wrong. Something in his voice went against the easygoing nature Maggie had ascribed to him.

But before she could pursue the puzzling thought

she felt his hands slide to her shoulders to untie the narrow bows; then the wisp of fabric slipped down her body in a silken caress. He took a step backward, releasing her reluctantly, and explored her naked loveliness with hungry eyes. She felt his scorching gaze on her small, rounded breasts, heard his ragged breathing as her nipples hardened into taut peaks under his concentrated stare. Then his eyes glided down past her trim waist and gently curving hips to the curling triangle of hair that guarded the center of her awakening passion.

Maggie stood perfectly still, reveling in his rapt survey, feeling long-repressed desires surge to the fore. She was primitive woman, born especially for this moment of revelation. Her eyes were filled with new, indescribable yearnings as she took in the strength of his shoulders, the symmetric beauty of his chest, with its mat of curling hair that narrowed to a slender trail down the flat plain of his stomach, then spread to embrace his hard, aroused masculinity. She stared unashamedly at him, sucking in her breath as she saw the athletic strength of his thighs, the lean grace of his hips.

As though the exquisite torture had broken all restraints, he pulled her urgently to him. She felt the thunderous pounding of his heart against her naked breasts, heard his harsh, labored breathing in her ear, and the knowledge that she could affect him so deeply sent her mind whirling giddily.

Bending abruptly, he lifted her high in his arms, a barbarian triumphantly claiming his plunder, and walked to the bed to lay her gently upon it. With one knee pressing into the bed, he stretched out a hand to stroke her cheek. "This is the picture

I couldn't get out of my mind," he whispered hoarsely. "Your body gleaming like ivory satin in the darkness."

Maggie lay trembling, waiting. Aching for his body to cover hers. Her breathing came in short, shallow gasps as his words flowed through her veins, hot and heavy like an aphrodisiac. She moaned in hungry impatience and reached up to pull him to her.

Giving in to the pressure of her hand on his neck, he laid agonizingly sweet kisses on and around her aching lips. "Is this what you want, Maggie?" he whispered, punctuating the question with another brief kiss.

"Please, Mark," she murmured, pleading for the solid feel of his mouth on hers.

"Easy, princess." Lying full length beside her, he stroked the side of her neck. "Let it come sweet and slow. We've got all the time in the world."

Sweet and slow. Slowly, he eased her into a fascinating new world of pure sensation, sending shafts of sharp, electric desire pulsating through her body. His hands and lips found all the secret places, and, sweetly, she yielded to the magic of his touch.

His long fingers glided with fairy lightness down her body, learning the rounded curves of her breasts, the silken length of her thigh, and Maggie moved sensually under his touch, shifting her body to meet his hands, his lips as he began an exhilarating symphony of movements. He made love to her breasts, first teasing the hard tips with circular strokes of his warm, moist tongue, then sucking them deep into his mouth, releasing one to taunt the other. He smoothed the soft inner flesh of her thighs with deft strokes, wordlessly urging her to part them to facilitate his erotic play. She writhed with a frustrated longing for his touch at the center of the pulsating intensity, moaning deeply when he moved his hands over her hips to clasp her buttocks firmly with both hands, squeezing and kneading the flesh in urgent, sensual rhythm.

Just as the fire he had kindled in her loins threatened to rage out of control, just as she felt she could no longer contain the fierce pleasure, he pulled her to him, molding her trembling softness to the long, hard length of his body. As he pressed her close, she felt alive as she never had before, every inch of her flesh tingling with sensation.

Her breasts met his chest, the taut nipples discovering the smooth skin beneath his mat of curling hair. She moved her body slowly, her stomach sinuously stroking his. Then they lay for soul-shaking moments, heated flesh meeting heated flesh, undulating feverishly in an erotic, naked pas de deux.

Then, as though their minds had touched as intimately as their bodies, she lay back against the silk sheet while he rose above her, entering her with a swift, sure stroke. She moved to greet his long-awaited possession, feeling him hot and hard between her thighs, gasping with unbearable pleasure as she felt that warmth reach deep within her.

"Magic, Maggie," he said in an urgent whisper, his movements asking—demanding—that she meet each thrust with an ardor as fierce as his own.

Maggie gripped the hard muscles of his shoulders as the pressure in her lower body mounted incredibly. Just as she felt she could not bear one second more without screaming, she heard a harsh, pagan cry from deep inside Mark and, as though the discovery of his delight had shown her the way to her own, she felt rippling, sizzling waves of pleasure lift her into an explosively violent climax and release her gently into peace.

Maggie lay in the darkness, staring at the shades of gray and black in her charcoal-drawn surroundings. She turned her head languidly, a delightful floating sensation pervading her body, leaving her with the feeling that everything was happening in slow motion. She looked lazily at Mark's face, memorizing every detail from his strong brow to the silver eyes that glinted in the dark, watching her closely as though trying to gauge her emotions, to the small cleft in his aristocratic chin.

"You wanna suck on my toes?" she murmured, her speech slow and slightly slurred.

His shout of laughter shook the bed, filling the room with the sound of his startled pleasure. He hugged her to him exuberantly. "Oh, love," he sighed, closing his eyes tightly. "Will you never cease to surprise and delight me?" He opened his eyes and held her chin in one large hand. "I'd be happy to nibble on your toes if you have your heart set on it."

Turning her head to kiss the palm of his hand, she explained. "Carrel thought I was silly to worry about what would happen here tonight. She said you'd had every opportunity to smear me with homemade jam while we were in the cellar if that was what you wanted. She was right. I was silly to worry." Maggie glanced up at his face, moving to lay a soft kiss on his firm, warm lips. "Mark?"

"Shh," he hushed her, grinning devilishly, his eyes closed. "I'm still visualizing the removal of the jam."

"Mark!" she gasped laughingly, pulling back to look at him. "You're a hedonist. But that's exactly what I mean. I can't think of a thing you could do to me that I wouldn't adore."

He chuckled softly. "You mean I didn't have to hide all the orgy apparatus?"

"Orgy?" she asked, scrambling to her knees, her eyes widening in curiosity. "Have you really had orgies?"

With cunning swiftness, he pulled her on top of him, nuzzling her neck playfully. "Not until tonight, princess."

"Are we going to have an orgy?" she asked, unconcerned, as she angled her head to give him access to the full length of her neck.

"We're having one now."

"Now?" she asked doubtfully. "I thought an orgy was louder. You know, with various and assorted bacchanalia, lots of serious debauching, and—"

"I hate to interrupt you in mid-debauch, love, but the correct definition is uncontrolled indulgence in any activity. I plan on indulging in a particularly delightful activity tonight"—his voice dropped to a husky whisper—"And I lost what little control I had the minute your robe hit the floor."

"Oh, Mark," she sighed, wrapping her slender arms around his neck and hugging him in an excess of unrestrained joy. "It was lovely, wasn't it? It was the most . . ." She paused, jolted by an unexpected thought. "Mark! My hiccups are gone. You cured me. Even the doctors weren't able to get rid of them that quickly. You're wonderful!"

"I must say, you're a little slow," he said, smiling at her enthusiasm. "Most people come to that conclusion a lot sooner. But I'll forgive you, because"—he slapped her gently on the derriere—"you've got such a cute fanny.

"Now," he said, rolling over to gently press her body into the soft bed, his voice dropping to a tantalizing whisper, "finish what you were saying about how lovely it was being in my arms." But before she could utter a word he lowered his head, and suddenly bacchanals seemed tame sport as her lips met his in a breathless rekindling of passion.

## Chapter Seven

A butterfly lit on her cheek, and Maggie smiled. It was a tiny, pale-yellow butterfly that fluttered a soft caress, then, having taken the time to greet her, flew away to take care of other, more pressing butterfly business.

Maggie lifted her hand to touch the still-tingling skin but found it captured by strong, lean fingers. She opened her eyes slowly, looking at the face of the man lying close beside her on the pillow. "Mark," she murmured, smiling as memories of the night before flowed through her, warming her. "You were the butterfly."

He halted the process of kissing each knuckle to look at her quizzically, his eyebrows drawn together, almost meeting. "I've always considered myself more of a daddy longlegs, but if you want me to be a butterfly, I'll do my damnedest."

Laughter bubbled up inside her. Grasping his

face with both hands she placed a frim, smacking kiss on his lips, then scrambled from the bed and opened her arms to the world. "I can fly," she laughed, whirling around in delight, then looked back at his reclining figure. "What did you do to me? Why do I feel champagne bubbles in my veins and sunshine coming from the inside out?"

Rising from the bed he took a deep, pleasurable breath, as though he too found the very air intoxicating. He walked to her, putting his arms around her bare waist, pulling her close. "I'm not going to take the rap for this one, sweetheart," he said in a very bad imitation of Humphrey Bogart. "It was you," he whispered. "You cast a spell, sang your siren song, and I'm helpless." Sliding his hands to her ribs, he lifted her high in the air and held her there, smiling complacently. "And now you're helpless, so you know how I feel."

"Put me down," she said, laughing.

He looked at her smiling face for a moment as though considering her request, then shook his head slowly in regret. "No, I'm sorry, I can't. After careful consideration I've decided I like you dangling before me. Now, any time I want to nibble on your . . . belly button"—he ducked his head to demonstrate his point, accompanied by her squeals of laughter—"I can. Yes, now that I come to think of it, this is very convenient."

"Marcus Wilding," she said, swallowing her laughter in gasps, struggling for a stern expression. "If I were standing on the floor I would have great difficulty using my knee effectively. But from this position? . . ." She looked down suggestively.

"That was truly a low blow," he reprimanded, setting her gently on the floor. "If I weren't so wonderfully magnanimous I'd make you pay for that one."

"Why, you pompous . . ." she sputtered.

"Temper, temper," he murmured, walking to the window. He moved the curtain aside, and the brilliant sunshine fell on his naked body, burnishing the strong flesh, giving it a deep golden glow. "Look at the world, Maggie," he said, his voice full of a curious, childlike wonder. "It's laughing. Not a silly little giggle, but a marvelously joyous belly laugh. It's out there waiting for us to join it. Let's—" He turned to catch her eyes on him as she memorized the sleek lines of his body. "Like I said"—he paused to clear his throat—"the world can wait." And he walked slowly toward her.


"Now, on your left, ladies and gentlemen, you'll find picturesque, bare-chested crewmen loading their picturesque cargo into picturesque leaky boats. And, of course, here"—Mark gestured to the left—"we have three thousand cruise ships— each and every one of them disgorging their load of"—he paused as a man with a camera around his neck not-so-gently elbowed him aside—"charming tourists."

Maggie giggled at his disgruntled expression, then sobered quickly as, with arrogantly raised brow, he commanded her attention for the rest of his lecture.

"If you'll listen closely you'll catch the beautiful calypso rhythm of the lilting down-island patois."

A loud voice floated across the crowd of rushing tourists to once again interrupt Mark's lecture. "So I says to George—who the hell cares, George?"

Roaring laughter greeted the comment, then the voice was once again lost in the crowd.

Maggie looked up at Mark with an ingenuous expression on her face. "Yes, I see what you mean. There is a kind of rhythm to it."

"Maggie, love," he said, smiling evilly, "how would you like to find yourself dangling in midair again?"

She laughingly ignored his threat as he pulled her along the busy waterfront street. The shops that lined it were delightful, carrying everything from Louis Vuitton luggage to Miss Piggy T-shirts. When they paused briefly to sample pan-fried chicken and a deliciously spicy homemade drink called maubey, Maggie found that the friendly islander who served them quickly, then bent again over the small brazier, did indeed have a beautiful, lilting accent. Mark looked down at Maggie with a smug "I told you so" smile before they walked on.

As they returned to the tiny car that also belonged to their absent host, Maggie found herself smiling at nothing. A deep contentment—no, contentment was too bland—an effervescent joy had filled her since she had awakened to Mark's kiss. She was like a teenager in the throes of her first passion.

Maggie looked at his strong, finely etched hands on the steering wheel as they drove through the labyrinth of roads that wound along the resort-filled coast. His hands should be carved in wood, she thought, only half listening to his explanation of the socioeconomic structure of the island. When she first met Mark she would have thought marble more elegantly appropriate to his character. But now she knew that stone was too cold and hard to do him justice.

With a small smile she admitted to herself that she had a full-blown crush on Mark. How could she not? He had brought her to life. He had given her a knowledge of herself that had always escaped her. She knew fulfillment at last, and she reveled in it.

But Maggie also knew that their closeness, the magical quality of their interlude, couldn't last beyond the Dallas–Fort Worth airport. The dream would end come Monday, when reality would remove the misplaced stars from her eyes. But somehow, knowing that it was a fantasy, that it wouldn't hold up to the bright lights of the real world, didn't diminish the wonder of what she felt for him right now.

Today, all through the day, she had felt the warmth growing steadily inside her. Viewing the lovely Brigadoonish island of St. John from the deck of a sailboat, swimming in the sparkling turquoise water—with Mark outlandishly ogling her brief maillot—and even waiting in a small café for him to complete his business, she had felt it burgeoning. So now, she felt she would burst any minute from the sheer pleasure of his company.

"Was it my description of the rum-making process that lost you? I can't actually hear you snoring, love, but I'd swear you're asleep."

Mark's deep voice broke into her reflections, and she glanced at his face to find him staring at her inquiringly. He is such a nice man, she thought, staring at his face. She smiled as she thought of the scathing remark he would make if she dared suggest aloud that he were anything as unexciting as nice. So she simply said, "I like you, Mark."

Pulling the car over to the side of the road, he

stared at her, a curious intensity filling his face, changing the atmosphere in the car. He reached out slowly to touch her face, a gentle stroke on her cheek. "It's a start," he whispered softly. Closing his eyes tightly, he repeated with a strange fierceness, "By God, it's a start." When he opened his eyes again the intensity was gone, replaced by silver sparks of amusement. "Did I or did I not convert you, love?"

Maggie shook her head dizzily, forcing herself to keep pace with his quickly changing moods. She would save the memory and examine it later. "I wouldn't call it converting," she said, chuckling. "I would call it brainwashing."

"I refuse to argue semantics with you. It's not important anyway. What is important"—he leaned over to give her a brief, hard kiss—"is the fact that once again I'm victorious."

"And once again your humility is inspiring to witness."

"Quite."

Their laughter filled the car, floating out into the growing darkness as they drove through the narrow, winding streets to return to their borrowed haven. Mark let Maggie out at the front door while he parked the car. She entered the dim hall remembering how spooky the shadows had looked the night before. Glancing around, she suddenly realized the only rooms she had seen clearly were the bedroom and bath. And those two rooms certainly didn't have the look of a tropic hideaway. There was not a stick of rattan in sight, and no potted palms to bring the lush scenery indoors.

Maggie was walking toward the living room to explore when she heard the front door close. She looked back over her shoulder and saw Mark leaning against the door as he had the night before. Once again his mood had changed. He looked at her without speaking, the sensual vibrations filling the air between them with sizzling sparks. Without a word he quickened her pulse rate, making her come vibrantly alive. Obeying his silent command, she began to walk toward him.

"It's been years, Maggie," he whispered when she stood before him. "No—it's been eons—since I felt your magic."

"Yes," she murmured in agreement.

Without fuss or pretension he put his arm around her shoulder and they walked to the bedroom, neither finding any need for words. Inside the bedroom he picked her up in his arms to carry her to the bed.

They came together as though they had been lovers for years, each meeting the other's needs instinctively in a warm, wonderful pleasuring that was like nothing Maggie had ever felt. It was like seeing a light at the end of a tunnel. Like suddenly finding yourself in familiar territory after being lost. It was like coming home.

Later Maggie lay in the curve of his arm, listening as his breathing returned to normal. She had been more deeply moved than she dared admit. Something extraordinary had happened to her. Something that would take a lot of soul-searching to explain. She couldn't—wouldn't—face it now. Looking through the darkness at his strong face, she kept her voice carefully casual as she asked, "Tell me about your life, Mark. I know almost nothing about you."

"There's really not much to tell," he answered slowly as though he too were having difficulty coming back to earth. "My mother died when I was five, and old Marcus, my grandfather, raised me. When I was fourteen he started grooming me to take over his empire—a job for which I was and am totally unsuited. But he wouldn't believe that, so when he died I inherited the whole mess. I manage to ignore it most of the time, but occasionally—like this weekend—I have to play tycoon. The rest of my time is spent avoiding anything that sounds like work," he finished drily.

"Did you never want to marry?"

"I always considered myself too young to marry," he said facetiously.

She laughed, watching the shadows on his face change when he smiled. "How old are you?"

"Thirty-eight."

"That's too young?"

"I always thought so," he said, then grabbed her hand to kiss the back with exaggerated continental elegance. "But if you'll have me, my lady, I promise to change my dastardly ways."

Maggie laughed and playfully punched his shoulder, unaware that he had flinched when he heard her laugh. "I ought to take you up on that just to teach you a lesson," she said, kissing the spot she had assaulted. Remembering his earlier words, she added, "You said your grandfather had raised you. Where was your father during all the grooming?"

It was a moment before he spoke, his voice strangely stiff when he said, "He was there, but he wasn't *there*, if you know what I mean. Dad was always a little vague, especially after Mother died. I don't think he considered himself a fit guardian. Actually, Jake was more of a father to me than Dad or old Marcus." He paused, and his voice took on a lighter tone. "Speaking of Jake, I have a confession to make."

"Confessions already?" she asked, smiling. "Let me guess. You're taking the kids and leaving me for a mezzo-soprano with the New York Metropolitan Opera?"

"That's close." He chuckled. "The truth is, the day that I stopped to ask directions, I already knew the way to Jake's place."

"No!" she said in feigned surprise.

"Oh, yes, but that's not all," he said, trying to sound contrite but not quite succeeding. "There is no lull in the middle of a tornado."

" 'O what a tangled web we weave,' " she quoted righteously, then said, "Mark?"

"Yes, love?"

"I have a confession to make, too." She paused briefly. "I knew there was no lull in the middle of a tornado."

He raised himself on one elbow, surprise showing in his handsome face. "You knew? You little fiend. Here I was feeling guilty for having tricked you, and you knew all along." He looked at her as though struck by a sudden thought. "If you knew, why didn't you call my bluff?"

She was silent for a moment, then said slowly, "I asked myself that same question all last week, and, although I've only recently admitted it to myself, it was because I liked being in your arms. It felt . . . oh, I don't know how to explain it—it just felt right."

"Yes," he agreed, pulling her closer. "That's exactly how it feels—just like the third bowl of porridge."

Maggie wasn't sure she liked being compared to a bowl of porridge, but she knew what he meant.

Being held in other arms had always been "too" something or other. Only with Mark was it just right.

The next day they arose early and Maggie had a chance to view the other rooms in the large house. Someone had obviously gone to great expense to furnish it, but Maggie found it a little formal for her taste. They were served fresh-baked croissants in a small breakfast room—which overlooked the landscaped grounds—by a shy young Puerto Rican girl who came in daily with her mother and brother to keep the house in order. As they ate, Maggie pestered Mark to tell her what he had planned for the day, but he would say only that it was something special, so she should shut up and eat breakfast.

Leaving the car in the garage, they walked down the hill that rose steeply from the harbor. They passed beautifully maintained manors—a legacy of the Danish aristocracy—then pastel frame houses standing all jammed together in a soft rainbow of colors.

Maggie, finally tiring of trying to keep pace with the man at her side, pulled him to a halt. "Mark, dear," she said patiently, "look down at your legs."

Looking down at the limbs in question, he said, "Yes?"

"Now look at mine."

He obliged by staring at her slim, tanned legs below the white shorts. He spent an inordinate amount of time inspecting them before smiling in pleasure and murmuring, "Yes, love."

"I don't know right off what it's called," she said, drawing his attention away from her legs, "but there's an irrefutable law of physics that states that these"—she pointed to her legs—"cannot possibly go as fast as those," she finished, pointing to his.

"The Law of Diminishing Returns?" he suggested, then laughed and hugged her briefly. "I'm sorry, love. I didn't realize I was going so fast. I'm in a hurry to get to the boat."

"The boat? Are we going sailing again?"

"Just be patient and you'll see," he said, smiling mysteriously, then began walking, more slowly this time.

Closer to the shopping district they met early-morning shoppers and enthusiastic tourists. When they passed a tiny old woman with smooth, dark skin, Maggie once again pulled Mark to an abrupt stop. She indicated the ancient woman's armful of packages. "Those things are too heavy for her, Mark. Maybe we should help her carry them home."

"The islanders are used to carrying things, especially the women. She probably grew up carrying baskets to and from the market on her head."

"But not now," Maggie protested stubbornly. "She's too old."

Mark sighed, seeing the sympathy shining out of Maggie's brown eyes. "Oh, very well. I'll carry them for her."

Maggie stayed where she was and watched as Mark approached the elderly woman, who was now struggling up the stairs of a pale-pink house with her packages. At the front door he returned the parcels to her and listened patiently as the woman smiled and spoke in a strange, musical language, the words foreign to Maggie's ears.

When Mark caught up with her, Maggie said in satisfaction. "You see how much she appreciated your help." She looked up at Mark's face, but instead of pleasure at having played the Good Samaritan, his features showed blank astonishment. "Mark?"

"I'm not completely sure," he said in bewilderment, glancing back at the pink house, "but I think she either propositioned me or put a curse on my offspring for the next three generations."

"What are you talking about?"

"That's what I'm trying to tell you. I don't *know* what I'm talking about. At least, I don't know what she was talking about," he said in confusion. "Her dialect was hard to understand, but I could swear I heard her say something about my 'increase.' "

"And you think she put a curse on them. Now, why on earth would she curse them for three generations?" Maggie asked incredulously, her laughter at the stunned look on his face threatening to spill over at any second.

"I don't know," he said irritably, still glancing warily at the pink house. "Perhaps that's when the warranty runs out."

At that, Maggie could contain her laughter no longer. She leaned against Mark, doubling over helplessly as he looked on with a sour expression. "Oh, Mark," she gasped. "I'm so sorry. Your first venture into selflessness and you get smacked in the face with a . . . curse."

"Yes," he said haughtily. "But of course, your genuine contrition at having caused my downfall makes up for a lot."

Maggie struggled to straighten her face and said, "I promise I won't force you into any more good deeds."

"I'll bet," he said doubtfully, then smiled reluctantly as she began to laugh again. "Come on, trouble, or we'll miss the boat."

Instead of finding the sailboat waiting for them that Mark had hired the day before, Maggie was surprised to find Mark had decided to take out their host's cabin cruiser—which had been furnished with supplies for the day. Today they were completely alone. No friendly crewmen to show them the sights. Just Maggie and Mark and a brilliant blue sky.

Mark insisted on keeping their destination a secret until they anchored in a tiny cove on one of the many uninhabited islets that surrounded the main island. He carried her ashore, calling out to imaginary pirate cronies to come and admire his booty, then returned to the boat for their supplies while Maggie looked around.

It was paradise, a tiny heaven on earth that seemed to whisper the secrets of love and life to anyone who would take the time to listen. And today Maggie was taking the time. Tomorrow would come soon enough, bringing dull things like responsibility and sanity. Today Maggie would grab her bit of paradise and savor every minute.

"Well, how do you like it?" Mark asked from close behind her, his arms reaching around her to pull her back against him.

Turning in his arms, she took a deep breath, inhaling an exotic mixture of Mark, the perfume of the yellow genip flowers, and the salty tang of the ocean. "It's wonderful. A place out of time. It makes me feel we could stay here for years yet on our return find that only hours had passed."

"You want to try it?"

"I'd love to," she said, laughing. "But while I wouldn't be missed, I have a sneaking suspicion that your diligent Mr. Lowe would find us all too soon."

"I suppose you're right." He sighed regretfully. "But it was a lovely thought." His voice sounded strangely wistful, and there was a faraway look in his eyes. Then he looked down at her and smiled. "So we have to make the most of the time we have. Are you ready for a swim?"

"But I didn't bring a suit."

"Oh, dear," he said, grinning slyly. "Did I forget to tell you we would be swimming?"

"You," she said, shaking her head, the gold tips of her hair glinting in the sun as she tapped him on the chest with one accusing finger, "are totally wicked."

"Yes," he agreed complacently. "Now, come on. We're wasting time."

Their hours on the tiny island were enchanted ones. A lovely, shining gift from the gods. They were carried back to a freer, more innocent time when clothing was an unnecessary encumbrance. They laughed and played like children, absorbing the sun and the sea and the beautiful silence.

Mark insisted that Maggie relate the entire story of her life, beginning with the day she was born, and, though she was unable to start quite that early in her life, she did her best to fill him in without boring him too much.

She told him about her loving but strict parents and about her two younger sisters, who had always seemed to be Maggie's special responsibility. It seemed that she had been pulling them out of scrapes for as long as she could remember. They still called occasionally with a frantic request for aid, and Maggie always gave in to their pleas.

"So that's why you take life so seriously," he

murmured thoughtfully as he sat under a coconut tree, leaning back against a large rock. "You had adult responsibilities even when you were a child."

"Do you think I'm too serious?" she asked, frowning.

"I didn't mean it like that, Maggie," he said. "You have a wonderful—if occasionally sadistic— sense of humor."

"Sadistic?"

"Well, it certainly seems sadistic when you're laughing at me," he said ruefully.

"Would I laugh at you?" she asked innocently, raising up on her knees and leaning across to tweak the hair on his chest.

"Yes, you little demon, you would. And now that I know all about your past, why don't you tell me about your future?"

"Aren't you sick of listening to me? Why don't you tell me about your childhood? I'll bet you were an—" she paused, glancing up at him impishly, "interesting child."

"I'll have you know I was a perfect child. Just as I'm now a perfect adult."

"Perfect?" she scoffed.

"Almost perfect," he said, falling suddenly to the blanket and pulling her with him. "I have one small fault."

"Only one? And what's that?"

He began running one long finger down her throat and across one firm, round breast, then whispered softly in her ear, "I have no patience at all, princess. And I've waited long enough for one day." He then began to make their perfect day complete.

•  •  •

As they lay on their blanket in the sand, replete with food and love, Maggie saw in one terrible flash what waited for them tomorrow, and she wanted to hold on to the magic for a little longer. She knew this was fantasy and would end when reality forced its way upon them, but for one brief moment she wanted to turn her back on the real world and give herself up to the dream.

"What are you thinking about?" Mark murmured in her ear.

"Oh, dull things like tomorrow." She turned over on her side and ran her hand over his chest, ruffling the fine hair. Stubbornly, Maggie pushed away the picture of the future and replaced it with one that would stick in her mind forever. A picture of Mark standing knee-deep in the ocean, his face raised to the sun, his blond hair darkened to gold by the water.

"Dallas isn't exactly St. Thomas," he said quietly, "but no place is dull if you're with the right person." He turned his head to face her. "Maggie, about tomorrow . . ."

Maggie tugged playfully at the short curly hair. "I don't want to think about tomorrow or Dallas," she said, grinning mischievously. "I want to think about a handsome blond beachcomber and a tiny turquoise cove."

"I love the life of a beachcomber," he said, pulling her over so that she lay on top of him, molding and smoothing her buttocks as though they fascinated him. "You find such interesting things that have washed ashore." Threading his fingers through her hair to pull her head to his chest, he sighed against her forehead and said, "I'm afraid it's time to leave paradise, love."

Then suddenly he framed her face with his

hands, holding her head so that he could look into her eyes, his own turning a deep, steel gray and containing something that looked almost like fear. "Let's stay, Maggie," he whispered urgently. "Let's never go back."

For the moment she was caught up in the unknown vision that held Mark in its grip; then she shook it off to scramble to her feet. "We can't stay, silly. Where would I buy nail polish?"

"The ever-cautious Maggie," he murmured softly, his eyes closed, then rose slowly to his feet. "Okay, woman," he said, slapping her on the rear, "let's stow this gear."

That night Mark had the nightmare again. He woke Maggie with his muffled cries, his face drenched in perspiration, a look of anguish twisting the strong lines of his face. And again Maggie held and soothed him, responding to his terrible urgency with a desperation of her own. The night before had been a leisurely, magical pleasuring. Tonight was raw need—a primitive, hungry mating. They came together in a wild, passionate coupling that touched the hidden depths in each of them, bringing them to a soul-shaking culmination that rocked their little piece of earth. And there was no peaceful sleep for them afterward. They lay holding each other, making love again and again, as though they were storing the loving away to hold them through harder, leaner times.

The next morning Maggie tried to act as though it were just another day, as though it weren't the end of a beautiful dream. But Mark was silent, watching her closely as she packed, and throughout the long trip back to Dallas, a look of reluctant resignation grew in his eyes.

They were met at the airport by the same attractive young man, but this time Maggie made no attempt to respond to his smiling enthusiasm. She looked around her at all the signs of civilization and realized that the invisible labels that separated her world from Mark's were already beginning to show. She carefully avoided his eyes as she slowly let go of the fantasy that had held her in its grip for days.

On their arrival at her apartment, when the bags had been transferred to her strangely foreign living room and the young man had returned to the car to wait, Maggie turned finally to meet Mark's eyes.

"That's it, then, isn't it?" he asked quietly. "You've had your frivolous fling and now it's back to normal, with no room in your orderly life for a court jester."

"Mark," she began, struck for the first time by the uncomfortable feeling that she had used him thoughtlessly, "I—"

"There's no need for explanations, Maggie. I'm not accusing you of anything. You made it very clear why you came with me." Reaching out, he gently smoothed the curls from her forehead with one long finger. "I suppose I hoped you would come to feel differently about it." Leaning down, he touched his lips to her brow, giving her a tender, lingering kiss. "Goodbye, love."

As he walked away she saw him once again, standing knee-deep in the ocean, his face lifted to the sun. She smiled a small, wistful smile, then murmured softly, her voice shaking unexplainably, "Goodbye, Mark."

# Chapter Eight

He was there again.

Maggie could see him leaning against a lamp-post across the street, nodding affably to the passers-by, pretending he wasn't following her. All week long she had seen him. Every time she left the office he was there, somewhere in the crowds that lined the downtown streets.

At first she had thought she was mistaken, that it was not him at all, but only someone who looked like him. But when she caught a glimpse of his silver eyes, a new thought took hold. Perhaps her week of ceaselessly dreaming of him had conjured his lean figure to pacify her fevered brain.

Then, exactly one week after they had said goodbye, she was looking into the display window of a department store and there he was, standing behind her, carefully studying a garish brass unicorn.

Turning to the two plump shoppers standing beside him, he said, "Yes, I agree, ladies. He is well worth the money. But then, of course, I'm only a man. What we need is a woman's opinion. I'm sure my wife will be glad to help." He turned to Maggie then, his gray eyes sparkling with fun. "Don't you think he's lovely, dear?"

"I think he's totally unprincipled," she whispered before walking briskly away from him, feeling the curious stares of the duo beside Mark. As she walked her face was completely composed, but her heart, her unruly heart, was bursting with unexplainable joy.

Mark didn't come after her that day, but in the week that followed she saw his blond head above the crowd, felt his eyes following every step she took. He was there when she went to lunch and when she walked to her car every evening. And when she and Carrel joined hundreds of other lunchtime shoppers in bargain hunting—he was there.

Maggie didn't try to hide from Mark. She simply did her best to ignore him. But of course, that was easier said than done. Mark was certainly not the easiest man in the world to ignore. And Carrel didn't help matters at all. Several times Maggie caught her waving to him when she thought Maggie wasn't looking.

Maggie had tried, without success, to convince Carrel that she was handling things in the only way she knew how. One evening as they shared a pizza in front of Maggie's television, Carrel again brought up the subject that was constantly in Maggie's thoughts.

"Explain it to me again," Carrel said as she reached for another piece of pizza. "Explain why you ignore a man who is handsome and charming and rich and—judging by the gleam in your eyes when you look at him—fantastic in bed. All that and crazy about you, too. Tell me again, and maybe this time I'll understand."

Maggie stood and began to pace around the room. Then she stopped and turned to look at her friend. "Don't you remember the discussion we had before I went away with Mark? You said you could see how any kind of relationship between us would be a disaster. Remember?"

"I may have said something like that," Carrel hedged.

"You said exactly that," Maggie said. "Then you decided that a fling would be just the thing I needed. Well, I've had my fling and now it's over."

"Why are you so defensive about it?" Carrel asked calmly. "And don't tell me that you went with Mark because I told you to. I refuse to believe that when he made love to you, you gritted your teeth and pretended he was castor oil."

"Of course I didn't." Maggie sighed. "I went because I wanted to and I enjoyed—" Maggie stopped as the inadequacy of the word struck her. "I loved every minute of it," she amended. "It was beautiful, but I can't relate it to my real life. I can't relate Mark to my real life."

"That's what you keep saying. How do you know you can't? You haven't given him a fair chance."

"A chance to what?" Maggie asked, beginning to pace the floor again. "Be reasonable. Can you really see Mark unobtrusively slipping into the kind of life I live? Can you see him sitting here eating pizza off a paper towel and watching a bowling tournament on television?"

"It's baseball, but I see what you mean. And no, I guess I can't imagine him here."

"Okay, then, can you see me slipping comfortably into Mark's way of life?"

"You could," Carrel insisted, turning sideways on the couch to watch Maggie's pacing. "You could if you wanted to."

"And that's the key," Maggie said. "If I wanted to. I like Mark. I like him a lot, but I don't want to change my life for him. And I would have to if I continued seeing him. Or at least, one of us would have to." She paused, her voice becoming calmer as she continued. "I won't rush into anything again. It makes me uncomfortable, as though I weren't in control of my own life any more. I like to think things over, look beneath the surface, and see how I'll be affected by any particular action in the future."

She stopped pacing and turned to face Carrel. "And there is no future of any kind for Mark and me."

Carrel shook her head sorrowfully. "You're thinking like a computer again, Maggie. I thought you were going to work on that."

"I can't help the way I think. It's part of me. I've got a brain and I've got to use it."

"But can't you see how much you're missing? You say acting impulsively makes you uncomfortable, but wasn't your trip with Mark worth a little discomfort?"

Maggie couldn't answer Carrel's question for a moment. She had to stop and think. Wasn't her time with Mark worth anything? Would she trade what they had shared, those wonderful, magical days, for logic? Maggie didn't have to give much thought to the question. She wouldn't give up her memories for anything.

"It was worth it," she admitted softly, then shook her head as though that would rid her of the confusion. "But it was only a dream. It only existed there. You can't bring dreams home with you in a suitcase, like a seashell. They dissolve when they're exposed to the air in the normal world."

Carrel didn't speak for a moment, and her eyes narrowed thoughtfully as she looked at Maggie. Then she murmured, "I wish I could figure out why you're trying so hard to convince yourself that this thing with Mark wouldn't work."

Maggie sighed in exasperation. "I'm not making this up, Carrel. These are facts. Indisputable facts."

"But what about feelings? You're getting so hung up on those damn facts that you're forgetting about emotions. You haven't said a word about how you feel."

"I feel like I'm being tracked by a bloodhound," Maggie said, smiling wryly. 'Now are you satisfied?"

"I don't think you've given yourself a chance to think about how you feel," Carrel said. "Why is that? You always examine everything so carefully. Why haven't you taken your emotions out and examined them, too? Is there something you're afraid of, Maggie?"

Maggie couldn't stand any more. She felt as though her brain were being pulled in a dozen different directions. She walked around to sit beside Carrel and said quietly, "I can't think about it any more tonight. Would you just take my word for it? I know it's wrong, and that's why I'm pretending he's not there."

Carrel did not want to accept Maggie's evasion,

but she knew her friend well enough to drop the subject—for the time being. After that night she resorted to subtle hints and gentle reminders that effectively kept Mark in Maggie's mind—even when she could not see him—yet didn't force her into a confrontation of her feelings for him.

"Maggie," Carrel said one day, picking up the banner again as she casually glanced at Mark who was looking through the merchandise on a sale table. "I think you should at least give him "E" for effort. He certainly doesn't give up."

"He warned me once that he doesn't handle defeat well," Maggie explained wearily, tiring suddenly of fighting herself as well as Carrel and Mark. "I'm the one who got away." They moved along then to another table, with Mark close behind. "You know how the mind can blow things like this out of proportion," she added, trying to convince herself. "It's the chance that you missed that always afterward seems like the golden opportunity."

"Maybe," Carrel replied doubtfully. "But I still think there's more to him than meets the eye."

And of course there was. Maggie knew very well that Mark had hidden depths, but she also knew that she could not continue seeing him without being hurt. That much she would admit to herself. If they picked up the affair where they had left off, Mark would absorb her completely. She would not be able to keep him separate from what she considered her real life. And if the affair went a step further, into a more permanent relationship, deep down Maggie was afraid she would come to feel the contempt she had secretly held for Barry. She couldn't risk losing the beautiful dream they had shared on St. Thomas for a less-than-beautiful reality.

So she continued to ignore Mark, pretending she didn't see him following her, just as she was pretending now that she didn't see him crossing the street and walking toward her. She quickly turned down the little side street where her car was parked, walking faster when she heard footsteps close behind her. She was only a few feet away from her car when she felt his hand on her arm, pulling her to a halt, turning her to face him.

"Hello, Maggie Simms," he said softly, looking into her eyes with a hesitant, slightly crooked smile.

The hesitancy, the uncertainty of his touch, broke her. All her carefully formulated objections flew right out of her head. She couldn't have remained aloof with a will one hundred times as strong. "Oh, Mark," she whispered, her lower lip quivering uncontrollably as he hauled her into his arms, holding her fiercely, oblivious to the stares of the passing world.

# Chapter Nine

In the weeks that followed, Maggie saw not one trace of the uncertainty that Mark had shown when he had confronted her. He teased and laughed and gave ridiculous excuses for having pursued her so persistently, but the hint of vulnerability was gone, leading her to believe that it was just one of the many guises he could pull at will from his enormous repertoire.

But it didn't matter. His vulnerability—assumed or not—had merely served as a catalyst that brought her own to the surface. She wanted to be with him. It was as simple as that. However mismatched they were, she wanted him. So she had called on the age-old trick of ignoring the unpleasant facts in favor of those she wished to see. While she knew that eventually things would come to a head, she decided to take things as they came and handle the problems if and when they surfaced.

Carefully closing her mind to the nagging voice of her Calvinist background, she gave herself up to the deep, abiding pleasure of Mark's presence. She let the tide of laughter and sensual feeling wash over her and carry her away from her logical, orderly world.

Three weeks later, as they drove through the quiet countryside on their way to see Jake, Maggie faced the fact that soon she would have to deal with problem number one. Although she was with Mark physically every night and mentally all through her working day, she could see that this arrangement was rapidly becoming inadequate for their needs. Mark was already spending more time in her home than he was his own. And it was getting more and more difficult for them to say good night at the end of each evening when he went home.

So what did she do? Suggest that he move into her tiny apartment? Or should she give up the home she had made for herself to move in with him until the affair ended? Mark was being very careful not to tread on the sensitive toes of her independence, but she knew that the situation was harder on him than it was on her. He was the one who had to leave each evening.

She looked around to find that they had turned off on the narrow oiled road that led to the lodge, and Maggie shelved the problem with a mental promise to attack it at the first opportunity.

"You've been awfully quiet," Mark said as they pulled into the small gravel parking lot. "Is something wrong?"

"I'm just enjoying the quiet. It's been a hectic week."

He watched her closely as they walked to the

large wooden door, then said quietly, "Just say the word, Maggie, and we'll fly away to a place where they've never even heard of a sales consultant."

"Don't tempt me." She laughed, then turned to greet Jake as he opened the door for them.

She had seen Jake on many occasions in the past, but now, knowing he had helped to make Mark the man he was, she looked at him with new eyes. How could this rough, homey man have been even partially responsible for the suave Mark? Whatever Jake had given him must be beneath the surface, hidden from the naked eye.

Jake welcomed them warmly into the large, open room that looked out over the small, twenty-acre lake. He had no guests, for the room was empty and no boats were visible on the lake.

After Mark had seated himself beside Maggie on the long, low sofa, he said, "Well, old man, what's this I hear about your falling in the lake again?"

"Again?" Jake asked gruffly. "You're gonna give Maggie, here, the idea that I make a habit of tryin' to drown myself."

"Well, don't you?" Mark asked, grinning widely. "I seem to remember a time a few years back when you took a nose dive off the dock into shallow water and came up spitting mud and curses a mule skinner would have been proud to use."

Jake shook his head sadly, his pale eyes twinkling with merriment. "You've got the devil in you for sure, boy. You had it then, and I sure don't see any signs of its dissipating."

"Surely you don't blame me," Mark said in mock surprise, then turned to Maggie to explain. "I was twelve years old at the time and I had just caught the granddaddy bass of all time. I would have landed him just fine if Jake hadn't gotten so excited that he tripped over his own legs and fell in the lake."

"For shame, Mark," Jake reprimanded. "Filling Maggie's head full of lies like that. Don't listen to him, darlin'. That long-legged limb of satan stuck out his foot on purpose just to see me take a dip."

"A vicious canard," Mark replied sadly. "Nothing but a vicious canard."

"Oh, talk English for once," Jake muttered. "And if that means the God Almighty truth, then I agree."

Maggie laughed along with the two men, enjoying their good-natured banter. The argument was apparently an old one, for soon the insults were coming fast and furious, each one more outrageous than the last.

Mark finally ended it by saying, "I don't care what you say: the truth is, you caused me to lose a record bass. Now, tell me, who threw you in the lake this time?"

"It's that damned dock. It should have been replaced years ago," Jake said, rubbing his weathered jaw. "I was leaning down to check one of the posts and lost my balance."

"Was the post rotted out like you thought?"

"Yeah, there's three of 'em that need replacing," he replied. "I'll get Harv and Shorty on it next week."

Mark stood. "Why don't I have a look at them while I'm here?"

"Now, sit down, son. There's no need for you to do that. The men will get to it when they have time."

"I want to, Jake." He turned to smile at Maggie. "You don't mind if I leave you with this old reprobate, do you?"

"Of course I don't mind," Maggie said over Jake's indignant snort. "Jake and I can compare notes about a certain self-satisfied man we both know."

"That sounds vaguely ominous." Mark laughed. "Perhaps I should stay to protect my image."

"Oh, go on, boy. Git," Jake said, shooing Mark away. "Me and Maggie are going to have a nice talk. If your image is just one-half as good as you think it is, it'll hold up."

As Mark left the room chuckling, Jake turned to Maggie. "Now tell me what that scoundrel's been up to, Maggie. I can't tell you how tickled I was when he told me you two had gotten together."

"Thank you," Maggie murmured. "I still find it hard to believe he's your nephew."

"So do I sometimes," the old man muttered, more to himself than to Maggie. "He used to practically live with me and Jennie. You never met Jennie, did you, Maggie?" He smiled slowly, his eyes taking on a soft, reminiscent quality. "She was the most beautiful thing God ever put on this earth. And she thought the sun rose and set in Mark's eyes. When we found out we'd never have kids, I thought her heart would break in pure sorrow. Then Mark came along. His mama was sickly, and Jonathan—Jon's my brother—he never seemed to have time for the boy. So me and Jennie got him every summer. That is, 'til old Marcus decided he was old enough to start learning all about big business."

He sighed heavily, a tired sound. "I sure hated to see him stop coming—mainly for Jennie's sake and because I loved him myself, but partly because I knew what my father and his circus of fools could do to a person. He tried the same thing on me fifty years ago."

"He wanted you to take over?" Maggie asked, finding it hard to imagine this man, with his stooped frame and his gnarled, work-roughened hands, in Mark's world.

"He sure did. He knew Jonathan would never have a head for business, so I was his only other choice. When I saw which way the wind was blowing, I lit out. I roamed around the country for a couple of years, picking fruit and washing dishes. Then I discovered East Texas and my Jennie." A light shone deep in the old man's faded gray eyes, and for a moment they looked remarkably like Mark's. "I knew the minute I saw her that she was what I was looking for—and I didn't even know I was looking. She was the little, bittiest thing you ever saw. And she was true clear through to the middle. I gotta tell you, Maggie, for a while I was tempted to go back and take old Marcus up on his offer, just so I could give Jennie the fine things she deserved. But she knew. Yessir, my Jennie knew what I was thinking, and she turned as stubborn as an old mule. She said she wasn't cut out to be high society and all she wanted was me and a house full of my kids. So I bought this place from Dan Kingman for her. God didn't see fit to give us those kids, but he made it up to us by sending Mark. If I didn't love Mark for himself, I'd love him for the happiness I saw in Jennie's eyes when she looked at him."

He sighed and seemed to draw himself back to the present. "I don't think I've said so many words in one sitting in twenty years. I didn't know I still had that much wind left in me. You're a good listener, Maggie." He reached across from his chair and patted her hand. "Now tell me what you think of my boy."

"That's a tall order, Jake," she said, shaking her head ruefully. "I've asked myself the same question dozens of times. Sometimes—usually, in fact—I think I don't know him well enough to have an opinion. I just know I love being with him."

"That's enough for now. The rest will take care of itself. Now let's go see if our supper is about ready."

After they had stood for a while in the kitchen talking to his large, cheerful housekeeper, Jake sent Maggie out to tell Mark that dinner was almost ready. She walked slowly in the direction of the dock, thinking about her conversation with Mark's uncle. All through their talk she had had the strangest feeling that he was trying to tell her something. Jake was not a man to give unasked-for advice. He had been making a statement of some kind and was evidently leaving her to figure it out on her own.

As she neared the dock a splash drew her thoughts away from the puzzling conversation, and she focused on a figure standing on the far side of the dock. It looked like . . . no, it couldn't possibly be Mark.

"Mark!" she gasped as she drew near enough to confirm her suspicion. "My Lord, you're covered with . . . mud!"

He looked up from the post he was pulling loose, to see her standing on the bank, then looked down at his bare, mud-smeared chest. "Why, yes. So I am," he replied, giving the post one last hard yank, then walking to lay it on the bank. "But on me even mud takes on a new elegance, don't you think?"

"You're impossible," she said, backing away as he threatened to hug her. "How are you going to sit down to dinner?"

"I keep a few clothes here. Now, stop backing away from me. Haven't you ever made love in the mud?"

"No. And I'm not about to start now. I still can't believe you're actually out here playing in the mud. I've never seen you mussed before."

"If I can't carry off a little mud with dignity and style, then I've lost my touch," he said haughtily, then laughed as she continued to stare in astonishment. "Come on, love. We'd better get back before Jake sends out a search party. I presume he sent you to fetch me."

"Yes. Dinner's almost ready," she said, walking beside him but carefully avoiding bumping into him.

"So what did you and Jake talk about? Did he let you in on the secrets of my past?"

"A few."

"And did you let him in on the secrets of my present?"

She smiled, thinking again how little she really knew about Mark. "I'm afraid your present secrets are still secrets, because I haven't a clue. I'm simply riding in your wake."

He stopped walking to look down at her. "Is that the way you see it?" He smiled a strange little smile. "How odd," he murmured, then began to walk again, changing the subject before she could comment. "How do you think Jake looks? I've been worried about him lately. The last time I was here—on the memorable weekend that we met—he was recovering from a bout with pneumonia."

"He seems fine to me. I've never known him to talk so much. He told me about your Aunt Jennie."

"Did he? We don't usually talk about her. It's

been twenty years since she died, but we both still miss her."

"She must have been a very special person," Maggie said. Mark's voice held the same quiet sadness that Jake's had when he had spoken of his Jennie, and Maggie wondered what kind of woman could have made such an impression on these two strong men.

"She was the best," he said simply.

They entered by the back way to avoid tracking mud into the living room, and Maggie stayed to talk with Jake about Maggie's aunt and uncle, while Mark went to shower. Later they joined Mark in the living room to wait on the last-minute preparations for dinner.

Mark sat on the sofa, pulling Maggie down beside him after mixing them both what he termed the perfect après-mud drink. Jake reclaimed his former position, watching them with a peculiar look in his eyes.

All through dinner he rarely took his eyes off Maggie and Mark, listening closely to their lighthearted teasing, and he seemed to grow more uneasy as the night wore on.

When they were preparing to leave, Jake took Maggie aside, out of range of Mark's hearing. "Maggie," he said hesitantly, "sometime soon do you think you could come back to see me . . . alone?"

"Of course, Jake," she said, puzzled by his request. "Was there anything in particular you wanted to discuss with me?"

He started to reply, but when he saw Mark moving in their direction, he seemed to change his mind and said jokingly, "Oh, just this and that and the price of shoes, darlin'. Now, you better go. Mark'll get jealous seeing you whispering secrets with a fine-lookin' man like me."

"I heard that, you old derelict. Trying to steal my woman, are you?" Mark asked, grinning.

"All's fair, boy. All's fair."

Jake stood in the door, waving as they drove away. Maggie turned around in her seat to give one last wave, then leaned back with a sigh, saying, "He's a wonderful old man. So warm and natural. You were lucky to have him and Jennie."

"Although I agree with you, love, I think I'm also a little jealous. I'm the only man you're supposed to find wonderful." He pulled the car over to the side of the road. "Do you see where we are?"

Maggie looked around. They were parked in front of her aunt and uncle's house, which lay in darkness. "Yes, but why are we stopping? Aunt Sarah and Uncle Charles always go to bed with the sun."

Leaning over, Mark put his arm around her and whispered in her ear, "There's a mound of dirt behind that house"—he nipped her earlobe gently—"that covers a cozy little cave"—he moved to kiss the sensitive skin behind her ear—"which holds some very lovely and some very frustrating memories. If I weren't afraid your uncle would shoot us as prowlers, I would carry you into that cavern and finish what we started there."

Excitement shot through her veins, singing dizzily in her ears. She turned her head, touching his neck softly with her lips. "I wouldn't want you to feel cheated," she murmured huskily. "We could always turn off all the lights in my apartment and sleep on the floor."

"Once I get you alone in your apartment, I doubt we'll get past the living-room floor," he said, his breath hot on her lips as his head descended. "I could eat you up right now." He traced the line of her lips with his warm, moist tongue before plunging it into the sweet depths of her mouth. Maggie met his tongue hungrily as the urgency built in each of them.

"My God, princess," he groaned, clasping her head to his chest. "What am I going to do with you?"

Maggie snaked her hand around his waist, feeling the warmth beneath his clothes. "I could make a few suggestions," she whispered shakily.

Giving a broken laugh, he released her slowly. "We had better leave now, before we risk shocking your relatives."

The drive back to Dallas seemed to take years, and when they finally arrived at Maggie's apartment, she found Mark's prediction to be accurate. They made it no farther than the furry living-room rug before giving in to the passion that raged in them both.


"Maggie, for heaven's sake, what are you doing?" Mark asked as he stood waiting for her to catch up with him. "Our reservation was for eight and it's eight-fifteen now."

She looked up belligerently as she walked to stand beside him. "And whose fault is that? I was ready to go. You're the one who had to watch the rest of that dumb situation comedy."

"It wasn't dumb," he protested, taking her arm as they walked. "It was a sensitive portrayal of the problems encountered by a transvestite hockey player."

144

"You idiot." She laughed. "It was about an advertising executive and his wife."

"Oh, was that his wife? I suppose it was the mustache that threw me off."

Maggie's laughter was interrupted by increasingly loud shouts from across the parking lot. The vulgarisms seemed out of place in the beautifully landscaped grounds of the Greek restaurant where they were about to dine. Maggie leaned around Mark to find out what was going on and saw three men standing under a tree, their angry curses attracting the attention of several people leaving the restaurant.

"Mark, they're bullying him," she gasped.

Mark tightened his hold on her arm and continued walking toward the entrance. "Stay out of it, Maggie," he said firmly.

"But he's just a boy."

He stopped abruptly, turning her to look at him. "Maggie, you cannot butt into other people's personal business." He gave her a little shake. "Now, no one is being hurt. They're simply arguing."

"But he's so young, and I saw one of them shove him." She looked up, her eyes pleading. "Couldn't you just check to make sure he doesn't need help?"

"You promised you wouldn't get me into this kind of thing again," he reminded her, then looked into her eyes and sighed in resignation. "Okay, okay. But you stay right here."

She watched in tense silence as he walked toward the trio. They turned as Mark approached, eyeing him curiously. From where she stood, Maggie couldn't hear what was being said, but she could tell the three men were listening closely to what Mark was saying. Then suddenly all she could see were flying fists and she ran toward them, shouting as she went. When she arrived, out of breath, the trio was walking away and Mark was leaning against the tree, holding his handkerchief to his eyes.

"Mark?" she said hesitantly. "Are you all right?"

Slowly he lowered the handkerchief, exposing some angry-looking scratches and a red and puffy eye which promised to be the most vivid shiner she had ever seen. He looked at Maggie, his eyes blazing, and spoke through clenched teeth. "If you ever . . . so much as look like you're about to volunteer my help again, so help me, Maggie, I'll hold you up by your toes until that busy little nose of yours turns blue."

"I promise," she said, torn between laughter and tears. "Never. Never again." She reached up to touch his face. "I'm so sorry, Mark. I seem to make a habit of saying that, don't I? Does it hurt much? It looks"—she swallowed a semihysterical giggle—"awful."

He looked suspiciously at her sober face, then said irritably, "I'm not exactly fond of pain, but no, it's not bad. And you can stop squelching that laugh. I can't hear it, but I can definitely see it in your eyes."

"No, you're wrong," she protested. "At least, I'm not amused by your pain. It's just . . ." She paused and looked again at the crimson and swelling skin that she had been carefully avoiding. "It looks so strange." His eyes told her immediately that she had said the wrong thing. He looked at her as if she were a pesky fly that had irritated him once too often, so she said hurriedly, "Why don't we go home so I can put an ice pack on it? I can fix you something to eat and . . ." She stopped as something besides irritation began to form in his eyes.

"And what, Maggie?"

"And . . . oh, I don't know. I guess I can apologize for getting you into a scrape and try to make up for it."

"And just how do you propose to do that?" he said, making no effort to hide his growing amusement.

"Well, certainly not the way you think," she fumed. "And if you're not going to be gracious enough to accept my apology, then you can just forget the whole thing."

"But I always accept everything you offer me graciously, love. And if you truly want to make up for being the cause of my excruciating pain, I'm sure we can work something out." He was laughing openly now.

"You are the most—" she began, her eyes blazing.

"Adorable, intelligent, handsome, *forgiving* man you've ever met," he finished for her. "That is what you were going to say, isn't it?"

Maggie looked into his eyes, ready to blast him, when suddenly her anger died. It was impossible to stay mad at him. He was so damn cute. "Yes," she murmured. "Now that you mention it, I guess that is what I was going to say."

For a moment he looked as though her answer had taken him by surprise, then slowly he began to smile and together they walked back across the parking lot to his car.

Back at Maggie's apartment, Mark consumed an enormous cheese omelet, then lay on the sofa, his head in her lap so she could apply the ice pack and a soothing hand to his brow.

Looking up at her with one gleaming silver eye, he asked, "Did you see which of the malodorous cretins dropped the Brooklyn Bridge on my face?"

"Well, actually . . ." She hesitated, avoiding his eye.

"Which one, Maggie?" he demanded.

"It was the boy," she admitted with a sigh.

"That pimple-faced little cur?" he shouted, pulling off the ice pack to stare in surprise. "But he couldn't have weighed more than a hundred and twenty pounds."

"He sneaked the punch in when you weren't looking," she soothed. "And anyway, I think you broke the fat one's nose."

"Did I?" He looked somewhat mollified by the information, replacing the ice pack with a sigh.

"Mark, why did they start punching? What on earth did you say?"

"I simply asked them politely to move their quarrel to a less public location, but they made it quite clear that they resented my interference." He removed the ice pack again to look at her. "Maggie," he said quietly. "I'm not Sir Lancelot. Not now, not ever. I would fight the city of Dallas en masse to keep you or Jake from being hurt, but I can't play Don Quixote even for you."

"I don't expect—" she began.

"But you do, love," he said, sitting up and pulling her into his arms. "Maybe not consciously, but somewhere inside you, you expect me to be something I'm not and never could be." He tilted her chin with his fingers. "Couldn't you possibly accept me as I am?"

Maggie laughed uncertainly, looking away from his observant eyes. "Don't be silly. Why should I not accept you the way you are?"

"Ah, love." He sighed heavily, closing his eyes as though disappointed in her answer. Then he opened them to murmur, "What happened to your plans to make it up to me for causing me to become entangled in a common brawl?"

Maggie smiled and slowly began unbuttoning his shirt, loving the feel of him, unaccountably relieved that the discussion had been postponed. She spread his shirt wide, running her hands across his chest, wondering if their lovemaking would ever be ordinary and mechanical. They had been together for over a month and still came together each time with a renewed hunger. Each time was new and wondrous and so right. And as long as this was right, all the rest seemed to fade into the background for Maggie.

She leaned her head forward, her tongue beginning to tease the stiff male nipples that her fingers had discovered. But Mark, breaking under the erotic torture with a deep growl, grasped her head suddenly between his hands, pulling her up to meet his lips—and the magic began again.

Maggie woke the next morning in Mark's arms, immeasurably glad she had asked him to spend the night. The warmth of having him beside her reached more than her flesh. She felt it all the way through her body. If she could only bottle the feeling, she felt she could cure the ills of the world.

Stretching lazily she caught sight of the clock on the nightstand. "Oh, Lord," she moaned. It was six-thirty already. If she didn't move quickly, she would be late for work. She turned to slip from the bed, but felt a large, warm hand snake around her bare waist to detain her.

"Deserting one's post is a serious offense," he murmured huskily, moving to half-cover her body.

"I know," she whispered regretfully. "But time

and Howard Electronics wait for no man. It's Monday and I have to go make peanut butter money."

Smoothing the curls from her forehead with a gentle, lingering touch, he said, as though the idea had just hit him, "Maggie, why don't you quit? No, wait and let me finish. We could get married. Then you wouldn't have to work and I wouldn't have to go home to an empty bed each night."

Maggie felt a whirling rush of warmth spread through her veins. She hadn't anticipated his proposal, and she certainly hadn't anticipated her reaction to it. What was wrong with her? Before she could gather her chaotic thoughts enough to form a reply of any kind, he continued.

"It would be such fun, love. We could go where we please and do what we want."

Fun? she thought, her heated blood cooling with the word, a shaft of deep, unexplainable pain striking her dead center. But of course he wanted fun. What had she expected, undying love? She closed her eyes against the thought, taking a deep breath to gain control, then opened them to find him watching her. "You're a nut," she laughed shakily. "People don't get married to have fun. At least, sensible people don't."

She slid from his grasp and walked to the closet to remove her robe. As she pulled it on she said, "I know this arrangement hasn't been too convenient for either of us, but we can work something out. Something a little less drastic than marriage."

As she walked into the bathroom for her shower, Mark lay where she had left him, silently examining the ceiling, but by the time she had finished showering and dressing, the carefree manner had reappeared, and before she left for work, he had arranged to pick her up for dinner as usual.

Maggie wished it were as easy for her to return to normal. Confusing thoughts pounded away at her head and by lunchtime had taken their toll, leaving her with a blinding headache. She sat in a little sandwich shop with Carrel, toying with her sandwich until Carrel could stand her lassitude no longer.

"Maggie," she said, the exasperation in her voice making Maggie flinch in pain. "What on earth is wrong with you? You've been a zombie all day. It's positively eerie."

"Mark proposed," Maggie replied dully.

"But that's wonderful!" Carrel said enthusiastically. "Why are you acting like the bottom just dropped out of the market?"

"It's not wonderful. It's—"

"Yes. It is," Carrel insisted. "I've been so worried about you. I could see how much you loved him and I was afraid you'd be hurt, but if you're going to marry him—"

"Love?" Maggie asked, shock widening her eyes. "I don't . . ." She stopped as the truth hit her with a sharp pain. "Oh, God," she moaned. "Of course, I love him. How could I be so stupid?"

"Now what's wrong? You love him. He proposed. What could be more perfect?"

"Carrel," Maggie said, the pain in her chest restricting her speech. "He wants to marry me because it will be fun."

"Of course it will be fun," her friend replied in confusion.

"You don't understand," she whispered, biting her lip to control the quivering. "He doesn't love me. He wants me and we have fun together, but he doesn't love me. And I want to be loved, Carey.

I want to be loved by him. The way Jake loved—still loves—Jennie. The way I love Mark."

"Oh, honey," Carrel said, laying her hand on Maggie's. "Don't you think you're asking too much? The kind of love Jake had for Jennie—that's a one in a million thing. Don't you think you should take what you can get? Believe me, it's more than most people get a chance at."

"I just don't know." Maggie sighed. "He didn't even mind when I turned him down."

"So tell him you've reconsidered, marry him, and then work for what you want," Carrel said urgently. "You've got a good start, Maggie. Build on it."

The rest of the day was a total loss as far as Maggie's work was concerned. She couldn't get Mark out of her mind. Build on it, Carrel had said. Build on what? All they had going for them was Maggie's love and an overpowering physical attraction. They were worlds apart in every other way. How could they build on such shifting sand? And would Mark even want to? If it got to be too much of an effort, if it stopped being fun, wouldn't he simply give up? Then where would Maggie be? She'd be out in the cold, much worse off than she was now, because she would have gotten used to loving him, would have built up her hopes so high that she would be completely devastated when it was over.

She couldn't imagine any pain worse than what she was feeling now, but logically she knew that it would be much, much worse later, when she had come to depend on him. And that would be like trying to depend on a butterfly.

No, she had to get out of it now, before the damage was too great. She had to call him and break their date for this evening, then find a way to tell him it was over. It wouldn't be easy, she knew. Mark really cared for her in his own way, and she didn't want to hurt him. But she was fighting for her life now, and she would find the strength somehow.

Picking up the phone, she dialed Mark's office number and asked for Mark when she heard the soft, feminine voice of his secretary.

Mark's voice was warm and low as he asked without greeting her, "How did you know I was thinking of you?"

Maggie swallowed hard and closed her eyes. She had known it would be difficult, but she could never have imagined the pain she felt at simply hearing his voice. "I guess I'm psychic," she said, her voice strained.

"Is something wrong, love?"

"Well, actually there is, Mark." She paused, feeling his tension through the wire. "Something's come up, and I won't be able to see you tonight." The words came in an awkward rush, causing the silence that followed to sound deafening in her ear.

"I see," he said finally. "Well, if it can't be helped, it can't be helped. Shall I call you later this evening?"

"No," she answered quickly, before her nerve failed. "I'll call you tomorrow or"—her throat constricted—"something."

This time the silence drew out until she felt she would scream. Then his voice, stiff and slow, came over the line again. "Very well, Maggie. If that's what you want." Then the phone was dead.

No, she moaned silently, it's not what I want. I want you. I want your love. Maggie took a deep breath, the muscles of her face tightening to keep the pain from overflowing. She suddenly felt someone watching her and looked up to see Carrel leaning against the partition wall.

"Why?" Carrel asked.

"He could break me," Maggie whispered through tight lips. "When he flew away to something that was more amusing, it would kill me. I know it would."

Carrel turned away, shaking her head in disgust, then looked back at her to say quietly, "You're a coward, Maggie." She picked up her purse and left without looking back.

And so went the beginning of the end, Maggie thought as she drove home. If the pain is this bad when I try to break one date, what is it going to be like when I try to explain that it's over? And what can I possibly say that will make any sense at all? Maybe, she thought desperately, when the time comes I'll know.

But the time came sooner than she had anticipated. When she walked wearily to her apartment door, she found Mark there, his hands shoved in his pockets in an uncharacteristically awkward pose. She stopped short the minute she saw him, then covered the remaining distance slowly. "Hello," she said hesitantly. "I didn't expect to see you tonight."

He made no comment, but waited silently for her to open the door, then followed her into the living room. His face held a look Maggie had never seen there before. He looked older, harder. Maggie glanced away, searching for something to say. She looked back at him, and the words she had been forming died in her throat as she met his eyes.

"Do you want to tell me about it, Maggie?" he asked, a terrible flatness in his voice taking the place of the usual animation.

There could be no hedging now. She couldn't stall or try to make light of the situation. She owed him the truth. "I can't see you again," she began slowly, her pride demanding that she look him in the eye, her failing courage urging her to look away. Pride won, and she continued. "I'm getting too involved with you, Mark. More deeply than I ever expected or wanted."

"And that's bad?"

"Not bad," she corrected, "but wrong. Wrong for me and, I believe, wrong for you. Can't you see? We're totally different. Not just on the surface, but underneath, where it counts. I can't live the way you live without its eating away at me. And you've already told me you can't live my kind of life. Work bores you silly, and in time so would I."

He stood there, his silver eyes penetrating her skull, not speaking for interminable minutes. Then he said softly, "So you've got it all figured out, have you?" He turned and walked to the window. "But what if you're wrong, Maggie? Have you even considered the possibility? Suppose our lives could mesh out of bed as well as they do in it. Suppose you've been mistaken in your evaluation of my character and in the depth of my feeling for you."

"Have I?" she asked, almost begging him to confirm it. "Am I wrong, Mark?"

He turned to look at her, his eyes growing perceptibly darker for a moment. Then he sighed, his breath coming from his throat in a rough, raspy sound, and said wearily. "The infallible Maggie wrong? Not likely, love. Not likely."

And before she could move, before she could beg him to stay and give her whatever he had to give, he was gone.

# Chapter Ten

This time Mark didn't come back. There was no blond head showing above the downtown crowds. No silver eyes following her movements as she waded drearily through the routine that had seemed so important to her before.

It took Maggie two weeks and three disastrous dates with faceless men to know that she had to do something. She either had to come to grips with the situation as it was or make a move to change it. Mark hadn't been out of her mind for five consecutive minutes in the past two weeks.

She had seen him constantly in her mind, reliving the events of their affair. Mark shaking out the burlap bags to make a bed on the floor of the cellar. Mark holding his hand over his heart, telling her with that ridiculous Southern drawl that he fancied her. Mark standing beside her, his naked body gleaming in the sun.

Oh, God, she moaned silently, her hands covering her face as she sat in her dark living room, fighting a losing battle against the memories of Mark. Then, suddenly, different memories flooded her mind. The look in his eyes when she had told him she wouldn't respect herself if she slept with him. The way he had drawn back, refusing to seduce her when she had had too much to drink. The vulnerability that had shown in his face the day he had confronted her on the street. His concern for Jake. His unfailing tenderness, his gentle understanding.

A terrible heaviness settled on her chest, and she knew then that she was admitting for the first time the things she had always known. Mark was a man to be admired. A man who enjoyed life, and, for her, made it worth living. She had been so caught up in the care-for-nothing facade Mark showed the word that she had ignored the sensitive man underneath. And she had had many glimpses of the sensitive Mark. How could she have been so blind? How could she have not seen the man she had fallen in love with? The sensual Mark had held her body captive. The court jester had captured her imagination. But it was the vulnerable, sensitive Mark who had won and held her heart.

And she had let him go.

No, she hadn't let him go—she had shoved him away. And not for anything so noble as principles. For stupid, crippling pride. Maggie was afraid of failing again. It was that simple. She was afraid she didn't have what it took to hold a man like Mark. So she had given up before the battle even started.

As that realization sank in, the pain became

unbearable. It screamed inside her head and ripped at her chest. She was dying. She was sitting in this dark, quiet, lonely room and she was dying. And she had brought it on herself. Her damned stupidity, her abominable pride, her . . .

"My God," she whispered, standing abruptly and wiping the dampness from her cheeks with trembling hands. "I'm getting maudlin. Why in the hell am I sitting here moaning and feeling oh, so sorry for myself? I've got to *do* something."

She would go to see him, she decided, walking quickly into the bedroom to change. She reached in to pull out a dress, then let her hand fall back to her side. She couldn't confront him, out of the blue, with her feelings. It wouldn't be fair. He would feel obligated to pick up their affair again, and from his silence in the last two weeks it was clear that he had adjusted quickly to being without her.

But Maggie had to let him know the real reason she had sent him away. She had to tell him how she had closed her eyes to his true character. She couldn't let him continue to think that she held a low opinion of him—and Maggie needed to tell him of her love.

Finally deciding a letter was the only way to handle it fairly, she sat down to write. A letter would let him know her feelings yet call for no response on his part. He could throw it in the trash and forget it if he wished.

After three hours of trying to explain on paper, only to crumble each effort in disgust, she finally settled for a simple statement of fact. It read:

Dear Mark,

    This is the most difficult letter I've ever tried to write. I've searched desperately for a way to excuse my behavior toward you during our association but have found none. You were wrong, Mark. I'm not infallible. In fact I'm probably the most fallible person you could find. I've thought of you constantly for the past two weeks, and one thing has become clear. You're a man such as I've never known before. Maybe that's why I was so slow to open my eyes. I was blind to your sensitivity, your tenderness, and your strength. I was also blind to the fact that I love you.

I hope you can forgive me for running scared from the unknown quantity of my love for you. I know I never will.

Maggie

Maggie read it through again, dissatisfied with the inadequacy of the words, the thoughts it contained. It didn't hold a fraction of the things she needed to tell him, but perhaps it said what he needed to hear.

Resolutely, she folded it, placed it in an envelope, and sealed it. She tried to tell herself not to expect too much, that her main reason for writing was simply to let him know she had been wrong. But Maggie knew she was lying to herself. Selfishly, she wanted the letter to make a difference, to bring a response from Mark that would show her that he returned her love even in some small measure.

She mailed the letter the next morning, then began an interminable period of waiting. She kept reminding herself not to get her hopes up, but she couldn't keep the warmth from welling up inside every time she thought of him.

Friday was the day she had decided the letter

would reach him, and when it came and went without a word, a feeling of defeat settled heavily on her spirit. After spending Saturday morning listlessly gazing out her window, she decided she would go to see Jake. She didn't even try to fool herself into believing she was going simply to talk with a sweet old man. She wanted to be near anyone who reminded her of Mark.

Two hours later she pulled into the gravel parking lot. She had called before she left, to make sure Mark would not be there, and had been surprised to find that Jake sounded anxious to see her. As she walked to the front door, she remembered the way he had taken her aside the day she had been here with Mark. Maybe Jake could give her a clue to Mark's feelings that would at least ease the questions in her mind so that she could settle down to a future without him.

The housekeeper showed Maggie into the living room, where Jake sat in front of a fire. The air was just beginning to hold a little nip, and the fire looked warming.

"Hello, darlin'," Jake said, rising stiffly. "I wondered when you were going to get around to paying me a visit."

"How are you feeling, Jake?" she asked, taking the hand he extended.

"I think old age is finally catching up with me," he said, chuckling softly, then settled back in his chair as Maggie sat on the sofa.

He looked at her suddenly, his pale eyes amazingly sharp. "What's going on between you and Mark, Maggie? He hasn't been to see me since he brought you, but when he phones his voice sounds tired. Tired and old." He raised an eyebrow, and Maggie caught her breath as his resemblance to

Mark struck her forcibly. "That boy has never been tired in his life. What happened?"

Maggie opened her mouth to heap the blame on her own head once more, then stopped suddenly. "I'm sick of telling myself how wrong and stupid I was, Jake," she said vehemently. "It wasn't *all* my fault. I know I was a coward, but, damn it, he didn't make it any easier. He deliberately played the fool and hid himself from me. If he had been more open, maybe I could have been, too, and we wouldn't be in this mess now." She leaned back against the sofa and closed her eyes. "What difference does it make anyway?" she asked wearily. "He's made it perfectly clear he doesn't want to see me. I wrote to him and apologized. I took all the blame on myself, and he ignored it."

"Maybe he's hurting too bad to see you right now," he suggested softly. "Are you sure he's already gotten the letter?"

"Yes, I'm sure. It's had more than enough time to get to him."

"I was afraid something like this would happen. I could see the way things were going when you were here before. That's why I wanted to talk to you. Mark wouldn't thank me for interfering, but I think there are some things you are entitled to know about him."

He paused as though to gather his thoughts, then began to speak slowly and quietly. "When Mark was staying with Jennie and me, he was the most open, loving boy you could ever hope to meet. He wasn't any angel, so don't get me wrong, but he was an outgoing, lovable, normal boy. Then, when he was fourteen, old Marcus took over. At first it didn't seem to make much difference, and I hoped that Mark would come through it all right.

Then"—he paused, closing his eyes briefly and clearing his throat before he continued—"then Jennie died. It was like his anchor was torn loose, and in my grieving I couldn't seem to help him. The open, loving boy got buried somewhere deep inside him, and a man I didn't know took over. Every now and then I'd catch a glimpse of the Mark I knew and I could see he was hurting, but there wasn't a damn thing I could do about it. He had closed himself off to everyone—me included." He sighed heavily. "I didn't have to ask him what was happening. I knew. I had been there before him. I know what superficial, money-worshiping people can do to person's soul, especially a man like Mark. When I was in that trap, I ran—as far and as fast as I could. Well, Mark did the same thing. He ran and hid—only, he did it in his head. He pretended that none of it bothered him. He saw the greed and those slobbering jackasses trying to lick his boots and he laughed. It was the only way he could find to fight it. He knew if he showed his grandfather and his so-called friends his true face, they would rip it to pieces. So he showed them a face they could accept."

"But me?" Maggie whispered, making no attempt to check the tears streaming down her face. "Couldn't he have been honest with me? Did he think I was like them?"

"Think about it, Maggie. This was not an overnight process. Think about how many years it took, how many times he got slapped in the face before he learned his lesson." He hesitated, then seemed to come to a decision, and continued. "I saw him looking at you the night you were here. He looked at you the way I used to look at Jennie. And I saw fear in his eyes, too. Maggie, yours is the one slap that would break him. I guess he just couldn't risk it. He learned his lesson too well."

"So what do I do now?" Her voice was tight from the hopelessness she felt. "I've told him I love him. What else can I do?"

"Just wait, Maggie. And don't give up on him. I have a lot of faith in him. He'll come through, all right."

I hope you're right, Maggie thought as she drove home. Oh, Lord, Jake, I hope you're right.

The rest of the weekend dragged, and by Monday morning as she dressed for work, Maggie decided that Mark had had long enough to make up his mind. It was time to take things into her own hands. What they had was too important to let slip through their fingers. She would dog his steps if she had to, as he had done with her. She would make him admit he loved her.

Please, she begged silently, let him love me. Then she shoved away the insidious doubts and picked up her purse on her way into the living room. She was walking toward the door to leave when the doorbell rang. Expecting a neighbor or Carrel, she opened the door—and found Mark standing there.

Momentarily paralyzed, she stood in silence. She couldn't have spoken if her life depended on it. His dear face was set in stern lines, but for a moment his expression made no impression. All that mattered was the fact that he was there. He had come, just as Jake had said he would. Maggie felt joy exploding in her mind, racing through her body, leaving her weak. He knew she loved him and he had come. That had to mean something.

Then, as he continued to stand there with that closed, hard look on his face, the doubts began to creep in again. The knowledge that she loved him evidently brought none of the joy to Mark that she was feeling. He made no move to touch her. He simply stood and stared.

"Mark," she began huskily. "I—"

"I want you to come with me, Maggie," he said, his voice stiff and unbending. "I have something I want to show you."

He took her arm, giving her no chance to accept or reject his stilted request, and spoke not one word to her until they had driven downtown and were in the elevator on their way to his office.

"Why did you bring me here?" she asked quietly.

"Because there are some things you need to know," he replied, his voice chilling. "I had hoped that this wouldn't be necessary, but apparently I was wrong. I went back to St. Thomas last week, and it gave me a chance to think. I finally decided that I would give you hard facts, since feelings don't seem to matter to you."

"You've been out of town?" she said in surprise. The possibility that he could be out of town had never occurred to her.

He looked at Maggie as though she were a little stupid. "Yes. I returned yesterday. Why?"

He hadn't received her letter. He couldn't have if he had only returned yesterday, for she had sent the letter to his office. So he didn't know.

"Mark," she said urgently, "I've got to tell you—"

"We can talk later, Maggie. I want you to have the facts first."

"But—"

"Later," he repeated sharply as he ushered her into his office.

John Lowe was seated in a chair beside Mark's desk. He rose as they entered, and shook Maggie's hand before Mark indicated that she should sit in the chair placed in front of his desk. He moved to sit in his own high-backed, swivel chair, then nodded to John.

"Miss Simms," he began after clearing his throat. "Mr. Wilding has asked me to bring you up to date on some of the activities he's been involved in over the past few years. I believe you'll find it a very impressive list." He smiled and glanced at Mark, who had turned his chair sideways as though uninterested in the proceedings, then cleared his throat again and continued. "When Mr. Wilding took over the company ten years ago it was still in the age of the dinosaur. It wasn't easy, because there were many who opposed him, but he brought it up to its present efficiency in just a few short years. What he did in simple terms was to . . ."

Maggie sat silently as Mr. Lowe began to lecture on the innovations Mark had made, not only in the parent company, but in all of the Wilding holdings. From there he went on to the labor reforms he had instituted, his work with charitable organizations, his activity as the prime mover behind the renovation of several historical sights around the state, and his periodic lectures at various Texas universities. She was bombarded by innumerable facts and figures for the next two hours. Then, smiling and nodding, John Lowe gathered his papers and left the room.

For several moments a heavy silence filled the office. Then Mark began to speak quietly. "Do you have any idea how demeaning it is for a man to have to convince someone he loves that he is worth her attention? After you politely suggested that I get lost, I told myself that if you couldn't love me without my having to prove myself, then I was better off without you." He turned to look at her, a strange, mocking smile appearing on his face. "But of course, that view didn't last long. After a hellish week without you I was brought forcibly to the conclusion that I would do whatever I had to do to get you. I can't say the realization made me ecstatic. It didn't. It made me feel weak and spineless. It's a very uncomfortable feeling, Maggie, and it's going to take me awhile to come to grips with it. Until then I think it would be best if you leave. Maybe later we can work something out, if you like, but not now." He closed his eyes and repeated, his voice strained, "Not now."

It took Maggie some time to absorb what he was saying. She had latched eagerly onto the fact that he had said he loved her, and the rest seeped in slowly through the cozy fog that enveloped her. He wanted her to leave. She had to tell him, make him understand that she loved him and had wanted him before Mr. Lowe's report.

"Mark, there is something that you should know."

"Please, Maggie, would you simply leave?" He leaned back in his chair. "I'm tired and I've got a half-dozen things to do before I can go home."

Maggie rose from her chair and walked to stand beside him. If she could touch him, she knew she could make him understand. "Listen to me, Mark. I sent . . ." She glanced down, and there, on top of a stack of mail, was her letter to him.

Mark's eyes followed hers, took in the letter, but showed no signs of comprehension. He stared at her for a moment, then rose abruptly to move away from her, saying, "Damn it, Maggie. What are you doing? If you have those blasted hiccups again, so help me, I'll strangle you." He moved to a wooden cabinet to pour himself a drink. "I have an appointment in five minutes, so we don't have time to discuss anything now."

She stared at him as he swallowed the drink in one gulp. Then she glanced back at the letter and shrugged. There was nothing she could do now. Eventually he would have to read the letter, and then he would know and understand. "Okay." She sighed. "If that's what you want." She turned and left the office.

What a holy mess, she thought as she took the elevator down to the lobby. She couldn't decide whether to laugh or cry. Every time it seemed as though things were going to work out between them, something else happened. It was all so crazy. She loved him and he loved her and they were still apart.

Mark loves me, she thought giddily, blocking out all the problems as the words formed again in her head, and they seemed so loud and clear that she looked around the elevator to see if anyone had noticed. But apparently no one had heard the joyous words, for they all seemed to be staring at the ceiling. She wanted to grab the world by the shoulders and shout, "He loves me."

As she walked down the street away from his office, Maggie smiled at strangers, perused the merchandise displayed in the windows—and took in absolutely nothing. Stopping before a small shop, she realized that it was familiar. This was the window that had held the brass unicorn. The unicorn had been dethroned by a red ceramic pig, and Maggie paused to stare at it, remembering. She had looked up that day and seen his reflection in the window.

Maggie looked up, and suddenly her reminiscent smile faded, her eyes widening in surprise. There, standing behind her, gasping for breath, was Mark. She whirled around to face him. "Mark!"

"Maggie, you little fiend," he said, breathing hard. "I'm too old to be chasing you down the street. Why in hell didn't you tell me about that letter?"

Before she could even formulate an answer he grasped her arm and began walking toward his office, pulling her along with him. She managed somehow to keep up with his long strides as he hurried her down the street and through the lobby to the elevator. She leaned gratefully against the elevator wall, trying to ignore the amusement of the other occupants.

When they reached the floor housing his office, she then had to face the curious stare of his secretary before finally reaching the solitude of his large office.

"Now," he said, closing the door behind her and leaning against it, "let's try to get this straight. You wrote that letter last week. Right?"

Maggie nodded silently.

"So my great martyr act was unnecessary?"

Maggie stifled a smile and nodded again.

"And you were trying to tell me about it when I very dramatically threw you out of my office?"

Maggie couldn't keep her lips from twitching as she nodded once more.

"And you're not going to make it one bit easier for me, are you? You're just going to stand there and let me make an even bigger ass of myself. Right?"

The smile could no longer be contained, and

she grinned openly as she said, "Right," then walked into his open arms.

"Oh, God, princess," he growled in her ear as he tried to meld her body into his own. "It's been so long. And I've been so hungry for you."

"I know," she whispered, burying her face in his chest, clutching him fiercely. "It's been awful."

"I thought I would go crazy," he murmured as he eased her down on the couch that lay along one wall of his office. "I would stay up until all hours of the night thinking of you. Then, when I would finally drift off to sleep, I would dream of you. And wake up to nothing."

"I'm sorry. I'm so sorry," she whispered urgently, touching his face, his throat, needing to confirm his presence. "It was my fault. I was so stupid."

"Hush," he said softly. "It doesn't matter now. All that matters is that you're here in my arms, where you belong." Pressing her back into the firm couch with his body, he buried his face in her throat, tasting the velvety skin with voracious kisses, smoothing the way with fingers that trembled. The buttons of her cream silk blouse were flimsy obstacles that fell quickly under his urgent siege. Then, without pause, he unclasped her lace bra, spreading the fabric of her blouse apart with hands that lingered on her swelling breasts. He watched with hungry eyes as her dusky rose nipples tautened and stood firm under his stroking thumbs.

Maggie caught her breath sharply as she felt his touch on her skin like tiny electric shocks. The pleasure sizzled through her flesh, and she moved convulsively as the tingling concentrated in her lower body. Without her volition, her hands reached up to draw his head down to her tumultuous breasts, and a groan, part pain, part pleasure, began in Mark's chest and was muffled against her rounded flesh.

He grasped her breast roughly with his hand as he nipped and stroked and sucked the erect tip avidly into his greedy mouth. He seemed to have lost all control, straining against her, pressing first one breast, then the other, into his heated mouth. He raised suddenly to jerk off his jacket and tie, then began to unbutton his shirt. Maggie reached up to help him but found her shaking fingers too uncoordinated to be of any use.

When the last button was freed, Mark leaned down slowly, his breath coming in short, raspy gasps. He was torturing her with his slow movements, and she felt she would shriek in frustration if she didn't feel his flesh against hers soon.

When the frustration had reached unbearable proportions, he reached down to slide his arm under her back and raised her the least fraction of an inch to meet him. She whimpered as the relief and pleasure—so incredibly acute—spread through her. She felt weak, as though her bones had been removed. Unable to move, she could merely lie there and feel.

But Mark suffered no such affliction. He moved against her urgently, each movement sending waves of sensation through her body. His hand slipped under her pleated skirt and slid down inside her panty hose, fondling her buttocks, squeezing them tightly before sliding around to clasp the heated, throbbing warmth between her legs.

Maggie cried out in unbelievable pleasure, writhing against his hair-roughened chest, his seeking fingers.

"God, princess," he whispered hoarsely. "I need

your magic now. I don't know if I can wait until we get home."

"I know, I know," she said softly through dry lips, her hand stroking his head soothingly as it lay on her breasts. "But someone could come in at any minute." She laughed shakily. "You certainly don't look like a dignified businessman right now."

"I don't feel like one, either," he said, turning his head to kiss her smooth, slightly tender flesh. "I've got a terrible problem, sweet."

"Oh?" she murmured, shivering in delight as she felt his lips touch the soreness of her breasts.

"Yes," he said. "I've got to figure out how to get us to your apartment without letting you out of my arms."

"That's a tough one, all right," she said, smiling in sympathy, then pressing his head closer. Although his voice sounded lazily casual, she could feel the frustration in his body. She wanted to soothe him, to bring him back from the high-pitched intensity of their interrupted lovemaking. She began to stoke his back, smoothing the taut muscles. But what began as aid to the man she loved soon turned into an exercise in tactile delight.

Her hands wandered over the warm, hard flesh, discovering every bone, every sinew in his strong back. She slid her palms down the ridge of his spine, over the sides of his trim waist, then back to slide her fingertips under his belt. Unable to stop the mesmerizing strokes, she moved her hand slowly around his side, then suddenly felt her fingers grasped and halted by his.

"Maggie," he said, his voice tight and hoarse. "I know you're trying to help, but if that's supposed to calm me, it's a total failure."

"Oh," she gasped, suddenly realizing what she

had been doing. "I'm sorry. I didn't mean . . . I was only trying to—"

"I know. And I appreciate your concern, but I don't think I can stand much more of your soothing without taking some definite and untimely action."

"Oh, Mark," she said, laughing at his rueful expression. "I've missed you so much. And it was all so dumb—I was so dumb."

"For heaven's sake, Maggie. Stop saying that." He raised up to look at her, then lay his head down again with a sigh. "You weren't any 'dumber' than I was. In fact, you showed remarkable intelligence compared to me. I knew what was happening. I could see so clearly where we were headed, but I couldn't—no, wouldn't—stop it. I didn't have the courage." He brushed his lips against her in an unconscious gesture, his eyes clouded with memories. "I was the clown, the court jester. I was afraid if I told you how desperately I loved you, you would laugh and make light of it, the way you did every time I hinted that I wanted more than an affair."

"But I thought you were joking," she protested, tightening her hold, feeling the hurt he must have felt at the time.

"I know, love," he soothed. "It wasn't your fault."

"Yes, it was," she insisted. "At least partly. I was all hung up on seeing you as a frivolous, superficial playboy, and I wouldn't let myself believe the evidence that was staring me in the face. And for the same reason as you: I was afraid. Afraid of failing again. What we had—have—was so beautiful, I couldn't take a chance on screwing it up." She laughed in disgust. "So I screwed it up."

"You didn't. You couldn't," he said softly. "I don't think anything could. Why do you think I pursued you the way I did? I knew that eventually, no matter what happened, we would be together. We had to be," he whispered, "or I would have lost myself, like in my dream."

"Your dream? The one you had in the cellar, then on St. Thomas?"

"That's the one." He shuddered and held her tighter. "The first time I had it was that night in the cellar." He grinned suddenly, his face looking years younger. "I was after you that night, love. From the first moment I saw you, I wanted you. And I'm not ashamed to say that I went to sleep that night with highly lustful thoughts filling my head. Then I had the dream. At first it didn't seem like a nightmare, merely a very strange dream. I was standing in a huge room—a ballroom perhaps—and I was surrounded by nebulous figures. Faceless people. Some male and some female, but all with a blank space where their faces should have been. At this point I began to feel a little uneasy. I began recognizing the figures as people I had known during my life. Don't ask me how. It wasn't as though I could see identifying marks or anything like that. I simply knew suddenly who they were. I remember seeing one of my closest friends, whom I had had dinner with only a few nights before. And standing next to him was the girl I was engaged to when I was twenty-four. The past and present were all jumbled together. And still I wasn't frightened. I simply knew that I didn't want to be there among all those faceless and, it seemed, soulless, people. Then I saw a huge gilded mirror hanging on one wall, the area around it deserted. I was drawn to it. I began to walk toward it even though I didn't want to. The closer I got, the stronger the feeling of dread became. I think I knew what I would see even before I stopped in front of the mirror, but that didn't make the shock, the horror, any less. When I looked into the mirror I saw that I was one of them. I was a nonperson, like everyone else in the room.

His voice was low and rough as he recalled the dream. Maggie shivered, stroking his face, sharing the terror with him as he took a deep breath and continued. "It was the most spine-chilling thing that had ever happened to me. You know how nightmares are. There's no logic, no reason, just overpowering terror. I was standing there facing the loss of my reality. Then I felt a peculiar sensation, as though the mirror had lost some of its power over me. I turned away and saw you." He hugged her closer, kissing her neck in a gesture of gratitude. "You were standing there in the middle of that ghoulish crowd, and reality seemed to shine out of you like dawn breaking on a dark night. In that moment it was as though I had X-ray vision, as though I could see clear to the heart of you, and I saw truth. You smiled at me, and the terror disappeared. You walked toward me then, and, Maggie"—he closed his eyes, remembering—"I seemed to swell and grow inside. When you stood beside me we turned together and looked again into the mirror. Somehow having you stand beside me had pulled me away from that false, nebulous world and I could see my own truth, my own reality, reflected in the mirror. As I stared at our images, I felt that I was on the verge of an important discovery. There was something I couldn't quite grasp, but I knew it was vital. Then you smiled again—a sad little smile—and began to walk away. The moment you left my side, my features began to blur and that debilitating terror returned. Then I woke up."

His voice faded and died, leaving an echo of the fear behind. Maggie had been so caught up in his nightmare, she felt weak with relief that it was finally over. "Lord, Mark," she breathed. "I can understand how it must have affected you. But if your love for me is based on that dream"—she paused and looked into his eyes—"I don't think I can live up to it. I'm not truth, justice, and the American way. I'm just me. Not all bad, but definitely not all good. Like I said in my letter, I'm totally fallible."

"Yes, I know, love," he said, chuckling as he raised himself on one elbow to kiss her. "That's what makes you so adorable." He kissed her again, slowly this time, then sat up, pulling her into his lap. "It took more than one dream to convince me. But still, I couldn't get it out of my mind after our night in the cellar. I also couldn't get your response to my lovemaking out of my mind," he added. "That's why I couldn't take no for an answer. Why I had to follow through. I had to know what the dream meant. I had to know if you held the key to my reality in your small hands."

"I guess I know what you mean," she murmured softly. "I had no dream, but during these past two weeks I've come to realize that you make me real. Only when I'm with you do I come to life."

"Oh, love," he sighed, laying his head back. "That's what I wanted but didn't dare hope for. When we were in St. Thomas it was so perfect. We came together as though we had been born specifically for the purpose of loving each other, and

I hoped—God, how I hoped—that you would love me back."

"You loved me then?" she asked incredulously.

He chuckled and gave her a bruising hug, his hand coming to rest on her bare breast. "I suspected I was in trouble the night I blew my chance to seduce you. Then in St. Thomas when you got those damned hiccups I knew I was lost. I wanted to hold you and protect you, even if it meant protecting you from myself. But of course"—he paused to kiss the tip of her nose—"you simply would not be protected and insisted on throwing yourself at me."

"I what?" she said indignantly. "I did no such thing, Marcus Wilding. You . . ." She stopped for a moment, then began to smile. "Come to think of it, I guess I did."

"Yes, you did," he said smugly. "For which I am eternally grateful. I was trying so hard to act honorably, but I'm afraid if you had held out much longer, honor would have gone right out the window."

"Ah, yes," she said. "My black knight. But you can't fool me any longer. You were the one who had Mr. Lowe read that interminable list of your virtues. So don't try to tell me you're a scoundrel."

"About that list, love," Mark said slowly, a grin beginning to spread across his features.

"Don't tell me you got that sweet little man to lie for you," she asked suspiciously.

"No . . . not exactly. It's just that those charitable things he told you about are forced on any man who is in my position. It's expected of me. So don't go thinking I'm your Sir Lancelot after all."

"Of course not," she said, smiling inwardly. It would take awhile before he trusted her enough to come out from behind his protective screen. Maggie wouldn't push it now. They had the rest of their lives. "I would never accuse you of being anything less than totally corrupt. But even if your armor is slightly tarnished, you happen to be the only knight I'll ever want."

"I'd better be," he said, framing her face roughly between his palms, then he repeated softly, "I'd better be." He lowered his head to kiss her lips, gently at first, then with a growing hunger. "Maggie," he murmured against her lips.

"Yes, darling?"

"Hadn't we better go home and get to work on curing those hiccups?"

She ran her hand over his chest, fascinated by the feel of him, then drew back to look at him as his words sank in. "But I don't have the hiccups."

He fastened her bra, then began to button her blouse before finally looking up to smile and say, "Don't you believe in preventive medicine?"

She stared at him and began to smile, then to laugh, and soon the sound of their laughter filled the room in a joyous premonition of the years to come.

## Chapter Eleven

And the years that followed *were* filled with laughter, and some tears, and they overflowed with love. As Jake's health began to fail, Mark gradually broke away from his grandfather's empire. He and Maggie moved into the lodge, giving Jake the dubious pleasure of the presence of Marcus Wilding the Fifth.

Buster, as Jake dubbed the boy, was a scamp from the minute he was born. He had his mother's brown hair, his father's silver eyes, and a hard-headed personality all his own.

By the time Buster was born, Mark had stopped having the nightmare, but for the first year of their marriage he would periodically wake Maggie in the middle of the night as he writhed in the grip of the old horror. When he reached out for her in the darkness, she would soothe him in the only way she knew, with her body and her love.

One morning as Maggie turned back to the stove to finish cooking Buster's breakfast, she thought again of the relief she had felt when the dream finally let go of Mark. She'd known then that she had his complete trust.

She turned the bacon, then shoved two slices of bread in the toaster. And as she lifted her eyes from the toaster, she caught sight of Mark, standing outside the window, his face lifted toward the morning sun. And suddenly they were on the island again and she could see him standing naked and golden in the bright tropical sun. She felt the sensual touch of the sand beneath her feet, and her heart began to pound with desire.

He turned to see her watching him and walked closer to the window. But when he saw the hunger in her face and shining from her eyes, he switched his course and walked to the back door.

"Let's go back to the island," she said when he held her in his arms.

"The bedroom is much closer, love," he said against her throat. "Why don't we go back to the bedroom now and go to St. Thomas next week?"

"I didn't mean right this minute." She laughed. "But you do want to go back, don't you? I mean to our island. We've been to Charlotte Amalie to see Paul, but we haven't been back to that little turquoise cove."

"Yes, we'll go back," he whispered in her ear. "And we'll swim and we'll spread our blanket on the beach and . . ."

Before he could complete the intriguing sentence, they were interrupted by a small voice. "Mom! You're burning the bacon . . . again," the voice said in disgust.

"I'm sorry, Buster," she said, hurrying to remove the smoking skillet from the burner. "I'll make you some more."

"You'd better let me do it," he said in resignation. "When you and Dad start kissing, a person could starve to death. And besides, I'm almost as good a cook as you are."

"And modest, too," Mark said, pulling Maggie back into his arms.

Buster turned to look at them, and Maggie caught her breath as she saw her eight-year-old son's silver eyes sparkle with fun.

"Quite," he said casually, then turned to select another skillet.

Mark and Maggie looked at each other, stunned into silence for a moment: then they began to laugh under the indignant eyes of Marcus Wilding the Fifth.

# His love for her is madness.
# Her love for him is sin.

## Sunshine and Shadow

### by Sharon and Tom Curtis

## COULD THEIR EXPLOSIVE LOVE BRIDGE THE CHASM BETWEEN TWO IMPOSSIBLY DIFFERENT WORLDS?

He thought there were no surprises left in the world ... but the sudden appearance of young Amish widow Susan Peachey was astonishing—and just the shock cynical Alan Wilde needed. She was a woman from another time, innocent, yet wise in ways he scarcely understood.

Irresistibly, Susan and Alan were drawn together to explore their wildly exotic differences. And soon they would discover something far greater—a rich emotional bond that transcended both of their worlds and linked them heart-to-heart ... until their need for each other became so overwhelming that there was no turning back. But would Susan have to sacrifice all she cherished for the uncertain joy of their forbidden love?

"Look for full details on how to win an authentic Amish quilt displaying the traditional 'Sunshine and Shadow' pattern in copies of SUNSHINE AND SHADOW or on displays at participating stores. No purchase necessary. Void where prohibited by law. Sweepstakes ends December 15, 1986."

Look for SUNSHINE AND SHADOW in your bookstore or use this coupon for ordering:

*Heirs to a great dynasty, the Delaney
brothers were united by blood, united by
devotion to their rugged land . . . and
known far and wide as*

# THE SHAMROCK
# TRINITY

Bantam's bestselling LOVESWEPT romance line built its reputation on quality and innovation. Now, a remarkable and unique
event in romance publishing comes from the same source: THE
SHAMROCK TRINITY, three daringly original novels written by
three of the most successful women's romance writers today. Kay
Hooper, Iris Johansen, and Fayrene Preston have created a trio
of books that are dynamite love stories bursting with strong,
fascinating male and female characters, deeply sensual love scenes,
the humor for which LOVESWEPT is famous, and a deliciously
fresh approach to romance writing.

*THE SHAMROCK TRINITY—Burke, York, and
Rafe: Powerful men . . . rakes and charmers . . .
they needed only love to make their lives complete.*

*RAFE, THE MAVERICK by Kay Hooper*

Rafe Delaney was a heartbreaker whose ebony eyes held laughing
devils and whose lilting voice could charm any lady—or
any horse—until a stallion named Diablo left him in the dust. It took
Maggie O'Riley to work her magic on the impossible horse . . .
and on his bold owner. Maggie's grace and strength made Rafe
yearn to share the raw beauty of his land with her, to teach her
the exquisite pleasure of yielding to the heat inside her. Maggie
was stirred by Rafe's passion, but would his reputation and her
ambition keep their kindred spirits apart?

 LOVESWEPT

## *YORK, THE RENEGADE by Iris Johansen*

Some men were made to fight dragons, Sierra Smith thought when she first met York Delaney. The rebel brother had roamed the world for years before calling the rough mining town of Hell's Bluff home. Now, the spirited young woman who'd penetrated this renegade's paradise had awakened a savage and tender possessiveness in York: something he never expected to find in himself. Sierra had known loneliness and isolation too—enough to realize that York's restlessness had only to do with finding a place to belong. Could she convince him that love was such a place, that the refuge he'd always sought was in her arms?

## *BURKE, THE KINGPIN by Fayrene Preston*

Cara Winston appeared as a fantasy, racing on horseback to catch the day's last light—her silver hair glistening, her dress the color of the Arizona sunset . . . and Burke Delaney wanted her. She was on his horse, on his land: she would have to belong to him too. But Cara was quicksilver, impossible to hold, a wild creature whose scent was midnight flowers and sweet grass. Burke had always taken what he wanted, by willing it or fighting for it; Cara cherished her freedom and refused to believe his love would last. Could he make her see he'd captured her to have and hold forever?

# THE SHAMROCK TRINITY

*On sale October 15, 1986
wherever Bantam LOVESWEPT Romances are sold*

# Only in a lost world could she discover passion's true treasures . . .

## *Fiery Obsession*

## by Lynne Blackman

Innocent and lovely Sloan Hyland's dreams of sensual passion—and fears that they will never come true—are all she knows . . . until her uncle Dean, a powerful New York art dealer, takes her with him on a feverish journey in search of a priceless artifact. Deep in the steamy Mexican jungle, Sloan meets Dominick, the daring, enigmatic leader of the expedition . . . the keeper of Sloan's dreams and captor of her unspoken desires. As the promise of golden riches lures them ever deeper into the exotic, shadowy paradise, Sloan's mind and body are overwhelmed by a secret, heated obsession—a fiery dream that will explode into reality on sacred tribal grounds, where rituals of love and the mysteries of the ancients flourish as if time did not exist.

## Fiery Obsession

Look for it at your bookstore or use this coupon for ordering:

Heiress to one of the world's great fortunes, a temptation no man could resist—she was drawn into a lush and frenzied world of grandeur . . .

MIRELLA: intelligent, passionate, and voluptuous. She seeks the ultimate in pleasure and lasting love.

RASHID: playboy, hedonist, master of eroticism. Behind his suave charm lies the threat of betrayal.

ADAM: dedicated archeologist, a man of vast sensual power. From his marble palace in exotic Istanbul he dreams of taking Mirella in the

# Soft
# Warm
# Rain

As they explore the limits of luxury and pleasure, they will experience delights beyond their wildest fantasies. And before their bodies are sated, they will lose their hearts.

Look for it at your bookstore or use this coupon for ordering: